D0229752
3 800

Consumed

DAVID CRONENBERG

FOURTH ESTATE • *London*

Fourth Estate
An imprint of HarperCollins*Publishers*
77–85 Fulham Palace Road
Hammersmith, London W6 8JB
www.4thestate.co.uk

First published in Great Britain by Fourth Estate in 2014
First published in Canada by Hamish Hamilton in 2014

1 3 5 7 9 10 8 6 4 2

A catalogue record for this book is available from the British Library

Hardback ISBN 978-0-00-729915-7
Trade paperback ISBN 978-0-00-755224-5

This book is a work of fiction. Names, characters, places and events either are products of the author's imagination or are used fictitiously. Any resemblance to actual events or places or persons, living or dead, is entirely coincidental.

Text design by Laura Brady

Printed and bound in Great Britain by
Clays Ltd, St Ives plc

FSC™ is a non-profit international organisation established to promote the responsible management of the world's forests. Products carrying the FSC label are independently certified to assure consumers that they come from forests that are managed to meet the social, economic and ecological needs of present and future generations, and other controlled sources.

Find out more about HarperCollins and the environment at
www.harpercollins.co.uk/green

For Carolyn

1

NAOMI WAS IN THE SCREEN. Or, more exactly, she was in the apartment in the QuickTime window in the screen, the small, shabby, scholarly apartment of Célestine and Aristide Arosteguy. She was there, sitting across from them as they sat side by side on an old couch—was it burgundy? was it corduroy?—talking to an off-camera interviewer. And with the white plastic earbuds in her ears, she was acoustically in the Arosteguy home as well. She felt the depth of the room and the three-dimensionality of the heads of this couple, sagacious heads with sensual faces, a matched pair, like brother and sister. She could smell the books jammed into the bookshelves behind them, feel the furious intellectual heat emanating from them. Everything in the frame was in focus—video did that, those small CCD or CMOS sensors; the nature of the medium, Naomi thought—and so the sense of depth into the room and into the books and the faces was intensified.

Célestine was talking, a Gauloise burning in her hand. Her fingernails were lacquered a purply red—or were they black? (the screen had a tendency to go magenta)—and her hair was up in an artfully messy bun with stray tendrils curling around her throat. "Well, yes, when you no longer have any desire, you are dead. Even desire for a product, a consumer item, is better than no desire at all. Desire for a camera, for instance, even a cheap one, a tawdry one, is enough to keep death at bay." A wicked smile, an inhale of the cigarette with those lips. "If the desire is real, of course." A catlike exhale of smoke, and a giggle.

A sixty-two-year-old woman, Célestine, but the European intellectual version of sixty-two, not the Midwestern American mall version. Naomi was amazed at Célestine's lusciousness, her aura of style and drama, how her kinetic jewelry and her saucy slump on that couch seemed to blend together. She had never heard Célestine speak before—only now had a few interviews begun to emerge on the net, and only, of course, because of the murder. Célestine's voice was husky and sensual, her English assured and playful, and lethally accurate. The dead woman intimidated Naomi.

Célestine turned languidly towards Aristide. Smoke tumbled from her mouth and nose and drifted over to him, like the passing of an evanescent baton. He took a breath to speak, inhaling the smoke, continuing her thought. "Even if you never get it, or, once having it, never use it. As long as you desire it. You can see this in the youngest babies. Their desire is fierce." As he spoke these words, he began to stroke his tie, which was tucked into an elegant V-necked cashmere sweater. It was as though he were petting one of those fierce babies, and the gesture seemed to explain the blissful smile that suffused his face.

Célestine watched him for a moment, waited for the petting to stop, before she turned back to the unseen interviewer. "That's why we say that the only authentic literature of the modern era is the owner's manual." Stretching forward towards the lens, revealing voluptuously freckled cleavage, Célestine fumbled for something off camera, then slumped back with a small, thick white booklet in her cigarette hand. She riffled through the pages, her face myopically close to the print—or was she smelling the paper, the ink?—until she found her page and began to read. "Auto-flash without red-eye reduction. Set this mode for taking pictures without people, or if you want to shoot right away without the red-eye function." She laughed that rich, husky laugh, and repeated, this time with great drama, "Set this mode for taking pictures *without people*." A shake of the head, eyes now closed to fully feel the richness of the words. "What author of the past century has produced more provocative and poignant writing than that?"

The window containing the Arosteguys shrank back to thumbnail size and became the lower left corner of a newscast window. The now tiny Arosteguys were still very relaxed and chatty, each picking up the conversation from the other like experienced handball players, but Naomi no longer heard what they said. Instead, it was the words of the overly earnest newscaster in the primary window that she heard. "It was in this very apartment of Célestine and Aristide Arosteguy, an apartment near the famous Sorbonne, of the University of Paris, that the grisly, butchered remains of a woman were found, a woman later identified as Célestine Arosteguy." In the small window, the camera zoomed in on the amiably chatting Aristide. "Her husband, the renowned French philosopher and author Aristide Arosteguy, could not be found for questioning." In one brutal cut Aristide disappeared, to be replaced by handheld, starkly front-lit shots of the tiny apartment's kitchen, apparently taken at night. These soon swelled to full size and the newscaster's window retreated to the upper right corner.

Forensic police wearing black surgical gloves were taking frosted plastic bags out of a fridge, photographing grimy pots and frying pans on the stove, sorting through dishes and cutlery. The miniature newscaster continued: "Sources wishing to remain unnamed have told us that there is evidence to suggest that parts of Célestine Arosteguy's body were cooked on her own stove and eaten."

Cut to a wide shot of an imposing municipal building subtitled "Préfecture de Police, Paris." "Prefect of Police Auguste Vernier had this to say about the possible flight of Arosteguy from the country." Cut to an interview with the strangely delicate, bespectacled prefect of police in what appeared to be a large hallway crammed with journalists. His French voice, emotionally intricate and intense, quickly faded to be replaced by a gravelly, less involved American one: "Mr. Arosteguy is a national treasure. So was Madame Célestine Moreau. It was a French ideal, the two of them, the philosopher couple. Her death is a national disaster." A cutaway to the rambunctious crowd of journalists shouting questions, cameras and voice recorders bristling, then a return to the prefect. "Aristide Arosteguy left the country on a lecture tour of Asia three days before the remains of his wife were found. We have no specific reason at the moment to consider him a suspect in this crime, but naturally there are questions. It is true that we do not know exactly where he is. We are looking for him."

The squawk of the carousel buzzer pulled Naomi out of the Préfecture de Police and back into the baggage claim arena of Charles de Gaulle Airport. As the conveyor belt lurched into action, the crowd of waiting passengers pressed forward. Somebody bumped Naomi's laptop, sending it sliding down her shins, popping the earbuds out of her ears. She had been sitting on the edge of the carousel and had paid the price. Now she just managed to rescue her beloved MacBook Air by pivoting both feet up at the heels and catching the laptop with the toes of her sneakers. The Arosteguy report continued unperturbed in its window, but Naomi flipped the Air closed and put the Arosteguys to sleep for the time being.

NATHAN'S IPHONE RANG and he knew it was Naomi from the ringtone, the trill of an African tree frog that she had found somehow erotic and had emailed him. He was squatting on the floor of a damp, gritty, concrete back hallway of the Molnár Clinic, digging around in the camera bag in front of him, looking for something he suspected Naomi had taken, so it made sense that she would call him now, her extrasensory radar functioning in its usual freakish fashion. He kept digging with one hand, thumbing his phone on with the other. "Naomi, hey. Where are you?"

"I'm finally in Paris. I'm in a taxi heading for the Crillon. Where are you?"

"I'm in a slimy hallway at the Molnár Clinic in Budapest, and I'm looking in my camera bag for that 105mm macro lens that I bought in Frankfurt at the airport."

The slightest pause, which, Nathan knew, did not have to do with Naomi's possible guilt regarding the macro, but rather the fact that she was texting someone on her BlackBerry while talking to him. "Um ... you won't find it in your camera bag, because it's on my camera. I borrowed it from you in Milan, remember? You were sure you weren't going to need it."

Nathan took a deep breath and cursed the moment he had convinced Naomi to switch from Canon to Nikon so that they could pool their hardware; brand passion was emotional glue for hard-core nerd couples. What a mistake. He stopped digging around in the bag. "Yeah. That's what I thought. I was just hoping I hallucinated the whole handoff thing. I have lots of dreams about giving you my stuff."

A snort from Naomi. "Is that really going to hang you up? You've suddenly discovered you need a macro?"

"I'm about to shoot an operation. I never imagined they'd let me in there, but they're deliriously happy to have me document everything. I wanted the macro for my backup body. I'm sure there'll be great weird Hungarian medical stuff to shoot huge close-ups of. Maybe not for the piece itself, but for reference. For our archives."

Multitasking pause, a random interruption of conversational rhythm that drove Nathan crazy. But it was Naomi, so you ate it. "Sorry. Who knew?"

"Never mind. I'm sure your need is greater than mine."

"My need is always greater than yours. I'm a very needy person. I wanted the macro to shoot portraits. I've set up some clandestine meetings with some French police types. I really want every pore in their faces."

Nathan slumped back against the corridor's damp wall. So he was stuck now with the 24–70mm zoom on his primary camera body, the D3. How close could that thing focus? It would probably be good enough. And he could crop the D3's image files if he really needed to be close. Life with Naomi taught you to be resourceful. "Hey, honey, I'm surprised you actually want to get your hands dirty with real humans. What happened to net-surfing sources? What happened to the coziness of virtual journalism, where you never had to get out of your jammies? You wouldn't have to be in Paris. You could be anywhere."

"If I could be anywhere, I'd be in Paris."

"Hey, and did you say the Crillon? Are you staying there or meeting somebody there?"

"Both."

"Isn't that crazy expensive?"

"I've got a secret contact. Won't cost me *un seul sou*."

Nathan immediately fired up his internal jealousy suppressors in the old familiar fashion. Not that Naomi's secret contacts were always men, but they were all sketchy in some threatening way, dangerous. If you wanted to track her constantly tendriling social network, you'd have to apply a particularly sophisticated fractals program to her, mapping every minute of her day.

"Well, I guess that's good," he said, with a lack of enthusiasm meant to caution her.

"Yeah, it's great," said Naomi, not noticing.

A dimpled metal door at the far end of the hallway opened and the backlit figure of a man dressed for surgery beckoned to Nathan. "Come now to get dressed, mister. Dr. Molnár waits for you."

Nathan nodded and lifted his hand in acknowledgment. The man flipped his own hand in a hurry-up gesture and disappeared, closing the door behind him.

"Okay, well, cancer calls. Gotta go. Tell me what's up in two seconds or less."

Another annoying multitasking pause—or was she just assembling her thoughts?—and then Naomi said, "On to some juicy French philosophical sex-killing murder-suicide cannibal thing. You?"

"Still the controversial Hungarian breast-cancer radioactive seed implant treatment thing. I adore you."

"*Je t'adore aussi.* Call me. Bye."

"Bye." Nathan touched his phone off and hung his head. Just seal me up in this dank corridor and never find me again. There it was. There was always that moment of ferocious inner resistance, that fear of carrying the thing through, the resentment that action had to be taken, that risk and failure had to be confronted. But cancer called, and its voice was compelling.

IN HER SMALL BUT SUMPTUOUS attic room at the Hôtel de Crillon, Naomi was stretched out on an ornate chaise longue beside a short, narrow pair of French doors leading to a door-mat-sized balcony. From that balcony, she had already photographed the courtyard, with its intricate web of pigeon-repelling wires overhead, paying particular attention to details of decay, *comme d'habitude.* No matter how deluxe the hotel in Paris, you could count on the imprint of time to surprise you with wonderful textures. Now, having made her habitual nest of BlackBerry, cameras, iPad, compact and SD flashcards, lenses, tissue boxes, bags, pens and markers, makeup gear (minimal), cups and glasses bearing traces of coffee and various juices, chargers of all shapes and sizes, two laptops, chunky brushed-aluminum Nagra Kudelski digital audio recorder, notebooks and calendars and magazines, all of these anchored by her duffel bag and her backpack, Naomi reviewed her latest photos using Adobe Lightroom while watching a new video concerning the Arosteguys that had just surfaced on YouTube. And in another screen window, next to a photo of the hotel window's rot-chewed frame with its faded white-and-green-striped awning, striped also with streaks of rust from its delicate metal skeleton, was another intriguing display: a 360-degree panorama of the Arosteguy apartment, which Naomi idly controlled with her laptop's trackpad, zooming and scrolling, in essence walking through the cramped, chaotic academics' home.

There was the sofa shown in the earlier video, now patterned with blocks of sunlight streaming from a trio of small windows through which Naomi thought she could see a slice of the Sorbonne across the road. Behind the sofa were the densely populated bookshelves, but now swing around ninety degrees and more bookshelves, and piles of papers, letters, magazines, documents, littering every piece of furniture, including the kitchen sink, including the floor. Naomi smiled at the absence of cool electronics: a tape player, of all things; a small 4:3 tube TV set (could it actually be black and white?); and a phone with a cord. This pleased her, because it felt right for a hot French philosophy couple who were closer to Sartre and Beauvoir than Bernard-Henri Lévy and Arielle Dombasle. The Arosteguys seemed to belong to, at the latest, the 1950s. (She could see Simone Signoret, with her heavy sensuality, playing the role of Célestine in a movie, but only if she managed to project the intellect of Beauvoir; she wasn't sure who would play Aristide.) To drill into their lives was to drill into the past, and that's where Naomi wanted to go. She wasn't looking for a mirror, not this time.

A paragraph below the panorama window confirmed that this was indeed the apartment before the murder, documented by a web-savvy student of Aristide's—obviously using Panorama Tools and a fish-eye lens,

Naomi noted—as part of a master's thesis connecting the Evolutionary Consumerist philosophy of the Arosteguys with the couple's own ascetic—relatively—lifestyle. The writer of that paragraph dryly noted that the wretched candidate, Hervé Blomqvist, had been denied his degree in the end. Naomi had come across an internet forum conducted by students of Célestine that had the tone of a sixties French New Wave movie. Blomqvist was a frequent contributor who positioned himself as a classic French bad boy along the lines of the actor Jean-Pierre Léaud. He hinted that as an undergraduate he had been the cherished lover of both Aristide and Célestine and was later punished for daring to use his place in the private lives of the Arosteguys to anchor what he confessed was "a pathetically thin and parasitical thesis." Naomi emailed herself a note to connect with Blomqvist, a mnemonic technique that was the only one that seemed to work. Anything else got lost in the tangle of the Great Nest, as Nathan called the cloud of chaos that enveloped her.

The third window on Naomi's screen was an interview shot in the oddly shaped basement kitchen of the couple who were responsible for the daily maintenance of the Arosteguys' entire apartment block. The room was dominated by an immense concrete cylinder which suggested that half the casing of an exterior spiral staircase was bulging into their space. It was against this pale-green stuccoed column that a short, stout French woman and her shy, mustachioed husband stood speaking to an off-camera interviewer. The sound of the woman's surprisingly youthful voice was soon mixed down to allow the voice of a translator to float over it. The translator's voice, more mature, more matronly, seemed a better match for the woman's face.

"Never," said the translator. "No one could come between them, those two. Of course, they both had many affairs. They came here, the boys and girls, to their apartment just upstairs above us. We could sometimes hear them here behind us, laughing on the staircase, coming down as Mauricio and I had breakfast in the kitchen. He's my husband." A shy smile. "He's Mexican."

With a sweet, excited embarrassment, Mauricio waved directly at the camera. "Hello, hello," he said in English.

The woman—only now, clumsily, identified as "Madame Tretikov, Maintenance" by a thick-fonted subtitle—continued. "They slept here. They lived here. Sometimes, yes, their lovers were students. But not always." She shrugged. "For the students, it was a question of politics and philosophy, as always. The two together. They were in agreement. The Arosteguys explained it to me and Mauricio, and it seemed very correct, very nice."

Naomi maximized the video window. With the screen filled, she could feel herself inside that kitchen, standing beside the camera, looking at that couple, the chipped enameled stove, the cupboards of moisture-swollen chipboard, damp kitchen towels spilling out of open cutlery drawers. She could smell the grease and the under-the-staircase dankness.

As if in response to the newly enlarged image, the cameraman zoomed slowly in to Madame's face, zoomed because he saw moisture welling up in her eyes, like blood to a shark. Madame came through for her close-up, biting her quivering lip, tears spilling. Mercifully, the translator did not try to emulate the tremor in Madame's voice.

"They were so brilliant, so exciting," said Madame. "There could be no jealousy, no anger between them. They were like one person. She was sick, don't you see? She was dying. I could see it in her eyes. Probably a brain tumor. She thought so hard all the time. Always writing, writing. I think it was a mercy killing. She asked him to kill her and he did. And then, of course, yes, he ate her." With these words, Madame took a deep, stumbling breath, wiped her eyes with the threadbare dish cloth she had been holding throughout the interview, and smiled. The effect was startling to Naomi, who immediately began to analyze it in the email window she had left open in the corner of the screen. "He could not just leave her there, upstairs," Madame continued. Her smile was beatific; she had a revelation to deliver. "He wanted to take as much of her with him as he could. So he ate her, and then he ran away with her inside him."

THE MEDICAL GOGGLES were getting in the way. Nathan could barely see through the viewfinder of his ancient Nikon D3, the plastic lenses projecting too far from his eye, the goggles slewing and popping off his nose when he pressed the camera close, their elastic band pulling at his hair and crumpling his baby-blue paper surgical cap. "Everything changed after AIDS," Dr. Molnár had just explained to him. "From then on, blood was more dangerous than shit. We realized you can't afford to get it into your eyes, your tear ducts. So, we put on ski goggles in the operating theater and we schuss"—here he made slightly fey hip- and arm-twisting motions—"over the moguls of our patients' bodies." Now Dr. Molnár bent close to the Nagra SD voice recorder hanging around Nathan's neck in its bondage-style black-strapped leather case, and into its crustacean-like stereo cardioid microphone breathed, "Don't be shy, Nathan. I'm notoriously vain. Get close. Fill your frame. That's rule number one for a photographer, isn't it? Fill your frame?"

"So they say," said Nathan.

"Of course, you wrote to me that you were a medical journalist who was forced by the 'swelling tide of media technology' also to become a photographer and a videographer and a sound recordist, so perhaps you are now somewhat overwhelmed. I will guide you."

Naomi had also, quite independently, bought one of the recorders, hers a now-discontinued ML model (it would kill her when she realized that), at Amsterdam's Schiphol Airport. Electronics stores in airports had become their neighborhood hangouts, although more often than not they weren't there at the same time. It got to the point that they could sense traces of each other among the boxes of electric plug adapters and microSD flashcards. They would trade notes about the changing stock of lenses and point-n-shoots at Ferihegy, Schiphol, Da Vinci. And they would leave shopping lists for each other in emails and text messages, quoting best prices spotted and bettered.

"I'd really like to take the goggles off, Dr. Molnár. They weren't designed for photographer-journalists."

"Call me Zoltán, please, Nathan. And of course, take them off. You'll have your huge brick of a camera in front of your eyes to protect you anyway." Dr. Molnár laughed—rather a phlegmy, unhealthy laugh, Nathan thought—and swirled away to the other side of the operating table, past the array of screened and opened windows which let in the muted insect hum of the street below and a few splashes of early morning light that painted the room's grimy and crumbling tiled walls.

Nathan took some shots of Dr. Molnár as he danced, and the good doctor's body language conveyed his pleasure at being photographed. "Unusual to have open windows in an operating room," Nathan couldn't resist observing.

"Ah, well, our infrastructure here at the hospital is in disarray, you know, and so the air-conditioning is not functioning. Fortunately, we have the window option. This building is very old." The doctor took up his position at the side of the operating table, flanked by two male assistants, and waved his arms over the table as though invoking spirits. "But you can see that the equipment itself is beautiful. First-rate, state-of-the-art." Nathan dutifully began to take detail shots of the equipment, gradually leading him to the face of the patient herself, hidden behind a frame draped with surgical cloth, also baby blue, which separated her head from the rest of her body. The autonomous head seemed to be slumbering rather than anesthetized, and it was very beautiful. Short black hair, Slavic cheekbones, wide mouth, chin delicately pointed and cleft. For the moment, Nathan resisted taking her photograph.

"I notice you don't seem to need to change lenses. The last photojournalist we had in here had a belt full of lenses. He made quite a lot of cinema twisting those lenses on and off his camera."

"You're very observant," said Nathan. It was obvious that you could not compliment Dr. Molnár too much; it gave Nathan perverse satisfaction to find oblique ways to do it. "I sometimes do have a second camera body with a macrophotography lens. But these modern zooms have actually surpassed a lot of the old prime lenses in quality. Are you a student of photography?"

Dr. Molnár smiled behind his mask. "I have a half-interest in a little restaurant in a hotel downtown in Pest. You must come. You will be my special guest. The walls are covered with my photographs of nudes. I wouldn't use that thing, though," he said, pointing an oddly shaped forceps at the Nikon. "I'm strictly an analogue man. Medium-format film for me, and that's that. It's slow, it's big and clumsy, and the details you see are exquisite. You can lick them. You can taste them." The doctor's mask bulged with the gestures his tongue was making to illustrate his approach to photography. He had already established in his first discussions with Nathan that it was the sensuality of surgery that had initially drawn him to the practice; sensuality was the guiding principle of every aspect of his life. He was making sure that Nathan wouldn't forget it.

And now, in a very smooth segue—which Nathan thought of as particularly Hungarian—Dr. Molnár said, "Have you met our patient, Nathan? She's from Slovenia. *Une belle Slave.*" Molnár peeked over the cloth barrier and spoke to the disconnected head with disarmingly conversational brio. "Dunja? Have you met Nathan? You signed a release form for him, and now he's here with us in the operating theater. Why don't you say hello?"

At first Nathan thought that the good doctor was teasing him; Molnár had emphasized the element of playfulness in his unique brand of surgery, and chatting with an unconscious patient would certainly qualify as Molnáresque. But to Nathan's surprise Dunja's eyes began to stutter open, she began working her tongue and lips as though she were thirsty, she took a quick little breath that was almost a yawn.

"Ah, there she is," said Molnár. "My precious one. Hello, darling." Nathan took a step backward in his slippery paper booties in order not to impede the strange, intimate flow between patient and doctor. Could she and her surgeon be having an affair? Could this really be written off as Hungarian bedside manner? Molnár touched his latex-bound fingertips to his masked mouth, then pressed the filtered kiss to Dunja's lips. She giggled, then slipped away dreamily, then came back. "Talk to Nathan," said Molnár, withdrawing with a bow. He had things to do.

Dunja struggled to focus on Nathan, a process so electromechanical that it seemed photographic. And then she said, "Oh, yes, take pictures of me like this. It's cruel, but I want you to do that. Zoltán is very naughty. A naughty doctor. He came to interview me, and we spent quite a bit of time together in my hometown, which is"—another druggy giggle—"somewhere in Slovenia. I can't remember it."

"Ljubljana," Molnár called out from the foot of the table, where he was sorting through instruments with his colleagues.

"Thank you, naughty doctor. You know, it's your fault I can't remember anything. You love to drug me."

Nathan began to photograph Dunja's face. She turned towards the camera like a sunflower. He regretted that he had decided not to use a video camera on his assignments, a fussy rejection that had to do with worries about media storage, peripherals, and other arcane techie calculations. Of course, if he'd been able to afford the new D4s, which could also record decent video ... but he couldn't keep up with the inexorable hot lava flow of technology, even though he desperately wanted to. Naomi was never so prissy. She just wasn't *wary*. She'd already bought a new high-def no-name Chinese camcorder at Heathrow and had downloaded an obscure Asian editing program to work with its difficult files. Even if she'd had to shoot with her BlackBerry, she'd have caught, in all its coarse grain, the weird banter he had just heard. Oh, well. He had the voice recorder cooking, and he could append a sound file to each photograph using the camera's microphone if push came to shove.

"Nathan? I think you are very beautiful," said Dunja, just before she faded back into unconsciousness.

Nathan began to line up a 24mm low-angle shot with Dunja's face in the foreground and her anesthetist—beefy, hairy, silent—behind her. "Nathan, forget about the face. It's the breasts you want to see. Come over here beside me." Nathan took his shot, then stood up and joined Dr. Molnár. Molnár pulled back the surgical cloth—orange, for some reason—covering Dunja's chest. Her breasts were very full, and very blue and surreal in the cold light pouring from the lamp cluster which towered over the table. Capturing the effect of that light was exactly the reason Nathan rarely used flash, which would overpower the ambient light. Each breast had a dozen clear plastic wire-like tubes running into it, making it look like an umbrella that had been popped inside out by a strong wind. "Take pictures of those, would be better. If they're good, I'll print them and hang them in my restaurant."

"You have medical photos hanging in your restaurant?"

"No, no. Yours would be the first. You think it would derange the eating?"

"It would derange my eating, I can guarantee you that."

Dr. Molnár burst out laughing. His surgical mask pumped in and out with the pneumatics of his hilarity. He bent at the waist with laughter. Nathan thought the mask would pop a seam. He scanned the others in the room. One of them winked and shrugged. It was just Doc Molnár. No worries. Molnár straightened up and gained control with some effort. "Do I shock you? We are very playful here. It's a good tone for an operating theater. It is a theater, after all."

"Yes," said Nathan, "so you've told me." He put the camera up to his eye, regretting the absence of the macro lens. He would get as close as focus would allow and crop into the shot later. When you got close, the breasts became complete animals, possibly marine, attached, perhaps, to auto-feeding tubes. Nathan began to think that some anesthetic fumes were floating around the room, affecting his perception. He shook it off. "Do you want to shock me, Dr. Molnár?" he said, moving gently over the woman's multi-penetrated breasts, rolling his finger on the shutter with delicacy. His nose was mashed, as always, against the camera's rear LCD screen—he used his stronger, left, eye—and he spoke out of the right side of his mouth, the way smokers swiveled their lips away from you while exhaling their smoke. "I have a feeling that you do."

"I want to be entertaining," said Molnár, picking up a small stainless-steel bowl. He fished around in it with his index finger, like a prospector panning for gold. "For your big *New Yorker* article. I've always wanted to be the subject of a piece in the 'Annals of Medicine' section. It's good for business, good for my vanity."

Still shooting, Nathan laughed. "*The New Yorker*'s a long shot. I'm doing this on spec."

"A 'long shot,' yeah, sweet expression, but we must all live in hope. I hope for *The New Yorker*."

"Frankly, I have the same hope. Unfortunately, my credits aren't quite up to snuff. I never did make it through medical school."

Molnár stopped fishing and looked up into Nathan's lens. "Well, neither did I. That hasn't prevented an illustrious career. I'm sure it won't stop you either." Nathan couldn't help glancing over at Dunja to see if she had heard. Her head was rolling dreamily from side to side, and her mouth kept morphing into various modes of smiles, but her eyes were closed. She was somewhere else. Molnár picked this up immediately. "She knows all about me. I learned my medicine during a turbulent era in Eastern Europe. Things were ... regularly irregular at that time. North Americans never understand. You want to see this? Would make a nice shot."

Molnár held out his bowl so that Nathan could see the dozens of tiny metal pellets in it. He rocked the bowl back and forth and the pellets glittered and rattled. It *was* a nice shot—for the 105 macro that Naomi had. Nathan cranked his zoom out to 70mm, then back wide to 24mm, knowing that either way he couldn't get close enough for the ideal portrait of whatever it was he was seeing. If Nathan stayed wide, though, Molnár's hands in the shot were interesting, especially as the doctor scooted the pellets around with his finger. Discernibly gnarled and arthritic even in their gloves, the grotesquely swollen knuckles and finger joints looked like goblins wearing translucent latex dresses. (Were there anesthetic fumes in the room?) Yes, the hands really were the subject of the shot now. How subtle could those stricken hands be during an operation? Nathan wondered if there was a Nikon dealer close to the hotel. Probably get screwed on the price, but when would he see Naomi again? He needed that macro lens. He found himself more and more drawn to the macroscopic level of medical endeavor, though he wasn't sure what he could do with it. There were plenty of medical specialists in the field, their stuff mundane, workmanlike, ugly. They weren't artists. But was Nathan? "It is pretty, but what is it I'm seeing, Zoltán?"

"I am preparing to perform a multiple lumpectomy. The patient has many discrete tumors in her breasts, but they are not very aggressive, and so, flying the pink flag of breast preservation, I shall remove only the tumors, thus sparing the breasts. Accordingly, I am about to inject one hundred and twenty radioactive pellets, which are radioactive iodine isotopes—iodine-125—encapsulated in these titanium seeds, into each breast, surrounding the tumors that are growing there." Molnár gestured expansively at the machines and monitors surrounding the table. "This is our three-dimensional ultrasound guidance system. We must locate each lump to within hundredths of a millimeter of exactitude within a chaotic inner space. I feel like I'm flying an airplane with only radar to guide me."

Nathan worked his way around behind Molnár. He found a lovely angle which included Molnár's hands and the shimmering pan in the foreground and Dunja's bewebbed breasts in the background. The light over the table combined with the D3's exquisite low-light sensitivity gave him enough depth of field that he could just hold both the foreground and the breasts in focus. As he fired off his shots, the Kevlar/carbon-fiber composite shutter hammering echoes off the blasted tiles of the room, Molnár shouted out for all to hear, "It's a good thing you are not shooting film, I must admit to myself. Her breasts will soon be radioactive, and your film would be fogged as a result!"

2

NAOMI THOUGHT SHE WOULD end up meeting Hervé Blomqvist at a little brasserie somewhere near the Sorbonne, something appropriate to a Truffaut film, something with small marble-topped tables and in keeping with the Léaud French bad-boy image she had taken from Blomqvist's various web manifestations. Instead, she found herself sitting in L'Obélisque, one of the restaurants of the Crillon, the only place the kid would meet her once he heard she was staying at the hotel. Fortunately, he did not seem to know about the hotel's other restaurant, Les Ambassadeurs, which used to be the ballroom of the dukes of Crillon and was even more expensive. L'Obélisque was described as informal and bistro-like in the hotel's brochures, but for Naomi its wood paneling and black-suited waiters with their gold Crillon pins—an art nouveau capital *C* topped by a crown—were intimidating and a bit of a strain, wardrobe-wise. She had unrolled her emergency no-name black cotton T-shirt dress and dug out her strappy, wedgy heels, the ones that weren't stilettos and didn't get trapped by Euro cobblestones and grates. And now she sat there, burning.

Earlier that day, she had been standing just outside the ornately formal entrance of the hotel, leaning against what she thought was a green metal electrical junction box across the street from the American embassy compound, madly texting Blomqvist about their imminent meeting, when she felt her shoulder being nudged. She turned to find herself facing a French cop carrying a submachine gun. He had walked across the narrow road behind her from his post at the corner of the embassy and now stood, just off the curb, forbidding and incongruous in his sunglasses and his dark-blue uniform complete with bulletproof vest and lobster-like body armor covering his shoulders, legs, and feet. Lying against his collarbone were two looped plastic zip-tie handcuffs held by flaps on his shoulder plate, ready for instant action. All that was missing was a helmet, but instead he wore a soft canoe-shaped garrison cap. "What are you doing, standing there playing with your cell phone?" he asked. He was very young and very handsome, and he smiled, but he was not friendly. A white-and-red shield-shaped emblem on his chest plate read "Police Nationale, CRS." Their specialty was riot control, Naomi knew, but the street, which ran into the Place de la Concorde, was absolutely serene, and the square was thronged with oblivious tourists. There was even a farcical group of Americans balancing uncertainly on two-wheeled gyro-stabilized Segways, listening to a briefing from their Segway tour leader before setting off into the crazed traffic.

"I'm waiting for a friend," said Naomi, her French more hesitant than it would be in a week's time. "I'm staying at the hotel, the Crillon, right here," she added lamely, gesturing behind her, and then was immediately angry with herself for giving him anything for free.

He took one hand off his weapon and made a flicking motion, shooing her away like a child. "Wait for your friend over there, on the other side of the hotel entrance. Away from this control box."

Naomi now realized that she had been leaning against the controller for a huge steel cylinder that would rise out of the tarmac at the swipe of a security card, blocking all traffic from the side street between the hotel and the embassy. The American embassy compound, ringed with metal barriers and tightly spaced concrete bollards topped with brass acorns, was a wasp nest. Agitate it at your peril. In silent revenge, Naomi had taken many long-lens photos of the windows of the embassy from a corridor window on her floor at the Crillon. Most of the embassy windows were opaqued, but she had a shiver that soon there'd be a kicking-down of her attic-room door and a brutal arrest, complete with those no-nonsense plastic handcuffs and perhaps a hood over her head. The incident had rattled her for some reason, but did it have to do with America in France, general outrage against authority, hot policemen, or just bondage/victim/humiliation fantasies? She resolved to research a piece on the eroticism of the Compagnies Républicaines de Sécurité. There was a glossy Paris-based gay magazine that would die to have it—if they hadn't done it already.

The Jean-Pierre Léaud clone swept into her space and sat down. He smiled and—of course—swept back his unruly lock of straight dark-brown hair. To her shock, he was wearing a narrow-fitting suit and a skinny tie. And a white shirt. And he was carrying a conservative dark-brown valise, which he carefully placed on the floor, propping it against the table leg. He watched her closely for a moment, then stuck his hand out across the table, weaving it neatly through the red- and yellow-tinted water glasses and the candles to reach her. She was not surprised at the tentative, intellectual's handshake. "Hello," he said. "You are Naomi Seberg—that's a nice movie-star name. I'm certain you have guessed that I'm Hervé Blomqvist." They had agreed, in the text messaging that had followed their first, relatively public, contact on the Célestine A. forum, that they would speak English. He needed the practice, he said, and would not speak French.

"I didn't have to guess," Naomi said, "because I've seen videos of you. In fact, you sent me a couple."

He withdrew his hand, unweaving it carefully. His brow furrowed in mock intensity and his lips pouted. He knew how to work his cuteness.

"I always had the illusion that I was impossible to capture on video. My essence, I mean." He felt so young to her, even though she was only six years older than his twenty-five. He had had a precocious passage through French academia, but, as was often the case, maturity in other matters had not kept pace, had most likely been sacrificed. All this from the forum, delivered to him by well-wishing but critical friends and to any troll who cared to absorb it. Like Naomi.

"I think you're right about your essence," said Naomi. "I have no insight into that. But your face … I recognize that. What I don't recognize is the suit and tie. You're always in jeans and a T-shirt on the net. Did you dress up for me?"

"I've never even walked past the door of the Crillon before. I was afraid they would discover me and throw me out. I borrowed the suit from my brother. He's an advocate. It's unusual for a journalist to stay at the Crillon, isn't it?"

"It would be unusual for a journalist to *pay* for a stay at the Crillon, yes."

"You don't pay?"

"Not with money."

"With sex?"

Naomi laughed. It was her best laugh, the one she always hoped would come out when she laughed. It was husky and genuinely mirthful, and it was like that because Hervé was so appallingly, boyishly hopeful. "No, not with sex. With photography."

"Ah, yes. Photography." Hervé pressed fingers to his temples and closed his eyes. "Is that a coffee you're drinking?" he asked.

"Yes. Double espresso. Do you want one?"

"I'd like just a sip of yours, if you don't mind. I need something, but not too much." He opened his eyes and smiled. "A touch of migraine." He pronounced it "*mee*graine," like the English.

She shrugged and pushed her cup across the table. "Be my guest."

He picked up the cup and made a show of inhaling the fumes. "Mm. It's dangerous. I get too hyper." He did pronounce it "*ee*pair," but there was no way Naomi was going to comment, even though in his texting he had expressed enthusiasm for "ruthless linguistic corrections." He sipped with exaggerated sensuality, his lips and tongue working overtime, looking her deeply in the eyes as he did it. Naomi closed her eyes and shook her head. She felt like his mother. When she looked up at him again, she affected a stern, flirtation-killing look. She pulled her voice recorder out of her bag, switched it on, and placed it on the table.

"Hervé," she said, "I'm recording you now, as we agreed, and my first question to you is: Is this how you were with Célestine Arosteguy?"

He froze for a beat, then put the cup down. "How I was? I was just me, as always. I don't understand what you mean."

"You're being very seductive with me. Did you seduce your professor, or did she seduce you?"

"I see," he said. "You want to play the role of Célestine with me. You identify with her."

"No, I'm really not playing at all. I want to know how it was with them, with the Arosteguys. From someone who knows. From you."

"It was full of sex with them, but more than just sex. But you're just interested in the sex, aren't you? You want to make a sensational conversation. You want to hurt them, don't you?"

"Why do you think that?" Naomi was genuinely thrown by this, and Hervé could see it. "We went through all that on the net. I thought you understood me."

"I understood you," said Hervé. "But I never believed you. How *sympa* you were, how you loved them, how their philosophy and their love story so inspired you."

"Then why are you here, drinking my espresso?"

A compact Gallic shrug. "I wanted to see what a room in the Hôtel de Crillon looked like."

THEY ENDED UP ordering room service. While they waited, Hervé agreed to pose for some stills, sitting on the chaise longue in the bedroom by the open balcony doors while Naomi squatted with the camera, shifting from side to side, trying to find the revealing angle. She was using the Nikon D300s, the cousin to Nathan's D3. It was more compact and lighter, and she prized unobtrusiveness and mobility above all things. The muted light was soft, diffused by the pigeon netting and the trapped bounce of the courtyard, and it brought out the femininity of the boy's face. He played the lens expertly, as Naomi expected he would, given his self-promotion on the Arosteguy forums, which involved endless videos and stills documenting the many moods and musings of Hervé Blomqvist. His general approach was coy/mysterioso, and Naomi knew just how to use the natural light and her angles, the brow, the dark, full eyebrows, the liquid brown eyes in the thin face, to make that pop.

"So, Naomi, what are you going to use these photos of me for?" He spoke between shots, timing her rhythm so that he wouldn't be caught in an ungainly mouth move. "Are you planning an Arosteguy picture book? Maybe for the coffee table?"

"I don't know what I'm doing, Hervé. Do you have any suggestions?"

"I do have a suggestion. I think you will be afraid of it."

Naomi paused and rested her camera on her knees. She felt strange in her dress, but at least she was now in bare feet. She looked up at Hervé, who smiled down at her with benign, unfocused eyes, like a priest. Annoying.

"Go," said Naomi. "Let's hear it."

Hervé stood up and began undoing his tie. "I propose a book that shows every lover that the Arosteguys ever had, starting with me. And they will all be in the nude. And they will say what their experience in fucking them was. And they will talk about the influence that Célestine and Aristide had on their lives."

Naomi sat on the floor, her back against the foot of the bed. "Are you taking your clothes off?" she asked.

"Yes," said Hervé.

"You want me to shoot pictures of you naked?"

"Yes."

"I'm not going to have sex with you. Really. I'm not."

Hervé had taken off his tie, jacket, and shirt, and was working on his belt, a fussy alligator-patterned thing with a dual-pronged buckle and a double row of holes which seemed to be giving him trouble. He was hairless and thin through the chest, just as Naomi thought he would be. All those New Wave movies. "If you have sex with me, I will show you something special that Célestine liked very much. It's unusual what she liked."

Naomi lifted her camera and casually began to snap away.

"Oh, I like your camera," said Hervé. "It looks like it's carbon fiber. Is it?"

"No. Magnesium body." She stopped shooting, hefted her Nikon, juggled it from hand to hand. "I have a feeling carbon fiber is next, though. It would be nice if it were even lighter." Then back up to her eye, shooting again. "And what about Aristide? Was there something special that he liked?"

Hervé finally got his belt undone and his trousers down. He was wearing black Calvin Klein bikini briefs. She had hoped for something more exotic. "Yes, certainly," he said, stepping out of the trousers. "It will be a little more difficult, but I can show you that too."

DUNJA LAY PROPPED UP in a bed in the Molnár Clinic's basement recovery room. There were a dozen beds, skeletal and primitive, creepy, but she and Nathan were alone in the room. He sat in an unstable plastic chair beside her bed, his camera on his lap, his voice recorder still hanging from its lanyard around his neck, its jewel-like red power light staining Dunja's sheet, so dark was the room. Dunja was still dreamy, but Nathan suspected it was emotional exhaustion more than the effect of the anesthetic. She nodded towards him. "I didn't expect the camera. In the operating room. I thought you would just take notes on a notepad, like a proper journalist."

"We're all photojournalists now. It's no longer enough just to write. We have to bring back images, sound, video. I hope you don't mind."

Dunja stretched, and it was somehow voluptuous despite the depressing threadbare hospital gown and the shunt in her arm. "I don't mind. Soon, that'll be all that's left, so the more the merrier. Something to remember me by."

"Why do you say that? Don't you have confidence in Dr. Molnár?"

Dunja laughed. "Look at this place. This is my strategy of last resort. No one else in the world would commit this operation on me. Only Dr. Molnár was arrogant enough. And you can quote me."

"I *will* quote you."

"And you? You were so impressed by Dr. Molnár you came from New York to write about him?"

Nathan's turn to laugh. "I saw him in a documentary about illegal organ transplants. He was very defiant and very engaging. I came to talk to him about the international organ trade and then discovered he was a practicing breast surgeon. I'm not sure yet what the piece I'm writing is really about, but that's not so unusual for me." He lifted his camera. "May I take a picture?"

"Why not? Send these images of me through the internet out into the universe, where I will continue my out-of-body existence."

Nathan checked the light metering through the viewfinder, then cranked the camera's ISO up to its maximum of 25,600. (The new D4s, the one he didn't have, could shoot at a surreal ISO 409,600—it could see in the dark—but that didn't bear thinking about.) The photos would be extremely noisy, grainy and splotchy, but would have a painterly quality, pointillist, perhaps, or impressionist. The camera somehow felt even more sensuous, more instrument-like, at that setting. He began to fire.

Dunja sighed. "Of course, for all eternity I won't look my best. Is there any pose you'd like from me? I'm not shy."

Nathan thought of what Naomi would say to that. She was a fashion photographer at heart, maybe even a celebrity shooter—a paparazza?—and wouldn't be shy about directing a subject as pliant as Dunja. "I don't really want you to pose. We're pretending that you don't know I'm here." Nathan stood up and moved around her, shooting with the lens wide open, with little depth of field, the floating images of her face driving right into his brain. Her eyes had a creamy darkness, and she seemed able to look into the lens without actually noticing it. Stunning.

Nathan paused and went back to his camera bag. He dug around in it for his flash. "Just to be on the safe side, I'll take a few with some bounced flash. There's not much light in here." He slid the foot of the flash into the hot shoe and locked it. "We can just do the same thing you were doing." He pulled up the flash's little plastic bounce card for eye light and began to fire.

"Oh, but now, with that flashing, I feel like a movie star," she said. "And I want you to see the best part of me." She pulled open her gown and presented her breasts, which were bruised and peppered with tiny swollen red dots. Nathan immediately stopped shooting. "What's wrong?" she said. "Too ugly? Too horrible?"

"No, on the contrary. It's, um, too sexy. In a fetishistic way. Or something. Maybe too Helmut Newton. I don't think I'd know how to use it for, you know, a medical article."

"Then just take some for yourself," said Dunja. "So that you remember me afterwards in a nicer way." She smiled the warmest smile at him, and then tears began to seep from her eyes. She did not wipe them away. "And can that camera function under water?"

DUNJA SPLASHED WATER at Nathan, targeting his camera but missing it, soaking the knees of his jeans. Somehow she still managed to look voluptuous in her clinical gray one-piece cotton bathing suit, in part because it was thin and unstructured, clinging. A white medicinal rubber bathing cap hid her hair completely. "I was sure they wouldn't allow you to take photos in here," she laughed. "And you're wearing jeans!"

Nathan was squatting next to a stylized stone lion-head fountain that drooled complex mineral water into the pool. He stood up and followed her, warily snapping, as she waded along the edge of the shallow end of the pool. "I got Dr. Molnár to pull some strings. Getting me in with jeans was the hardest part, apparently. But what about you? Every other woman here is wearing one of those blue plastic shower cap things. You're not in regulation dress either."

"The matron in the locker room is very strict, but she's also half Slovenian, from my father's town of Jesenice. I told her why I needed a special hat to keep the water out of my ears. I made her cry. I think she's in love with me now."

They were in the main swimming pool room of the Hotel Gellért, on the hilly Buda side of the Danube. The room was vast, more like an opulent art nouveau ballroom than a pool, and was bordered by a series of twinned, intricately tooled marble columns, arcades, and ornate balconies bearing potted ferns that projected from the spacious upper gallery. Thin morning light drifted in through its arched yellow glass roof.

"And what about that bathing suit? Is that yours too?" asked Nathan.

"You don't like it? They rent them here. I think they were designed by Stalinists."

Somewhere deep inside the pool's mosaic-tiled heart, motors fired up, and the entire pool became a frothing, sulfurous Jacuzzi. Dunja ducked under the effervescing water and disappeared, leaving Nathan to stalk along the edge of the pool, tracking her among the other swimmers as they churned out their slow, orderly laps or clung to one of the many pulsing jets on the pool's floor. He dodged the columns and the fan-backed plastic chairs strewn randomly along the arcaded hall. When she surfaced, laughing, the bathing suit a sexy-astringent commie second skin, he started shooting again, the shutter rattling like a submachine gun, ignoring the wary looks of swimmers who got in the line of fire. Playing the camera all the way, Dunja pulled herself out of the pool and sat in one of the chairs—*her* chair, evidently, because she pulled around her the towel that had been draped over its back. Nathan pulled up another chair and sat close to her.

"So, you're actually staying here, at this hotel?"

"Part of the Molnár Clinic package," she said. "It included business-class tickets on Malév. Flying me right from my hometown deep in the wilds of Slovenia. Where are you staying?"

"Holiday Inn. My expense account is limited."

"Is it nice?"

"Well," said Nathan, "you can park a bus there. Great if you have a bus."

Dunja peeled the bathing cap off her head. She let it flop into her lap like a jellyfish and combed her fingers through her black crop. "You really should stay here. Would you like at least to see my room? For your writing? And of course you could take pictures. It's very ... proto-Hungarian."

"Aren't you going to try the thermal baths? They're supposed to be very healing."

"Oh, I did that when I first got here. I really don't think they'd be very good for me right now. Besides, Dr. Molnár forbids it. I think those little pellets will come popping out of my breasts like blackheads if I get all steamed up. He's seeing me again tomorrow. I wouldn't want to upset him. I won't even tell him I went swimming."

DUNJA'S SUITE WAS A DISAPPOINTMENT. It was large and blandly comfortable, with a nice partial view of the historically strategic Gellért Hill and the sinister, sprawling stone Citadel that topped it, but Nathan had been hoping for something more exotic than just bourgeois familiarity. He had, he realized, hoped for the swimming pool, the florid thermal baths, converted into a hotel suite.

But Dunja was not a disappointment. She was wearing a waffle-pattern bathrobe, looking at herself in the mirror over the writing table. The bathrobe was open, and she was holding her breasts, one in each hand, palpating them expertly, clinically, without sensuality. Nathan sat on the bed and took photos of her through the mirror.

"So? My breasts are now officially radioactive. I'm not allowed to hug pregnant women for at least three months. What do you think of that? Journalistically."

"I don't know. Can you hug non-pregnant men?" Still firing. The constant clucking of the camera had become part of their repartee, Nathan rolling his firing finger over the shutter release as exclamation, as rimshot, as query.

Dunja turned to him, her bathrobe still fully open, hands still holding breasts. "Nathan, I'm a very sick woman. Does that turn you on?"

Still firing. "Well, I told you, I'm a failed medical student. Now I'm a medical journalist. So, yes, I guess sickness does turn me on in a way."

She approached him and gently took the camera out of his hands and placed it behind her on the writing table. "What about death? I could be dying. Is that exciting to you?" She took his hands in hers and placed them on her breasts. "They ache a bit, you know. After all, they've been penetrated by two hundred and forty tiny titanium pellets. Like asteroids and a cosmic dust shower. Look. Look at all those needle marks. I'm like some weird junkie, crazy for titanium." She laughed. "Don't be shy. They feel better with some pressure on them." He squeezed her breasts tentatively and kissed her.

After a beat, she pulled her mouth away. "I've discovered that most men are repulsed by disease, especially when it starts to be visible." She took up his hands again and placed them on her groin. "You feel those lymph nodes, how big they are? My shape is changing. It's really starting to become a not-human shape. I had a boyfriend in Ljubljana, you know, for eight years. When he felt those, he told me it creeped him out, his exact words—well, the Slovenian equivalent. Then he noticed these." She took his hands and placed them around her throat, then pushed them up under her jaw. "You feel those? They're hard, aren't they?"

"Yes," said Nathan. "I noticed them when you were swimming."

"They spoil my jawline, don't they? It used to be very strong, very elegant. Now it's lumpy and I look like an old toad. No, worse, because they're not even symmetrical. A lopsided old toad. And so my boyfriend left me for a German tourist he was showing around the city. He worked as a guide in the summers. Now he lives with her in Düsseldorf. They go hiking. Marike's a very healthy woman. He sent me a book of poetry by Heinrich Heine, who was born there. He says his German has gotten quite good, and he hopes I'm getting good medical treatment. That's thoughtful of him, isn't it?"

Nathan slid his hands down around her throat and kissed her deeply. Once again, she pulled away, this time laughing. "Maybe you're not normal. Or is this part of your research? Do you always have sex with your subjects?"

"You're not my subject. Dr. Molnár is my subject, and I'm not going to have sex with *him.*"

"Maybe you can ask him again why I have these swollen lymph nodes. He tells me it's the cancer but that no one really knows what causes the swelling. I think he's being evasive. I think I have cancer everywhere, not just my breasts. Look at these." She twisted away from him, shrugged off the bathrobe, and held up her arms. "You see these? Near my armpits? They're so big, they're almost like two more breasts." She dropped her arms and shrugged. "But maybe four tits is nice for you, who knows?"

Dunja turned and strolled over to the bed. "If you make love to me, who will be shooting the photos?" She lay down on the bed languorously, head propped up on one hand.

"There's always a way, if you really want that. There's a self-timer on the camera." Beside the writing table stood a large armoire that held the TV aloft, flanked by miniature fluted wooden Greek columns, presenting the screen as though it were an oracle. Below that was a pair of doors, which Nathan now opened to reveal the scuffed, refrigerated minibar; sitting on it was a wooden tray that held snacks and sundries. Nathan slid out the tray and started rummaging through its chaotically scattered contents. He picked up a black cardboard box with red stripes and turned it over, looking for a label. "It would be tricky to get the best porn angles, though. We'd have to ask the concierge for help. Or maybe see what the doctor is doing right now. He seems to be a connoisseur of nude photography."

"What are you looking for?" she asked.

"I think they have something here called a Pleasure Pak. Has gels and condoms and things."

Dunja sat up on the bed. "Nathan, forget that, please. I've had enough technology shoved into my body." She spoke softly.

"Really? But aren't you ..."

"I'm not anything. In the last two years I've been irradiated from head to toe, inside and out. Nothing inside me has survived. Believe me. And besides, I don't have much of a future to worry about, so if you have the clap, or even something worse, I don't much care."

HERVÉ SAT CROSS-LEGGED on the chaise longue with Naomi's old MacBook Pro on his lap. He was wearing his white shirt and loosened tie and his Calvins. On the bed, Naomi used her BlackBerry to email a certain Dr. Phan Trinh, Célestine's personal physician, whose address had just been given to her by Hervé. The boy was proving useful beyond her wildest imaginings. She was beginning to suspect that he was some kind of police asset at the Sorbonne, and that he had been informing on the Arosteguys, who were, along with everything else, contrarian political activists. "Dear Dr. Trinh," she tapped. "I wonder if you would agree to speak to me in confidence about the medical condition of Célestine Arosteguy. I believe that many destructive rumors have tended to damage the reputation of this wonderful woman, and I, a woman myself ..."

Hervé jumped up unexpectedly from the chaise and started fanning his crotch with a copy of *Les Inrockuptibles,* an amusingly unruly French movie/culture mag he had brought with him in his brother's valise. He was very proud of a short movie review he had written for the magazine, his first ever published, and had read it out loud, very slowly, to Naomi, cracking up at every delicious instance of his own insolence. "Shit. Something in your computer just tried to grab my balls."

Without looking up from her screen, she—mother Naomi—said, "I told you not to sit that way. I always feel some weird magnetic-field hot tingling when I have it on my lap and the hard drive's spinning, and I don't even have balls. If you thought your Peyronie's was bad, wait until you try testicular cancer."

"If it was good enough for Lance Armstrong, it's good enough for me. A lot of people in France believe that his cancer treatment turned him into a sci-fi monster super-racer, even before the normal sports drugs."

"If you say so." All Naomi could do was shake her head. Lance and cycling had loomed large in Hervé's failed attempt to seduce her. It turned out that his secret sex weapon was Peyronie's disease, which he believed he had acquired by riding his carbon-fiber Colnago bicycle along the entire arduous route of the Tour de France two summers ago. Certainly, for a skinny kid, he had amazing quad muscles; they were so out of proportion to the rest of him that they looked like implants, or maybe CGI sweetening. They were a pleasant shock to Naomi when his trousers came off, but really not enough of a novelty to get her into bed. Nor was his mildly bizarre penis.

Hervé had already researched his condition, could at least name it—François de Lapeyronie had been surgeon to King Louis XV (what resonance!)—but Naomi found him to be very selective in what he retained, more romantic than medically astute. She did her own quick web search, which revealed that Peyronie's involved the mysterious growth of a hard, inelastic fibrous plaque along one side of the penis just under the skin, causing it to bend alarmingly when erect. Hervé's particular version of the condition had his long, thin, uncircumcised organ making an almost full right turn of ninety degrees two-thirds of the way up from its root, its tip thus looking at his right hip. Was it scar tissue caused by trauma? The idea of a scarred penis, that it had been through the wars of sex, had its rough charm. Was it an autoimmune system assault? Not so appealing.

Hervé felt it was a cycling problem. He had first asked to use her laptop because he wanted to show her his bicycle, whose photos were posted on one of his many websites. Still naked, he turned the screen towards her to show a loving shot of an ornately painted racing bicycle hanging from rubber-coated hooks screwed into the living room wall of his flat. "This is the machine that did it. It's so beautiful, it's hard to believe it would do that to me." He flicked through the detail close-ups. "You see that three-leaf-clover symbol, like in playing cards? That's the Colnago logo. The seat isn't original equipment. I had it fitted. It's carbon fiber too. It's not very merciful, but it's incredibly light. I'm addicted to the carbon fiber."

He had described to her the evolution of his attitude to his new sex organ, whose altered form had apparently just appeared one morning, no warning, while he was showering and thinking erotic thoughts. At first, of course, he was appalled. His sex life was obviously over, laughable. "I kept getting these spam emails about lengthening your penis and making it harder and thicker. I used to mock of those. Then suddenly I found myself hoping to see one about straightening it out. I would have been tempted, even if I had to FedEx my cock to Nigeria." That was the first laugh he had gotten intentionally from Naomi.

He had been abstinent from that morning on, ashamed not only of his warped tool but also of the bourgeois embarrassment which gripped him. Even masturbation had become abhorrent. It was the Arosteguys who rescued him from sexual despair, though it was a side effect that came from their work with his more dangerous philosophical despair. At times, the Arosteguys gave a lecture together, normally in the modest Amphithéâtre Turgot, with its steeply raked floor and simple wooden desks. But occasionally they would hold court in the magnificent sky-lit Grande Amphithéâtre, its hundreds of green-baize-covered seats and benches jammed and bristling with students, and it was at one of these that Hervé first conceived the idea of attacking his new problem through the medium of a philosophical treatise concerning the body as commodity, a concept at the core of the Arosteguys' politics.

Inevitably, his huddle with the couple at the end of the lecture led to an invitation to a private tutorial at their flat, something for which they were deliciously notorious. They were genuinely excited by the boy's use of his own physical reality to leap into the powerful waves of Arosteguyan speculation. They were also excited by his sex, which Célestine called her "bat penis," although further net-searching by Hervé did not come up with any validation of her pet name. The images he found revealed that bats, especially fruit bats, or flying foxes, had very humanoid, long, straight cocks that put his to shame with their fearful symmetry. The bats were also capable of licking their own glans to keep it clean while hanging upside down, and looked rather joyful doing it, too. This first sexual encounter, which announced the potent presence of Hervé in the lives of the Arosteguys, was sketched in some detail on the boy's Facebook page, but the chiropteric element had been excised.

Hervé now kneeled on the floor in front of the chaise, the malignant laptop safely at arm's length in front of him. "Okay, Naomi. I now have something wonderful for you."

Naomi was finishing off her plea to Dr. Trinh, whose photograph she had just found. A posed office photo of the type meant to sell the compassionate competence of a private medical clinic presented a small, neat, perfect Vietnamese woman in an elegant tailored suit who smiled out of Naomi's phone. "What would that be, Hervé?"

Hervé rolled sideways on the carpet so that he could lounge with studied cinematic insouciance against the sill of the balcony doors. "I've just told Aristide Arosteguy all about you. He wants to meet you in Tokyo."

THERE WERE SEVERAL IMMENSE, empty tourist buses in the parking lot of the Holiday Inn. Nathan schlepped his way past them, camera bags over shoulders, iPhone in hand, having just been dropped off by the hotel's shuttle. Naomi had texted him to call her ASAP, but for some reason the reception on the minibus had been poor. He had dialed her the second he stepped off. "How's your beautiful, expensive hotel?"

"Appropriate. How's yours?" said Naomi.

"I'm looking at it as we speak. Let's just say ... functional. More appropriate."

"More?"

"Yeah. 'Cause I know that yours is too good for a journalist."

"It's that darn rich-girl problem again. And speaking of girls, how was she? Your patient?"

"Beautiful. She was really beautiful."

"In a doomed beautiful sort of way?"

"In a Slavic sort of way."

"That sounds dangerous," said Naomi. She meant it.

"She *was* dangerous. Literally radioactive. The seductiveness of decay. What about Arosteguy? I've seen him in interviews. Pretty devastating. Gorgeous, in that irritating French intellectual way."

"I'll let you know when I find him. Nobody seems to know where he is, including the prefect of police." For some reason, Naomi wanted to hold back her new contact with Arosteguy, even though that was the reason she had called Nathan. Was it the Slavic-beauty comment? "I think Célestine is really our September cover, though. She's even more seductive. Beautiful but dead is always killer." *Killer* was what they loved at Naomi's primary magazine, *Notorious,* whose editor, Bob Barberien, was himself notorious for drunken office rants that somehow became sensational articles that you had to read; they generally involved unimaginable acts of murder. *Notorious* mimicked the 1950s scandal mag *Confidential* in its starkly aggressive cover graphics and even its retro typography. Naomi loved its recklessness and its ironic naïveté; it provoked her own.

"Yeah, and will he really have anything interesting to say? 'I murdered my wife and then I ate her.' How do you follow that up?"

"Nobody seems to want that to be true," said Naomi. "There's a weird national protectiveness about that pair. It's all denial, even from the police. From what I can see here, it's possible that one of her student lovers killed her out of jealousy." It had occurred to her that Hervé might know something about that. Or might even be the killer himself.

"And students are notorious for not eating properly. I'm getting into the elevator now. If I lose you, I'll call right back." His room was on the third, and top, floor, and he did lose her, and waited until he was in his room to redial. "So I guess the only photos you've taken with my macro lens are shots of your laptop's screen."

"Very funny. And what about you? Are you going to send me shots of your beautiful doomed patient?"

Just the slightest pause from Nathan, but it hurt Naomi. "I only got a few during the operation. But basically, she wouldn't let me. She felt diseased and ugly."

"You've never let that stop you before," said Naomi, fishing.

"I got stopped this time. Stopped in my tracks."

A big pause from Naomi before she said, "I can't wait to see you. Amsterdam or Frankfurt?"

"I need Amsterdam. My connecting flight to New York's already been paid for. I land on the fourteenth. Work for you?"

"The fourteenth works for me. Bye, darling."

"Bye, darling."

Nathan thumbed his phone off. That was life with Naomi—disembodied. Nathan realized he had almost no awareness of getting to his room other than the disconnect in the elevator. No smells, no sights, no sounds. He had been in his phone, Naomi a voice in his brain. On his laptop, he scrolled through the photos he had taken of Dunja—the operation, the spa, the sex they had together in her hotel room. It did not bother him that the photos aroused him in a weirdly objective way, as though he had stumbled upon a stash of celebrity sex photos that hadn't hit the mainstream yet. Nathan was a connoisseur of his own sexuality, and its twists and turns amused and delighted him. And speaking of pictures, Dunja did look beautiful but doomed, and never more so, oddly, than in the snaps he had taken later in Molnár's restaurant on the Pest side of the river. It was perverse of her, he had thought, to want to go there, to a restaurant owned by her cancer doctor, where nude pictures of his patients covered the walls, and while she was in the middle of an intense cancer procedure. And worse, Dr. Molnár himself had threatened to greet them there, to fuss over them and introduce to them in excruciating detail each dish, which he would personally serve them; perhaps, he hinted with a twisted twinkle, he would hover over their special corner table until they had each opened their mouths and, with exquisite care and sensuousness, tasted.

Molnár had not been there when they arrived. The maître d' could not give them the corner table and had no record of special treatment to be accorded them, no reservation in fact. It was a relief—even to be forced to leave for some other restaurant would have been better—but there was a table, or at least two chairs side by side along a run of small square tables pushed together. Dunja and Nathan were on the outside, facing a framed mirror and a pair of solitary eaters who paid no attention to each other. The mirror made it possible for them to eat and talk and watch each other's responses as though they were characters in a charming Czechoslovakian movie from the sixties. The seating lottery also absolved them of any need to study Molnár's wretched and scandalous photographs—the opposite wall was blocked from view by a thick stuccoed pillar—which were all portraits of his patients shown in the most vulnerable, if not drugged, circumstances, with a clinically salacious eye for nakedness, both emotional and physical. Nathan had to reluctantly flash Dr. Molnár's card at the maître d' to get permission to use his camera in the dumpy restaurant, which was inexplicably called La Bretonne. His first attempts to document the good doctor's artwork were intercepted by two waiters and a busboy, certain, no doubt, that the photographs were a rich treasure in danger of illicit duplication and dissemination. As he framed the Molnár photos in his viewfinder, Nathan was disturbed to find himself responding to them with a profound and hopeless sadness. One or two of the shots he had taken of Dunja could have fit seamlessly among those of the women—all women—nailed to the rough-hewn dark wood of the walls, and it allied him with Dr. Molnár in a way that made him queasy. The large black-and-white prints, Nathan had to admit, were gorgeous; the fine grain of medium-format film, with its deep contrast and subtle shadows conveyed by silver gelatin on rag paper, produced a startling hyperreal effect.

Nathan made his way back to Dunja from the far end of the restaurant. She was cradling a glass of red wine in her beautiful long-fingered hands—bigger than his own, he had noted; he felt the oddness when they held hands. He immediately swung the Nikon around on its strap and fired off a few shots, the crack of the shutter easily swallowed by the surrounding boisterous murmur and cutlery clatter. But Dunja snapped her eyes up at him in anger, and it surprised him. Thus chastised, he sat beside her and stuffed the camera into its bag, which he jammed between his feet on the floor, not trusting the raucous flow of patrons and waiters behind him. And it would be those snaps, taken solely by the light of the candles on the table and the warm incandescent sconce lights on the wall in front of her, that revealed a pain and despair that Nathan had not seen in photos of her taken in much more vulnerable circumstances. She was going to die soon; she knew it in a profound way, and now that awareness had been reignited by the camera and was hot in her mind.

"Nathan," she said, "will this be the first time you've made love to a dead woman?"

Nathan fumbled for his own glass, which he had not yet touched. "You mean you?" he said, taking a sip. The wine was very rough. Not good. "You're not dead. I can personally confirm that."

"No, but I mean, after I die, you'll have memories of sex with a woman who's now dead." She smiled a dangerously innocent smile. "Will that be a first for you?"

"Except for my mother, yes. She died when I was fourteen."

"Different kind of sex, then. The Freudian kind. Doesn't count." She paused. He sipped again to fill in the gap—nervously, he was surprised to note. Weirdly giddy. "While I was waiting for you in my hotel room," she said, "I watched a nature show. A young deer fell into a deep snowbank and couldn't get out. A grizzly bear found it and jumped on it from behind. The deer tried to look around. Its eyes were wild and excited. The bear gently grabbed the deer's muzzle in its mouth. It was so sexual. Sex from behind. The bear loved the deer, it was obvious. It ripped the deer's throat out, and then licked the dying deer with the most passionate affection. I thought of you and me."

DR. TRINH KEPT BECOMING Japanese. It was Hervé's fault, of course. The possibility of meeting Aristide Arosteguy in Tokyo had enormous gravitational density, enough to warp every nuance of Naomi's day. And here, in Dr. Trinh's perfectly elegant office on the medically chic Rue Jacob in the Sixième, this warping manifested itself in a subtle shifting of the doctor's delicate Vietnamese features and her complexly accented English towards the rougher features and Japanese schoolgirl diction of Yukie Oshima, Naomi's old Tokyo friend. Naomi had already calculated that Yukie would have to be a major ally in any Tokyo/Arosteguy initiative she might undertake and was finding it hard not to think of the constantly morphing

Dr. Trinh as, well, Yukie in Paris. But Dr. Trinh was not an ally.

"Please put away your camera," she said, as Naomi set her Nikon on her lap. "I regret every moment that I allowed myself to be recorded or photographed. I am talking to you only to undo the damage which that demented cleaning lady has done by talking about Célestine Arosteguy. I will probably regret this too."

Naomi gently caressed her camera as though demonstrating its innate harmlessness. "It's really just proof that I actually spoke to you. You'd be surprised how many interviews are just patched together from things on the internet and presented as face-to-face conversations." Naomi imagined Nathan chuckling and shaking his head over her shoulder as she said this. Somehow, Naomi was of another, newer, generation than Nathan, despite the fact that they were the same age. Nathan seemed to have absorbed his sense of journalistic ethics from old movies about newspaper reporters. For Naomi, internet sampling and scratching was a completely valid form of journalism, presenting no ethical clouds on its open-source horizon. To not be photographed daily, even by oneself, to not be recorded and videoed and dispersed into the turbulent winds of the net, was to court nonexistence. She knew she was being disingenuous with Dr. Trinh as she talked to her about proof, but the only effect her awareness of this had on Naomi was to make her feel more completely professional. It was the way of the net, and it was liberating.

Dr. Trinh was tougher than she looked. "Even photographs and recordings can be easily tricked these days, so what you say makes no sense here in my office. Put your camera and voice recording device away, that little thing hanging around your neck which I see advertised in all the chic fashion magazines, or you can leave right now." Her face and tone were absolutely neutral as she said this, and Naomi could feel her own face start to burn, her skin telling her that she had been deeply, instantly unnerved before her brain or gut knew it.

"Well, off the record is certainly one way to do it, if that's what makes you feel comfortable," said Naomi, unclipping her rarely used Olympus micro-recorder, glossy black like a little piano and reserved for stealth recording, and packing it and the camera into her camera bag with as much nonchalance as she could muster. She hated her own volatility, the cycling so easily between manic confidence and crushed, hopeless insecurity. Maybe drugs would help. Probably not. Naomi had a sudden suicidal urge to ask the doctor if she had any bipolar patients, but Dr. Trinh was not designed to be natively helpful, at least not to Naomi.

"There's nothing about this situation or about you that makes me feel comfortable. Let's talk about that cleaning lady, that Madame Tretikov, the Russian."

"Yes, yes. That maintenance woman … she seemed certain that Célestine Arosteguy had brain cancer." And now Naomi could look up from fussing with her camera bag and jab back, however delicately. "Now, Dr. Trinh—I hope I'm pronouncing that correctly—Dr. Trinh, you're not a cancer specialist, not an oncologist, for example, are you?"

The doctor took a deep breath. "What's that pin you're wearing? What does that designate?"

Naomi was completely thrown. Pin? Oh, yes. "This pin?" She unclipped the gold Crillon pin she had been given by her hotel contact and tossed it onto the leather writing pad on the doctor's desk. "It's the symbol of the Hôtel de Crillon. I've been staying there. It's held on by this big round magnet. You see? They're very nice at that hotel. Not snobbish at all." Dr. Trinh picked it up and examined it with weird intensity. The doctor's paranoia was suddenly exciting to Naomi, comforting rather than insulting, helping her to cycle back up. It meant that the doctor had something to hide, or at least to protect. "Were you … were you thinking it might be a microphone?"

Dr. Trinh tossed the pin back on the pad and immediately forgot it existed. "There was nothing medically wrong with Célestine Arosteguy. Nothing beyond the normal complaints of a woman of her age. I was her personal physician. I was the one who sent her to specialists when she needed them. Something like cancer … I would have known."

Naomi desperately wanted to pull her notepad out of her bag, the one that was spiral-bound at the top, had a montage of newspaper pages decorating its cardboard cover and labelled itself "Reporter's Notebook/Bloc de Journaliste"—naturally, Nathan had given it to her—but she could feel the fragility of the situation through her skin and didn't dare. "What would you consider the normal complaints of a woman of her age?"

Dr. Trinh actually smiled, though there seemed to be some pain involved in the act. "Perhaps you will simply look up menopause on the internet and your question will be answered."

A small, intimate explosion went off in Naomi's brain, triggered by the unexpected mental juxtaposition of "menopause" and "crime," two things she had never remotely linked before. She needed to remember this tiny epiphany somehow, and she needed to delve into the most heavy realities of menopause and womanness, a place she had never thought to go before. She generated a marker in her mind, one that would pop up whenever Célestine's age was mentioned. "Why do you think the Arosteguys' landlady thought that Célestine had a brain tumor? Isn't that an odd thing for an ordinary person to just invent?"

"Have you ever met this woman, this Tretikov?"

"I've seen an interview with her."

"Yes, of course." Dr. Trinh stood up, brushing the front of her suit with her tiny hands as she did so, as though Madame Tretikov had covered her with breadcrumbs. "Yes, she's an ordinary person who has unconsciously used the power of the internet to create a new reality concerning Madame Arosteguy. And it has caused me and my medical colleagues a lot of anguish, I can tell you." A contemptuous snicker. "She's the kind of superstitious old woman who believes that thinking too much, or even thinking certain thoughts, can give you brain cancer. And I want you to correct that. That is why I agreed to talk to you." Having made her statement, this figurine of a woman sat back down and resumed exactly her former position. "The media have now accused us of negligence in our treatment of a woman who was considered a national jewel. They talk of misdiagnosis, of carelessness, of political pressure on us that forced us to ignore her deadly condition, and so on."

"And none of that is true?"

"None of it."

"And Célestine didn't tell her husband that she had brain cancer, and she didn't ask him to kill her?"

At this, Dr. Trinh produced a sad smile, and it struck Naomi as a genuine smile at last, one which illuminated the doctor's eyes and altered her breathing, which summoned the earthy presence of Célestine Arosteguy into her fussy, controlled office. "Célestine always used to say that she was doomed and that she had a terminal illness. She said that to her students, to me, to everyone. It was not a complaint, you see. It was almost a promise. But then, anyone who read her writings deeply would know she didn't mean anything medical."

The smile was still on Dr. Trinh's face as she looked down at her doll-like hands, lost in secret memories of the doomed, womanly Célestine, and Naomi found herself wanting to destroy it, to punish her for it. In particular, Naomi was annoyed with herself for not having read even a précis of the Arosteguy oeuvre and could not therefore call the doctor on this evasion. The necessary weapons, however, were close at hand. "And would she ask just anyone to kill her?" It occurred to Naomi that she had very recently fallen back on the expression "just kill me" in a conversation with Nathan in which he had again carped about his missing macro/portrait lens—the lens on her camera right now, sitting in the bag at her feet—but she doubted it would be part of Célestine's lexicon.

"Of course not."

"But someone did kill her. Who do you think it was?"

"I have no idea. She had many friends."

"That surprises me. You think a friend killed her?"

"She knew many people."

"You don't think a stranger killed her."

"These are things I know nothing about."

"She would say to you, her personal physician, that she had a terminal illness, and you felt that she was being philosophical? You didn't take it seriously?"

Dr. Trinh had been talking to her hands, but now she raised her eyes to Naomi, searching as she spoke for verifying signs of Naomi's stupidity, her profound American ignorance. "It was an existential statement," said Dr. Trinh, "about the death sentence we all live under. She had an affection for Schopenhauer, which led her at times into a kind of fatalistic romanticism. I tried to get her to revisit Heidegger, not so different in some ways, the Germanic ways, but at least a shift away from that sickly Asian taste for cosmic despair." As if summoned from the ether by that last phrase, a tiny silver crucifix hanging from a bracelet around the doctor's left wrist caught the raw daylight bouncing onto the desk from a corner mirror and caught Naomi's eye. Naomi's friend Yukie was also a Christian, an anomaly that was somehow a disappointment to Naomi. Shintoism, Confucianism, Taoism, Buddhism, perhaps. So much more interesting. What bracelets would they wear then? Dr. Trinh continued: "But she couldn't get past the man's politics, the Nazi associations, the anti-Semitism. We disagreed on that point, that a man's politics should negate the value of his philosophy.

She could not see how a separation of that kind was possible. A perfectly French attitude, of course."

Naomi met the doctor's eyes and her inwardly directed smile with a smile of her own, but she had no confidence that she could disguise the evidence of her immediate downward spiraling, brought about by her intense regret that she had initiated talking to another human being, live. If she had been in front of her laptop, she could google these two Germanics, get a feel for them, but in a strictly oral context she had no idea how to even spell their names, much less respond intelligently to Dr. Trinh. It was one thing to toy with Hervé, bright though he was. Nathan was the one with the classical education, or whatever you called it. He was the reader. Where was he? Naomi was struggling to keep her head above water with the doctor. A street brawl was the only way out.

"Has anyone done an autopsy on Célestine's brain to see if she had a tumor?"

"Based on the diagnosis of a cleaning lady? I doubt it."

"Are you aware of the report that Célestine's severed head was cut open and that her brain was removed by her murderer or murderers? Why do you think they did that?"

A smile was still there on Dr. Trinh's face, but it was no longer the same smile. It had become a smile that said, "I knew you were my enemy when you walked in here, and now here is the proof, and it makes me happy to see how right I was." Dr. Trinh stood up and with special force brushed some more crumbs from the front of her suit, this time very dirty, greasy, ugly crumbs that had been sprinkled by Naomi herself. The little silver crucifix—had Vietnam been converted by French Catholic missionaries?—bounced at the end of its chain like a freshly hanged man. And still Naomi couldn't help herself. "Dr. Trinh, off the record, did Célestine ask you to kill her and then eat her? As a kind of womanly, compassionate sacrament, perhaps?"

Dr. Trinh came out from behind her desk for the first time and walked to the door. She opened it for Naomi without a word. Naomi noticed the doctor's shoes. They were stilettos with an ankle-strapped bondage component, very severe in their stitching and their shape, but shockingly colorful—red, yellow, blue, green, black—like rare Australian parakeets. As Naomi left the office, she could not help thinking that Dr. Trinh's shoes were somehow significant.

3

DR. MOLNÁR HAD ARRANGED for him to be upgraded to elite business class—the Duna Club Lounge!—on his Malév flight to Amsterdam. Even so, Nathan found himself wandering restlessly through the generic steel and glass of Terminal 2A at Ferihegy Airport. Unlike Naomi, who would immediately bury herself in her laptop the instant she arrived, Nathan considered airport downtime an opportunity for people-watching; but today, a drizzly, chilly summer day whose gloom seemed to have seeped into the airport, the only person Nathan was watching was Dunja, who was playing continuously on a screen in his mind. Trailing his roll-on camera bag behind him like a little red wagon, Nathan heard her say the terrifying, outrageous things she said she couldn't help thinking but had no one to say them to until she met Nathan.

"What will I do when you leave me? Who will want me?"

"I'm not so special. If *I* want you . . . You're gorgeous. You'll have as many lovers as you want."

"So many women have cancer now. Do you think a new esthetic can develop? Cancer beauty? I mean, if there could be heroin chic, the esthetic of the death-wishing drug addict? Will non-cancerous women be begging their cosmetic surgeons to give them fake node implants under their chins and around their necks? Under their arms? In their groins? So sexy, that fullness. And it works so well as an anti-aging technique, to fill out that sagging turkey neck. Who wouldn't want it? And the jewelry, the titanium pellets piercing those tits. So S&M/bondage." Dunja kept talking in Nathan's head as he segued into a parallel inner dialogue with her about health and evolution, about the theory that concepts of beauty were not just concepts, but perceptions of indicators of reproductive potential and therefore of youth, about selfish genes using our bodies as vehicles only to perpetuate themselves, about how perhaps cancer genes could begin to make their own case for reproductive immortality as well, and so they too would put immense pressure on cultural acceptance of formerly taboo concepts of beauty, concepts which used to indicate disease and nearness to death but now mesmerized and seduced and mimicked youth and ripeness and health, and so her little fantasy of a culture forming around her own dire straits could theoretically ... It wasn't a conversation they actually had, but if he were Naomi, he'd probably be texting or emailing or instant-messaging Dunja right now using that Naomiesque stream-of-semi-consciousness that had flowed over him so often in the four years they had been together.

Naomi never let anybody go, and she used her unique, potent mixture of technology and witchiness to do it, whereas Nathan was only too happy to disconnect, to remove you from his Friends list and leave you dangling in the ether of cyberspace. Naomi thought that Nathan was ruthless with his friends; Nathan thought Naomi was compulsively, obsessively possessive. But what was Dunja? Despite the sex and the intimacy, she was the subject of a piece, and his subjects often tried to keep up a correspondence with him, sometimes clinging, with an unhealthy, creepy desperation, to that special moment in their lives; they couldn't accept that their time was up, that the piece about their arcane, provocative medical condition had been published, and that Nathan was now permanently out of their lives. Naomi's subjects usually ended up behind bars or executed, and that neatly limited flowback, as Nathan called it. Of course, Dunja was certain she would be dead in a few months, and that would neatly limit flowback as well.

Their last conversation had taken place in the Molnár Clinic's horrid recovery room, after her breasts had been duly cut open and many small tumors had been removed under the cold blue surgery lights that transformed her flesh into silicone and her blood into magenta paste. He sat on the same plastic chair, although this time she was in the bed by the door and there were three other patients rustling and moaning in the room.

"Did you enjoy that?" she asked. "It made it easier knowing that I had an appreciative audience."

"Molnár seemed confident of success. I enjoyed that part of it," said Nathan.

Dunja laughed. "Molnár is just talking about the mechanics of tumor removal. That's his success. He knows I'm not going to last long, but he doesn't really consider it to be his problem."

"Would it hurt for you to be more positive?"

"Oh, Nathan. It hurts when you become sentimental and ordinary. Why would you ever do that?"

"Ouch!"

"Did you get good pictures? Were they shocking? Will Molnár put them up on his wall to excite his customers eating their goulash? Should I make a pun about ghoulash? Ghoul lash?"

"I get it, I get it," said Nathan, still stung, unable to smile. If she did recover, what would they talk about? Her dream of going back to architecture school at the University of Ljubljana and building luxury houses on the banks of the Sava with her father? How ordinary and sentimental would that be? "I got some very good shots of your operation. I'm not sure that you'll like them, but I'll email them to you if you want me to."

Dunja took his hands in hers and pulled him towards the bed. He tried to lurch his chair forward, but it was too flimsy, bending and twisting until it popped out from under him, leaving him standing in a half-crouch like a jockey. She laughed again, and he took a step and settled on the bed, the lowered metal side rail digging into his thighs no matter how he shifted his weight. "Did it turn you on when Zoltán cut into my breasts? I almost convinced him to give me just a local anesthetic, but he copped out." Nathan enjoyed Dunja's sporadic sixties drug/rock lingo and wanted to ask her exactly who she learned her English from, but it never was the right moment.

"Dunja, I'm not a sadist. I'm not a bondage freak. It really brought me down to see you getting cut up." Dunja became quiet, still. What he had just said, his expression of sexual normality, was not what she wanted to hear; he knew she would take it as rejection. He spoke very gently, skating on perversely thin ice. "When you recover from this, when you've healed completely, you'll still be incredibly attractive to me. I mean, your disease and your treatment are not what make you sexy and beautiful."

Dunja's elegant big hands covered Nathan's, squeezed them gently and pulled at them, shook them in slow motion, as though trying to reason with him through them, hoping that unspoken arguments would travel up his arms and down to his heart. "Nathan, oh, Nathan. You are really so sweet and lovely. But I have markers in my genes that say my cancer was destined to metastasize; and it has, it's everywhere in my body, in my lymph nodes, you've felt them and caressed them, and you know it's true. I'm not going to get out of this one, I'm really not."

"But Molnár told me ..."

"Molnár is a very strange and flaky man. He is a surgeon, a mechanic. He doesn't want to know about things he can't attack with machinery. I was completely surprised to wake up and find that I still had tits at all. I was sure he'd get so excited that he'd cut them right off. I was almost disappointed to see them, and looking only a little battle scarred too. He's referred me to another clinic, this one in Luxembourg. It sounds very sketchy to me, just like Molnár, but I have a marker in my brain that means I'm destined to go there too, to let them do things to me until I'm dead."

Nathan could only just manage to keep looking into her searching eyes, feeling at that moment very sentimental and ordinary, and therefore mute. Could he really say anything about classical concepts of art, and therefore beauty, based on harmony, as opposed to modern theories, post-industrial-revolution, post-psychoanalysis, based on sickness and dysfunction? Could he make a case for her new, diseased self as the most avant-garde form of womanly beauty? He didn't dare, but she did.

"While I'm still alive, I'll have nothing special left to seduce with except the scent of dying. That will be my lethal perfume. And I want it to be what seduced you, you see? Because that's my future, and I don't want to live it alone. So you might find me calling you to give advice to my next lover. I might want you to encourage him to go deep into me and not be afraid. Or I might call you one night and ask you to fly to me and then strangle me to death while you fuck me from behind. Why not? Why waste the situation?" Dunja paused, her eyes never stopping their desperate search of his eyes. She smiled a freakishly kind, loving smile. "Would you come to me, Nathan? Would you come to me then, if I called you?"

Nathan headed for the sliding glass doors of the Malév Duna Club Lounge. As he walked in, he recalled Naomi saying, "Just kill me," when he complained to her about something on his cell. Approaching the check-in counter, he thought about strangling Naomi to death while fucking her from behind. Her hands were tied behind her with a terry-cloth hotel bathrobe belt. His hands were powerful around her long throat. Her face was twisted into a beautiful, open-mouthed, terrifying expression of ecstasy, and the fantasy-Nathan knew that it was the end of sex, that there could be no more sex after this sex. At the desk, an extremely unattractive and excessively uniformed matron—that cloying red scarf printed with little multicolored stylized wings—explained to Nathan why the photocopied membership card and other obscure paperwork Molnár had given him was not valid, and that she therefore had to deny him entrance to the promised land of the Duna Club Lounge. As he rollered away from the lounge and headed towards his gate, Nathan could only marvel at the Molnáresque perfection of it all.

CHARLES DE GAULLE was undergoing extensive renovations. After walking for miles past dormant moving sidewalks, Naomi had to lug her roller bag up a double set of stairs—the small glass elevator was *absolument* for disability use only—then over a platform randomly strewn with cafeteria chairs (but no tables) that were served by a huge, lonely, lopsided automatic drinks machine, then down another set of stairs which led her into a dense mass of travelers standing numbly in a corridor with no seats at some distance from a gate with no seats. The horror of it was exacerbated by the near impossibility of getting out her laptop and opening it without cracking someone in the head. Naomi dug her BlackBerry Q10 out of the roller's side pocket. She preferred it to Nathan's iPhone in any text-intensive context like the ones she usually found herself in; she needed real, physical buttons (you couldn't type on an iPhone when you had decent fingernails) and was dreading the possible imminent collapse of the BlackBerry empire. Such was the perilous life of the ardent tech consumer.

As she fired up the Q10, she remembered with a pointy shot of adrenaline that she had left her Crillon pin on Dr. Trinh's desk, so rattled had she been when she left her office. This was especially annoying because the entire day and a half in Paris after that had been tainted—a strange metallic taste in the mouth and a general warping of colors, like a migraine aura—by the Dr. Trinh debacle. Not only had she not gleaned anything useful from Célestine's doctor, she had unexpectedly bumped into the limits of her intellect, or at least her education, and felt bruised by the collision.

Or was she selling herself short? The Crillon pin, for example. She could imagine Dr. Trinh picking it up from her desk with ancient silver North Vietnamese surgical tongs and sending it out to her favorite counter-surveillance lab for analysis. But it was a perfect excuse for further contact with the doctor, if Naomi could devise a more efficient tactic for dealing with her. She could send Hervé to pick it up, primed with some innocent French bad-boy questions which, coming from him, the doctor would feel safe in answering. How close a collaborator could she afford to make Hervé? As if in answer to that question, her Q10 began flashing its email alert light. It was him.

"You did not get a very good review from Dr. Trinh," he wrote. "She was very quick to contact me and to let me know that I should stay away from you because you obviously wanted to do damage to the memory of our dearest Célestine. She also said that she did not feel that you were very intelligent, or maybe you were just American, she's not sure, and that you used shock tactics that reminded her of American military policies in Vietnam. I asked her if she would pose nude for me, for my book that you liked the idea of. She said that her culture forbids it. We had a nice discussion about cultural assimilation and the sensuality of the East. I do not think she will do it."

Naomi's thumbs began to fly. "I'm very disappointed to hear about the doctor's reaction to me. Did she really talk about the Vietnam War?"

"Ha ha, got you there. No, I made that up. She did say that she didn't trust you, though, and that you deliberately left some pin or something in her office as a kind of symbolic marker or presence. Do you know what she's talking about?"

"Did you really ask her to pose nude for your book?"

"Yes. All that is true."

"Does that mean that she was Célestine's lover?"

"Yes. I was once in bed with both of them. One day I'll tell you about that. It was very interesting. It made me think of Karl Marx."

"Was there anyone in the Arosteguys' life together that they didn't . . ."

The corridor, which was lined with glass, had become unbearably hot as the sun edged over it, and the constant irritated nudging through the waiting crowd by passengers trying to get to their baggage or some other flight was ramping up the general hostility. Someone stubbed his foot on Naomi's roll-on and rammed her with his shoulder so hard she could feel the density of his bone and muscle—it felt intentional, a punishment, and Naomi gasped—causing her to inadvertently hit the Send button on her phone. Now other people started to wedge their way through the gap that Naomi had left as she stepped forward under the blow, and she was separated from her camera bag. She rotated herself on the spot so she was confronting the surge and worked her way back to her roller. Facing that direction, she saw the marquee of an airport electronics chain, and with her bag safely back in hand, she plunged towards the oasis of the kiosk.

IN THE CORNER of the room between the minibar and the TV dresser unit crouched two sets of unopened bags: two camera rollers, two backpacks, two small black Samsonite four-wheel Cruisair Spinner suitcases with faux carbon-fiber-weave finish (Naomi and Nathan aspired to Rimowa Topas, the sexy German dentable aluminum stuff, but that was, for the moment, out of their range). It was not so much that they had the same taste in gear, but rather that they collaborated on their consumerism; it was a consumerist dialectic that led to the same commodity. That's what Naomi was thinking in the floating part of her mind as she sucked Nathan's cock—so delightfully, boringly, not curved much at all, not a mutant organ in any way, but a classic, modern circumcised penis—in room 511 of the Hilton Amsterdam Airport Schiphol Hotel. And she was surprised to find herself thinking in Marxist terms, because up until that moment at the electronics kiosk, in which she discovered three books by the Arosteguys—cheap-looking rushed editions in American English pumped out to take advantage of the philosophy-cannibalism scandal—she had barely heard of Karl Marx or *Das Kapital*. And yet those books, small, with large, inviting typefaces, and so easy to read, like owner's manuals for hitherto undiscovered parts of the brain, made her feel as though she had been born a Marxist economist. Not that Marxism was the subject of the books, but that the lexicon of Marx somehow underpinned the Arosteguys' evidently profound understanding of contemporary consumerism—and of Naomi herself, as it turned out.

The lack of an available direct flight, which would have been a short hour-plus hop from Paris to Amsterdam, meant a seven-hour ordeal involving a layover in Frankfurt. But the time dissolved in an odd way, because instead of wandering among the randomly strewn high-tech shops of that stainless-steel commercial kitchen of an airport, punctuated by intense bouts of Wi-Fi hotspotting, Naomi found herself settled into a lounge chair near her gate, submerged in the deep inner sea of the Arosteguys—a warm sea nurturing a coral reef inhabited by the most bizarre and engaging creatures—continuing a dive she had begun on the flight from Paris. By the time she came up for air, she had been transformed into a quiveringly, giddily passionate Arosteguyan.

And now those three books—*Science-Fiction Money, Apocalyptic Consumerism: A User's Manual,* and *Labor Gore: Marx and Horror*—lay innocently on the glossy desk by the window as Nathan unexpectedly, and somewhat unsportingly, came in Naomi's mouth, phlegmy and bitter. It was her breasts that did it, or rather, it was all four breasts—two of Naomi's, two of Dunja's, superimposed on each other, the image fermented in Nathan's brain and downloaded through his penis into Naomi's hot, distracted mouth. Or so it felt to Nathan, absorbing Naomi's jet lag and distraction as his own, and confusing her breasts, beautifully wobbling as she sucked, with Dunja's larger, mutilated ones, and somehow even adding Dunja's swollen armpit glands—six breasts?—to the mix. He had his arms behind his head and wasn't even touching Naomi's breasts. It was the distance that made the hallucinatory laminating of breasts possible, and his usual come-control ineffective. Or had he even tried to exercise that control? Was he like a small dog who punishes his mistress for staying out too late and leaving him locked in the kitchen? Naomi never swallowed unless she was very drunk. Naturally, she had a rationale. It was more porn-like to just let it dribble out of her mouth, to let it form a stringy bridge to his penis and his pubic hair. She did it now, not startled, exactly, but maybe puzzled by his betrayal of their routine, which was that they would decide in advance of her mouth enclosing him whether this was foreplay or this was it for now. Naomi didn't like sexual surprises. She was always willing to play, but she wanted structure.

And so it was a surprise to Nathan, then, that Naomi, abstractedly wiping her lips with the back of her hand, said, "What do you think about Marx and crime, Than?" No sexual reprimands, and a reversion to her infantile name for him, Than, suggesting a thumb-sucking, asexual state of mind.

"Well, I'm not sure, Omi. It's a huge subject, I guess. You've been deep into it? Marx? That's a first for you, isn't it?"

Naomi rolled onto her back, flattened by the enormity. The ceiling was a stained plaster swirling. It matched her mental state. "I've been deep into the Arosteguys."

"They're Marxists?"

"I've been reading them. I realize I have no education. It's intimidating and depressing. It hurts my head. I need the internet to read them. And exhilarating. I'm not sure what they are. Were. She's very dead. And dismembered." Naomi folded both arms over her eyes, shutting out the oppressive ceiling. "Omi, Than." Nathan began the cursory wiping of his penis with an obscure corner of the bedsheets, a habit Naomi had forced herself to decide was endearing. Was it a passive-aggressive statement? Did he hold off doing that when she swallowed? She couldn't remember.

"That's us," he said. "Omi Than. We sound like a Vietnamese gynecologist."

Naomi shook her head under her arms. "So weird that you say that. So weird."

"Because?"

"Because there *is* a Vietnamese gynecologist in my life. Or almost." Naomi unfolded and rolled back over to face Nathan, lips still sticky. "Célestine's GP. Dr. Phan Trinh. She definitely had an intimate knowledge of her patient's vagina."

"And a Marxist? A criminal?"

"Dr. Trinh? No, I was thinking about Aristide when I said that."

"A Marxist and a criminal?"

Naomi rolled off her side of the bed and squatted beside her camera roller. She dripped a few drops of lazy viscous fluid into the carpeting as she unzipped the bag and groped its innards. "I was thinking more like a Marxist and *therefore* a criminal. I mean, the way he—they—wrote made me dizzy-crazy, made me feel intelligent and deep, and you know how seductive that is for me, you used it yourself to get me into bed that first time." And now she flopped back onto the bed, a white-and-silver iPhone 5s in her hand. "Lemme take a shot of you cleaning your cock."

Nathan stared at her in disbelief. "You have a bag full of the highest of high-tech photographic shit that you've lugged all over the globe, and you're shooting my manhood with a cell phone? And since when do you have an iPhone?"

"Since Charles de Gaulle. It's a natural segue from my well-documented-by-you desire for disembodiment. I want to junk the camera roller bag and travel with only this, this implement. It shoots HD video too. And you can edit it on the phone, while flying. Touch focus. Dual LED flash. Fingerprint security. Great macro. Look." And she swooped down to within centimeters of his cock-head and started snapping, the phone making an absolutely delectable shutter sound, reminding Nathan of the Australian lyrebird that would replicate the shutter sounds of forest paparazzi to seduce a mate. Or was it a more sinister thing? Was the iPhone a malevolent protean organism, the stem-cell phone, mocking him who had cameras with real physical shutters whose sound you couldn't turn off? Promising to replace every other device on earth with its shape-shifting self—garage door openers, solar timers, television remotes, car keys, guitar tuners, GPS modules, light meters, spirit levels, you name it? "And now *mit Blitzlicht*." The LEDs embedded in the glass back of the phone blasted the tip of his cock with 5,400 Kelvin degrees of cool-blue daylight. He thought he could feel it. She held the phone up to his face. "You see how the flash throttles down for the macro shot. Perfectly exposed, matches ambient color temperature, doesn't blow out your cock, as it were." She pulled the phone back to look at her photo, then, drawn by its ruthless intensity, kissed the image. Her lips left semen smears on the screen. Commodity fetishism at its finest.

Nathan rolled over on top of her and looked over her shoulder at the photo. He thought fleetingly of that shot of Galapagos lizards mating on a sun-drenched rock. Naomi flicked Camera Roll back and forth with her index finger, nail strangely not clacking, sorting through the varieties of flash and flashless, macro and micro, a shockingly quick dozen of them, some *mit* scrotal views as well.

"This is making me very nervous, Omi. Kind of existentially unstable."

She began to edit the photos in a cute retro app, making his cock look like it was shot with an Instamatic in the sixties, and then a Polaroid in the eighties. "You talk pretty, Nathan. But what do you mean? It's all good. I'm going to give you back your big mother macro lens. I won't need it anymore."

"Those are the most terrifying words you've ever uttered." He buried his head in her neck under her hair, nuzzling in a pathetic and desperate way. He spoke to the pungent nape of her neck. "You're giving me back my big mother cock. You won't need it anymore."

Naomi tossed her phone onto a pillow and twisted around under him until they were belly to belly. He thought fleetingly of that fifties French movie featuring Saint-Tropéziens mating on the beach. "You're very anxious. You don't have to be anxious."

"You just spoke German. Since when?"

"The Arosteguys. Reading them."

"Why not French?"

"Marx was German. *Das Kapital.* They quote him. They translate."

"Marx talked about *Blitzlicht*? He was into flash photography?"

"He was an all-rounder. A lateral thinker."

"So Marx. The guy who forced your French guy to murder and eat his wife."

"Maybe not forced. Induced. Inspired. That's the way I read it."

"That's the other thing. You're the one who doesn't read. Not books." Naomi tried to shrug him off, but he let his muscles go limp, made himself as heavy as that iguana. She had to breathe when he breathed. "Where's your BlackBerry?"

"I'm suffocating."

"Me too. Where?" Naomi grabbed his hair and pulled his head back and he spun off her. "Because—and I'll tell you before you ask me—because you've abandoned your faithful BlackBerry, your old friend and lover, the one that was cool with long fingernails, left him, now that you've got a new exotic toy to play with." Nathan pounced on Naomi's left hand and splayed her fingers, stroking their tips along the edges of her fingernails. "Yeah, right, and you've cut your fingernails for the first time since we've been together, and it's not for *Last Tango in Schiphol* reasons either. It's for iPhone touchscreen sex." He dropped her hand and she protectively hid it under her hip. "And I know you're serious about the Nikon withdrawal too. Nikon, that was our defiant consumerist thing, no Sony, no Canon, our badge of professionalism, our shared sex-tech. So now you'll go with cool eight-megapixel Jello-cam rolling shutter no-bounce-flash iPhone hipness. And you'll leave me, you'll fly to Tokyo to have an affair with the French-Greek philosopher guy, who will then kill you and eat your breasts. And photograph your corpse with your iPhone."

"That's really fucking horrible, to say all that. Wow." Naomi kicked at him with both feet in unison, like a cat on its back. "That's probably the meanest you've ever been to me." She jumped off the bed, grabbed the iPhone from the pillow, and began to delete the Nathan's cock portrait photos, one by one, with violent, short-nailed jabs at the trash-can icon while singsonging, "Nathan's penis: delete, delete, delete ..."

BUT OF COURSE a penis is not so easy to delete, and before long, Nathan's was happily ensconced inside Naomi. It had amused Nathan the first time he noticed it—what he later thought of as "theme sex." It was dizzy and dreamlike, like a Las Vegas sex room (or at least his imagining of that chimeric thing), and it had come after watching *Mutiny on the Bounty*, the Brando version, and his sex partner was Sheila Dahms, who was just dark enough of eye and hair to support the Tahitian-themed rec room sex, the drums, the waves, the grass-covered thighs and musky breasts. He felt he was underwater with her, it was so hot and humid, and there was a breeze, the drums, the first sigh of the East on his naked buttocks … And afterwards, after she had jumped up and gone to the bathroom to pee and maybe douche out, as they then did, she came back luminous and said, for a second there I thought you were Brando, and you were still wearing those white breeches and those shoes with the buckles, and we were underwater. It was never like that with Naomi. She didn't seem to have theme sex, ever. She admitted to distracted sex, thinking about arguments she'd had with her mother or her sister, even ratcheting up the anger and intensity to the point of orgasm. Nathan could not imagine that such a thing could be true, but she swore it was. Was she covering up her own version of theme sex? Maybe it was fantasy/celebrity sex and she was fucking some prepubescent rock star, male or female, and wouldn't cop to it. Once in a while she'd play and try to guess his theme of the moment, but mostly he stopped mentioning it, holding it back, keeping it private the way she felt that some of her sex things were too private, though he hated that, he wanted to violate every part of her, dirty it up and make it part of him too. And this time, of course, since the theme was Dunja, Dunja and surgery and sexual mutilation, he was not going to play thematic, especially since the doubling up had actually disturbed him, so specific had it been. He became the Hungarian surgeon, inserting the radioactive pellets into Naomi's breasts with his mouth, holding them between his teeth and pushing them, nuzzling them, into her flesh. And then they became Dunja's breasts, and Naomi became an amalgam of Naomi and Dunja and someone else—was it Sheila, was she making her comeback bid from the distant past?—and he became Arosteguy, terrifying himself, his conception of the man filtered through Naomi and the internet and those photos he had found with the safe filter off, photos you didn't want to see because they adhered to the inside of your skull and lacerated your brain. And that website called poundofflesh.com devoted to the eating of breasts. Nathan/Arosteguy ate her breasts right off her chest, ripped them off with his teeth, and then he came again so voluptuously that it terrified him.

Naomi pushed him off. "What the fuck was that? You actually bit me!" She pulled at her left breast, looking for bite marks on its underside. "I can't fucking believe it."

"It wasn't me. It was Arosteguy." Naomi's dismissive shrug. "Sex theme. I know you think they don't exist."

"They don't for me. I don't have sex fantasies."

"A sex theme isn't exactly a fantasy ..."

Soon Nathan had her D300s in his hands and was shooting a series of posed pictures. She was still naked, but he had wrapped the sheets around her lower legs so that only her thighs were visible. "Okay, now, can you guess?" said Nathan, hiding behind the camera. "I'm working on a pitch and you're one of my subjects. What's my article about?"

"Hmm. You've covered my legs with a sheet."

"Not just covered."

"You've ... hidden them."

"Not just hidden." Nathan squeezed off some clattery shots as punctuation.

Naomi's eyes went wide. "You've amputated them."

"Ah," said Nathan.

Naomi squirmed a bit, then readjusted the sheet. "It's that one where people want to amputate parts of their bodies because they just don't feel that they're the shape they're supposed to be?"

"They roam the earth looking for a doctor who will cut off a perfectly good arm or leg. An arm and a leg."

"Or else they do it themselves with a chainsaw or a shotgun. Yeah. What's it called?"

"Apotemnophilia."

"Yeah. Body dysmorphic disorder, on the street."

"Psychotherapeutic amputation."

"Amputee identity disorder, with a twist of bioethics. It sounds juicy."

"Speaking of ethics," said Nathan, getting very close to her with the camera, "I believe I might be experiencing a touch of acrotomophilia. What should I do about it?"

"Hmm," said Naomi uneasily, "I got the philia part."

"A sexual attraction to amputees." Nathan started to nuzzle her thighs.

Naomi whipped off the sheet and sat up. "I think you just managed to creep me out." She held out her hand. "Gimme my camera back."

"Aw."

"I don't do medical. You do medical, remember? I do crime. It's cleaner."

"Sometimes hard to separate them. But I thought you were giving me your camera. You were going iPhone solo, remember? I could use a backup."

Naomi snapped her extended hand at him and Nathan gave her the camera. She immediately started to delete the photos.

"I think you've just rejected my pitch, and that *is* a crime," said Nathan.

Naomi swung off the bed and started fretting the Nikon back into its roller. She spoke into the wall with her back to him. "Hey, aren't you supposed to be going to Geneva for that . . . what was it? Worldwide Genital Mutilation Conference? Honestly, I think that's more interesting than the amputation thing. There were so many articles about it for a while, then it tanked into hotness oblivion. It's interesting about diseases, how they peak and tank. The politics of genital mutilation, now, that's endlessly hot."

"Thanks for the encouragement. I was thinking that my apotemnophilia piece would segue into that exact meditation. But never mind. The Geneva mutilation piece is off. No, I stay here in this hotel and finish the Hungarian thing, just in case there's something in Europe I missed and have to pick up. I email it to my agent, shamelessly begging him to get me *The New Yorker*—"

"That's still Lance, isn't it?"

"It is the same old Lance. Then maybe I just go home to NYC. To where you aren't."

"I hate that part."

"The *New Yorker* part?"

"The part where we say goodbye," said Naomi, now sitting on the floor and playing with her new iPhone, still not looking at him.

Nathan stood up and leaned against the windowsill. "And you leave me alone in yet another hotel room," he said.

Naomi looked up and flinched, almost startled to see him, as though she had just discovered an exotic bird at the window. Using the High Dynamic Range option, she took his flashless backlit picture with the phone. "I leave you desolate and alone. And I go back to Paris."

NATHAN WAS FINISHING UP his solitary room-service meal. On a website called mediascandals.com was a page devoted to Dr. Zoltán Molnár. His iPhone quavered and he answered it. "Hi, it's Nathan."

A very little female voice: "Nathan?"

"Yes?"

"It's me. It's Dunja."

"Dunja? Where are you?"

"I'm at home. You know. Somewhere in Slovenia."

"Yeah." An awkward pause. Her voice was too little for comfort. "How are you?"

Dunja inhaled raggedly, suggesting to Nathan that she had been crying just before she called him. "Nathan, I think I gave you a disease. I'm so sorry."

"A disease? You mean, literally?"

"Roiphe's, Nathan. Roiphe's disease. Dr. Molnár just phoned to tell me. It showed up by accident in some tests …" Her little voice hung there, suspended, weightless.

Almost without thought, or rather exactly like thought involving memory and information, Nathan was googling Roiphe's disease and within seconds was downloading data into the conversation. Fingers flying and swiping.

"Roiphe's?" said Nathan, net-borrowed argument tinting his tone. "Nobody's had Roiphe's since 1968."

Dunja's tone was the flattened tone of unassailable logic. "I've been immune-suppressed for a long time, and I have it. And so do you, now, I think. Probably."

"The Roiphe's survived all that radiation?"

"Radiation is not a treatment for Roiphe's."

"No," said Nathan, "I see that."

"You … you see that? On your computer? On the internet?"

A photo of Dr. Barry Roiphe on the cover of *Time* magazine, May 1968. He looked lanky and shy, a bespectacled Jimmy Stewart. The caption, in screaming yellow, read, "Dr. Barry Roiphe: Sex and Disease." Dunja began to sob huge, liquid, globular sobs. For a moment, Nathan thought the sobs were coming from Dr. Roiphe himself, his apologetic, twisted grin now morphing into a rictus of grief and shame.

"I wonder whatever happened to him?" said Nathan.

"Who?" said Dunja, amid shudders.

"Roiphe. Dr. Barry Roiphe."

NATHAN WAS HAVING A PEE, and it hurt. He talked to the pain: "Ow, fuck, ow, shit, that really hurts! Barry, Barry, what did I do to you?" The pee dribbled to an uncertain halt, then dripped morosely. Nathan shook his penis angrily and reached over to his shaving-kit bag. He took out a large magnifying glass with a ring of battery-operated LEDs, swiveled around to the sink, flicked on the LEDs, flopped his penis over the edge of the basin, and examined its tip. The word *suppurating* came to mind. "Fuck," said Nathan. "Fuck, fuck, fuck!"

Back in the Schiphol Airport Lounge, despondent, he sat with laptop closed while others browsed with professional intensity. He hadn't finished his Hungarian piece, his Slovenian, Dunja piece. The hotel room had started to feel like a disease ward, a holding compound for infectious disaster. His phone released the frog trill that said Naomi. He would have to consider changing her ringtone. The endangered frog species thing. Spooky, symbolic, something not good. Slide to answer. "Yeah, hi. Nathan."

"I hear airport. Are you in an airport?"

"Yeah. Checked out early. You home?"

"Well, the Crillon. Not exactly my home away from home. Comfy."

"I'll bet. You sound edgy."

On Naomi's laptop was a grid of several horrific black-and-white photos under the heading "Arosteguy Crime Scene Images." The photos showed the torso of Célestine Arosteguy, which was missing various pieces: one breast, half a buttock, the soft area around the belly button. Bite-sized lesions everywhere. "I'm back in my room, and I'm alone and I'm freaked out."

Nathan was surprised to hear Naomi mention being alone, something she never did; with social media, net, phone, camera, recorder, she never seemed to feel alone. "Yeah? How come?"

"Oh, the CSI photos of Célestine Arosteguy. They're hideous. How could the guy do that? I just can't believe it. He's such an attractive character, but . . . I dunno. Maybe. God. I'm sending you the URL."

"Maybe don't," said Nathan. An African lady with a pushcart came around cleaning up bottles, cups, cans, newspapers. She took Nathan's cappuccino before he was finished with it. "I'm not in the mood."

Naomi got up from the desk chair and twirled onto the bed. She got under the duvet with all her clothes on, including shoes. "I need your advice, Than. You have to see this stuff. I can't have it in my head all by myself. He ate pieces of her. I mean, I knew that, but now I'm seeing it."

Nathan lifted the lid on his own Air, the third generation one with no SD card slot. It was actually Naomi's hand-me-down. She needed that slot, she said. Needed it for photos, especially now that those little cards had become ubiquitous, even on pro cameras. He couldn't bring himself to press the power button. "Is this crushing loneliness I feel just for you, or is it really, underneath, the harsh metallic edge of existential longing?"

"That's the airport talking."

"Could be."

"Well, it's all for me, honey. Don't try to sidestep it. Feel it."

"I do feel it."

"Soon you'll be back home in our apartment and you'll feel cozy again," said Naomi.

Nathan began to feel the eyes of his loungemates flicking up at him. Why would they be listening? "I'm not going right back to NYC. I've been diverted to Toronto. You know, Canada."

Under her covers, Naomi felt a twinge of ... could it be separation anxiety? Her nest wasn't busy enough. She slid out of bed and began to gather electronic devices, dumping them on the duvet as she found them. "But you're not in the air yet. How can they divert you?"

"I diverted myself. I'll email you the address and stuff."

Naomi jumped back under the covers again, the nest reconstructed, ramparts, moats, drawbridges. "What's going on? Toronto? What, Sunnybrook Hospital?"

Nathan's voice went *sotto.* Paranoia thickened in his brain like Alzheimer's plaque, as it always did when he got that shiver of a great idea for a piece. "You remember Roiphe's disease?"

"Oh, sure. The thing that killed Wayne Pardeau. But they cracked it, didn't they? Extincted it. Only samples left in stainless-steel containers. After that, *pas grand-chose,* as I recall."

"In itself, as diseases go, ultimately, *pas grand-chose,* no. But extinct, also no."

"You have a brilliant angle on it?"

Nathan's sharp, involuntary intake of breath went unremarked. "Let's say compelling. I have a compelling angle on it."

By now Naomi was on the same pages Nathan had been on—with the Air, not the old MacBook Pro for the moment—and she was looking at Roiphe's house in Toronto in Google Street View. A freshly built faux chateau, Victorian kitsch pastiche of the worst kind. Oh, well. What did you expect? An old Canadian Jewish doctor with some money. But nice leafy street. "Roiphe's there, isn't he? In Toronto. You're going to see him."

Nathan had heard the rustle of Naomi's keyboard, but out of his inexpressible guilt he wanted to compliment her. "Hey, that's pretty good for somebody who doesn't do medical. Try this. Do you know Roiphe's first name?"

"Are we playing Faster Fingers or are we thinking?" Faster Fingers was their code for supplanting brain/memory with Google Search.

"Too late for the first-name thing, I guess."

"I'm looking at Barry's face right now," said Naomi. "Rabbinical Jimmy Stewart, somehow. Holy Blossom Temple or something in my Toronto past. Do you know Alzheimer's first name? No fingers."

"Sure: Aloïs. But did you know that Alzheimer's assistant turns out to be Creutzfeldt of Creutzfeldt-Jakob's? You know, human mad cow disease? Sort of?"

"I forgot what you do."

Nathan, starting to cook now—and it was in articulating things to Naomi that the cooking really happened, part of their closeness, though he worried it didn't really work in the opposite direction—edged himself down lower into the lounge's carpeting, bringing the phone closer to floor level. He didn't want his lips read. "What happens if this guy, Barry Roiphe, the guy the disease was named after, what if he's lucky enough to discover another hot disease? Do they call it Roiphe's 2?"

"That would be lucky?" Naomi was drifting, fingers of her left hand working the iPad, her right the Air, both all over the net and some juicy SMSs rolling in on the iPhone. The juiciest: "Greetings from Tokyo, Naomi. Here's the email address you wanted: hmatsuda@j.u-tokyo.ac.jp. Let's talk soon." The avatar in the message bubble was an actual photo of a pleasant-looking young Japanese woman that was framed like a painting; a little 3D-rendered brass plate at the bottom of the antiqued frame bore the signature "Yours, Yukie."

Nathan was himself drifting into an imagined conversation with Dr. Barry Roiphe: "It helps with the research grants if your particular field of study touches a public nerve, don't you think?"

"Is that it?" said Naomi. "Is that your hook? Roiphe's 2: The Sequel?" Naomi was never intentionally cruel unless attacked, but when she was browsing, her attention thinned out into dismissiveness. But Nathan was really pitching his story to Roiphe, not Naomi.

"But it's a *great* hook. I mean, it's about medical fame and all that comes with it. It's about the politics of medical grant-giving, repression from the religious right, etcetera. It's about becoming a household name that's more feared than Creutzfeldt ever was. What kind of man would want that fame? Would he get depressed when they found a cure and his name disappeared from the front pages?"

"It's workable. Will it get too sensational? Have you placed it?"

"It's another spec piece. Self-financed. Feels like *The New Yorker*, though, doesn't it? 'Annals of Medicine'?"

"Everything feels like that to you."

"This is different."

"Something about it is driving you."

"Something. Must be."

Triggered by the Yukie text, Naomi had quickly left Roiphe to unearth new Arosteguy crime-scene pages, all of them murky and suggestive of viral infections and weird Russian and Chinese spoofed URLs. That the pages themselves should feel diseased and virulent seemed appropriate, even oddly comforting. As though tracing her thoughts directly through her fingertips into its touchscreen, her iPad (she named it Smudgy) disgorged a close-up of Célestine's severed head in the small refrigerator of the Arosteguy apartment.

"Oh, god," said Naomi. "Oh . . . I just got another Arosteguy atrocity hit. I think the killer must have taken these photos himself. I don't see any crime-scene guys around in them. But who posted them? I'm sending you that URL too."

Nathan stood up and stretched. Something resembling a flight announcement was resonating through the lounge. It wasn't his flight, but he held the phone out a bit to pick up the metallic garble for authenticity and then brought the phone back to his mouth. The disease dissonance was getting to him. "Well, maybe I'll look at them in Toronto. Gotta go now. They're calling my flight. Adore you. Don't crumble."

"*Je t'adore aussi.*" Naomi touched the red End button, and was instantly back in the Arosteguy apartment.

4

NATHAN GOT OUT OF A pumpkin-and-mint-green Beck cab in Toronto's Forest Hill Village in front of the Coach Restaurant, a faded greasy spoon with the graphic of a silhouetted coach-and-four hanging over the door. Seniors leaning on walkers shuffled, a few girls in gray-and-burgundy uniforms from nearby Bishop Cornwall School drifted in and out. Carrying no camera, no visible recording device of any kind, he walked in through two sets of doors and stood by the vintage National cash register—embossed brass, color-coded glass keys, marble and wooden base.

A man who could be one of his own senior customers came slowly up some back stairs and approached him. "Can I help you?" he said, dropping a pad of order forms behind the ornate machine and punching the orange No Sale key. The National's cash drawer slid open and a bell chimed.

"Is Dr. Roiphe here?"

The man—manager? owner?—smiled a wry, snorty smile without looking up and lifted a hinged lead-weighted bill holder so that he could riffle through the banknotes in one of the drawer's cubbies. "You think this is a doctor's office?"

Nathan played it straight. "I'm supposed to meet him here, but I don't see him. Dr. Barry Roiphe."

"If you don't see him, then you're blind," said the man, not looking up but sticking an index finger into the air.

"I think I see one finger," said Nathan.

The man lowered his finger and pointed to an obscure booth in the back. In it sat a gangly gray-haired man wearing big non-chic plastic glasses. Cardigan and flannels. Straw hat. "I was wrong. You can see after all."

"Thank you."

Nathan walked over to Roiphe's booth and stood for a moment while the doctor tried to saw through one of his three pork chops, face low to the plate, oblivious. Nathan subtly swayed on his feet, studying the man. He had by now of course watched lectures, interviews, and news footage of Roiphe, and had read his learned papers—no trace of humor there—which often included photos of the man going back to his graduation from the University of Toronto medical school, class of 1957. But he had not recognized him: the collapsed posture, the big glasses with those distorting bifocal blobs, the weird hat. Roiphe's head eventually came up, the eyes smeared behind the lenses, the glasses crooked on the notched, reddened nose. The doctor looked puzzled. Why was this young man just standing there? Was he a waiter?

"Dr. Roiphe? Nathan Math. Thank you for agreeing to meet me."

A hint of a delay, like an old transatlantic phone call, and then a thin-lipped smile. "Oh, yes. Sit down, sit down. Just having a couple of pork chops. They're tough, but I need the exercise." Roiphe worked his jaw comically; the effect was grotesque. Nathan slid into the narrow booth and felt the rough texture of the scarred seat through his jeans. "You want anything?"

"No, no thanks," said Nathan. "Hope I'm not taking you away from your patients."

"Oh, no. Man's gotta eat, doesn't he? And, too, I'm pretty much retired. Well, I still practice a bit. Just to keep my hand in. I've become a bit of a tinkerer, though. A bit of an experimenter. So, tell me again. What's this all about?"

From his research, Nathan had calculated that Roiphe would respond to a fairly melodramatic pitch about his life and his work; he came across as a failed but still eager self-promoter. "For one shining moment, you were the king of fear," he said.

Roiphe's eyes managed to startle into sharpness behind the bifocals. "What? What are you talking about?"

"Roiphe's. Roiphe's disease. You made the cover of *Time* magazine."

Irritated, Roiphe went back to his pork chops. The way he chewed suggested false teeth, but Nathan couldn't be sure. The doctor's jaw sawed sideways; maybe it was an eating style. Still chewing, Roiphe came up for air, blinked, spoke. "Not me, for god's sake. The disease. Surely you don't equate the two. And the politics surrounding the disease. All sex, all hysteria, very American." He wiped his mouth with a thin paper napkin. The stubble on one side of his poorly shaven chin shredded it, so that in effect he wiped his mouth with his fingers. He sucked those fingers as he squinted suspiciously, as though trying to focus on an especially noxious varmint. "Why is it, exactly, you wanted to talk to me?"

Nathan figured he had to scale back the drama. "I'm writing a piece about medical fame. The scary kind. You know—Alzheimer's, Parkinson's. Names that people are terrified to hear. Afraid that their doctors will speak those names to them."

The doctor burst out laughing, a short, liquid bark that spewed shreds of chop across the table. "Roiphe's disease was a leaky pecker or a mucky twat. Hardly in the same league."

"But Roiphe's could be lethal if it was left untreated. I mean, Wayne Pardeau died of Roiphe's."

"Who?"

"Wayne Pardeau," said Nathan. "A famous country-and-western singer."

"Never heard of him. But it was probably drugs that killed him. Usually is."

"Do you have an inferiority complex about Roiphe's? Was it not a potent enough disease to bear your name?"

"What an odd young man you are. You sound like a headline in a Victorian yellow newspaper. I suppose you've heard of yellow journalism? Sounds like you practice it."

"Did it ever bother you that it seemed at one point to have been cured? Wiped off the face of the earth? Did that not consign you to some kind of medical oblivion? Of historical interest only?"

Roiphe fastidiously scraped the apple sauce off his remaining chop with the butter knife, wrapped the chop up in a napkin, and stuffed it into his pocket. Nathan was sure the grease was already weeping into his cardigan. Rising with some difficulty, Roiphe said, "Maybe you should be talking to Dr. Alzheimer while the talkin's good. I assume that you're getting the check."

Nathan twisted himself out of the booth and without being too obvious about it blocked the cramped aisle. He pulled out a neatly folded pink diagnostic report and held it out to Roiphe. "Doctor, please take a look at this."

Out of some ancient reflex, Roiphe snatched the report, unfolded it, and began to read, face close to the paper and head twitching from side to side, as though he were smelling it rather than reading it. Nathan had spent a week getting to know Toronto in preparation for Roiphe, and that had included a visit to a walk-in clinic for STDs on Queen Street West; he could look forward to twenty-eight days of Ciprofloxacin, mild diarrhea, genital irritation, and the possible but unlikely advent of ruptured tendons, psychotic reactions, and confusional states. "Looks like you have a hefty dose of Roiphe's. Makin' a comeback, I guess. Your triglycerides aren't that great either." He looked up and shook the paper before handing it back, as though to purge it of dust or mites. "Does that mean I owe you something, or do you owe me?"

Nathan tried to peer around the reading blobs in the doctor's glasses to get at the real eyes. It then occurred to him that at this close distance, which didn't seem to unnerve the doctor at all, it might be preferable to look through those blobs for better eye contact. The result was a palsied head movement that suggested extreme shiftiness on Nathan's part. "I would like to discuss the narrative of my infection with you," he said breathlessly, his chest tight.

Roiphe barked out another laugh, sounding particularly like a Jack Russell. "The narrative of my . . ." He shook his head. "Look, son. I long ago left the field of venereal pathology, if that's your hook. I'm just not very interesting. That's the real problem. Now Parkinson, there was an interesting man."

"Why don't you let me decide that? What kind of patients do you have now? What are you experimenting with?"

Roiphe studied Nathan for a beat, jaw thrust forward, lips pursed, then took his glasses off. His eyes were large and smeary even without the bifocal blobs, but they were also the most amazing, unnatural turquoise, and they shocked Nathan. He was sure those eyes could see things that normal eyes couldn't.

"You could come by the house tomorrow, if you'd like. Just around the corner. My office is in the house. Tomorrow. Not too early. I've never been a morning person, believe it or not. Just show up."

SURROUNDED BY MARBLE in the bathroom of her suite in the Crillon, Naomi sat having a pee, and it was hurting. She watched herself in the door mirror howling in pain like a child. "Ow, ow, ow! That hurts!" She looked down at her white cotton panties—a little threadbare around the elastic, she noticed—and saw what looked like a mayonnaise stain in the crotch. "Fuck, fuck, fuck!"

Sitting on her bed with the Air on her lap, new panties on, travel yoga pants on, diagnostic wad of Kleenex in panties providing reassuring pressure, Naomi watched another downloaded clip of Arosteguy lecturing, this time with the tinny Air sound turned off. She gazed intently at Arosteguy's image, then, provoked by that image, bounced off the bed and started to set up an image-making session of her own.

She wasn't sure she was ever serious about giving her Nikon gear to Nathan and riding off into the sunset with only her BlackBerry and her iPhone and her iPad and her laptop as image-making devices—was there anything now that did not take pictures and video?—and when it came to rolling out the door of their room at Schiphol, she didn't hesitate to take it with her. She would not feel like a pro without the Nikon gear. And she would not have been able to do what she was doing now: placing two wireless Speedlight flash units—diffusers for softer lighting clipped over the flash heads—on a chair and a dresser, then the camera on a tripod next to the laptop, then setting the timer, then beginning to take portraits of herself artfully lit by the flashes and the soft window light.

Later, back on the bed, sorting through the shots with Photo Mechanic, her favorite fast photo browser, she began to settle on a few that presented her as beautiful but moody, intelligent and intense. She laughed at her topless variants, but she couldn't quite bring herself to delete them; the light on her breasts was so soft and voluptuous, they might never look that good again, though what was that mole doing on the left underside? Was it bigger than the last time she looked? Was it redder? Pinker? Less symmetrical? She zoomed in on the mole, put a window around it large enough to encompass the slighter paler circle that surrounded it, dated the window, and saved it as a TIFF to her "Body Horror" file, the one that stored images of every scary part of her body, the iffy, unstable, volatile parts. Now kill the ADHD. Focus. Back to that email.

"Dear M. Aristide Arosteguy, I'm writing you this email and attaching several photos of myself that I've just taken with the very object you discuss in your wonderful and inspiring online essay 'The Anatomy of a Perfect Object.' My purpose is simple, though the results might well be complex: I want to fly to wherever you are and interview and photograph you."

Naomi reread her email a few more times, leaning forward on the bed to add to it, finesse, backtrack, elaborate. The Arosteguy essay concerned consumer objects and the possibility of beauty that could equal or exceed natural beauty, given the industrial/technological new state of man. Natural beauty became atavistic, nostalgic. Real objects of the innate lust for beauty were now commodities, industrial products. She was not sure that photos of herself posed with some of her nest objects really said anything at all about the anatomy of a perfect object, but she was confident enough in her own beauty to feel that Arosteguy, who was, after all, both French and Greek, would want to meet her in Tokyo. She added two of the best topless photos to the "attached" list and hit Send.

NATHAN STOOD IN FRONT of what Naomi had mocked as a faux chateau in the heart of Toronto's Forest Hill. A quick swivel to right and left confirmed what Nathan had seen from the taxi. Roiphe's castle was not alone; the street was aswarm with synthetic stone facing, copper-trimmed turrets, and authentic-looking slate roofs, though it had to be said that a kind of neo-Victorian mausoleum variant was also well represented. Nathan shouldered his tripod case and pulled his reluctant camera roller up the cobblestoned pathway to the front door. The stone porch was shaded by a fan-shaped, art-nouveauish tinted glass canopy. The front door was huge, exotic wood and pebbled glass. Nathan was searching for a doorbell button when the door opened with a vacuum-lock whoosh. A beautiful willowy woman wearing a disturbingly clinical white cotton dress with long sleeves and a high collar stood in the doorway. She seemed to be about thirty.

"Hi," said Nathan. "I'm Nathan Math." The woman just looked at him, no affect whatsoever. An awkward pause. "I, uh, I have an appointment with Dr. Roiphe." No reaction. "An appointment with the doctor?"

Her eyes were so large that they narrowed suspiciously without seeming to get smaller. "You don't have an appointment with the doctor."

"I don't?"

"The doctor doesn't take new patients. You are new. You would be a new patient."

"Oh, right, no," said Nathan, exhaling in slightly exaggerated self-directed mirth. The woman had rattled him without actually doing anything. "I'm not a patient. I'm a journalist. I write on medical/social issues. I'm interviewing him. Dr. Roiphe. About his career."

"What's wrong with me?" she said, brushing her blond hair back, her voice unaccountably hard.

"What?"

"Diagnose me. You do have some medical training, don't you? How could you write meaningfully about the doctor if you had no medical training?"

"Some medical training. Some. Is there something wrong with you?"

"Well, yes, of course. I wouldn't be a patient if there weren't something wrong with me."

"You're a patient? Of Dr. Roiphe?"

It seemed to Nathan that the woman was on the verge of slamming the door in his face, and he was calculating his response to that when a crusty voice reverberated from deep within the house. Nathan could practically hear all of the house's marble floors in the acoustics of that bellow. "Chase?" called Dr. Roiphe. "Is that our own private paparazzo? Bring him on in!"

"Welcome, Mr. Math. Please, do come right in," said Chase, suddenly genial. She swung the door open wide and curtsied an ironic curtsy as he sidled by her, his tripod case thumping the door frame, his roller bumping and twisting over the raised granite sill. She bent towards him and whispered, "Consumption. That would be *my* guess."

Her face was uncomfortably close to his. "Consumption? You mean tuberculosis?"

Still whispering, still too close. "No. I mean consumption." She straightened up, smiled, and said, "Follow me!" in quite a different tone, too loud and too declamatory, then turned and marched off into the house leaving Nathan struggling to follow her. Center-hall plan, polished wood staircase, black-and-white-streaked marble floors everywhere. Chase veered off to the right and stood just inside the living room, waiting with exaggerated patience for Nathan to pull his roller up to her. The room was furnished in a very traditional way, as befitted a Victorian fantasy of a French chateau, and this was yet another level of fakery because it looked as though the house had been bought complete with the real-estate agent's staging furniture and never touched again. She gestured to a plump brocaded wingback chair. "That's where you'll be."

"And where will you be?" said Nathan, fussing the tripod case off his shoulder, trying not to swipe the pottery animals off the side table by the sofa, which matched his assigned chair.

"I'll be in limbo, Nathan. Come see me there when you have the will."

By the time Nathan could lift his eyes from the gear he'd just settled on the floor, Chase was gone, leaving him to imagine the set of her face, and to wonder whether she could possibly be coming on to him. As he sat in the indicated chair, he felt rather upbeat about the demeanor of this young woman, whose strangeness immediately suggested that he was on to something with this Roiphe thing, this Roiphe who was not as interesting as Parkinson.

Roiphe entered through a set of French doors which led onto a small flagstone patio. He turned and closed the doors, a bit shaky with the latches, and met the rising Nathan with an outstretched hand. They shook and sat down, Roiphe on the matching sofa.

"Nathan."

"Dr. Roiphe."

"Please, please call me Barry. I've always found it bizarre that the Americans call their ex-presidents 'Mr. President' for life. I am retired, you know."

"Except for ... Chase, was it?"

Roiphe looked puzzled. "Chase?"

"The young woman who assigned me this chair. She said she was your patient."

Roiphe doubled over until his chest touched his knees. Nathan, startled, thought he was having a heart attack until the doctor straightened back up, his face crumpled with silent laughter. It took a moment or two for the sound to come, a good, hearty, roaring laugh flecked with phlegmy wheezes. "Well, yes," he said, still heaving, "that's one way of looking at it."

"She's not your patient."

"Whatever she is, she's sure darn full of surprises. I haven't heard that one before. But no." He leaned forward, pulling on his knees to enable him to slide his torso closer to Nathan. "She's my daughter, Nathan. Now, there's a sense in which all children are constantly being diagnosed by their parents, wouldn't you say? So, I guess that's fair of her to say, metaphorically, I guess. But like I say, never heard that one before."

"Does she live here with you?" Nathan felt that the general strangeness of the situation allowed him to ask that question.

Roiphe let go of his knees and relaxed back into the pillows of the sofa. "I guess this is the beginning of the interview, is it? The new art form. The art of the interview." He flicked a hand towards the roller. "And is that your camera? You said you were a photojournalist. I love that word. *Photojournalist.*"

Nathan tipped over his roller and unzipped it, revealing a tightly packed group of lenses, flashes, spiraled flash cords, and cleaning tools. He slid the big Nikon out of its padded cubicle, the rhino-like 24–70mm lens attached, and hefted it in his hand. "It's a digital SLR, if that means anything to you. Digital single-lens reflex camera. It means you can see exactly what the lens is seeing when you look through the viewfinder. They've been around for a long time, film first, of course, and now digital, but this is the latest incarnation. Well, almost the latest. It's hard to keep up with the technology when you're on a budget. It's heavy, and it's probably obsolete already. It just doesn't know it. Is this too much information?"

"Hell, no," said Roiphe, holding out his hand, wanting the camera. "I was a passionate amateur nature photographer in my time. Haven't come to grips with the digital thing yet, though." Nathan suppressed his urge to deny Roiphe his camera and handed it over. "Maybe this is something you can teach me. We'll be quid pro quo-ing all over the place here." Nathan countered his equipment anxiety by busying himself setting up the Swiss Nagra Kudelski SD audio recorder on the glass coffee table in front of Roiphe. The insanely expensive radio-quality recorder was overkill for a print journalist—though these days there was no such thing in the purest sense—but Nathan had spotted it at an electronics booth in the Zurich Airport and couldn't resist. He and Naomi both used technology to enhance their credibility as professionals, and he knew that she would never really give up her Nikons for an iPhone until it was an acknowledged cool-but-pro way to go. Too much insecurity involved, always the sense of being a poseur. While he was deciding which Nagra plug-on microphone to use—the stereo cardioid was good for ambiance plus voice, which could be interesting when Chase was around, but the mono was best for focused, undisturbed voice recording—Nathan watched Roiphe out of the corner of his eye as the doctor dug around clumsily in the sunshade of the zoom lens, trying to pry off the lens cap.

"Are you trying to get the lens cap off? Just squeeze it in the center. It's spring-loaded."

Roiphe chuckled and popped the cap off. Nathan slid the Automatic Gain Control switch on the side of the Nagra to On, figuring that manually riding the recording levels would be a distraction. Roiphe in turn managed, after a quick survey of the many buttons, dials, and switches on the Nikon, to turn the camera on, and in no time was snapping photos of Nathan, happily cranking the zoom in and out like a delirious child.

"Well," said Roiphe, after the mirror had clacked up and down about thirty times, "that seems to work. I guess a camera is a camera. Oh, look at that. There's you, right there on that little TV in the back. Hmm. Somehow makes you look kinda sinister. See? Something in the eyes." Roiphe handed the camera over to Nathan, who felt he had to assess his own image to be polite. Roiphe was right. Nathan looked nasty and untrustworthy—though in a darkly handsome way.

"Good shooting," said Nathan. "Very good."

The last photo Roiphe had taken was a zoomed-in close-up of the Nagra, and he now pointed to it with a twitching index finger. "You haven't turned that on yet, have you?"

"No. May I?"

"Not yet," said Roiphe, and he held his knees and pulled himself forward to his confidential position. "We need to make our deal."

"Our deal?"

"Yeah," said Roiphe, drawing out the word to give it a slightly comical street feel. "Innarested?"

Nathan leaned forward to match the intimacy, clasping his hands like a choirboy. "I . . . sure."

Roiphe laughed a small dry laugh. "You're not *too* sure, are you? But you will be. Listen. I've tried writing a book, you'll be surprised to hear. I'm no good at it. Not on my own, I'm not. Chase researched you on the internet—she's so clever, that kid. She's already read half of what you've written. And we came up with something, she and I. You know the work of Oliver Sacks? *The Man Who Mistook His Wife for a Hat? Awakenings?* That was made into a great movie with De Niro. *An Anthropologist on Mars?*"

"I know his work and I've met him a few times."

"Oh, really?" Roiphe's tangled eyebrows shot up in challenge.

Nathan had to respond, to authenticate. "Yeah. He's got this weird thermostat problem. He's always too hot. He's always leaving the restaurant to stand outside. That's why he loves to swim in those cold mountain lakes. I've got an interview with him in the works. And he wears weird shoes." Nathan was immediately ashamed of throwing in the data about the thermostat. It was true, as far as he knew, but mentioning it smacked of desperation to impress.

Roiphe was very excited. "That's super! That's titanic! Oliver Sacks is a doctor, a neurologist, and also a brilliant writer. I'm a doctor, you're a writer. Math plus Roiphe equals Sacks. Get it? I was a neurologist first, you know, not a urologist the way people think. I specialized in genital pain, and ouch, there was Roiphe's waiting for me."

"Things I didn't know." Relieved, Nathan conjured up the enthusiasm to say, as though with enlightenment dawning, "So, we collaborate on a book!" but then was immediately uneasy as the possible implications sank in.

"Medical fame," said Roiphe. "Your subject. You want to get to the marrow of it? This is your big chance."

"But a book about your life? Your work? Your retirement years?"

Roiphe sank back heavily into the brocaded pillows. "Are you being sarcastic?"

"I'm being nervous. I'm worried about being co-opted by my subject. They warn you about that in journalism school." Nathan released a pathetic chuckle which was meant to show that he knew he was being superficial and paranoid. "This could be a classic case."

"Not a co-opting. A real collaboration. I don't censor you. You don't pass judgment on me."

"Okay," said Nathan. "Okay. This isn't exactly what I had in mind, but it's interesting. I'm loose, god knows. I'm flexible. But you have a subject in mind, don't you? Something very specific."

"My experiments. My recent work. With my most recent subject."

"Who is?"

"My daughter, of course," said Roiphe. "Chase. But you. Good instincts. We're gonna need 'em for what comes next."

5

NAOMI WAS ON HER JAL flight from Charles de Gaulle to Tokyo Narita. Her laptop was on her seat tray, displaying a photo she took with her iPhone of the elegant first-class toilet in the Boeing 777. She especially appreciated the small orchid in the milky glass vase glued to the lav's mirror, even though she suspected it was artificial. In her ear, Nathan was complaining. "You flew right over me and I never knew it. I'm crushed."

Naomi spoke quietly into the airphone, resisting the temptation to talk louder to compensate for the airplane drone. She hated it when she could hear everything that everyone said. And she had a very large Dutch male seatmate—she had seen his burgundy Kingdom of Netherlands *paspoort* when it slid out of his computer bag onto her seat—who was sitting very close to her because she wasn't in first class but what they called Premium Economy, which featured something called the Sky Shell Seat. "You fly east to Japan from Paris, not west."

"Oh, god, that means you're flying away from me," said Nathan. He was sitting at the desk in his room in the Bloor-Yorkville Holiday Inn, trying not to be depressed, speaking into his laptop's mic using a VoIP app. He was looking at one of the nude apotemnophilia photos he had taken of Naomi, talking to it; she had not managed to delete them all.

"Why the sudden romanticism? What's going on there in Toronto? Should I worry?"

"Things are strange here and I miss you, that's all," said Nathan.

The Dutchman beside Naomi ordered a vodka martini. It was not his first. He was very tall, and Naomi could not be sure that he wasn't actively eavesdropping. "Tell me about the strangeness."

"Roiphe's syndrome. A new thing, nothing to do with the old Roiphe's disease. That's the sole subject of his past year's work. I don't know if he's inventing it or defining it. He doesn't want to talk about anything else, and he won't even give me a hint of what's involved unless I agree to do this book deal." Nathan had emailed details of the book-deal gambit to Naomi for vetting. She had thought it would be the perfect challenge to get Nathan out of his journo rut. A book—even if it ended up only being an e-book—how could it not be a good thing?

"And it's really his daughter? She lives with him and he studies her? She's his project?"

"Chase. That's her name," said Nathan, struck for the first time by the name's comical appropriateness. "That's what the situation seems to be."

The Dutchman's vodka martini arrived with a cup of nut-like lozenge-shaped snacks. Earbuds plugged in, he was watching a bizarre Japanese game show on his seatback screen, and Naomi wondered idly if he could really understand what was being said. He did chuckle from time to time.

"That sounds just sick enough to be yummy," said Naomi, now working her own screen through some general data regarding the University of Tokyo. She was trying to imagine Arosteguy's life in exile, and was struggling. It wasn't just the opaqueness of Japan that was the problem; it was the idea of a French-Greek intellectual murderer in Japan that was the problem. But of course also the source of excitement. She had stumbled across the case of Issei Sagawa, a Japanese student at the Sorbonne who killed and ate his classmate, a Dutch woman named Renée Hartevelt. Judged unfit to stand trial by reason of insanity, he had returned home to roam free in Japan, a minor celebrity who painted nudes, wrote restaurant reviews, and worked the talk-show circuit. Although it made Naomi extremely nervous to think about it, the idea of having Sagawa interview Arosteguy aroused her almost unbearably. It was just sick enough to be yummy.

"I wasn't looking for that approach exactly."

"Your pieces are as sensationalistic as mine are. They're just dressed up a bit. Make sure you don't sign anything," said Naomi.

"He's a cagey old codger. I can't read him yet."

"Tell him you need a taste to see if it's going to be deep enough for a book. You can always go with the short piece if you have to."

"It means holing up here in this hotel for weeks. Maybe longer. I'll practically have to live with them. In fact, he's already shown me his nanny suite. In the basement."

"I'll come visit you. After Arosteguy."

"But listen, isn't it too creepy? I mean, would you do it? Move into a subject's house? Have a shower in the same shower as your subject?"

"You'd just be another embedded journalist. It's all the rage."

"You've arranged to meet Arosteguy? He really is in Tokyo and is willing?"

"I got the email address of an intermediary. He wants to tell his story. The boys at *Notorious* are excited. They said go for it. He agreed to meet me."

"Hey, the guy could actually be a murderer. Where are you going to meet him?"

"Wherever he says, I guess. There's speculation that he has a house in the city."

"That's dangerous."

"Well, *he's* dangerous. But that's the hook, isn't it?"

An awkward pause. Nathan was flashing to a sex romp between Naomi and the French-Greek woman-killer in a spooky little Japanese house—did they actually have houses in Tokyo?—after which she confesses to Arosteguy that she's infected with Nathan's dose of Roiphe's, so Arosteguy kills her in a rage and eats her.

"What?" said Nathan.

"I've developed some weird discharge," said Naomi, reading his mind obliquely as usual. "It's annoying." The Dutchman turned his head slightly towards her. He must have heard. Well, let him.

"Maybe it's just your routine yeast thing."

"No. This smells different," said Naomi, raising her voice ever so slightly for the Dutchman. She wondered if he knew about the Dutch connection with the Sagawa murder. Was it iconic in Holland in some way? That might be an interesting avenue to explore. "I'll have to get it checked out. So boring."

A pregnant pause and a sigh from Nathan. Naomi was on instant alert, fully in the airphone now, the screen pulled out of focus. "Naomi, the last time we were in bed together. In the Hilton. Schiphol."

"Yeah? What?"

"I had a dose of Roiphe's disease. You probably have it now too. I'm sorry. I didn't know. Fuck. You should get yourself checked out."

"What? You incredible schmuck! I can't believe this. You want me to get myself STD gynoed in Tokyo? By some weird Japanese gyno? Fuck!" At this, the Dutchman actually pulled his right earbud out, the one on Naomi's side, in order, she was certain, to hear her better. When she glared at him, the Naomi Death Stare, he smiled shyly and turned away. But he left the earbud out.

"I know, I am, I—"

"Who the fuck did you get it from, you unbelievable asshole? Or do you even know?"

"I do know. It was that breast-cancer patient I covered in Budapest. Dunja Hočevar."

"Oh, yeah, you really covered her but good! Talk about embedded journalists! Fuck!"

"It was a mercy fuck," said Nathan. "I was into the story and I was vulnerable. I dunno. I mean, she was immune-suppressed and . . . I dunno."

"Listen, I have a suggestion for you. Why don't you mercy-fuck Barry Roiphe?"

Naomi slammed the phone back down into its cradle in the armrest, jarring the Dutchman's vodka martini. He grabbed it just before it toppled over and smiled an oily smile.

"Sometimes I think these airplane phones are not such a good idea," he said, but Naomi was already back in her screen, communing with images of Arosteguy.

"NAOMI! OVER HERE!" Yukie was waving wildly as Naomi pushed her baggage cart with its streamlined wheel covers out through the glass doors of the immigration area. "So wonderful to see you again, my honey!"

"Yukie, hi! Oh, thank you for coming to meet me. You're such a doll." Yukie was wearing a bizarre dark-brown faux-fur coat with mauve and purple highlights, magenta leather gloves, a pink-striped fluffy scarf, and thick, clear-plastic oval sunglasses—all normal for her. Her hair was still long and full down her back, and it gave Naomi comfort to see her looking the way she remembered her.

They took the Narita Sky Access bullet train to Nippori Station, and then they were in a cab nudging its way through the Tokyo streets to

Yukie's flat. In the cab, Naomi was slightly disappointed that their cab driver wasn't wearing white cloth gloves, but at least the white-doily-draped seatbacks and headrests—so frilly and lacy they seemed Victorian—and the right-hand drive matched her internet-researched expectations. Yukie was taking photos of Naomi with her iPhone, and Naomi reciprocated by clacking away with her Nikon.

"Oh, it's so good to look at you again," said Yukie. "You know, you look so more mature now, not so little girl."

"Does that mean old?" said Naomi, hiding behind her viewfinder.

"No, of course not. I'll show you photographic proof." Yukie scrolled through her shots, chose one, and held it out for Naomi to see. Even front-lit by the phone's LED flash, smiling sweetly as she peeked out from behind her camera, Naomi did look pretty good still, looked viable, she thought, whatever that meant.

"C'mon, I mean really," said Yukie. "Look how glamorous and sexy. It must be the marriage thing. Nathan must be a terrific, sexy, supportive husband."

"You know we're not married, Yukie."

"It's a modern marriage," she said. "It's what marriage has turned into, and you're it. You're married. Cyber-married. Somehow, the internet is involved."

Yukie's place was in Shinsen, just west of Shibuya Station, on a small side street of slightly shabby concrete-and-tile buildings. Just outside her apartment door, Yukie turned to Naomi and put her hands on her shoulders. "I'm going to make all the usual single Japanese working-girl disclaimers. It's small and ugly and crowded, and I'm embarrassed to have you see it, much less stay in it."

Naomi gave Yukie a quick kiss. "All the more reason for me to thank you. It's the best place in Tokyo for me, believe me." Once inside, Naomi was disappointed to see a quite neat, clean, and modern little space that could have been a studio in Brooklyn or Queens. No tatami mats, no futons, no shoji screens. She shouldn't have been surprised, she thought, since Yukie herself was neat, clean, and modern, though following Japanese tradition they both took off their footwear just inside the door.

"Are you needing to hide out, though, really?" said Yukie, as she hauled Naomi's big duffel bag into the kitchen. Sheer white curtains closed off the kitchen from the bedroom, which was also the living room. "Even my friends can't seem to find me here, so you should be pretty anonymous."

"I'm not sure," said Naomi, thinking about her Dutch seatmate and his continuing interest in her as they waited for their baggage. He kept smiling and nodding at her, trying to catch her eye as though they shared an intimate secret, and it creeped her out, induced paranoid fantasies. "I wouldn't be surprised if someone on the plane wanted to follow me."

Yukie laughed dismissively and closed the substantial metal-clad door behind her. She took Naomi's hand and led her to the bed, where she sat down and patted the sunflower-pattern bedspread. Naomi left her roller and shoulder bag on the pink carpet and sat beside her, Yukie still wearing her coat and gloves. "You can take the bed. I'm used to sleeping on the floor in my sleeping bag."

"That doesn't feel right," said Naomi. "We'll work something out. Maybe I'll sleep on your kitchen table."

"Oh, yeah, right," laughed Yukie. "It's actually not even big enough."

Naomi was feeling that deep, heavy jet lag, now that she could let go, could stop traveling. She was almost delirious enough to be serious about the kitchen table; she imagined lying on it on her back, her legs hanging over the edge, dangling slippers. Her eyes felt dead from the inside out, but Yukie's eyes were luminous with excitement. "So, really? Is there a story for me in this? You know, a unique Japanese angle? Something you wouldn't want but you can give me? My boss has been hating everything I bring him lately."

Naomi was very comfortable with Yukie's guilt trips—they were so gentle you could ignore them—but she did owe her, and she did need her. Yukie was a media relations agent at Monogatari PR, one of the most powerful public relations firms in Japan—their specialty was spin-doctoring celebrity catastrophes, particularly the political variety—and though she was a junior agent, she knew everybody in the highly incestuous and regimented Japanese media world. "I'm meeting a very dangerous man here in Tokyo. Nobody knows about it."

"Not even Nathan?"

"He knows about it, the asshole."

Yukie's eyes went even wider. "Uh-oh." She looked down and took Naomi's hand again, and without looking up said quietly, "Maybe, Naomi, you should give me the name of some contact or something? Just in case? Maybe not just Nathan?"

"I'll do that, Yukie. That's a good idea. And meanwhile, I need a contact from *you*."

"Oh, yeah?" Having said the fearful thing, she was able to look up into Naomi's eyes again.

"Who's your gynecologist?" said Naomi.

"WE HAD A WONDERFUL Portuguese housekeeper living down here for a while, but we lost her to a better offer," said Roiphe.

"Oh?" said Nathan.

"Boyfriend married her. Swept her away."

"She forgot to take her flag," said Nathan, tipping his head towards the small plastic Portuguese flag on the wall. Next to it was a voluptuous poster depicting a Moorish castle in the Sintra Mountains near Estoril, the Vila de Sintra coat of arms prominent in the lower right corner, where the poster was slightly torn. At that point, stuffing his underwear into the light-birch veneer Ikea dresser which sat under the poster, Nathan was already feeling like a Portuguese housekeeper, desperate to create a window in her windowless basement bedroom with the windswept vista of the poster. He would keep that, but the flag had to come down. And why was there no mirror in the room?

"She disappeared overnight. Left a lot of her junk. Must have been pretty hot stuff," said Roiphe, hunkered down and shamelessly poking through Nathan's open camera bag on the furry floor. Shag. Visions of seventies carpet rakes danced in Nathan's head. Or was shag carpeting really making a comeback? This variant was a muted dark slate, not what you'd consider a 1970s color. Was this insane? Was he really doing this? Would he actually be able to sleep down here, and then wake up, and then function?

Nathan decided to laugh. "Well, I could probably fill in a bit if things get slow. I'm particularly good with a feather duster."

"Damned if I won't take you up on that, things get hectic. Hey, you've got some crackerjack gear in here." Roiphe held up Nathan's wireless flash trigger. "Now what the heck is this gizmo? It says," he began reading the label, "that it's a Nikon Wireless Speedlight Commander SU-800. Sounds pretty impressive to me."

Nathan decided to use his iPhone's LTE personal hotspot to generate a private wireless signal. Roiphe had handed him his house Wi-Fi password—"Network Name: DoctoR; Password: inFeKt1On!!"—shakily hand-printed in silver Magic Marker on the back of a ten-dollar Pizza Pizza/Toys "R" Us savings card. "I'll want that back once you've logged in," he had said, obviously not fearing the revelation of his home's Wi-Fi password to the administrators of the Pizza Pizza redemption program. The old codger protested his technological ignorance too much; he seemed absolutely clear and savvy about all things *i* and *e*, and Nathan was convinced that feeling paranoid in the Roiphe household was simply being realistic. He was sure that if he used the DoctoR network, every keystroke would be duly logged, every email kidnapped and archived, and every Skype conversation transcribed for later sinister use. Or did he just need this to be true to make his story more compelling than it threatened to be?

Certainly Roiphe, after his major song and dance about wanting a lawyer-certified, bulletproof contract binding them together in secrecy and artistic collaboration in such a way that liability and patient-abuse litigation and other such medically inspired legal chicanery would be made impossible, seemed quite nonchalant about dropping the whole matter once Nathan agreed to move in. He had even dropped, for the moment, his demand that they funnel their book deal through a credible literary agency—"I figure maybe Oliver Sacks's own Wylie Agency"—before he allowed Nathan to record a word or take a photograph. He now seemed perfectly content with some vague understanding whereby they would magically fuse into an alternate-reality incarnation of Sacks, with a movie, an opera, some delicious parodies, and of course vicious attacks by colleagues fueled by jealousy following the release of their book, tentatively entitled *Consumed: A Curious Case History*. The doctor rehearsed defending himself against accusations of exploitation: "It's in the hallowed tradition of the clinical anecdote, what we're doing. Freud did it, Charcot did it, Luria did it. And we're doing it! It's an educational procedure, intended to provoke discussion, perfectly legit." Nathan was happy to let Roiphe's enthusiasm carry them as far as it might without the complication of paperwork, lawyers, book deals, agents. He needed to feel that he could walk away, literally, in the middle of the night, trundling his camera roller after him, with no goodbyes and no regrets.

To seal the deal, Roiphe had brought his home office's Pixie—with two sleeves of gray-coded Roma capsules—down to Nathan's subterranean domain after Nathan had confessed his addiction to Nespresso. He had never seen a Pixie in the flesh. This one was the adorable titanium-colored version, which spookily matched the shag carpeting. "It's okay, don't thank me, I have the big mother deluxe one in the kitchen. I won't go caffeineless." Nathan was drinking a Roma right now out of the supplied cup and saucer, both in elegant white ceramic with the swooping split-N logo embossed within a beveled square recess, green capped letters on the bottom of each proclaiming "Nespresso Collection, Made in Portugal," which of course evoked the poster on the wall and the former housekeeper. Synchronicity? Nathan took it to mean that what he was doing there in Roiphe's basement had cosmic support. There was an undeniable shape to it.

He had decided to keep the Pixie in the bedroom—on the dresser for now—instead of the tiny but workable nanny's kitchen just around the corner from the slate-floored sitting room. He wanted it to feel like a European hotel-room adventure rather than a move-in-completely-and-hopelessly situation—move in with your recently widowed father, for instance. Nathan had done that, and it had been bitter and desperate in too many ways to bear experiencing it again, even analogically. Picking up on Naomi's line of thought, Roiphe had joked that there was no separate entrance to the embedded reporter's suite, the better to keep an eye on him, but everything worked, including the bathroom with shower.

It had to be admitted: he was down here because of Chase. He wanted to be in the same house with her. He was not sure why. She was certainly attractive, but immediately gave off those convulsive, anaphrodisiac waves of looniness that tell you not to bother fantasizing. But where in the house was she? Did she know yet he had moved in? Would he be able to hear her? Could she hear him? Would she visit him down here? After finishing the Roma, he tried several times to email, text, and phone Naomi, without success. Then he called Dunja's Slovenian mobile number, also without success; her phone disconnected after nine rings without accepting any messages, and a disconsolate Nathan wondered if, overwhelmed by guilt at infecting him, she had committed suicide.

ON THE HONGO CAMPUS of the University of Tokyo, familiarly known as Todai, Naomi walked down the broad, tree-lined avenue leading to the fortress-like Yasuda Auditorium with its dark-red tiles and incongruous stone-arched entranceway, then turned right on the heavily wooded path that would take her to Sanshiro Pond. She could walk with confidence because, of course, she had Google Mapped and YouTubed her route to death before venturing outside Yukie's flat, whose wireless signal was surprisingly robust. Yukie had insisted on covertly entering the flat's wireless network password on Naomi's various machines herself, not letting Naomi watch, a touch of paranoid strangeness that chilled Naomi's feelings for her. She had to shrug it off. So, experiencing that comforting but oppressive net-preview déjà vu, down the curving series of stone steps she went, past a group of students sitting on large rocks in the pond feeding the carp and koi, past the tiny waterfall, and on to the simple wooden bench upon which sat Professor Hideki Matsuda of the Faculty of Law. In their email exchange brokered by Yukie, Matsuda had made it clear that he did not want to meet Naomi anywhere too public, but he also wanted to be respectful, and the ancient pond seemed a fitting compromise. In response to his wariness, Naomi carried only her iPad in its dedicated Crumpler shoulder bag, and a black nylon shopping bag from La Grande Epicerie in Paris for her mundane stuff and her Sony RX100 compact camera, just in case.

The professor rose from the bench as Naomi approached and bowed slightly, not extending his hand. "Naomi, so nice to meet you."

"Thank you, Professor Matsuda. I'm very grateful for your help."

An awkward beat of silence filled by the shouts of students talking to the fish and one another which rose from the other end of the pond. It was obvious to Naomi that there was considerable stress involved in their meeting for this neat, delicate man of about fifty, his suit and tie impeccable, his glasses of fine stainless steel. Eventually, he took a card from an inside jacket pocket and offered it to Naomi with both hands as though it were a business card. She took it similarly with two hands, but it was just a note card, and completely in Japanese—perhaps intended to convey to her that Matsuda did not want her to know anything about him beyond what she already knew. She would need Yukie's help with the card. They sat down together opposite a tiny, lush island.

"The philosopher can be found at this address, at the time I have written on the card. It is his current home. He is interested to meet you."

Naomi was sure that Matsuda would be happy to leave it at that, to say goodbye right then and there, or perhaps stroll around the pond a bit, elaborating on its creation in 1615, its special heart shape, and its informal renaming to reference the 1908 campus novel *Sanshirō* by Natsume Sōseki—all safe topics, all charming and congenial. But Naomi was not charming and congenial.

"Professor, you are a personal friend of Aristide Arosteguy, is that correct?"

"I would not say personal friend, no. We are colleagues in philosophy; he, professionally, and I, well, philosophically, as an outgrowth of my interest in justice and international law. We have run into each other occasionally at various venues."

In her face, which she felt sure was burning red, Naomi could feel the wet vegetable heat coming off the pond. Matsuda looked cool. "Have you seen him recently?"

"No, not recently. We correspond by email. He is a controversial figure on campus, as one might imagine."

"As controversial as the cannibal Issei Sagawa?"

Matsuda flinched away from Naomi a few centimeters, as though the words had shoved him in the chest, but his expression did not change. "That is . . . not a valid comparison, Naomi."

"Professor Matsuda, I will be seeing Monsieur Arosteguy alone. Completely alone."

"Yes."

"Should I be worried?"

Matsuda adjusted his glasses with both hands. "There are so many levels to that question."

"The level that I'm concerned about is the physical safety level. Will I be in danger from the philosopher? I don't mean philosophical danger, or emotional danger. I mean physical danger." Matsuda seemed unable to answer. He just stared at Naomi, blinking as a small flock of birds swept over the pond. Naomi pushed. "Some French policemen consider him capable of murder."

It was apparent now that Matsuda could not bear these words. There were beads of sweat on his forehead. He stood up. "Please give the philosopher Monsieur Arosteguy my regards when you see him." He bowed, turned, and strode off along the verge of the pond, a briefcase, which Naomi had somehow not noticed before, held stiffly at his side, not swinging.

6

NAOMI STOOD IN A residential street in Western Tokyo that looked more like an alleyway than a street. Yukie had assured her that, yes, there were houses in Tokyo and they were much more common than, say, houses in Paris, some of them very large and luxurious, some of them miniature modernist jewels. But as her cab left her, picking its way gingerly past the bicycles, potted plants, baby strollers, plastic garbage cans, and random furniture lining the street, she could see that Arosteguy's house was neither luxurious nor jewel-like.

It was after 8 P.M. and the light was fading fast. Naomi pulled out her camera—the compact Sony RX100 again; better to look like a tourist for now—and began snapping off shots in all directions. She steadied the camera against whatever wall or pole was handy to compensate for the low light levels and the resulting slow shutter speeds. The gathering twilight combined with the mercury-vapor street lamps and the incandescent light spilling from house windows made for pleasingly surreal 3D-feeling images. She could almost hear the little camera's computers buzzing madly in their attempt to balance the color temperatures of the varied light sources.

After documenting the shop across the narrow street, its steamed-up windows displaying mysterious aluminum, ceramic, and glass containers, Naomi turned her attention to Arosteguy's gray-stuccoed two-story house with its sad garden just inside the entrance. It was streaked with dirt and crumbling, its ironwork gate pocked with rust and its garden a rotting, garbage-strewn mess. There was some thin light showing through the second-floor windows, but the first floor was dark. After exhausting every imaging possibility she could think of, scrolling through her shots to see if anything jumped out at her, Naomi put the camera in her bag and crossed the street, trailing her roller behind her.

On the outer wall, just beside the open gate, a stainless-steel mailbox featured stenciled white numbers—"13-23"—on a blue rectangle. Another blue rectangle contained impenetrable white Japanese characters. Walking through the gate and into the courtyard, which was fitfully lit by stained orange garden lights built into its raw concrete walls, Naomi was tempted to take out her camera and start snapping again—so many wonderful depressing details expressing the decay of this man's life (as the accompanying copy would have it)—but she resisted. There would be time.

Facing the sliding wooden doors, Naomi vainly tried to see through their narrow, full-length vertical panes of pebbled glass. She thought she saw a security camera in a hat-like galvanized steel housing above and to the right of the doors, but it proved to be an electricity meter. Electrical wiring crawled haphazardly all over the building's stucco, many of the corroded screws and clamps barely hanging on. She looked for a buzzer or a doorbell, but there wasn't one, so she knocked on the glass, which rattled at her touch. After a moment, a dim, watery light came on somewhere deep in the room beyond, there was a scuffle of locks, and the door slid open.

Arosteguy stood in the doorway, his face hidden in shadow, a large, imposing, shaggy presence. This surprised Naomi; from her YouTube experience of the philosopher, he was small and fastidious about his appearance. She wondered for a moment if this man at the door was someone else, or even if she had the wrong address, but after warily looking her up and down, he spoke, and the voice and the accent were Arosteguy's.

"You've brought your suitcase. That is good."

Naomi glanced down at her camera roller, nervous. "Oh, this? It's my equipment roller. I keep my camera and flashes and things in it. I thought it'd be okay to bring it. We talked about photo shoots, documenting your life here ..."

Arosteguy reached down and picked the roller up by its top handle. "Heavy. Heavy equipment." He hunched his shoulder to move the roller out of Naomi's way and slid the door open wider with his knee for her to enter ahead of him. "Take your shoes off and come in," he said, assuming she would be oblivious of that protocol despite his stockinged feet and the presence of his own oxblood brogues sitting in the *genkan* just before the step up into the house.

Arosteguy served green tea to Naomi, who sat floor level in a dumpy beanbag chair in a generally dumpy small living room. The light remained as sickly as it had looked through the front-door panes, adding to Naomi's tightening unease. Greasy sliding glass back doors opened out into darkness. Naomi could now see that he was haggard and unshaven, his long hair—gray with some black streaks still—unwashed and wild, his clothes rumpled and slept in. It all somehow made him even more attractive, and Naomi was aware that this, not fear, was the source of her unease.

"Thank you," she said, taking the tea.

Arosteguy sat opposite her on a futon folded into a couch and sipped his own tea, cradling the cup as if for warmth. A fragrance, vaguely Japanese in character and not unpleasant, seemed to emanate from him. "And so, yes, you brought your camera. That's good. You'll want photos. I've taken some photos myself. Very strong photos."

It was the last phrase that added intimidation, and perhaps now at last fear, to the established substratum of unease. Naomi had to work hard not to imagine this man, still trailing a fragrant effluvium, meticulously photographing his wife's half-eaten head. Were some of those photos she found on the net posted by him, posted in defiance, perhaps, or perversity?

She had to hasten to fill the lapsed moment, almost stuttering. "Have you? Photos? Um, were they journalistic photos or art photos?"

Arosteguy laughed a ropey laugh. He lit a Japanese cigarette that he had some trouble shaking out of a pack beside him on the couch, then laughed some more, emitting short snorts of smoke towards her.

"I only smoke Japanese now. I want to become Japanese. I'll never speak French again. Never. They say that Tolstoy learned classical Greek very quickly once he put his mind to it. I'm learning Japanese very quickly. Until then, I speak English or German. For philosophy, at least, you have to speak German. Perhaps I will make Japanese essential for contemporary Western philosophy. If I live long enough."

Naomi was groping. "Photography has no language. Is that why you're so interested in it?"

"I think you've seen some of my photographic work," said Arosteguy. "You can tell me whether it's journalistic or artistic. I myself think that it's both."

"I've seen your work?"

"On the internet. Those famous photos of my wife. I posted them from Todai, from the university." Another small laugh, a phlegmless one this time. "They don't know it yet."

"Your wife?" said Naomi. She wanted it to sound lame, and it did, but she was positioning herself for the moment as the naïve and easily shockable North American—familiar journalistic role-playing.

"Before, and after. Mostly after. Those are the ones everybody's interested in. I'm sure you've found them. On the arosteguyatrocity dot com website."

Arosteguy rose and leaned over Naomi to pour her more tea. Her teacup was still almost full. Was it a threatening, a challenging move? Reflexively, she shrank back ever so slightly. "Maybe you'd like to take some pictures of me now? Our first meeting? Historic. You said you brought your flash units. I don't like bright light in my house. I can't think in bright light. But a flash of inspiration is always good."

NAOMI HAD SET UP her three wireless Speedlight flash units with the chunky black wireless SU-800 Commander, which controlled and triggered the flashes using infrared pulses, locked in her D300s's hot shoe, and was snapping away as Arosteguy sat and posed, drinking tea and smoking, effortlessly playing the role of rumpled sage. The lighting setup, for now, was simple and unadventurous: one flash lighting the background, splashing the walls and the narrow wooden staircase behind the couch; one above right, sitting on the radio's speaker—there seemed to be only one—giving her the key light on Arosteguy's face; and one directly off to the left, sitting on a pile of books, which provided the fill light. Naomi's Nagra recorder—a model ML, one generation behind Nathan's Nagra SD—was working on the side table next to Arosteguy's couch. So smooth was the philosopher that he timed his sentences to her flashes, never once being caught with his mouth half open or his eyes half closed. In this, he reminded her of Hervé. Had one of them schooled the other?

"That's a very big camera you have. Very professional. Of course, that's to be expected. I myself also use a digital camera, but a small one, a 'consumer camera,' they call them. I would like very much for you to teach me professional photographic methods. That's one of the reasons I insisted that you live here with me for the few days that you do your interview. At least I will gain something."

Naomi constantly checked her shots as they popped up on the camera's rear LCD screen, something the pros derided as "chimping" but all did obsessively anyway. So accurate had the screens become in terms of both resolution and color that you really knew exactly what you were getting. She knew nobody who was nostalgic enough for the days of film to actually shoot with it other than as a masochistic retro-gesture. "Monsieur Arosteguy, you know I haven't agreed to stay here. But do you really think photo tutorials are all you have to gain? I thought you wanted to tell your story. I thought it had never been told."

"Ari. You must call me Ari if you are to stay with me. But I am working on a book that will tell my story. I don't expect you to be that objective, or rather that subjective."

"In my experience, a good journalist can tell a subject things about himself that he never knew."

"Really?" said Arosteguy. "That would be interesting. Very interesting."

NOT TOO MANY HOURS LATER, Naomi took over Yukie's spindly metal kitchen table to assemble all her electronics in preparation for taking them to Arosteguy's house. Yukie leaned against the front door, watching Naomi while of course texting, Facebooking, Twittering, Instagramming, playing video games, and watching cartoons using a massive clamshell phone of a type unknown to Naomi which was covered with cute/sinister anime/manga stickers.

"You know, I think you're crazy," said Yukie. "Maybe suicidal."

Naomi liked all her cables, connectors, and adapters packed away in old padded mailing envelopes, and each time she packed, she was presented with a new puzzle: which things went where. She stood over the table, hands on hips, watching the spread-out tangle of devices and envelopes, waiting for clarity. At random moments, she would attack one or another set of devices, like a cormorant diving into the sea for eels, and stuff it into its mysteriously appropriate sleeve, then pull back and wait for the next illumination.

"It's just an overnighter. I'm leaving most of my stuff here, if that's okay. He says he wants me to teach him photography."

"Honey, it's either sex or murder he wants. Probably both. At the same time."

"Nice," said Naomi, diving in once more. "I'll make sure to send you photos."

"And speaking of sex, you haven't told me how it went at the Ladies Clinic. Did you find the English-speaking gyno?"

"I ended up with a French-speaking gyno. At first he wanted to give me the Blue Lotus Course."

"Sure. That's for women who work. I mean, in offices and stuff. Was he okay? I should have gone with you."

"He was okay. I found the career-women thing kinda odd. I had to convince him I was only interested in STDs. I think I shocked him a bit."

"The Germanium Course. I know it well."

"Do you? Really? Yukie?"

"I've had some bad boyfriends. Nothing at the level of your philosopher, though."

"Please. Don't gross me out. But why Germanium? Why is a Japanese examination for sexually transmitted diseases named after a weird metalloid discovered by a German? Blue Lotus is a lot sexier."

"Japanese medical people are traditionally very strange and creepily poetic. You should have just asked the doctor."

"I didn't want to distract him. He correctly diagnosed Roiphe's—with a bit of help—and gave me this script." Naomi dug the prescription form out of her jacket pocket and handed it to Yukie, who barely glanced at it.

"Sasagaki. I didn't know he spoke French. Garden-variety antibiotic. We can get this filled for you at the pharmacy down the street. You'll have to come with me. It looks like about two months' worth. Are you planning to have sex with Monsieur Arosteguy? You might have to wait a bit. Or do condoms work well enough with this STD?"

"Thanks for the lovely stream of consciousness, Yukie. It really clarifies things for me."

"No problem."

AROSTEGUY HAD TO MAKE two trips to carry Naomi's camera roller and her duffel up the cramped stairs of his house. There wasn't really much of a hall upstairs, just two bedrooms and a bathroom jammed together. Arosteguy opened the door to one of the rooms, so small he could drop the duffel on the narrow wooden bed from the doorway, and turned to Naomi as she followed him. "I decided to give you the room right next to mine. You'll want to know my every move, of course. From here, you'll know each time I get up to urinate in the night. I do that very often now. Man's fate."

Naomi squeezed past him—he actually inhaled his belly so that she could get past—and unslung her bag onto a small table near a window that looked out over a metal-strip balcony. There seemed to be no way to get onto that balcony except by crawling through the aluminum-framed sliding window. "Thank you. This is great."

"There's power there, see, just on the wall there, and also a telephone jack. I do not yet have a wireless network in this house. I assume you have a laptop and chargers for your camera batteries."

"Yes, I do. Thank you."

"I have learned the password of two of my neighbors' wireless home networks, so you can use theirs if you like. Be a parasite on their network. Global digital parasitism is the new Trotskyism. Connect to anywhere in the world you like. I'm not worried." Arosteguy ran his hand through his hair, which had flopped over his right eye when he was dealing with her luggage. He smiled a tight, wincing smile, as though something had just hurt him. "And also, please keep in mind that sex between us is very possible, if you like it." Naomi let her face register exactly nothing. Had he been talking to Yukie? For a moment she thought it was plausible and was overwhelmed by dark, sticky paranoia. Let's see: she had first contacted Arosteguy through Hervé Blomqvist, who was able to give her only the name of Professor Matsuda, but then Yukie had actually ferreted out Professor Matsuda, who had given her Arosteguy's address ... Naomi had wanted to avoid giving Arosteguy's address or any other contact data to Yukie because Yukie was a public relations flack with a journalist's instincts. Naomi hated to admit it, but on a certain level she didn't trust Yukie. Yukie was trying too hard to hide her excitement at the Arosteguy-scandal connection—she was playing it a little too cool—and though Arosteguy was a *gaijin,* it would be a stunning coup for her to bring him in to her demanding boss at Monogatari PR as a client looking for a public Tokyo makeover.

The Japanese vegetable scent—water lilies? ginkgo leaves?—that Naomi had caught her first day with Arosteguy now flooded over her as he called back on his way down the staircase. "Perhaps you would like to go out for a late dinner. Perhaps not. Let me know. We can eat here as well. I cook."

Later, Naomi had her laptop and cameras set up on the bedroom table and was sitting on the bed—there was no room for a chair—working over her first Arosteguy photos, cropping and color grading them in Adobe Lightroom, then Dropboxing them to her editor at *Notorious*. The photos she had created were very moody and dramatic, and showed that beneath the current shabbiness, Arosteguy was a refined and handsome man.

She dabbed at the trackpad, hitting the Upload button as though the Air might explode in her face, but it all seemed to work smoothly. She'd had to let Arosteguy mess with her computer, switching the keyboard to Japanese in order to type in the neighbor's network password, and it felt like a violation, not the less disturbing because it was a consensual one. As the photos churned away into the ether, her email chime went off. It was from Nathan, and it said, "Naomi, I need to talk to you about Arosteguy and Roiphe. Odd things, funny parallels. You told me your cell phone wouldn't work in Japan and it doesn't. You must have gotten a Japanese phone by now. Call me. Nathan." Naomi immediately replied, "Send me pictures of you and Roiphe fucking each other. I'll call you to comment." She was surprised by the spontaneous depths of her own vindictiveness, but rather pleased by them as well.

In the bathroom, she checked herself out in the plastic-framed mirror, leaning close to finesse the subtle eye makeup, the just-perceptible lipstick. She had put on the sexiest outfit she had that you could still do physical work in—formfitting beige light wool sweater, tight black cotton pants—without allowing herself to wonder why she bothered. She had started her course of antibiotics.

NAOMI HAD HER SPEEDLIGHTS and her Nagra set up in Arosteguy's tiny galley kitchen and was shooting him as he cooked. She had made a fetish of culinary ignorance, part of her integrity as a media professional somehow, and so she could only see that he was manipulating a lot of tiny shrimp and clumps of what looked like seaweed with a delicate knife. A small jug of warm sake and two mismatched cylindrical ceramic cups sat beside the sink. They both drank randomly.

Arosteguy too had cleaned up a bit: he was shaven now, and had washed, or at least brushed, his hair, though she hadn't heard him in the bathroom. He had also changed his clothes, looking very professorial in a thick sweater and corduroy pants. Zooming in on her D300s's LCD screen to check her focus, Naomi could see thin, transparent wires trailing from his hairline down into his ears. "Are those hearing aids in your ears," she asked, "or are you listening to music?"

"Bionic enhancements. And through them, I am in constant contact with certain satellites."

"You're kidding, right?"

"I have no sense of humor. But my Greek father, a violinist, and my French mother, a pianist, were both quite deaf before the age of fifty, and they both wore hearing aids. Of course, they were analogue then, and very primitive, but now they're digital. I like the French word, *numérique,* better. It's more descriptive, and it doesn't confuse with the reference to human fingers, to the digits." He turned and waggled his fingers at Naomi. They were short and powerful, and with them he pulled a hearing aid from his left ear and let it dangle in front of his face so that she could shoot it. A rather shapely silver capsule—to match his hair—fitted behind his ear, and a transparent plastic lead containing the thinnest of wires fed into a translucent twin-domed bud—it looked like a tiny jellyfish—that plugged into his earhole. "It's made by Siemens. German, of course. They're not as good as real ears, but they're good." He gently coaxed it back into his ear and turned again to his cooking. "This moment reminds me of a famous family moment in Paris when my mother was cooking and somehow, adjusting the clip that held her hair back from her face, she popped her hearing aid out of her ear and into her bouillabaisse without realizing it. And I was the one who ate it." Arosteguy began to heave with laughter at the memory. "The toxicity of the battery was of some concern, as you can imagine. They were much bigger then. But they couldn't imagine how to get it out of me at that time in French medical history without the possibility of doing terrible damage to my young stomach and intestines, so we just waited for the inevitable. My mother found it quite annoying to be unbalanced in her hearing for all that time, and ultimately they gave her a new pair, even better than what she had."

Naomi was zoomed in on a shot she had just taken of his cheekbone, which was very shapely but smeared with a light discoloration that reminded her of her grandfather, a dermatologist, who had told her that the skin became a garden of weird life-forms when you aged. "Cover it with makeup when it happens," he had said. "You can't fight 'em. Too damn many of 'em."

"Do you always shave at night?" said Naomi. She asked questions partly to get Arosteguy to turn towards her so that she could find new angles on his face, which was beginning to seem endlessly interesting to her.

"I hadn't spoken to anyone for a week before you. I realized with a shock that I did not look very civilized."

"You look like a three-star French chef at home now."

"That alarms me. I don't cook French anymore. I cook Japanese. Well, I'm trying. My friend Matsuda-san is actually a wonderful cook. He's teaching me. I can only do the simplest things. So subtle, so subtle and complex what he can do."

"Professor Matsuda? I got the feeling that he wanted to distance himself from you."

"In public, yes, of course. Not in private."

"Well, his teaching must be good. Even your posture is starting to become more Japanese. And you look like you know what you're doing."

"Yes," said Arosteguy. "You too."

"Yeah?"

"Photos of the cannibal Arosteguy cooking a meal. Later, photos of the cannibal eating the meal. I'm sure you will be able to sell these around the world."

"What about video?" Naomi hefted the D300s in her right hand. "This thing shoots decent video. And I have a microphone and earphones to go with it."

"Maybe. When we get to know each other better. And I have some lawyers I need to consult with. They are already angry with me for the event of you. The event of Naomi. They are basing everything on the lack of an extradition treaty between Japan and France, but there are delicate circumstances which complicate things, and public outcry and opinion are dangerously involved."

"Well, you're not wrong about the cannibal thing. It's pretty potent stuff. But you don't object? You don't mind?"

Arosteguy turned to her and pulled his mouth open to one side with his index finger. The effect was grotesque. Startled, Naomi lowered the camera. Arosteguy let go of his mouth. "Into the very mouth of the cannibal. Don't you want that picture?"

"Are you sure you want me to take it?"

"Take it," said Arosteguy.

He pulled his mouth open again. Naomi began shooting. She changed lenses quickly—an extreme wide-angle lens now—and continued snapping, getting very close, optically spreading his face and his mouth, distorting them. Arosteguy played it seriously and intensely, his gums and teeth—quite good, really, with only slight tobacco discoloration—completely exposed on one side and somehow perversely naked. Naomi lowered her camera and checked the LCD screen. The photos were very disturbing.

"Enough for now," said Naomi. She reached for her sake.

"Call me Ari," said Arosteguy.

"Enough for now, Ari." She drained the cup and poured herself more.

7

THE DOOR TO NATHAN'S basement bedroom opened a crack, letting in a slash of light that cut across his face, waking him, befuddled, still dreaming himself a child with his white underpants on his head to keep his wet hair from soaking the pillow, something he had worked out with his mother, who tended to remember he needed a bath just before bedtime. When he awoke, the underpants—worn and frayed, the elastic popping out everywhere around the waistband—were always miraculously gone and his hair was dry, just as it was now. And the unutterable sweetness of that dream suffused, in a bizarre, wholly inappropriate way, the sinister shadow that appeared at the entrance to the room, hesitated, then slid elastically over the door frame and the dressing table. When the shadow reached Nathan, it liquidly merged with a silhouette that was Roiphe, tiptoeing in comic fashion.

"Nathan? Are you awake?" The sweetness quickly leached away at the touch of Roiphe's nasal voice, leaving a sourness tinged with anxiety, which, Nathan understood, was his default reaction to Roiphe.

"Not really," said Nathan. "Do I have to be?"

"Well, get awake and grab your camera," said Roiphe. "I was going to wait till we had some major prep time, but it's happening now, so let's take it at the flood."

"Flood?"

Roiphe shook his head in mild exasperation. "It's time to observe the nocturnal habits of an odd creature. Get up, boy."

Nathan's sense of being a boy in his childhood bed was palpably enhanced by his pajamas and slippers, which as an adult he never wore. The slippers were white Crillon hotel slippers bearing the elegant golden, foliate, and crowned letter *C* logo, given to him by Naomi, of course, who knew he'd be staying in places that did not hand out free slippers; the garden-variety striped flannel pajamas with the big white plastic buttons he had bought at the Hudson's Bay department store, anticipating that he'd toss them once he was no longer a resident at the Roiphe Hostel. Just the thought of sleeping naked in that basement under that thin, clumped-up acrylic duvet provoked revulsion. And yet it was the pajamas and the slippers, the protective apparel, that transported him to a strange and unexpected place as he followed Roiphe through the darkened house, which sported sly, unexpected nightlights everywhere. Slithering in the sloppily fitting backless Crillon slippers up the teakwood staircase, clinging to the handrail of the wrought-iron balustrade—also foliate in a pseudo art nouveau style—Nathan listened to Roiphe whispering that the series of rooms on the third floor, which they were approaching, had been built "against code." The trick had been to leave it unwalled and unfinished until after the final building-code inspections had been carried out, and then to have the rooms miraculously appear to the first buyers of the house in all their beautifully executed, dormered glory as "architectural workspace." Said space now occupied solely by Chase Roiphe. But Nathan was also slithering in his childhood moccasin slippers, slithering downstairs by the light of the potent chromed-aluminum Eveready flashlights that he and his fragile, thin-limbed sister, Shelley, held, making their way before dawn to their living room, which was all but filled by an upright piano and a Christmas tree decorated with everything commercial and nothing Christian—candy canes, reindeer, elves, tinsel, cotton-batting snow, edible stars. There were presents of every size and shape under the tree, of course—the point of the whole exercise. Nathan had sent a SantaGram to the North Pole, and Santa had come through in the most satisfying way.

LATER, THEY SAT DOWNSTAIRS, with what Nathan thought was perverse appropriateness, in the kitchen. The granite-topped island, whose vast and immaculate surface was interrupted only by a stainless-steel offset double-bowl sink, provided a clinical workspace for what Roiphe, rocking pelvically, rhapsodically, on his spidery wrought-iron breakfast stool, called "our first strategic debrief." Nathan sat beside him on a sister stool, not rocking, his laptop on the granite in front of them, scrolling through the photos he had taken over the last hour. The fourteen embedded digital clocks strewn around the room, from the MacBook Pro to the ice-maker in the Sub-Zero fridge, the Wolf stove, the Jenn-Air warming drawers, Nathan's camera (which sat just beyond the laptop), to Roiphe's own odd cheap plastic wristwatch, all indicated that the time was somewhere between 4:06 and 4:09 A.M.

"So you see what we're up against here, son. What we're working with."

"Not really," said Nathan. "Honestly, I'm kind of in shock. That's really what I'm working with."

Roiphe managed to work some rhythmical sympathetic nodding into his rocking. "Uh-huh, uh-huh, I can understand that. And that's what we're doing here, right now. Want some ice water? Maybe coffee? Anything?"

"No, thanks. I'm good."

"'I'm good' is funny. Sounds funny to me. We never used to say that. We'd say 'I'm fine. I'm all right.' But they do say 'I'm good' these days. So what are we looking at here? What happened? What did you see? What did you shoot?"

"I'm having trouble believing what I'm looking at right now," said Nathan, squirming a bit on the stool. Its floral-print plastic cushion was coming loose at the rear left edge, and he was half-consciously trying to slide it back into place with his buttocks.

"I think maybe you should just verbalize. Keep it simple and direct and we'll get somewhere fast." Roiphe was still nodding and rocking, but now with a fierce-eyed intensity that was unmistakably masturbatory, urging Nathan on towards some obscure epiphanic orgasm that he felt was completely beyond him. He decided to keep it simple and direct.

"Your daughter, Chase, was cutting bits of her flesh off with a nail clipper, putting those bits onto little children's plastic toy plates, and then eating those bits of flesh using little children's toy utensils."

"Uh-huh. Uh-huh. And what do you think her state of mind was while she was doing this? Was she hurting herself? Was she in pain? Was she punishing herself?"

Nathan wondered if Roiphe was aware that he was recording their conversation through GarageBand on his MacBook. He had it running on Desktop 2, so the app was not visible (though only a three-finger swipe away), and it thus perhaps counted as semiconscious surreptitiousness. Like clocks, recording devices were everywhere embedded; everything was being recorded at every moment, like a huge, infernal Mac Time Machine backup system that created backups of backups regressing into infinity. Who would play these back? Who would pick among them like the survivor of a hideous bombing looking for the rags once worn by his dead and naked mother? He was not yet sure how much he wanted Nathan Math the character to feature in *Consumed: The Collaboration*, but at the very least his side of every exchange with the Roiphes—and who knew who else?—would provide context which might ultimately even have legal consequences, given the weirdness that was emerging from Roiphe's life and practice.

Nathan was running his photos within Lightroom, which allowed him to easily manipulate their quality as he and Roiphe reviewed them. He could pull down seemingly burned-out highlights to reveal startling details of expression, and open up clogged shadows to reveal tormented gestures; later, he could play with them as photographic art, tweak them towards meaning that was not yet obvious, though he could not imagine including them in their chimerical book. The "Annals of Medicine" piece had more future reality to it, though it too was unstable, shimmering, flickering—morphing perhaps into a piece for "Annals of Psychopathology," no pictures allowed. And in playing with the photos, he experienced once again the phenomenon of non-presence, the photographer's non-authentic existence during the act of photographing; only in reviewing the photos did the event photographed emerge in experience, like the flowering precipitate caused when a crystal of sodium acetate was dropped into its supersaturated solution. But then the experience was moderated by the photo, the lens, the camera, the camera-eye's response to the light—and that was what Nathan was reacting to now. He was not sure he had actually seen any of these events with his real eyes, a feeling sharpened by the clattering of the big camera's shutter and mirror, which he could hear as he looked at the photos; the sound became part of his interpretation, even though Chase herself never seemed to react to it or notice it at all.

Nathan was acutely aware that he was looking at photos of a naked woman with her father sitting beside him, also looking. True, Roiphe was proving to be an unusual father, but some of the photos were, quite by accident, perversely erotic, and Nathan felt that no matter how elaborate and subtly graduated Roiphe's emotional filters were, he could not fail to see that. Not that there had been a hint of incest in their past that he could sense—at least, not yet—but disturbingly, Nathan felt as though his undeniably surging lust for Chase counted as incest because her father, almost shoulder to shoulder with him, breathing with ragged old-man intensity into the side of Nathan's face as he searched the screen for signs of something obscure, possibly something sublime, must surely be inhaling it. Once again, it was that paradigm of the retroactive experience: Nathan had not felt anything like this while taking the photos, so caught up was he in the mechanics of getting the shot, but now, looking at them with Roiphe guiding the zooming and the scrolling with surgical insistence, Chase's muscular nakedness, which revealed the massive scale of her macroscopic self-mutilation (almost every reachable square centimeter of her skin had been attacked as though by swarms of blackflies, the wounds puckered and weeping or scabbing), provoked unsettling reveries in Nathan. Did Chase's body remind Roiphe of his dead wife's body? (The former Rose Blickstein, as per the doctor's Wikipedia entry.) Did it fill him with a bittersweet sexual nostalgia, an incestuous melancholia?

"She does seem to feel it, feel the pain," said Nathan. "I see it there, for instance, in this shot. She's feeling the pain, and feeling the grain of her skin as the metal of the cutting edges separates the cells of her skin, bites through the layers of her skin and the tissue underneath it. But the pain makes her laugh, a weird silent laugh—see there, it's not subtle, really. So she feels the pain, but she wants the pain, looks for it, like a bodybuilder wants the pain and searches for it."

"Happy to be punished? Looking for punishment?"

"The bodybuilder?"

"Fuck the bodybuilder. The girl."

Nathan zoomed into the photo in front of them. That was ecstasy on her face as she cut herself, not self-pity, not masochistic pleasure. But why ecstasy? The ritualistic elements of her trance—a classic fugue?—were complex and narrative; they were telling a consoling story to Chase, yes. Nathan was shaping the article as he reacted. He would have liked to record these thoughts, just say them to GarageBand so that he wouldn't forget them, but he was not yet comfortable enough with Roiphe to collaborate in that intimate way, to leave himself vulnerable to the old man's sarcasm and irony.

He scrolled to the eating shots, still zoomed. There were other people there with her, somehow, sharing the tiny bits of her flesh that she had doled out onto five little plates with butterfly and bunny patterns. She seemed to be taking on the roles of different characters, rotating through the plates, delicately eating from one, coarsely from the second, ravenously from the third. Bouncing the flash off the ceiling and the walls, he had gotten close to the plates and the teapot and cups, the plastic cupcakes with switchable toppings of vanilla, chocolate, and strawberry (each of these crowned by a convincing dimpled red cherry), and the shiny forks and knives in primary colors. The bounce absorbed the warmth of the terra-cotta walls and raked the covert tea party's flatware and hollowware with soft red-clay light, instilling sinister drama into the innocent child's set piece with its transient shadows and throwing into high relief the slivers of flesh and their smears of blood, which might otherwise have disappeared into the bright colors of the Fisher-Price plastic.

But it was the hands that were mesmerizing, Chase's hands, with their long, sinewy fingers and paradoxically perfect fingernails, hands that were out of proportion with the child-sized tea things and so seemed, especially when top-lit, to be monstrous as they delicately picked at the flesh bits and lifted them to her open mouth, her tongue extended and waiting. Very close to her now, he had been nervous about swiveling away from the child's table to follow the trajectory of the hands—she alternated left and right, as though picking berries in a deliriously fecund patch—but the graphic momentum soon carried him to Chase's face, which seemed swollen with contained excitement. When Nathan half-pressed the shutter release, a cross-hatched red laser pattern sprang from the base of the flash unit, allowing the camera to focus in low light. Caged by those red stripes she looked feral, like a wolverine caught by a self-triggered animal-cam in a remote boreal forest. She barely blinked at the brutal flashing that followed focusing, the harsh light, direct now, revealing scabbed notches taken out of the cartilage at the very tops of her ears, normally hidden by her hair, which was now swept back and held by a plastic tortoiseshell clip, its long, curving, interlocking teeth reminding Nathan of a sprung Venus flytrap. She was conscious enough of what she was doing, thought Nathan, even calculating enough, to avoid cutting her face and her hands—how could she cover up?—so where exactly was her mind now? The face in close-up currently on the screen, terrible, beautiful, used ecstasy as a mask and a shield. What was behind it? And she was talking, speaking for the invisible characters who sat around the chunky green-and-white circular plastic child's table, talking soundlessly, shuffling around the table on her knees, shifting the chairs about so that she could play each point of view with varying mien but consistent intensity.

"Okay. Here's where I do my healing thing. Keep shooting," Roiphe had said. In the photos that scrolled by now, Roiphe was partially lit by the Hello Kitty lamp on the night table in the corner, which he had flipped on so that he could unpack the beige corduroy Air Canada business-class toiletries bag he had stuffed into the pocket of his navy velour bathrobe. Roiphe was kneeling beside the oblivious Chase, intrepidly tracking down every fresh wound so that he could disinfect it with alcohol and Polysporin, dabbing with a rough precision.

"For her, we're not even here, boy. You see that," Roiphe had said as he worked. "You see how she manages to move around me without acknowledging my presence. Nice little modern dance." Nathan had caught some of that with his camera, and looking at the photos of Chase evading her father in sinuous slow motion, as though practicing an exotic variant of t'ai chi, he regretted not having been able to shoot video.

"She's very consistent in the pattern of her little spaceout. She's finished cutting and serving and eating, and now comes the funny social part where she talks to her party guests without saying anything."

"And how does it end?" Nathan had asked, still snapping, still finding the evocative angle, at times forcing Chase to weave herself around him as well. (Her arm brushed his hand at one point, and it was ice cold, though the room and the house were fairly warm.) It ended with Chase getting up from her knees and walking over to the metal-tube-and-canvas child's bed at the other end of the room, where she lay down with a blank face and pulled her covers—teddy-bear sheets and two Hudson's Bay blankets—over her. The images of her walking away from Nathan—again light bounced off the earthy walls—highlighted her long waist, muscular, low-slung buttocks, and short, athletic legs, a combination which Nathan had always found compelling, though the opposite of Naomi's short waist and long, slim legs.

"I don't think punishment is involved, Barry. I think she's reliving something, something that was communal. And she's playing all the roles." Nathan was leaning on his elbows, speaking to his screen more than to the actual Roiphe, but now he sat up straight and turned to the man himself. "I wonder what that something communal could have been?"

Roiphe snorted and fastidiously lifted his glasses off his nose with both hands, unleashing his turquoise eyes with deliberate dramatic effect. "Why don't you just ask her?" he said.

NAOMI AND AROSTEGUY ate the meal he had prepared. The dinnerware was spartan and shabby, but the meal itself looked good. A lot of warm sake, which they both poured freely. They used chopsticks and sat on the floor at the low table. Naomi's camera sat beside her tray, muscular and matte black, like a brooding cat. Her voice recorder sat beside the camera, its blue VU-meter LEDs rippling in response to words spoken, its microphone like the beak of a hummingbird straining skyward. Her cat and her bird watching over her, thought Naomi, and, thinking that, became aware that she was drinking too much.

"Please forgive the decor. Nothing in the house belongs to me. It sat empty for a long time. Tokyo is very expensive." Arosteguy poured more sake for both of them. "I love warm sake. How brilliant to create a drink at body temperature." He shook his head. "The Japanese. Feared by the West for so long, and now fading into their beloved sunrise. Or sunset. First militarily, then economically, and now, only gastronomically. And I need to become Japanese at a time when everyone wants to become Chinese. The Chinese call the Japanese 'the little people,' I've been told. That could have to do with the miniaturization of island species. I must do a study."

"Why do you need to become Japanese?" said Naomi, cross-jamming her chopsticks and dropping them into her plate. She fumbled them back into her hand and managed to pick up a shrimp.

"I cannot be French anymore, and I was never Greek, except with philosophical and familial nostalgia. So what can I be? I am a fugitive. It satisfies my sense of self-drama, but it racks my nerves."

"You must be lonely here."

"I was lonely in Paris."

"*Même avec Célestine?* Sorry. Even with Célestine?"

"That was the basis of our love. Our loneliness. Our isolation."

"But now that she's gone? There's no change?"

"Now I'm ... alone. It is different."

Naomi began to see their mutual drunkenness as an agreement, a contract, with clauses allowing almost everything, at least as far as words were concerned. She felt giddily unafraid. "Monsieur Vernier, *le préfet de police*, seems to believe that you're innocent, that you didn't commit murder." She seemed compelled to throw French words into the mix; she wasn't sure why. She really had no wish to provoke him, though he seemed to have no problem with the language at the moment.

"Oh?" Arosteguy snorted a tight little laugh which could have been an expression of self-pity. He had seemed immune to that up until now. "I've lost touch with the case, I'm afraid. To my surprise. It seems to belong to many others, but not me. To you, for example. It belongs more to you."

"He called it a mercy killing. Is that interesting?"

"A mercy killing followed by some elegant cuisine, possibly? The French love their cinema. I expect soon to feel the Hannibal Lecter resonances, and maybe then to pose for photographs with Sir Anthony Hopkins, perhaps in the small restaurant of the Hôtel Montalembert."

"You don't want his help?"

Arosteguy gave a particularly dismissive shrug. "He's a policeman. And not just for the city of Paris. The police of Paris are national police. Imagine the world he lives in."

Naomi rolled out of her sitting position and half-slid towards her camera bag. In it she found her iPad and, returning to her place at the table, began to scroll through the Notes app until she found the words and photos of M. Vernier and the Préfecture de Police on the Île de la Cité.

"He gave me a message for you."

"Really? He knew you would come to see me? He spoke to you and his words went into your ear, knowing that? It makes me feel that he's here himself. So strange. We've discussed Schopenhauer on three occasions, Auguste and I, once on the TV show *Des mots de minuit*. He seems to be obsessed with Schopenhauer."

Naomi read from her notes: "Tell him that I am conducting a philosophical investigation provoked by his case and I want him to help me with it as a good professional and an academic. To do this, he must return to France."

Arosteguy popped some noodles and shrimp into his mouth with a theatrical flourish. "You see me eating—look, see?—and of course that seems normal. But for me, to eat anything is not the same now as it was before. Afterwards, I could not eat for a week. I could barely drink water. I almost died here in Japan, such an alien country in any case. But in a way it was that very alien quality which allowed me to disconnect from Europe, from France, from the net of the so-called crime."

Naomi put her iPad on the floor beside her and picked at her food, very conscious now of the process of how the lips and tongue worked, the jaws, the teeth, the swallowing, but trying to return to normal unconsciousness.

"So you recovered fully."

"Yes. I hope you have seen that already. There's a basic life force that expresses itself even in me. It's crude and merciless, and very hard to overcome."

"Why do you say 'even in me'?"

"The arrogance of the intellectual. The delusion that we have more balls in the brain to juggle than most people."

Naomi made an effort to eat the largest shrimp on her plate before responding. "So, Ari, are you admitting to me that you ate the flesh of your wife, Célestine?" She almost gagged on the word *flesh,* but managed to turn it into a dramatic pause that involved catching some slipping noodles before they fell to the plate. "*Monsieur le préfet* made it clear to me that nothing, not that, not the fact of murder, had really been established."

Arosteguy drew a deep breath, then exhaled deeply, preparing for something special. "Let us say that the question of spousal cannibalism expanded in the media to the point where it took on a potent reality that was not really connected to my life or to Célestine. I was enveloped in that reality, enshrouded, until it became my own, until my own thoughts and emotions were displaced by those thousands that came from television, newspapers, the multiple internet sources, the YouTubes and Twitters, yes, even the car radio and the talk shows, and of course the people on the street, buses, the Métro. I lost possession of my recent past, and my long past, my history. I was colonized, appropriated. I had to leave my dead husk to shrivel and wither in Paris and become someone else, somewhere else. Become Japanese, or failing that—and I am failing that—to become an exile, an isolate, a disconnect. And I have been succeeding at that."

"You haven't really answered my question. Will you answer it in the book that you're writing?"

Arosteguy laughed. "That book seems to be a meditation on the philosophy of consumerism. As you might expect, I have a new take on it, though in a sense that's all I've ever written about. Consumerism ..." He shook his head, chuckling, then looked at Naomi with an intensity that shook her. "You know, everything that has to do with the mouth, the lips, with biting, with chewing, with swallowing, with digesting, with farting, with shitting, everything is transformed once you have had the experience of eating someone you were obsessed with for forty years." He smiled. "Of course, every one of those things also becomes a joke in the popular imagination, which is quickly becoming the only imagination that exists—the media imagination. I've seen the jokes on the internet. Some of them are very sophisticated, very amusing. Sometimes there are cartoons, even animated ones."

"Is that why you posted those photos of your wife's half-eaten corpse?" Naomi said, holding her breath. "To destroy the jokes? To bring the discourse back to human reality?"

Arosteguy put down his chopsticks and crawled around the table on all fours. He kneeled close to Naomi. He put his lips close to her left ear and whispered. His voice was somehow even more textured and forceful as a whisper. "If you want to understand, you must experience this mouth, the mouth of the cannibal, the mouth of a thousand bites, a thousand human atrocities." He didn't touch her, and he didn't bite her, and after many long, frozen seconds, Naomi forced herself to turn to him, her own mouth half open, an unformed word lingering. Arosteguy placed his open mouth forcefully over hers. It was not really a kiss—more like a cap being placed over a jar. Naomi was suddenly terrified. She didn't dare move. Arosteguy began to breathe air in and out of her lungs through his mouth. She had no choice but to breathe in sync with him. She was waiting for his tongue, not knowing how she would react when it came, but it didn't come. He took his mouth from hers and slumped down beside her.

"So pathetic," he said, with a grunt. "So sad. Such a cliché. You can be so fond of cinema, of world literature, the classics, but then, when you find yourself playing out a classic scene, you don't feel ennobled, linked to that greatness. You feel ... pathetic."

Naomi wanted to ask him what work of cinema or literature he felt was being replayed at that moment, but she was afraid to speak, and so there was silence, and she could only hear his heavy breathing and not any breathing of her own. Then he spoke as though they were in the midst of a discussion she had somehow missed.

"There are other photographs which you have not seen. I'll show them to you if you fuck me. I'll give them to you. Nice thick digital files. They are powerful and they will shock you and you'll be a star. But I need you to be my lover for a while, my Tokyo mistress."

"I ... Professor, I ..."

"Ari. That's my name to you. Aristide becomes Ari. We didn't establish this? No, you've barely said my name. Does it taste disgusting in your mouth? You know, Sagawa, the Japanese cannibal, who still lives right here in Tokyo, said that the Dutch girl's ass tasted like tuna prepared for sushi. That's enough to make it dangerous for any Dutch woman to visit Japan. He's considered a tragic hero here, a media celebrity. An artist. I can envision lineups of Japanese men waiting for the Netherlands tourist buses to unload, each with his *Suisin maguro bōchō* sharpened and ready." He drank some sake and muttered under his breath, an afterthought. "Of course, she was a Dutch girl. That made it somehow not so criminal. Maybe even praiseworthy."

The mention of Sagawa, whom Naomi had initially thought might be a clever stepping-off platform for her piece, now filled her with horror. It was obvious and vulgar and revolting, and it was making it hard for her to physically see Arosteguy. The way he held his face, he was starting to actually look Japanese. "Ari, I . . . I can't do that, what you ask," she said quietly, projecting, she hoped, thoughtful consideration, though there was nothing to consider. "I can't."

Arosteguy launched himself unsteadily upwards and stood over her, towering over the low table and filling the room with his anger. He screamed at her. "Then get out! Get out, get out!" He kicked at the table, lifting it a foot or so before it came crashing back down, scattering the food, the camera, the dishes, then stormed up the stairs, leaving Naomi shaking, her eyes wide and swelling with tears.

She flew out of the house dragging her roller with her, its contents hastily stashed, its exterior compartments bulging pathologically, cables hanging and jouncing out of the improperly zipped pocket mouths. Her momentum carried her into the middle of the street, which was dark, dingy, and completely deserted. Scared, stalled, and now acutely alerted to her drunken state by her inability to perceive depth, she pivoted on the spot like a pinball flipper, looking for a cab. There was nothing except Arosteguy, strolling casually out of the house and walking up to her, coming very close to her as though nothing had happened, speaking as though continuing an understood subliminal conversation that had to be finished. He took her arm gently, just holding it, not pulling her.

"We made love frantically, desperately, as though I could possess her and keep her from death," he said quietly. "But I couldn't, of course. She was going to die. Her body was changing. She had swellings and nodes and lumps and rashes. I had to forcibly change my sense of sexual esthetics to accommodate her new body. I needed it to still be beautiful for me, though it was changing every day, every hour. And finally, when the changes were all coming to an end, we wanted her to die while making love to me, not fucked by a dozen plastic tubes in a hospital. So we devised a plan, and we carried it out."

He bent down and picked up the roller, still holding her arm, and led her back towards his house, its door wide open, the pale fluid of its light washing the plant rags of the garden. She let him take her with him. "I strangled her while we made love. The swollen lymph nodes in her neck made it difficult, but more exotic. You know that in French an orgasm is *la petite mort,* the small death. And for the English metaphysical poet John Donne, 'to die' meant 'to come,' to have an orgasm. It was the most intense, exquisite moment in my life. It was a moment you never recover from. I kissed her while she died. Her eyes were full of love and gratitude. Her last breath came into my lungs like a hot tropical breeze."

Naomi stopped just outside the door, shrugging off Arosteguy's hand. Her voice was quiet and small. "I'm afraid of you, Ari. I thought I wouldn't be, but I am."

"And now she was dead, and I was alone. And what was I to do? Wave goodbye like a good bourgeois and soldier on with my life? Plead madness like the good Marxist professor Louis Althusser, who strangled his wife of thirty years in their special permanent apartment in the infirmary of the École Normale Supérieure, no less, and claimed he thought he was just massaging her neck? A few years in the asylum and then a comfortable exile to the provinces?"

He took her by the arm again and began to walk her into the house. He was giving her things, terrible, precious things. She didn't resist. "No.

I wanted to embody her, to incorporate her. I would have had to commit suicide if I had not been able to do that terrible, monstrous, beautiful thing."

He slid the door closed behind them.

"THEY SENT ME TO PARIS. I was afraid to go."

"Why afraid?"

"French."

"French the people or French the language?"

"The language of the French."

They were sitting in the living room replaying Nathan's first conversation with Roiphe there, Chase sitting on the sofa, Nathan in the wingback chair with the Nagra running on the glass coffee table. He was extremely uncomfortable, but it was an exciting discomfort; there was so much strangeness about the situation. If she really had been in some kind of trance, a fugue state, she would not know that Nathan could see right through her soft dress and sweater and striped knee socks to her ravaged skin. But did she really not know? Would she care if she did know? How could he find out? How direct could he be? Could her trance really be some species of bizarre performance art? If it was, was it designed for her father alone, or was Nathan's presence part of what induced it? And the project, the pretense for their current interview? Chase had suggested a half-truth: Nathan was there to do a book about her father, and that book would include a bit of family history as background—nothing too deep, nothing sensational, and all subject to review by the subjects. No photos, she had said. She didn't accept Nathan's line about using the photos only as a memory aid, to make sure he got his descriptions right; it wasn't going to be a picture book. She would perhaps do a photo shoot with him under controlled circumstances some other time, but she couldn't talk while being photographed. Something had happened in Paris that had changed her attitude to being photographed, and it was no longer something to be taken lightly, girlishly, playfully; too bad, but things changed, didn't they?

"What was it about the French language that scared you?"

"I learned my French in Quebec, while I was at McGill University in Montreal. I was passionate to learn the Quebec language, to acquire that strange, wonderful, ancient accent that got trapped in Quebec after the French Revolution. But McGill is an English-language university, and I learned my Quebec in the streets. Actually, worse than the streets, because I spent my summers in small towns where they spoke hard-core Quebec worse than anywhere in Montreal. I wanted my French to be rough, and it was."

"Why did you want that? I wonder."

Chase giggled and then, to Nathan's astonishment, dug into the green leather pouch tucked in beside her, pulled out a high-tech nail clipper, and began to trim her fingernails. The clipper had a matte titanium finish, a dimpled and contoured lever, and a pivoting plastic clippings catcher that reminded him of an old steam locomotive's cowcatcher apron. He was fairly certain it was the same clipper he had seen her using in her bedroom, though he had never gotten a clear shot of it. She worked the clipper at eye level and glanced mischievously over it. "Youthful rebellion expressed through the politics of language, mostly directed at my father. And then he twisted it back on me by suggesting that I use my hard-earned French to study at the Sorbonne. He used to joke that the Quebec language was not really French at all, and that I could prove he was wrong by speaking it in Paris. I would be studying with the most sophisticated writers of French you could imagine, and I was afraid. I would be Anglo Jewish from Toronto speaking bad street Quebec."

"What would you be studying? Who were those writers?"

"The Philosophy of Consumerism. The kids called it PhiloCon, which, I think I recall, can sound a bit naughty in French if you want it to. Do you speak French?"

"Not really. I can read a bit. If we took a second language it was usually Spanish. And those writers who were supposed to teach your PhiloCon course?"

"Aristide and Célestine Arosteguy. You've heard of them? A married couple. They were kind of controversial in the academic world. Ow!" Chase flapped her hand and then sucked a finger. "That hurt."

"What happened?"

"Nipped a bit of finger. I suppose it'll be trapped in this little clipping-catcher thing. See? You just flip it down when you want to toss the nail clippings. It stops it from popping the clippings all over the place, the way the old clippers do. It's a Sally Hansen. Stainless steel. Oh, there's some blood . . ." There was some blood, winding its way down her ring finger. She smeared it against her middle finger then sucked them both, watching him.

It had to be an elaborate construct by Chase, if not by Chase and Roiphe. They must have researched him on the net, somehow linking him with Naomi and her Arosteguy project. Naomi could be so cavalier about the net when she was in that mood, even though she knew all about lawsuits against Tweeters and mob actions against Facebookers. And the clippers, the blood . . . it was a brilliant miniature piece of theater and almost unthinkable that it was really an unconscious acknowledgment of a psychopathological state. But did he have a role in this drama, or was he just a recruited audience?

"Did you go, then? Did you do it? Study with the Arosteguys at the Sorbonne?"

"Oh, yes, I did. I spent two years there with them. I took a lot of other courses as well, but mainly it was them. The Arosteguys."

"And your French? Were you humiliated? Can you speak Parisian French now?"

Chase let her hands drop into her lap with an expressive exhalation, and then, in counterpoint, a giggle. "I can't speak any French now. Either brand of. None."

"Really? How come?"

"I guess I just forgot it all. It's been a whole year since Paris." Chase stood up, brushed at her dress, then sank gracefully to the floor and began picking at the carpet as though grooming it for lice. "I dropped some nail bits when I showed you how the catcher works. My father notices those things. I call him Laser Eye. He doesn't miss a trick. Gotta watch it with Dad." By the end of her little speech she was doing a good comic impression of Roiphe, verbally and physically, mimicking exactly his loose-limbed unsteadiness and affected vulgarity. She crawled to her feet using the coffee table for support and stood over him, cradling the invisible clippings in her hand and bouncing them gently up and down as if testing their weight.

"Did you get them all?" said Nathan. He could think of no other strategy than to play the Roiphe game as it unfolded.

"I think so," said Chase, with exaggerated musicality. "I do think so."

"Chase, have you been following the story about the Arosteguys?"

"How would I do that?"

"Well, probably on the internet."

"I've found the internet to be a very dangerous place. Especially for children. I don't go there anymore."

"But you're not a child."

She laughed. "On the internet, nobody knows you're an adult. Hey, have you heard of 3D printing?"

"I have, yes. Why?"

"Have you heard of 3D philosophical tissue printing?"

"No, that I haven't heard of."

"It's not even on the internet. Know why?"

"Why?"

She was still in jaunty Dr. Roiphe street mode. "Because some friends and me invented it, and we don't talk. Someday I'll maybe let you play with it." She turned away from him and disappeared up the stairs.

8

NAOMI SAT ON THE COUCH, Air opened on her lap, flickering Nagra and solemn camera (with soy-sauce-smeared LCD) restored to the tabletop, professionalism re-established. Arosteguy squatted on the other side of the table blotting up the spilled sake with a spice-plant-themed kitchen towel. "I need to tell what happened when Célestine was diagnosed. It destroyed the present tense for us, because it destroyed the future. It poisoned us. And it secretly destroyed our relationship with everyone we knew. Every laugh was a lie, every smile was a betrayal. Because we decided not to tell them. We knew it would destroy their present tense with us as well, and we couldn't bear it. It drew us closer together, but in a melancholy, sick way, and it compressed our existing isolation almost to the point of madness."

He balled up the wet towel, tossed it in the general direction of the kitchen, and segued into scraping up with a bamboo-handled spatula the remains of the meal he had scattered, carefully arranging the scraps of noodle, shrimp, seaweed, and tofu in a perforated red plastic shopping basket lined with newspaper. "We couldn't take photos after the diagnosis. Every photo displayed the lie. Every photo was already a memento of a life that was gone, a photograph of death. Compared with those innocent early family photos, the pictures I finally took of Célestine … afterwards … they were honest, they contained no betrayals, no lies, no deceit. So they were horrible, but they were pure."

"Ari, what doctor was it who did the diagnosing? You know that some people say there never was a diagnosis. That you invented it to justify the murder of your wife …"

He examined a shrimp on the blade of the spatula, then plucked it off and popped it into his mouth. "Who said this exactly? Dr. Trinh?"

"Dr. Trinh among others."

"Others on the internet? The Twitterverse? There were blogs established to promote exactly that view."

"Yes."

"The internet is now a forum for public prosecution. But you ask me who diagnosed Célestine," said Arosteguy. "The doctor who told her she had acute lymphocytic leukemia was Anatole Grünberg, a Nobel laureate for his work in hematological oncology. Who would doubt him?" A reflective pause. "They had been lovers when he was still in medical school at Paris Descartes, of course. They would meet, on and off. She liked to connect our work, so abstract, so interior, to the work of the human body. That is how she grounded our writing. Politics, the normal French mode of grounding, she found even more abstract and disconnected than philosophy. It never attracted her."

Fingers flying, Naomi was already checking out Grünberg on Wikipedia. The featured portrait depicted a man with wild, protruding eyes, fleshy lips, and thinning, muddled hair. "Of course, I've heard of Grünberg from the boating accident scandal. But he was still practicing medicine? Like a regular doctor?" Grünberg had narrowly avoided conviction on charges of *homicide involontaire*—manslaughter—in a tragicomic drunken boating accident on the Marne River in which two of his three illegitimate children had been decapitated, after which had followed much sour public discussion of the value of genius in the real world.

"That was the basis of all his revolutionary research. Patients like Célestine."

"You discussed that diagnosis with him?" asked Naomi.

"No. We knew each other socially, but he and I were cool to each other. Probably just primitive jealousy. We're not immune. But Célestine reported everything back to me. Medical diagnoses, obscure medical websites, this was our daily bread."

Naomi was incredulous. "He said nothing to you?"

"He was acting here as her doctor, her specialist. He had a professional rigor. He wouldn't discuss it like café gossip."

"You saw test results? Blood tests? Bone scans? CAT scans? MRIs? X-rays? Anything?"

Arosteguy shook his head at all of these—short, angry, contemptuous head shakes.

"Could Dr. Grünberg have been lying?" said Naomi. "Could Célestine have lied to you? Could she have not been sick?"

"I told you about the changes in her body. Those were real."

"Maybe they were caused by something else."

He snorted disdainfully. "A woman's natural aging? It's amazing what people will attribute to that. How they refuse to see things they are terrified to see."

"Dr. Trinh told me that there was nothing medically wrong with Célestine."

"Dr. Trinh was infatuated with Célestine. She adored her, worshiped her, could barely look at her without falling on her knees. It was embarrassing. She was pathetic. Célestine never went back to her after Anatole's diagnosis. And why would Célestine lie to me, tell me she was dying when she wasn't?"

"To induce you to kill her," said Naomi triumphantly. "A mercy killing, but not for the reasons you thought."

"A perversion beyond perversity! What a wonderful invention on your part. You are a dangerous writer after all."

Soon Naomi was curled up on the couch with Arosteguy, who had his arms around her and was caressing her throat. For both of them, the resonances of philosophical wife-strangling that were undeniably in the air were comforting, not disturbing, offering a linkage to richly textured past dramas full of meaning. Her eyes were half closed and her voice was drowsy.

"But it was hideous, wasn't it? The actual act itself—the eating, I mean? It was a horror show. Butchery. Those pictures. I've never seen anything so horrible. And Sagawa, he was eating a healthy young body. It's sick of me to say this. I'm shocking myself for even thinking it. But somehow, because Célestine's body was so ravaged by disease, it makes it more horrible. I can't believe I said that."

Arosteguy laughed a short laugh that quickly shaded into a husky whisper, a theatrical technique, thought Naomi, which was probably effective when he was lecturing; she liked it herself, and felt for the moment like a student with cozily limited responsibilities. "Healthy sick thoughts," he said. "Honest ones. But you are able to say that because you didn't know her. You didn't know her body with the intimacy that I did. You see a corpse, a dead, mutilated, anonymous—yes, diseased—body. But not me. I lived in the landscape of that body for so many years. As that landscape changed, my living changed with it. She never stopped being my Célestine. Never."

Arosteguy kissed Naomi with passion and hunger. She kissed him back with the same. Soon they were naked, half on the couch, half on the floor. "Are you going to bite me?" said Naomi. He did. And she bit him back, on the shoulder, the biceps, the neck. "And then, are you going to eat me?"

And he did—breasts, thighs, and then down to her pussy. She stopped him, grabbing his head, holding on to his hair.

"Oh, no, Ari. I forgot. My old boyfriend …"

"Your boyfriend, yes?"

"No, it's … he just told me that he has Roiphe's disease. You know. That venereal disease. I mean, I might not have it, Roiphe's, but I have something …"

Arosteguy snorted. "Do you know my age?"

"Wikipedia says you're sixty-seven."

"Wikipedia is correct. And what a force for global harmony that creation is!"

Naomi detected no irony. "What has your age got to do with my disease?"

"Well, we are both diseased, aren't we? For example, I no longer spurt. I just ooze, in a sinister way, like a popped pustule. For me, those come shots in porn videos, like cake-icing guns going off, they're pure sci-fi, they're CGI VFX only."

Naomi snorted back in deliberate imitation. "What else? Do I get the whole list now, or do I get a chance to make some exciting monstrous discoveries?"

"Over time, with these sexual disabilities emerging gradually, old couples gradually accommodate them, and they don't embarrass each other, they become part of the domestic seniors comedy you promise to write together, but your memories are thankfully not too good and you forget to do it. But for a youngster to be thrown into the den of the aging lion … I've experienced some difficult moments."

"With your students."

"The youngsters with enthusiasm and defiance, yes, which protects them from revulsion for a little while, but then …"

"You're lucky nobody's blown the political correctness whistle on you. I think those days are long over, even in France."

"There have been dramas behind the scenes. The French press has had a tendency to be a bit more discreet than the rest of the world, but with competition from Facebook and Twitter . . . All sexual adventurism is lethal now."

"Didn't some of your youngsters have sexual insecurities?"

"Oh, yes, all of them. Célestine and I took full advantage of them in the name of therapy and philosophy."

"And me? I have a few of those myself. Do you want my list, or do you want to make your own discoveries?"

"Honestly, I think a list would be charming. We can exchange them, and then see if reality matches."

"I'll start working on mine right away. But meanwhile, I'm serious about having my own oozing down there. You might catch something nasty. Do you have a pack of cute Japanese condoms lying around somewhere? There must be Hello Kitty condoms. Translated as Hello Pussy."

"I'm so tempted to say something that sounds like it came from a poorly translated Punjabi erotic tale, something like 'A cook must have a taste for sauces, no?' and then go down on you."

"Please don't say that."

"And please don't do that?"

"I didn't say that."

"BUT WHERE ARE YOU GOING? You booked a hotel? How can you afford that? And I thought you needed to hide out in Tokyo."

"I'm going to hide out even more," said Naomi, hustling her remaining gear and clothes into her bags.

Yukie watched her, shaking her head. "From me? You don't trust me?" Naomi turned away from the bed—she had colonized it and the kitchen table and a few other surfaces to organize her packing—and held Yukie by the shoulders. Yukie rolled her eyes up to her, and Naomi was surprised by the emotion she could read in them.

"Yukie, no, no. It's not like that at all. It's not." She hugged Yukie, who let her body stay limp, unresponsive, a full-body pout.

"Then what is it? I don't like the look in your eyes. I remember how wild you got that time in Santa Monica . . ." and just her own mention of the Santa Monica incident, which was a cornerstone of their mutual history and mythology, triggered an understanding in Yukie, hit her physically so that she flinched in Naomi's embrace and then pulled away, drifting to the end of the kitchen to get an objective look at her friend. "Not still that French guy," she said, shaking her head again. "Not the professor cannibal killer guy." Yukie started to pick nervously at one of her fingernails, each coated in pearlescent white and sporting a tiny black ceramic rose glued to it. One of the roses had partially broken off and Yukie was trying to scrape the rest of it away. Naomi had noted how delicate an operation it was for Yukie to pull on the tight gloves she was so fond of.

"A few days with him isn't enough to get the whole story."

"The whole *intimate* fucking story! You're as insane as he is!"

Naomi had wanted Yukie to be emotionally invested in her project, needed her to be at first, but now she felt the blowback of that setup, how it gave Yukie the right to be judgmental even in her genuine fear for her friend, though as always with Yukie there was that competitive thing, that career jealousy that surged to the surface and took a quick bite before you realized what hit you.

Naomi turned away and continued packing. "He's an incredible man. Very sweet, very sensitive."

Yukie began pacing back and forth in the kitchen. "Omigod. They won't even be able to bring you back to me in a body bag. It'll be two dozen freezer-quality Ziplocs."

"Don't get melodramatic on me, Yukie. He's not some dark force. He's just a man, a man who did something extreme, out of love and passion and obsession, did it once."

Yukie stopped pacing. She felt she could read the whole story from Naomi's body language, the whole story including the ending. "You fucked him already, didn't you? Your first night with him, and you fucked him. I can't believe it."

Naomi didn't turn around. "No, you can't understand it. That's what you can't. And I don't expect you to until you read what I write about it. That's really what it's all about, and you've lost sight of that. It's the writing. It's the story. It's fantastic and it's all mine."

"Wow. I'm shocked," said Yukie. "Does Nathan do this too? You compare notes? You torment each other's interviewees? You have some laughs about it?"

Naomi did laugh, her back still towards Yukie. "You know, that's not a bad idea. I'm going to give him a call."

NATHAN WALKED IN THE LEAFY, lush streets of Forest Hill, talking, improbably, to Naomi. The sun was hot, the light dappled. "I'm walking in the streets. I needed to get out of that house."

"I know the feeling," said Naomi. "Problem with me is, when I do that, I'm in Tokyo." She sounded relaxed—too relaxed for Nathan's comfort. It was the kind of relaxed you sounded when you'd had a lot of sex. The thought was floating at a subliminal level, and Nathan wasn't going to address it, but it was there, gnawing. Well, let it gnaw away, with its ferocious little yellow teeth. How *could* he address it? It was Naomi who had finally broken the airphone-call-debacle deadlock after Nathan had spent fruitless hours emailing, texting, SMSing, phoning, social-networking.

The shape of it was this: she hated his fucking pusillanimous guts and would never forgive him. He had mortally wounded and mutilated and deformed her love for him, not to mention the STD aspect. He was saved, she told him, only by the use to which she intended to put the whole sorry incident and, yes, their entire relationship. He should think of himself as about to embark on a particularly hideous *hors catégorie* mountain stage of the Tour de France, perhaps Mont Ventoux, or the Col du Tourmalet, jammed with scary, jeering, bizarrely costumed fans coming much too close, and he was going to suffer, suffer, and suffer more. Of course, she was thinking of Hervé and his carbon-fiber bicycle and his bib-style compression cycling shorts with their elaborate vented crotch pad and his Peyronie's penis when she said it—she should have just fucked him, what a mistake—since all her understanding of bicycle racing came from him.

And there was that one final element, which was Nathan's last email promising the revelation of a weird and unlikely connection between Roiphe and Arosteguy, which, Naomi had to admit to herself, might actually have tipped the thing over into reconciliation; there had to be something delicious and nutritious there, because Nathan just didn't have the devious creativity required to invent something like that. And so she was talking to him again.

"The irony of the whole thing is, you tell me that your murderer cannibal guy, Arosteguy, is saner than you ever imagined," said Nathan, "and now I have to tell you that my respectable old doctor guy is a complete fucking lunatic."

"You're kidding," said Naomi, stretching languorously, with kittenish sexuality. Or so Nathan imagined. "That sounds fantastic. I was afraid for you."

"Really? Afraid?"

"Afraid that your whole Roiphe thing would turn out to be boring. But no. Fantastic."

"I'm not so sure. I think the man is delusional. I'm finding it hard to believe that he was ever a real doctor. Maybe he has Alzheimer's."

"What is it that he's doing, exactly, that's so loony?" said Naomi, and then she said some more words, but they were digitally garbled.

"You're breaking up," said Nathan. "Can you hear me? I'll send you some photos. I'll send you some photos." But she was gone, Call Ended.

Nathan walked up to the front door of Roiphe's house and rang the incongruously plain doorbell, just a cube of black plastic with a white button, hidden away on the faux-stone doorjamb. The button lit up when he pressed it, but Nathan could hear no sound from inside the sealed mausoleum of a house. Eventually, Chase opened the door.

"Hello, Nathan. Forgot your key?"

"Um, I don't have a key."

"If you're going to live here, you should have a key." As always, Chase had almost every part of her body covered: suede boots, flared silk pants, and a long-sleeved blouse with a mandarin collar. He wondered when she would start wearing gauntlets.

"That would be … that would be nice." An awkward pause. Chase smiled but didn't move, deliberately blocking the doorway. "To have my own key," he said. Pause. "To your house." No reaction. Was this Chase's standard front-door mode? He decided to take a radical tack. "Want to go for a walk with me?"

"Oh, no, I couldn't," she said airily. "I'm in quarantine."

"Vraiment? Il s'agit d'une maladie sérieuse?"

Chase's smile disappeared into zero affect and she slammed the door in Nathan's face.

When some time later Roiphe drove up in his 1990s-vintage Cadillac Seville, parked in his driveway, and got out with tennis racket in hand, he found Nathan sitting on the steps of his house. "Lock yourself out, did you?" he said, crossing the lawn with a boisterous chuckle. His trim blue Puma tracksuit made the scrawny doctor look lithe and athletic.

"I was never in."

Having mounted the portico, Roiphe showed off his backhand, the racket breezing cheekily close to Nathan's face. "Lady of the house didn't answer the doorbell?"

"I made the mistake of speaking French to her and she slammed the door on me."

The doctor's face clouded over for just an instant. "Well, that's clever of you. Why would you do that, of all things?"

"She told me about studying at the Sorbonne. Said she had a complex about speaking French. Thought I'd take her by surprise, shake her up a bit. Guess I did. Was that a mistake?"

"Ah, well, French is part of her past, and at the moment the past is not part of her therapy. No Freudians allowed inside here!" Roiphe slapped Nathan on the back, swapping his Prince EXO3 to his left hand to do so.

Nathan stood up and shrugged. "Have I blown it? Am I banned from the ranch?"

"Far from it. We're gonna get you your own key. Now, how's that for a journalist's wet dream? The keys to the kingdom! You wouldn't abuse that privilege, would you? I know how you boys like to root around in the drawers and the underwear."

NAOMI HAD FALLEN ASLEEP after her call with Nathan. She had used Arosteguy's curiously long and slender Japanese LG flip phone to make things simpler; he had himself fallen asleep downstairs on the couch and she had gone up to her room to make the call. She had the sense that

Nathan could smell Arosteguy on her voice, and that pleased her and helped ease her into a very creamy sleep space. But now her iPad chimed the receipt of some email, and she was acutely sensitized to that sound; she could not sleep through it or wrap a protective coating around it. The iPad was on the table and she could reach it without getting out of bed or even wriggling to the edge of the bed. She lay back and held the glowing screen over her head, a hovering, benign presence, reassuring in a way that she needed. She could see from the Notifications panel that it was the photos Nathan had promised to send, the subject line "Shocking Non-Reality Photos ... and more!"

When she opened the photos in Preview, she was puzzled, and she sat up so she could cradle the device in her lap and manipulate the images. Who was this very pretty young woman caught naked on her knees in front of a child's table strewn with child's teaware? (All the teaware, Naomi couldn't help noting, was very North American, or pseudo-British at best; her growing ease with restricted Japanese space, and the novel strangeness of non-Japanese teaware, pleased her; it felt like the stirrings of a profound cultural change *à l'Arosteguyenne.*) But what was the woman in the photos doing? Pretending to be a child? The photos came in three medium-resolution batches, and these were followed by a separate explanatory note: "This is Chase Roiphe, Dr. Roiphe's daughter. She says she studied at the Sorbonne with the Arosteguys as recently as a year ago. She might have neat things to tell you. Wanna show some of these to your new pal? Maybe he'll recognize her. I get the sense she would've made an impression. Otherwise, your beautiful eyes only!!"

The mechanism of vengeance and love being what it is, Naomi was immediately panicked and hurt by that penultimate line. Apparently Chase Roiphe had made an impression on Nathan, and, given her beauty and her nakedness and—she had to be honest—her freakishness, which Nathan had always been a sucker for, especially if it proved to be not too self-destructive, she doubted it was entirely intellectual. A biochemical impression, then, the worst kind. But what kind of freakishness was it?

All of Naomi's sharpest analytical instruments immediately came into play, and the resulting dissections were unnerving. She could feel the camera in Nathan's hands as if it were in her own hands, and she could feel his accumulating attraction to this woman, this Chase Roiphe, as the camera moved from short-lens wide-angle and distant, to wide-angle and close, to long-lens intimate close-up; these corresponded to documentary objectivity morphing into evidence of love, or at least sexual attraction, if not obsession. The angles themselves told their own story: I am interested in you in a perfunctory way, but now I'm kind of intrigued by you even as I begin to fear you, and now, though I'm nervous about getting close (my shooting is very messy and ill-framed), at least you're letting me get close without reacting negatively, and now I feel that you're inviting me into your face and your body, and now I'm confidently finding the optical perspectives that show off your fearsome beauty and your provocative weirdness to their best advantage. By the end of the hellish portfolio, he was crawling all over her face and body—that sensational athletic body covered with what? Eczema? Mosquito bites? Blackfly bites? Had she been swimming nude on the Canadian Shield? And what was that she was eating? Bizarre macroscopic grazing with Nathan wanting to follow her fingers into her mouth, she could just tell.

Naomi tossed the iPad onto the bed. She was sure that Nathan would be fucking Chase in no time, and maybe he'd call it another mercy fuck. Or maybe this time it represented the new standard: embedded research. To her own surprise, Naomi started to laugh. She was sure that Nathan knew she was fucking Arosteguy, and that meant they had emerged into a new and exciting level of game play, one which braided their new lovers into each other's lives. And look how majestically it was playing out: for all she knew, Chase had fucked Arosteguy—and Célestine!—and what Nathan learned from Chase would illuminate the Arosteguy saga for her. He was obviously primed to share the Roiphes with her, and it could all lead to a tingling and dangerous place. She stretched out on the bed, arms and legs thrown wide, welcoming the vulnerability, the transparency, exquisitely aware of the old flimsy cotton happi coat she was now wearing, which Ari had found for her. It had a crazy-making indigo lattice pattern and was fraying around the edges, and, feeling the graze on her skin of its opaque history, she fantasized that it was something that Samuel Beckett would have worn in his last days in that depressing municipal old people's refuge called Le Tiers Temps (the Third Stage)—he called it "an old crock's home," his breathing machine wheezing in the corner—something that said despair and poverty to her, which translated into Japanese became joy and freedom. It had come with the place, Ari had said, stuffed into a window frame to keep out the winter cold. The image of Beckett brought Naomi directly back to Nathan, who was her only conduit to the playwright. He had begged her to read his article called "Beckett's Last Tape"—a meditation on Beckett's last year on earth—after sitting with her through a DVD of the Gate Theatre's production in Dublin of *Krapp's Last Tape* starring John Hurt, and she had liked the interplay between the tape recorder and Krapp's memory, linking it even then to her fascination with photography and its inexorable manipulation of memory. For her, Beckett was primarily that hair, that nose, those cheekbones, those brows—those ears!—a stunning photographic thing. She sat up and snatched the iPad, poised to reply to Nathan with everything she had just been thinking—let him feel the sinister electricity across an ocean and a continent, let him be jolted and insecure and frightened—but instead she found herself importing the photos into her Photosmith app for better image handling and then, once they had loaded, getting up and going downstairs in stealth mode, iPad in hand like a charged pistol.

The futon had been unfolded on its low wooden frame to form a platform specifically for sex, and Arosteguy, wearing only a French marine shirt, royal-blue-and-white stripes à la Picasso, was lying on his side, close enough to the fetal position that it choked Naomi with potent visions of her father in his last days in Sunnybrook Hospital in Toronto, shriveled and jaundiced and twitching towards death. At the same time, she was amused at how un-Japanese he looked in that compressed space, a big white spreading European man with thick hairy thighs and broad thick chest. He had shown her some Japanese porn on a fourteen-inch Sanyo tube TV playing through a chunky silver no-name VCR. It featured a seventy-three-year-old porn star named Shigeo Tokuda who had sweetly protruding teeth and a few wisps of hair, and a touchingly crumpled old body with a penis you could barely perceive through the pulsing, Mondrian-like censor's blur effect which was quite hypnotizing when that penis was moving in and out of the mouth or vagina of a large-breasted twenty-something girl. The video was called *Prohibited Elderly Care: Volume 17* and, as promised, presented sex in a nursing home for the elderly. He said that he had bought the video in order to segue gracefully into sex of the aged Japanese flavor, happily certain that he would never fuck a Caucasian woman again. The subtext of their CRT screening event was that Naomi was interfering with his desire to cast off as much of his Frenchness as possible in exchange for Asianness, and was meant as a compliment, but the sub-subtext was that old men were sexually viable, *n'est-ce pas*? Having found him overwhelmingly attractive from the first YouTube video she had seen of him, she really needed no convincing; Shigeo Tokuda, on the other hand, she found only comically congenial. She began to take photos with her iPad of Ari sleeping, the shutter sound effect turned off, worrying on some level that the very functioning of her brain would wake him in anger. She feared his anger. As she got close to him, she realized that he was gently snoring in a variegated and random way that was oddly expressive, as though he were talking through his nasal cavities. She briefly flirted with the idea of shooting video but didn't dare, though the thought of a documentary rather than an article or a book did cross her mind. She could almost feel his nasal septum quivering like the reed of a clarinet or a heart valve during a bout of atrial fibrillation, another oblique connection with her father's last days. She covered his entire body in loose frames and then tight ones. When she came around to the front of the futon to take a close-up of his face, she saw that his eyes were open and watching her.

He yawned and stretched and half sat up. "I suppose a photo of the deflated, semen-encrusted penis of the notorious French philosophy cannibal could be of interest, even if taken with an iPad."

"Only five megapixels, but a nice documentary quality. Probably all you need for a book." He pulled in his legs to make room for her and she sat next to him. "And speaking of documenting, there's something on this"—she waggled the iPad—"I want to show you. Or do you want me to make you some tea first? I think I've mastered those two crummy little rusty burners."

"I was endlessly fucking you in my sleep."

"Your snoring was very sexy."

"Snoring?"

She did her best to replicate his snoring, not sure if he simply didn't know the English word or was surprised to hear that he had been snoring. It came off sounding a bit like one of the mocking green pigs from Angry Birds, a free HD copy of which she had on that very iPad.

Arosteguy laughed. "You must do sound effects for me more often. You have a great talent there. But show me what you want to show me. I usually wake up with clarity that rapidly fades, so maybe now is the best time." He put his arm around her and pulled her close with a deep grunt in a way that she found disturbing, neither very French nor very Japanese, and perhaps quietly desperate; it didn't feel like part of whatever their relationship was, felt more like the incestuous embrace of a father and daughter (was this what Nathan meant when he talked about "theme sex"?),

Arosteguy sitting there with his exposed thighs and penis and balls, she naked under her skimpy, threadbare happi coat, and it gave what she was about to do—show him Nathan's photos knowing that they had explosive potential (though she wasn't sure what that would be)—an ultra-perverse sheen.

She unlocked the screen and angled it towards Arosteguy. "These are photos my friend Nathan took. He's working on a piece in Toronto."

"I know the city. Very nice. Friendly. I was there in 1996 for a Third World energy symposium. What are these photos? Who is that girl? Nice haunches. What is she doing?"

Naomi paged rhythmically through the photos, Arosteguy reacting with little grunts and exhales as though still asleep, until she paused at the first shot showing Chase in close-up. "Ari, do you recognize her?"

Arosteguy cantilevered his head forward and squinted at the screen. Naomi spread her fingers over the shot as though stretching out a membrane, enlarging it until Chase's enraptured, openmouthed face filled the viewer window. Arosteguy jolted back as though struck in the head, his right hand violently clenching Naomi's shoulder. He stood up, roughly raking his arm across Naomi's shoulders as he pulled away from her, backing away from the futon, eyes blazing with anger. Naomi felt herself shriveling up like a spider touched by a lit cigarette, but still had the presence of mind to activate the iPad's Voice Memos app, and this had a soothing, distancing effect, allowing her to float into that protected space which is *professional observer*, safely placing Arosteguy on that rotating specimen platform under the magnifying glass. He paced back and forth, muttering to himself, then snatched his tight-fitting navy corduroy pants off the floor and struggled his way into them without underpants, which he seemed never to wear. Thus armored, he sat back against the front windowsill, pushed his lips out into a flexing pout as though silently rehearsing his next sentence, and then said, "Who is your friend who sent these photographs?"

"His name is Nathan Math. He's a journalist. Lives in New York."

Arosteguy nodded. "Boyfriend?"

Naomi, shrugging with an insouciance she did not feel, said, "Sometimes."

"So, your boyfriend and you. A classic American journalistic conspiracy."

"Ari—"

"Why have you done this? How do you know Chase? What are you two trying to do to me?" He pronounced her name "Shass," which almost tilted the whole melodrama into farce for Naomi.

"I don't know her. And I wasn't sure that you did either. She's back home in Toronto with her father, a doctor, Barry Roiphe. She's in some kind of weird therapy with him, and Nathan is in their house to write a medical article about them. And she told him that she had studied at the Sorbonne with you and Célestine. That's all. A coincidence, not a conspiracy."

Arosteguy barked out a harsh, phlegmy laugh, and the phlegm seemed to remind him that he needed a cigarette. He roamed around the periphery of the room until he found the pale yellow flip-top pack with the bold red Japanese character crowning the letters *RIN*, and was soon inhaling deeply. Naomi was surprised that he smoked cigarettes with cork-tipped filters, her surprise a matter of style rather than smoking arcana (she had never smoked); she felt he should be a Gauloises man, just like Jean-Paul Belmondo in *Breathless*, Gauloises Caporal without filter in the classic soft French-blue pack with the machinelike winged-helmet logo; but of course he was resolutely turning Japanese. She had a very strong impulse to photograph his pack of cigarettes, could see even across the room that the same red Japanese character on the pack was printed on each cigarette just below the filter. Given the importance that consumerist impulse, passion, and identity had in the social philosophy of the Arosteguys, it seemed imperative that she eventually apply to the couple themselves their own approach to psychology: consumer choices and allegiances were the key to character and to all social interactions. She was sure Arosteguy was conscious of that as he struggled—how serious was he? was it merely ironic?—to become Japanese by consuming Japanese items. She could see the conundrum exemplified by Western versus traditional Japanese clothing; he was too proud, too aware, to allow himself to become a caricature of a Japanese man who clings to tradition—if he were to become Japanese, it would be a current and forward-looking variant of the same—and so it was left to minor items like cigarettes and food to carry the transformation.

"No, but really, I admire you and your boyfriend Nathan. A new and modern version of *Les Liaisons dangereuses.* A very compelling partnership for the Information Age. It should make for a very nice entertainment."

"Ari, I don't know what you're talking about." The smoke in his lungs really did seem to relax him, modulate his rage into sarcasm, a relief for Naomi. "I know it seems ridiculous, but it really is a complete coincidence. Nathan is with the Roiphes because of Roiphe's disease. I told you, he gave it to me and then decided to research it. That's how it all happened."

"An unexpected coincidence, then. Okay. And then some unexpected consequences?"

"What would those be?"

Arosteguy stubbed his cigarette out on the sill, folded his arms for a meditative moment, then walked back to the futon and sat down beside Naomi. He gently took the iPad from her lap and held it up in one hand. "May I play with these? The photos of Chase, taken by Naomi's good friend Nathan?" Naomi gave a shuddering, terse little nod, eyes wide, nervous, excited. He hunched over and began to examine the images, scrolling through them and expanding them with forensic intensity.

"What are you seeing?" said Naomi.

Without looking up, he said, "I am seeing that Aristide Arosteguy will soon be caught in a lie, and so he might as well tell everything to his priestess confessor."

"What was the lie?"

"That is exactly what a priestess would want to know. But isn't she curious about the mechanism of revelation? The priest of my childhood, for example, Reverend Father Drossos, a terrifying man, was obsessively, perhaps unnaturally, concerned with the mechanism of revelation. Of course, there were sinister and familiar reasons for that."

"Well, your former student Chase Roiphe will eventually tell Nathan some secrets about you, and Nathan will tell me, and I'll tell the world."

Arosteguy looked up at her now with an appreciative smile. "Very good, and no less than I would expect from Priestess Naomi." He offered the iPad back with a slight bow, holding it with both hands flat underneath it, palms up, like a sacramental plate—or a Japanese business card. "But the secrets have already been told without a word being spoken, and they are all right in here."

"GONNA HAVE KIDS someday, Nate?"

They sat side by side on the rough-cut stone patio overlooking the narrow lap pool and the fussy, overgrown rock pond harboring some very butch koi. Beyond that there was a slate-roofed coach house which looked original—that is, about a hundred years old—overlooked by a bland institutional apartment block. Nathan idly wondered how many tenants were watching them through binoculars and urban telescopes. He could hear the trickle of a small artificial stream or waterfall but couldn't see it from where he was sitting under the vast canvas teak-strutted garden umbrella that sprouted from a gasketed hole in the center of their table, also vast, also teak. A small, anxious Asian woman had brought them coffee and nuts and berries in bowls.

"I have no idea, Barry."

"You've probably got a steady girl somewhere, though, haven't you?" The sun was high and hot and Roiphe had polarized sunglass clip-ons over his glasses that were even bigger than the glasses themselves; the chromed lower edges of the clip-ons dug into the doctor's flaccid cheeks.

"I sort of do, I guess."

Roiphe was playing with a khaki mesh-vented Tilley hat, twisting the brim, crushing the crown and re-blocking it, putting it on and off his head. "Do I detect some sexual ambivalence there? You know, there was a big vogue a while back where GPs dabbled in sex therapy. I'm not sure how healthy that really was, but it was pretty darned common. You can see the psychopathology right there. I refused to get into it. A lot of my colleagues got into big trouble with it. Busted up a lot of marriages."

"Ambivalence, I guess. I wouldn't say sexual." The blueberries were especially good, but the raspberries had gone soft, mushy, and sour. "Just the commitment problem, I would say. Not just committing to a particular woman, but committing to a particular future. Kinda banal and ordinary." He rotated his Nagra so that he could be sure it was recording at a decent level given the heavy ambient noon traffic noise. "But speaking of psychopathology, I have to wonder about the deal here, you playing the role of shrink to your own daughter."

Roiphe chuckled and poured himself more coffee with a shaky hand, spilling a bit onto the brim of the hat that now rested next to his cup. "Aren't you the cheeky one. Well, to begin with, that's how I always approached being a parent. I'm naturally analytical. I'm clinical. I can't fight it. That doesn't mean I'm cold, although maybe my poor dead wife would've disputed that. But goddammit, what would you be doing? We sent her off to France, Rose and I, with the best of intentions—as you can imagine, given the expense. She was such a bright girl, Chase, and kinda European in her outlook. She didn't look to the States for excitement or inspiration.

Partially it was the language thing. Of course there's a lot of Spanish going on in the US, but she wanted the whole deal, a country where English was basically not spoken, and the culture was based around that language. And then, of course, there was the Quebec thing. She told you about that?"

"She did, yes."

"Okay, so anyways, we pack her off to France, she gradually stops phoning, then stops emailing, and then we just don't hear from her. Not a word. And then Rose dies, a big fat horrible surprise. She was in great shape for an old babe—we can get into that sometime, if you think it's relevant to the book, but it might not be, depending. So Rose dies, and I can't find a way to let Chase know about it, and so I get in touch with this Arosteguy guy, and I get a really weird vibe from him. So I fly over to Paris looking for her, and eventually I find her with the help of this kid, a student, Hervé Blomqvist—what a name; I can barely get my mouth around it—a colleague of hers. It seems she was living with him. Something traumatic happened to her, and she left that great little apartment on the Left Bank that we found for her and moved in with this Blomqvist. I guess that's a Norwegian or maybe Swedish name, but he seemed totally French to me. You know, kinda saucy and arrogant, but in the end really helpful and okay. You'd have to say that ultimately he was an okay kid. I think she would have been in terrible trouble without him. You might eventually want to look him up to get his take on the whole Sorbonne thing. For the book."

"I might," said Nathan, thumbing exactly that note into his iPhone's Notes app. "How do you spell that name, exactly?"

"I'll give you all the particulars when we get back inside. Never was much of a speller myself. I've got it lying around somewhere. And an address and a phone number. They're a year old now, but you never know. And now, speaking of the French language, when I got Chase back she was a helluva basket case, and it all seemed to do with speaking, or not speaking, French, and that the Arosteguys—turns out there were two of them, a man and a woman, married professors—said such terrible things to her in French that she was traumatized. And when I asked her what they could possibly have said that could do that, she said she couldn't recall it because they spoke the words in French, and French was gone from her brain—*exiled* was the word she used, exiled from her brain—as was French in general, and so she couldn't remember anything. And then she started doing these weird ritualistic things and eating bits of her own skin, stuff that you've seen, all in a trance, and I can't for the life of me see what that has to do with the terrible French words being spoken thing. And that's basically where we are. The old mystery wrapped in an enigma, or whatever the hell that was. And so that's having kids too. It's rougher than you can imagine. That's why I asked you."

"Barry, you mentioned 'experiments' in connection with Chase's condition. I wonder what you meant. What exactly is your course of therapy for her?"

"I'm attacking on all fronts, boy. And some of those fronts are weird, lemme tell you."

"For instance."

"For instance, up in that third-floor attic space that's all hers. I bought this house for her, really, you know. Rose never lived here. We've only been here a year. I bought it with all the furniture and lights and stuff that they put in to show off the house—what do they call it, staging, home staging. I just wanted a big space of our own when I saw what shape she was in, and that condo downtown on the waterfront that Rose and I had was just too small, too introverted. They couldn't believe I was serious, but I told them I had no taste and that everything they had done looked fine to me. The woman fought me on that, said the stuff was rented and it was deliberately bland so as not to distract from the house, the property, the space itself. Anyhow, I rolled right on over her and her bosses, and they made it work because it'd been sitting around unsold for over a year."

Roiphe stopped and took a tentative sip of his lukewarm coffee, lost in a sudden reverie. Nathan waited for him to continue but he seemed to think he had answered the question. "Barry, you were saying. Your weird course of therapy."

"Oh, yeah, yes. So I collaborated in a way with Chase on a solution to her distress, which she never really admitted to, and she said, 'There's a thing called a 3D printer, and I want one to play with, I think it might relax me.' That's the term she used, *relax me,* and it became our code for *cure me,* or maybe *heal me a little bit.*"

"She mentioned the 3D printer to me. Said she'd show it to me."

"Really? Well, that would be rare. She's sure never let me see her using it, I can tell you that. And hell, you should see the damned thing. Not cheap! She insisted on the best, and then, like I said, after setting up and outfitting the whole third-floor suite for her, three rooms and a bathroom, she won't let me see what she's actually doing with it in what she calls her workroom. Actually locks the door on me. I could break in, of course, but I'm scared to. Might set her back into that catatonia she was enveloped in when I brought her back from France. You should've seen her, stiff as a board and all bundled up with blankets even though it was as hot a summer as today. So she said she'd show you? Well, there you are, you're a part of my course of therapy. We collaborate on Chase as well as the book, and that gets her over some of her father issues too."

Nathan wasn't ready to delve into the father issues, but he suspected that they would have deep and tormented roots. "Wow. That's a bit of a stretch, don't you think? I'm just a journalist."

"These are radical times, boy. Can't you feel it? You need to stretch with the times, stretch to the breaking point. I sensed the second I saw you that you were ready for a life breakthrough, and this is it. No telling where it'll lead."

"I'm not sure how much she'll want to collaborate after the door slam."

"Just don't speak French to her again. I'm sure it'll be all right. She's kinda intrigued by you. She's been pretty reclusive since I brought her back."

"Have you ever heard of the book *Le Schizo et les langues*? Written in French by an American, Louis Wolfson, a schizophrenic who couldn't bear to speak English, or even to hear it spoken, and retreated completely into other languages, but mainly French. In his case, it was mother issues."

"Well, there you are, you see? Destiny has called in a specialist for me, and it's you, boy."

"WE COULDN'T TAKE PHOTOS *after the diagnosis. Every photo displayed the lie. Every photo was already a memento of a life that was gone, a photograph of death. Compared with those innocent early family photos, the pictures I finally took of Célestine ... afterwards ... they were honest, they contained no betrayals, no lies, no deceit. So they were horrible, but they were pure."*

The futon had been folded back into its couch configuration, and Naomi, now in yoga pants and gray fleece Roots zip-up hoodie, had taken possession of it, spreading all her electronic paraphernalia protectively around her: MacBook Air on lap with shield-like lid open, glowing Apple logo a talisman against Arosteguy, who sat on the other side of the low table, slumped in the segmented brown velveteen beanbag chair. She had originally recorded him using the Nagra's uncompressed WAV files, which were huge but so beautifully detailed; the lossy MP3s would have been more than adequate for transcription, but she wanted the full quality of Arosteguy's smoky voice, anticipating at least a radio program if not a video documentary. For the moment, though, she had been playing back a key passage of Arosteguy's Célestine testimony through her Air's tinny speakers—not resonant, but clear enough for condemnation. The Nagra sat on the table close to Arosteguy, its blue LED modulometer twitching in sync with the distant street sounds, waiting for him to speak. Naturally, he had tea and an RIN cigarette to play with while he generated a response, and he sipped and inhaled and exhaled with exquisite cogitation. Finally, he glanced up at her with calculated, sheepish charm and smiled.

"I apologize to my priestess. I underestimated her. I equated her with the global media, which is where I found those easily digestible raw materials for my banal and bourgeois account of *My Life with Poor Terminal Célestine*. There are so many blogs and articles in the 'Living' sections of online newspapers pouring out the synthetic emotions and the mundane details and the shocking bodily consequences of any disease you can think of or even invent. Honestly, Célestine and I felt we had to fully understand the phenomenon of the internet, because consumerism and the internet had fused, they had become one thing, even though on a certain level it was anathema to us, noxious to the strange, introverted, and, yes, relentlessly *snob* personal culture we had spent years developing together. But also we realized we needed the net in order to understand what was the basic human condition, what a current human being really was, because we had lost touch with that, our students made that clear to us, and so we were also using the internet to research our roles playing normal human beings."

He took an intense drag on his cigarette that was rich with unspoken, ironic drama, or at least Naomi interpreted it that way. She felt humiliated to have been deluded, suckered into a sympathy fuck, and at the same time triumphant and eager for a scoop that was beyond the internet's reach. Undeniably, it was Nathan's photos—their full meaning still cloudy—that had brought Arosteguy to heel, and it meant that she and Nathan were still some kind of team, perhaps not on the scale of the Arosteguys but pleasingly outlandish in its own way, and maybe she would encourage Nathan to fuck Chase Roiphe if he hadn't already, just to sharpen the parallels. The thought made her giddy, and some juices began to flow.

Arosteguy seemed to be fading away into his own head now, and Naomi reflexively became the interrogator. "Ari, let's start with the basics. Was Dr. Trinh telling the truth? Célestine did not have brain cancer or any other kind of cancer?"

Still pacing the inner landscape of his own skull, Arosteguy answered without looking up, as though Naomi were inside that skull with him. "Dr. Trinh, yes, she was telling the truth about that."

"And so ... why is she dead? What killed Célestine Arosteguy?"

"Célestine woke up in the middle of the night. She shook me to wake me up. When she could see the light swell back into my eyes, my consciousness, she said, with great, husky gravity, 'We must destroy the insect religion.'" He raised his head and looked at Naomi, but she felt, with a deep visceral chill, that he was looking at Célestine. "That was a pulled trigger, it was a terrifying shot fired into my brain directly from her mouth."

"I don't understand the reference."

Aristide laughed; he was now looking at Naomi. "No trigger for you, then. Because obviously you've never read the famous essay."

For Naomi, *this* was the pulled trigger, the terrifying shot fired into her brain directly from *his* mouth: her ignorance, her lack of depth. Yukie was able to flaunt this thinness, could flip the veneer into the structure, the wood-grain paneling becoming the table itself, just like all her social contemporaries; if you knew too much, if you were too aware or too educated, you were vulnerable to special varieties of pain and anxiety, and, worse, you were not cool. But Naomi was not Yukie. It caused her anguish that she had not read the famous essay, had not known it existed. But strangely, given any kind of handle at all, she could imagine it, and this had always been her quick, saving grace: not knowledge, exactly, but intuitive invention. "I'm sure I can find it on the net. Title?"

Arosteguy stubbed out his dying RIN and quickly lit another one. "The essay was called 'The Judicious Destruction of the Insect Religion.'"

Yes, thought Naomi as she netted madly, here it is: Weber. Capitalism. Vatican. Luther. Entomology. Sartre. Consumerism. Beckett. North Korea. Apocalypse. Oblivion.

9

THE TRIGGER WAS THE RELIGION of the breast, of the fluid of the flesh which is there to nourish, to create more flesh. And then there was an actual breast, Célestine's wonderful left breast, which was full, not of milk and milk glands, but a buzzing, bristling hodgepodge of insects of every shape and configuration. Yes. "My left breast is a bag full of insects. I don't know why it's attached to me, and I would like very much to ... disconnect it. You can have it afterwards, if you like. I know you're fond of it."

We were on the jury at the Cannes Film Festival, the only two members who were not moviemaking professionals. The year before, it had been an American opera singer and a computer-game designer. Sequestered in a deluxe villa in the hills overlooking Cannes, we were to discuss in the most leisurely and free-form manner all questions of cinema and society with our nine jury colleagues—including our president, the Serbian actor Dragan Štimac—while eating the most exquisite meals and wandering the most Arcadian gardens. Eventually, we would sit around the grand table in the impressive ballroom and vote for the various awards. There were twenty-two films in the competition for the Palme d'Or and several other intensely anticipated and analyzed prizes.

The villa was said to belong to a ninety-three-year-old Russian countess, a former beauty who was actually lurking somewhere on the premises, hidden from view, not wanting to be seen but thrilling to the excitement of judgment on art that thronged her halls. It was in the grotesquely Russianate pool anteroom, in a changing room tiled like the Hermitage, that Célestine pulled my face to her naked left breast and said, in a voice shivering with horror, "Listen!"

I listened. I heard her heart, trip-hammering. "Your tachycardia," I said. "Can you control it? Do you need your pills?" Her face was disfigured by fear; it was, I confess, a face I despised, a rare face. She squeezed her breast, jounced it like a bag of cherries. "Entomology," she said. "Bag of bugs. Listen to them in there. They would like to come out. Especially the Hymenoptera. They tend to be claustrophobic. Which is strange, of course, because my breast is very much like a wasp nest, and you'd think they'd be comfortable in there." She was really crushing and kneading her breast in her hands, and I gently pulled them away and held her wrists down on her thighs. She sighed, her face relaxed, and she laughed a small laugh.

I had never heard anything like this from her before. It shocked me and terrified me. It was as though she had had a stroke of some bizarre kind, and the strangeness of her face supported that thought. The pressure was also bizarre, because soon we would have to gather around that table with the jury and the chief of the festival and have solemn discussions and arguments and rancorous voting. I tried to turn it into a joke, a spontaneous piece of performance art. "This is your response to the North Korean film, isn't it? The North Korean film has burrowed into your breast, your left-wing breast, your Red breast." I knew the movie had affected her profoundly, and had already disturbed many sleeping Marxist dogs which never leave their French intellectual kennels. But she screamed at me, and moaned, and I was terrified that the jury would become a criminal jury and they would convict us and we would never be allowed to leave the czarist villa. No one came to monitor us, though. We had heard many shrieks and shouts and arguments and morbid moanings throughout the course of the evening before, then the night, then this Sunday morning, the Sunday of the *palmarès*. A passionate and creative group of cineastes.

And so the essay. It was really a letter to me, a confession she could make in no other way, published in the Paris magazine *Sartre,* though I had begged her not to. It was too intimate, I said. But she said, "Philosophy is intimate, the most intimate act of thinking." And so: "The Judicious Destruction of the Insect Religion," an essay by Célestine Arosteguy. Of course, those of us on the jury of that year would hear the resonance. The North Korean film was called *The Judicious Use of Insects,* and in her essay Célestine confesses that the movie triggered the "stroke"—of luck?—but reveals that the breast disconnect, the insect connection, had been building for years and so terrified her that she couldn't speak of it to anyone, not me, not her beloved physician. She describes the scene of the ultimate vote for the Palm. The president had asked the jury for the titles of all their proposed candidates for the Palm to be handwritten on a piece of festival paper—complete with golden embossed palm symbol—and passed to him. When he came across her paper, upon which she had written the title of the North Korean film, he took his cigar lighter out of his pocket and set fire to it, tossing it into the ashtray which he himself had brought every day to our meeting room in the Palais des Festivals and now brought to the villa in defiance of the non-smoking regulations. "I was not allowed to bring my nine-millimeter pistol," he said, with his characteristic sarcasm-dripping smile, "so this will have to do."

The festival's artistic delegate, who was there to certify the legitimacy of the voting procedure, was horrified at this barbarity and gently admonished the jury president. But he would not be cowed. "If this thing wins the vote for the Palm, or in fact for anything at all, I shall resign as president and I'll let everyone know why." And his look to Célestine was hideous, mocking, malicious, and misogynistic. I was there too, of course. I did not intend to vote for the North Korean film, but I had not yet revealed my own choice.

There was on our jury an aged, angry, exiled North Korean director, Bak Myun Mok, who was obviously an enemy of the director of the North Korean film in competition. He was prepared to do anything to prevent his entrenched countryman from winning a prize, and so he was campaigning—none too subtly—against him. He turned specifically to me and spread his hands in helpless despair. His translator, Yolanda, was a shy young Spanish woman with short, straight black hair that suggested she was trying to look Korean. Even the way she held her mouth was somehow Korean. Yolanda was not comfortable with what he was saying. "You are a philosopher," she said to me, beginning her translation, but then paused and looked at him apprehensively, almost begging him to say something other than what he was actually saying. In response to this insolence, the director picked up a pencil—we had all been provided with pencils and pads of paper, so charmingly retro—and prodded her viciously, twice, in her delicate, exposed clavicle. Though there was an eraser in the end of the pencil, it left an angry red mark almost immediately.

The translator turned back to me with wide apologetic eyes and continued. "You are a philosopher," she said, "and that meat dog of a wife of yours is also a philosopher. Both of you professional philosophers, whatever that means. Can you not explain to the bitch that the movie, even the title, *The Judicious Use of Insects,* is not philosophy, and not art, but politics of the worst, most repressive kind. And to give this wretched, sinister movie any prize would be to shackle the art of cinema to the wall of political expediency."

"'Meat dog of a wife'?" I said to Yolanda. "He really said that? And 'the bitch'?"

"Under his breath, yes, he said those things." Yolanda's voice shook with distress, and her eyes became shiny with tears. "I made sure that I did not misunderstand him. I asked him to reconsider what he was saying. And he said those words again, no longer under his breath." Then, as a tremulous pedagogical afterthought—Yolanda was trying to acquire a French teaching certificate—she added, "In Korea, meat dogs are called *nureongi* or *hwangu*, meaning 'yellow dog.' You don't let them into your house. 'Bitch' is girl dog."

He was not small, Bak Myun Mok, but he was arrogant and therefore slow and unprepared for my attack. Because we were not allowed to bring cameras and cell phones to our retreat, there are no photographs or videos of the expression of my rage, though the aftermath—Bak's broken cheekbone, his black eyes, his shredded lower lip—was duly recorded by the police photographer summoned to the villa. Through all of this, Célestine was profoundly absent and vacant-eyed, increasingly anesthetized by her own spiraling reactions to *The Judicious Use of Insects.* I won't go into the overall delicious scandal, which is well documented on the internet. Suffice it to say that the voting procedure was quite irregular, the *palmarès* was a satisfactory pandemonium, and the North Korean film won a Special Jury Prize—for "artistic subversion and visual elegance"—in consolation. Dragan, the president, voted against this, though he had clapped his hands in delight as Bak and I rolled around on the floor, exclaiming in several languages that this was real cinema and unsuccessfully encouraging the rest of the jury to join in. Bak also voted against the prize, his vote conveyed from a dentist's office in Cagnes-sur-Mer, where he was having emergency treatment on an upper-left bicuspid which I had loosened when I smashed his face into the replica Winter Palace Dutch tiles of the ballroom floor. When I grabbed his hair and dragged his head towards the solid ebony voting-table leg, the action had produced a satisfying smear of saliva, blood, and mucus on the tiles, mostly from that rocking tooth splitting the gum it was embedded in.

Bak later swore that he had been mistranslated and that he had a deep respect for all women, particularly intellectual women like Célestine, and was incapable of even thinking of words like that in relation to her. Yolanda later came to us in Paris, technically as a witness in the assault investigation proceeding against me, but emotionally to sob and whine about the loss of her festival job and the general degrading of her standing in the community of translators. She did ultimately end up in bed with me and Célestine, and was very sweetly needy and desperate sexually, which of course was a delight to me, and would normally have been to Célestine, but she was still benumbed. It was only when I forced Yolanda to describe our sex play in real time in the most obscene way in both Spanish and Korean that Célestine was somehow resuscitated.

I had entered Yolanda from the rear—not anally, you understand; she resisted that—and Célestine had her back up against mine. As she heard the breathy, ragged, dirty phrases coming from deep within Yolanda and mounting in intensity, she turned until her belly was against my back, reached across my head, and grabbed Yolanda by the chin and the hair. She rotated Yolanda's head until the shocked translator had to twist towards me to avoid having her neck snapped, and then, face to face now, Célestine said, "And the meaning of the title, then? You can explain it to us and reveal the sinister malignancy it encodes according to Bak Myun Mok? I saw you talking to him in the halls of the Festival Palace. You were flirting with him. He must have confided in you." At first Yolanda was understandably confused, firstly because Célestine spoke to her in her very imperfect Spanish, and then not least because she had seemed to be on the verge of a monumental orgasm, one which had a Moorish flavor somehow, or perhaps that was just my delusion, and now had twisted me out of her, leaving her to pump frantically against my right knee, which had been aching in its chronically unpredictable way, so that I had to shift her pudendum to my left knee.

Most of this melodrama is, as I have said, embodied in the famous essay, famous for the personal events that it revealed as much as for its radical, some say unhinged, approach to consumerist philosophy. What Yolanda said in our bed about the North Korean film did not satisfy Célestine. Bak Myun Mok's interpretation fell along traditional political lines: staggering under the burden of a crushing drought, the poor villagers in the film—who lived in a hermetically sealed fantasy of a timeless proto-Korean village—were forced by their rulers to supplement their protein-poor diets with insects, which were viewed as noxious and disgusting by the filmmakers, although of course considered legitimate delicacies elsewhere in the world. (Even in modern South Korea, *beondegi,* steamed or boiled silkworm pupae, looking unashamedly segmented and insect-like, are a popular street snack food.) The title word *judicious* was used with irony, in the sense of "desperate," "last-gasp." But in the stunning and brilliant new world of North Korean Juche Idea, or neo-Stalinist self-reliance, one would not have to resort to insects to feed one's children, and this was exemplified in the most didactic, programmatic way by the revolt of the peasants against their village elders, who were all members of a violent, repressive, shamanistic caste that promoted insect-eating as a religious imperative. Did not Célestine see the crude propaganda involved? Was she seduced so totally by the retro visual style of the movie, so strangely in color and camera movement like a lush Douglas Sirk Hollywood melodrama of the 1950s?

What Célestine did see was a work created expressly for her by, unaccountably, a North Korean movie director whom she had never heard of and who probably, given the geo-fencing of the country, had never heard of her. How was this possible? Of course, she recognized the inevitable theory that this was a solipsist reverie, but in the spirit of inner drama it didn't matter if it was: it had meaning for her, and gave her a philosophical project. Korean cinema, particularly North Korean, became an obsession for Célestine, but of course, given its unorthodox trajectory, it did not require study of Korean history or even the actual watching of Korean films. No. It required research of the subversive, subterranean kind, and so I came home one evening, for example, to find our apartment full of acolytes of Simon Sheen, also known as Shin Sang-ok. Shin was most famous for having been kidnapped in Hong Kong, along with his actress ex-wife, Choi Eun-hee, by the future dictator of North Korea, Kim Jong Il. Kim was a movie fanatic who understood the propaganda value of film, and also knew movie charisma when he saw it. And he didn't see it in North Korea, so he kidnapped it. (The evening proved to be dismal and awkward, with no narrative to speak of, though Célestine was enraptured by the Sheenians' somewhat confused presence.)

Célestine convinced herself that the director of *Judicious* was not Korean at all, but was in fact a kidnapped French director who knew her very well and was signaling her through his film. Bak had claimed that Supreme Leader Kim Jong Un himself was the movie's producer, following the principles set out in his father's book *On the Art of Cinema,* and so, given that the passion for movies still flourished in Pyongyang in tandem with neo-Stalinist ruthlessness under the guise of the Juche Idea, why would they not kidnap the best appropriate director? Why would they not kidnap Romme Vertegaal?

SO. "WE MUST DESTROY the insect religion," she said.

"Tina, are you really awake? Are you dreaming? Do you know what you're saying?"

["Tina?" said Naomi.]

["From Céles*tine*. And we both loved Tina Turner, the American singer."]

["Okay. So, Tina."]

"He would be forty-two now," she said.

"Who would?" I asked, though I knew the answer.

"Romme," she said. "He was almost exactly twenty years younger than me."

You need to know that while there was always Aristide, there were also what we called lacunae, intervals when we needed to be apart. And inevitably filling those lacunae for Célestine was Romme, a brilliant young and radical filmmaker who left his Sciences Po studies to communicate his politics through the art of cinema. Strange politics, and strange cinema: an obsession with Ike Eisenhower, China, the 1950s in America, and the films of Douglas Sirk. Romme Vertegaal was a student of Célestine's, and of course her lacunate lover as well. He was Dutch born and ridiculously tall, and he stressed to Célestine right from the very beginning that, perhaps in keeping with his extreme height, his eye was always on oblivion. "Blessed, blessed oblivion," the original Beats would have tattooed on their shoulders, and Romme had those words tattooed on his heart. It was clear that he intended to disappear, to "obliviate," and eventually he did, leaving Célestine quite devastated. We had just reconnected, filling our latest lacuna with ourselves, and the substance of our rekindled talks was this newly lost love of hers, and the unexpected pain it caused her hurt me too, because I thought she would never recover from it, and therefore any love between us would be experienced in the shadow of this holy, much greater, lost love. Romme was a spectacular young man even beyond his absurd, almost surreal height. Perhaps you have encountered some of his works on YouTube. They are stunning.

His friends were certain that he committed suicide in some fiendishly clever way that involved the absolute dissolution, possibly by automotive chemicals, of his body, and that was also the tentative official police version of his disappearance. Célestine, however, was sure he went to China and disappeared into the vastness of that country, despite his height. And then came *Judicious*, and Célestine knew that he had ended up in North Korea, making propaganda films for Kim Jong Il, and then real movies for his possibly more volatile successor, the boy-king Kim Jong Un, movies which had certain messages directed at her, Célestine, Romme's eternal and transnational love.

And so, that night when Célestine shook me awake to tell me that we must destroy the insect religion, I knew we were in trouble. I just didn't know what shape that trouble would take. Perhaps in the cards was an approach to whatever clandestine North Korean representatives in Paris we could find with the suggestion of a special visit to their homeland from two famous French philosophers, with an emphasis on the philosophy of cinema. Once there, Célestine would try to contact Romme Vertegaal, who worked under the pseudonym Jo Woon Gyu (the listed director of *Judicious*), and would elope with him, or rather would marry him under the auspices of Supreme Leader Kim, auspiciously replicating the forced marriage of Simon Sheen to his actress ex-wife after they were both kidnapped, and symbolizing the divine fusion of political philosophy and cinema in the Workers' Paradise of the North. Could Célestine really think in these terms? Profound emotion lay beneath all her thinking, but it never stopped her from being crystalline in her logic, rigorous in her doctrine. Everything connected with Romme, on the other hand, was soaked through with girlish lunacy, and was very disturbing and destabilizing to me and to us.

But even given all the time I spent living in her head and in her body, I never could have anticipated Célestine's actual Korean strategy.

WE DRIVE AN ELECTRIC Smart Fortwo in Paris. I took Célestine to a North Korean restaurant where she was to meet some mysterious collaborators on her Romme Vertegaal project; it was famous for its startling military-theme design featuring the graphics and colors of totalitarian kitsch. She asked me to leave her there; she would call me when she was finished. I became worried that she was getting into a potentially dangerous situation. I fantasized that she herself would be kidnapped and spirited off to Pyongyang. That she didn't want me involved troubled me even more: it meant she was communing with Romme, almost the only time that she could not also commune with me, and of course that was distressing. I confess that I parked our car some streets over and lingered across the street from the restaurant.

As I stood there smoking, sheltering in the entrance to a carpet shop, I mused, oddly enough, on the fact that even in his youth, Romme had worn hearing aids—originally Phonaks, but when last seen, Siemens—as a result of a childhood disease. When I finally accepted that I needed them myself, I thought of Romme's claim that they were tuned to the music of the spheres, and then, more seriously and mundanely, to certain satellite frequencies. He was never ashamed of or reticent about his hearing disability; he was more likely to be boastful and aggressive about it—he politicized it, like everything else—and so it became a cause. After he had worked you over in a café, you felt as though you ought to at least pierce your eardrums with a fork tine in solidarity with him, and also to experience firsthand the divine creation of Swiss and German audio technology. In a kind of audio-homage to him, I went to his own audiologist when it came my time to be fitted. By then, digital technology had enhanced the sophistication of these devices beyond science fiction to the point that they could be linked to cell phones, satellite GPS, and many other communications devices. It was commonplace to call them hearing *instruments,* an appellation with empowering artistic overtones, as opposed to hearing *aids,* a term unfailingly evocative of aging and infirmity. My own

Siemens instruments featured Bluetooth, six separate programs tailored for different hearing environments, rocker switches for program shifting and volume control, and a wireless controller that looked like a garage door opener. Mme Jungebluth cryptically assured me that she numbered several international intelligence agents among her clientele, none of whom was hearing impaired.

I was certain that any of those agents would have been listening to Célestine's dinner conversation if he stood where I did on that corner, and recording it and transmitting it to some distant Siberian outpost, but I was left, pathetically, only to imagine it. And then I saw Célestine emerge from the ornately carved doorway of the restaurant in the company of two Korean men in dark suits and ties, one middle-aged, one quite young. She turned to face them, paused, and hugged them, one after the other, with great, joyous warmth. The young one handed her a padded manila mailing envelope which he took out of his inside jacket pocket, and as she stuffed the envelope into the pocket of her coat, he put his hands together, bowed, and turned away. His companion did the same. As the two men walked off down the street, Célestine took out her old Nokia clamshell and called me. I quickly muted my own phone's ringer and turned my back towards the restaurant.

"Yes?"

"I'm on the street outside the Eternal President. Will you pick me up?"

"Of course. Give me ten minutes." But I stood there for at least five, watching her like a spy, like a curious stranger, like a talent scout for an Albanian sex-slave trader, analyzing her body language as she paced and smoked, rhythmically patting and squeezing her coat pocket to make sure that the envelope was still there, seeming to take pleasure and security from whatever was in it.

Back in the car, Célestine was distracted and joyful, a very disturbing combination. "How was it?" I said. "The Eternal President. I've never been in there. I assume the name refers to Kim Il Sung. The walls must be covered with glorious images of him in that Stalinesque North Korean style."

It took Célestine too many seconds to reply to what I said, almost as if she had to decide to absorb it first and then decide to respond. "Not just the walls, but the plates too. Kim Il Sung as the Sun King, laughing, happy, emanating yellow rays of light, encircled in red, adored by soldiers and workers of all ages. And the floor show: beautiful young girls in strictly cut, short-skirted military dress and cake-shaped peakless caps, but executed in cartoonish colors and fabrics, pastel chartreuse and fuchsia, performing perfectly synchronized choreography that seemed to mock military exercises while somehow glorifying them at the same time. And singing songs that did the same thing, pop versions of army songs, soldier songs, aggressive and cheerful and threatening. It was exhilarating in its alienness."

"And the food? You ate?"

"Oh, yes, we ate. Fish and soup—I think it was dog, honestly—fried dumplings, fritters, and kimchi, and a lot of things I couldn't identify. The music seemed somehow to mix in with the food. It made it humorous to eat, even ironic. My friends assured me that it was authentically North Korean, not South, but that only the elite there would experience the high quality we were presented with."

"Your friends were Korean?"

It was here that Célestine looked at me for the first time since she got in the car, almost surprised to discover that she'd been talking to another person and not to herself. "Oh, yes. They were Korean. South Korean, but very helpful."

"*But* very helpful? You mean you would have preferred North Koreans?"

"For my research, yes. That would have been better. More direct. But these were two lovely, helpful men." Célestine patted my thigh in an attempt to be comforting, but it only irritated me and made me more suspicious.

"They're film people?"

"No. They're insect people. I mean, they're from the Entomological Society of Korea. I was curious about the accuracy of that film, the *Judicious* film, its approach to insect life in Korea. I want to write a piece on it for *Sartre* magazine. Jean-Louis Korinth there is extravagantly enthusiastic. Of course he always is, and then he kills it when he actually sees it. He has an idea in his head immediately, and then what you write never matches what he has in his head ..."

She was rambling now, wandering off into the deep woods of the Korean Peninsula, her head turned away from me, not seeing the streets slip by. I wondered if she had drunk too much. Alcohol had really been deranging her brain these days, her short-term memory, her emotional responses. I tried to bring her back.

"And so they were able to illuminate some things for you? Insect life in North Korea as portrayed in the *Judicious* film?"

She turned back to me, and her face opened and blossomed and became joyous once again, this time without distraction. "Oh, they did more than that," she said, and she dug around in her coat pocket and brought out the manila envelope, which I had not dared to mention. "They gave me the movie. They gave me a DVD of *The Judicious Use of Insects*."

WE SAT WATCHING THE DVD as soon as we got home. Dinner for me was coffee and cigarettes, something that Tina would normally never allow, but I and my ragged metabolism did not at the moment exist for her. She stopped and started the movie as she made notes on her spiral-bound *bloc de journaliste,* her focus intense, her gaze transcendent. Our copy of *Judicious* had French and English subtitles and had obviously come from the Cannes Film Festival, where it had probably been used as a screener for potential distributors. Célestine had found, above a Korean travel agency on the

Rue de Rivoli, the minuscule Paris office of the Entomological Society of Korea—an outpost of shadowy purpose, one might imagine, for how useful could it really be?

But apparently the fraternity of entomologists and insect enthusiasts of all stripes was well established and seemed to be somewhat free of the usual politics. As I mentioned, she had gone there to verify the facts of village life as they pertained to the insect-eating depicted in *Judicious*. She had assumed that she would have to educate her new entomologist friends about the very existence of the movie, but to her surprise they had copies of the film and were very proud of their connection to it: the society had gotten a consulting credit which was very prominent in the end-credits roll. The two men she had met in the office offered to take her to the Eternal President for dinner after pointing out that credit to her, promising to discuss their involvement with the movie in detail, and then surprised her with the supreme gift of the rare movie itself. They also promised to send her a copy of the newly revised edition of *Korea Insect Names* when it became available, as well as enrolling her as a subscriber to their journal *Entomological Research*, which she said she preferred to see in Korean rather than in English, and assured them that she was already beginning her Korean language studies. They assured her in turn that to have the searchlight of the mind of a genuine philosopher illuminating the subject of Korean insect life was an excitement beyond imagining for them, and would surely be for their colleagues as well. They would eagerly await her *Sartre* piece on *Judicious* and would definitely consider it for publication in their official journal, as destabilizing as such a piece would be, nestled between "Evaluation of Larvicidal Potential of Certain Insect Pathogenic Fungi Extracts Against *Anopheles stephensi* and *Culex quinquefasciatus*" and "Electroantennogram and Flight Orientation Response of *Cotesia plutellae* to Hexane Extract of Cruciferous Host Plants and Larvae of *Plutella xylostella*."

Célestine believed they were just being fastidiously polite, but she would submit it eventually nonetheless. Her ineluctable attraction to hard science was not uncommon among professional philosophers, who often found themselves adrift in abstraction and politics and longed for what seemed at a distance to be gloriously earthbound and thus substantial and undebatable. It seemed to me now that she was playing entomologist in front of our sad, outdated, cathode-ray-tube Loewe TV (at one time the crème de la crème), whose blurry image frustrated her constantly, so that she sometimes fell forward on her knees to squint up at the screen, hunting for details, studying the world of the movie as though it were a tropical rain forest in Papua New Guinea and she were living inside it. I anticipated an eight-hundred-page monograph called *The Judicious Consumption of Korean Insects,* perhaps in the Korean language, perhaps in fifteen years. She had that look as she worked, that look into the far distance, the future, a ferocious look that always terrified and thrilled me.

Watching the movie with Célestine controlling it, rolling it backward and forward, freezing frames of obscure interest and providing a rambling, improvised narration, was to witness the creation of a new movie related only vaguely to the one the Cannes jury had judged some weeks ago. In the new movie, the one co-directed by Célestine in our humid, cramped living room, the enlightened elders of the fictional North Korean village of Chosun (an ironic reference to the ancient Hermit Kingdom of that name, immediately positioning the village as primitive and isolationist and floating in time) have decreed that insects of all kinds shall be bred and harvested as the main source of nutrition, and that the traditional crops of rice, maize, and cabbage shall be used only to feed those insects. In this version there was some bizarrely deformed—not to mention anachronistic—Atkins nutritional dogma about vital insect protein replacing woefully deficient and health-destroying grain carbohydrates which fostered dependency on the West and its stooges.

Babies are, of course, exempted from the new insect diet, and so there were seen in profusion the peasant breasts of the village women, always presented in connection with the breastfeeding of infants and never sex, or at least overt sex (some of us on the jury found the breastfeeding sequences extremely erotic; others did not). Though we of the jury had been assured that the version we saw was the official one approved by the Workers' Party of Korea, and that this version would be shown everywhere in the country with no excisions, there was great skepticism among us as we were wary about this possibly being a ringer tailored specifically for our decadent Western tastes. Would there really be bare breasts and engorged nipples on screens in puritanical Pyongyang, never mind Kaesong or Chongjin? Undoubtedly, these questions hurt the film during our voting, but of course they were irrelevant to Célestine, for whom *Judicious* was a love letter from Romme Vertegaal.

And the occult (in the medical sense) key to the message from the kidnapped film director seemed to be the sequences in which the now happy, radiant, nutritionally enhanced village is raided by a fierce mountain tribe of warrior priests who violently subdue the men and rip innocent babies away from their blissfully nursing mothers, not incidentally exposing those aforementioned engorged nipples. The warrior priests worship insects as sacred beings, and believe that the ingestion of insects ennobles man and keeps him from descending into bestiality; thus even infants are not to eat anything but the sinister black insect mush which forms the priests' diet. After the initial conquest of Chosun, there are occasional winklings-out of brave, clandestinely nursing mothers who have fled to the mountain forests, followed by their execution by strangulation.

Célestine was horrified and transfixed by these scenes, even as she was, in a sense, creating them; she clutched her left breast as she watched them (her larger breast, and my favorite, even though it was less perfectly shaped than her right; it was not just the size, it was the nipple, the areola, the elastic softness, the birthmark like the one on Elizabeth Taylor's cheek). For her, the message from Romme, the love letter's message, was: Cut off your left breast, that rustling bag of insects, because if you don't, those insects will spread their insect religion to your entire body, including, and especially, your brain. And then you will be done as a philosopher, and you will be of no use to Romme Vertegaal.

I soon saw this as Célestine's version of what we called apo, for apotemnophilia, though I was aware that it seemed not really to conform to the template of the syndrome. That template involved the desire for an amputation of one or more limbs as a correction to a body whose structure was not yet correct. My right leg does not belong to me, it is an extraneous appendage. I need it to be gone; I cannot be whole, I cannot realize myself, until it is gone. At my insistence, Célestine and I studied apo assiduously, because I could not accept her certainty that she had received a diagnosis from an old lover through the medium of a movie which mysteriously conveyed both a prognosis and a drastic course of treatment, all of which seemed accurate and acceptable to her.

Célestine indulged me in my desire to convince her that she was suffering from apotemnophilia, which, though exotic enough, was at least an acknowledged psychic construct supported by a body of technical medical literature and many websites of the afflicted. Research was ongoing. Discoveries involving skin conductance response experiments followed up by magnetoencephalography seemed to confirm the neurological basis of the syndrome; it could be argued that it was not in her neurotic imagining but was corporeal, a brain problem, and therefore "real." But the Célestine version of apo was perhaps too exotic even for this structure. She gently pointed out to me, as in a casual, sweet discussion (the devastating technique she used with her students which made them love her), that she had had no breasts in childhood and therefore had not as a child wanted them amputated; that a desire for breast reduction or even mastectomy was not a recognized part of the apo syndrome, but related more to gender change/confusion and other psychic states, and that it was not so much that her left breast felt as though it were not part of her body as that it was full of insects that were a danger to her, like ductal carcinoma in situ or full-blown breast cancer, and therefore the removal of that breast was calmly, rationally indicated.

And the element of religion was also far from a classic apo concern. Célestine's book *The Nipple and the Mouth*, about the universal religion of the nourishing breast, was of course the critical text here. It delineated how a pure, rigorous atheism required the rejection of some religions that were not recognized as religions but functioned as religions and thus needed to be exposed and dismantled—like the insect religion of *Judicious* as communicated to Célestine by her former Dutch-born French lover, Romme, now transmuted by the alchemy of kidnapping into a North Korean movie director. You see, then, what I was faced with on that waking from a dream, the dream that had been our life together up until that moment in the early morning in that villa high above Cannes. And so my unspoken struggle with Célestine was to be conducted on two fronts: her desire to amputate her left breast, and her desire to reconnect with the phantasm of Romme Vertegaal, aka Jo Woon Gyu.

Had she actually had a stroke, a cerebrovascular accident, while we watched *Judicious* in the jury box in Cannes? Had the stroke clouded her brain with cosmic portent while the images of peasants, warrior priests, and insect harvests flowed over us? (I thought of Philip K. Dick's post-stroke religious novel *The Divine Invasion*.) By the time we had got back to Paris, she was joking about our experience during the festival and suggesting that her little "philosospasm" had been caused by the overheated and overly critical public atmosphere of the festival itself. And did she have another stroke during the night which reanimated the power of the movie over her after it had lain dormant for several months? Could a stroke regenerate the effects of a prior stroke, effects which had flared and then shriveled away to nothing? I urged her to book a CT scan. I scanned her face myself, looking for telltale weakness, a slumping mouth, a drooping eye. I found nothing, and she felt nothing, and refused to see a doctor of any kind. It was a simple series of epiphanies, she said, the kind we often suffered together—*suffered* because they struck us as revelations that demanded action, that upset comfort, turned it over and dumped it on the polished hardwood floor. She was talking about philosophical and social awarenesses, breakthroughs of cognition which were inextricably mixed with potent emotional mandates. We would often force these moments into being while traveling when exhausted, or when writing while under extreme political duress. I could not deny the reality of these intangible and cryptogenic events; we had shared so many. Intellectually, for a nanosecond, it all seemed reasonable, and then it all seemed patently foolish and insane: amputate a perfectly healthy breast because, against all plausibility, its owner disowned it and feared its contents?

I insisted that Célestine let me study the results of her last mammogram. She did not resist. Its affirmed normality (with the usual technicians' disclaimers regarding the unusual density of her fibroglandular tissue seen bilaterally, which decreased the sensitivity of the mammography and thus possibly compromised an accurate assessment) did not faze Célestine. It was three years old, and so it contained the seeds of its own inadequacy; it represented a flawed and circumspect medical worldview which could not and did not address the plane of existence upon which human life is conducted. There had been ultrasounds, pictures of the inside of her breasts. We strolled through them as though they were old family photos. There were no insects in evidence. Of course not, she said. The onset of the insects is abrupt, barbaric, and absolute. It is a colonization, as per the village in *Judicious*, a first staging, to be followed by a total metastasis and subsequent subjugation. How did they get in there, into that beautifully sealed liquid dome? "They can burrow. They can tunnel. They can inject eggs. I'll be meeting with my entomologist Korean friends about it," she said. "We've already made a date to discuss global insect strategies."

"I'd like to be at that meeting. I'd like to document this … adventure."

"You can, of course you can. And you can do more than that. You can meet with your audiologist and see if she'll tell you where Romme is living right now. She will have been in contact with him, I'm sure. They had a special relationship, very complex and subtle, and his hearing—and so also his career as a filmmaker—in some ways depended on her. He won't have abandoned her, even at the distance between Pyongyang and Paris. I think now they can even reprogram your hearing aids for you over the internet. After all, they're just tiny Bluetooth-and-Wi-Fi-enabled little computers. I think you've even done it yourself, haven't you?"

I hadn't, but I had no doubt that it was possible. And I had no doubt that if anyone was programming the Dear Respected Leader's favorite movie director's hearing aids over the internet from an office in Paris, it would be Elke Jungebluth.

10

MY JOURNEY TO THE Jungebluth Audiology Clinic was more than just a short trip in an electric Smart Car, though on the most mundane level that is what I thought it was going to be. We allowed each other a number of "philosospasms" per year; these were episodes of obsessive/compulsive behavior, often involving sexual affairs with students, or periods of deep, intricate despair, or occasionally intense political adventures which made us very vulnerable to the media and the public and caused us great discomfort. But our agreement was that we would support each other during these spasms, and would treat that momentary reality as though it were the only true reality, which, of course, in so doing, it was. And so I trundled along the Périphérique, searching for the off-ramp to the Rue de Vaugirard, Porte de Vanves, which would take me to the Jungebluth Clinic, and soon, there I was, in the sleek, technichrome waiting room with my audiology records being studied by a very serious Sciences Po student who was working in the office part-time and pretended not to know who I was.

My initial foray into the world of hearing instruments spilled me out into a dismal series of suicide-inducing offices located in seniors' homes or clandestine impromptu workshops in basement apartments which resembled discount do-it-yourself furniture outlets. Though the technology was often sophisticated, the retailing was sleazy and amateurish. And every time you came back to plug your ears into the aud's computer, it was a different aud, and often a different program in the computer. The audiologists, in my experience, were all women, or rather, in most cases, girls, and girls who were not very comfortable with intense and demanding old men like me. They wanted to condescend, to help you insert your in-the-canal receiver with your trembling, gnarled, insensitive fingers; they wanted to simplify the technology of the devices (which were created by vast electronics industries incorporating computing power six thousand times that which launched the Apollo 11 moon shot) and hide from you the six separate programs that you could shape in infinitely variable ways, leaving you just a button that switched the things on and off. They did not want to confuse you.

It was only when I stumbled across Elke at Romme Vertegaal's insistence that I felt that the world of sound could flower for me in a serious, exciting way after years of muted, dulled, oblivious non-interactions. And now here we were again in Vanves, in consultation, which for her was a commitment involving the intertwining of two lives in a creative project of substantial magnitude.

Elke was the homely daughter of two German psychoanalysts from Cologne, her father a Freudian, her mother a Jungian, both hearing impaired. Her older brother was a musicologist who specialized in Elizabethan dance and had moved to Boston to teach at the New England Conservatory of Music; he was also hearing impaired. We see here, then, what Freud would have called a neat cathexis ultimately generating the Jungebluth phenomenon. As the only normal-hearing member of the family, and the youngest, Elke absorbed responsibility for the entire familial soundscape; to shape and enhance the aural world for them, and then for everyone she could reach, soon became the focus of her life. Though it's obvious that a psychoanalyst must be able to hear to function professionally, and a musicologist must as well, Elke found herself dealing with the familiar problems of denial of impairment, as she put it, her brother even going so far as to ask her to listen to recordings that he himself could barely hear, urging her to fill in the aural details with her descriptions. At times, her parents would surreptitiously record sessions of analysis with their patients and then play them for Elke, asking her to transcribe what was said and to offer comments on the nuances of the patients' modes of expression. Thus there was an immense life pressure placed on Elke as well as an intense sense of duty and responsibility, a potent and not uncommon mixture. And I was the beneficiary of it all.

As always, we sat in Elke's rigorously sleek consulting room. I've said she was homely, and she was: an impossibly thin and long face; dull, opaque, muddy-brown eyes of noticeably different sizes; lank and unhealthy-looking hair which was graying prematurely in awkward patches; protruding, comically alert ears; a dumpy, uncertainly shaped body which seemed to constantly be causing her distress of some indeterminate kind. But it was an intellectual homeliness, by which I mean her physical presence asked you to discount it and concentrate instead on her penetrating and holistic intelligence, on the immediate and effortless gestalt she created which enveloped you and nourished and even exhilarated you. The subject was Romme Vertegaal.

"Can you talk to me about him?" I said. "He referred me to you. Does physician-patient privilege operate in audiology? I know that audiologists are not physicians ..."

"Listen to the crickets," she said, nodding sagely as she spoke, understanding everything.

"Listen to the what? To the crickets? You mean the insects?" I had immediately thought of Buddy Holly and the Crickets (once even named the Chirping Crickets) and the wonderful naïve music of my youth—"That'll Be the Day," "Oh, Boy!" "Not Fade Away," "Maybe Baby"—which seemed at that time to flow seamlessly into my studies in Hegel, in Heidegger, in Kant, in Schopenhauer, informing them and infusing them with contemporary sexuality and emotional relevance. My head started to fill with that music, such potent wrappers for the emotions of my youth and the attendant wave of the passage of time, of mortality, that I had a pathetic and juvenile need to confirm that she was not referring to the band, knowing all the while that she could not be.

Imagine, then, my confusion when Elke lifted herself with cheerfully endured suffering out of her Aeron chair—the contortions of her body conveyed in detail through the austere fabric of her tightly tailored Jungebluth Clinic coat—crossed the room to crouch down before a low-slung stainless-steel cabinet, slid open its opaque glass door, and returned to me with a record album of the classic vinyl format in her hand. Had she in fact been referring to the Crickets, and was this an obscure rendering of one of their original albums? The title *Listen to the Crickets* unraveled on the cardboard sleeve in a loose, artisanal handwritten font in white across a dark-blue background. Below the title was a high-contrast black-and-white portrait of a middle-aged man with glasses who was not Buddy Holly but was Romme Vertegaal. Below the portrait were letter characters stacked into syllabic blocks which I could just recognize as Hangul, or Korean script. Was it simply the album's title translated into Korean? You can imagine my shock at seeing the image of Romme connected in any way with Korean words, not to mention insects. My avowed project—undeniably condescending at its core, but induced by forty years of love and intellectual intertwining with Célestine—of forcing reality into Célestine's absurd *Judicious*/Korean fantasy of the kidnapped Romme Vertegaal, was now shriveled into irrelevance by this unexpected validation—at least in part—of what anyone would have assumed was a pathological chimera.

"That's Romme" was all I could bring myself to say.

"Yes," said Elke. "Isn't it stunning?"

"I'm not sure. Are those Korean letters?"

Elke sat back heavily in her chair, carefully cradling the album on her lap but thoughtfully tilting it towards me so that I could revel in its splendor. It now caught the overhead light in a way that revealed its artful metallic treatment of the subtle shadows of the cover art, which I had not at first noticed. What I had thought was a solid dark blue was now a field of blue-green grass: we were down in the grass with the crickets.

"Romme has had business dealings with the Democratic People's Republic of Korea for some time, and this vinyl record album is the result of some of that work. Not just business, of course. Heavy North Korean technology is made manifest here. The Korean characters translate as 'The sagacious'—or possibly 'The discerning'—'use of insects in hearing technology.' Romme's North Korean partners are not quite as whimsical or poetic as he is." She slipped on a pair of delicate white cloth gloves that she took from her pocket and slowly, dramatically pulled the thirty-three-and-a-third licorice-colored vinyl disc from its sleeve. "This is the very first iteration of *Listen to the Crickets* in Europe. It might well be the only one at the moment. More will ineluctably follow."

"But what is it? Is it a compendium of insect sounds? Is it connected with the Entomological Society of Korea?"

"No," said Elke. "It's a tool created for programming hearing instruments in ways that their designers never imagined."

A completely retro vinyl recording interfacing with sophisticated digital hearing aids and their proprietary digital fitting platforms—I couldn't imagine it either. But then, I didn't have to, because five minutes later I was hooked up to Romme Vertegaal's North Korean venture and in the process of being … tuned.

"THERE ARE NOW laser turntables that do away entirely with mechanical tonearms and diamond needles and cartridges," said Elke, as she looped the lanyard of the Connexx wireless controller around my neck. "Using one of those would certainly make life easier for us humble audiologists who simply want to use the Vertegaal tuning method. But Romme won't have it. Each of us was forced to invest in one of these exotic monstrosities. They're hideously expensive and difficult to maintain, and that's why there are not many of us who do what I'm about to do for you. This one is over twenty years old. They were all created by an Israeli woman named Judith Spotheim-Koreneef who worked out of Eindhoven, Holland. Romme optimized *Crickets* to the audio parameters of her machines using the only sample in Asia at the time. There are a few more there now."

We were enclosed in Audio Booth 4, basically an audio recording cabinet floating on foam and designed to be sound-neutral. Words spoken in Booth 4 sounded unnaturally deadened, like inanimate objects. The walls of the booth, the floor, the ceiling, none of it added any energy or shape by reflectance or geometry to the sounds that came out of our mouths, and this had a mysterious effect on the meaning and the impact of the words themselves that was hard to calculate. It made me realize that total neutrality in human communication is destabilizing; there is a paper to be written there.

In front of me sat an enormous and complex device which could be called, simply, a record player, but whose presence was more like that of an impossibly gigantic specimen of zooplankton. Its use of translucent acrylic for its massive platter and various blocks and cylinders; stainless steel for the weights embedded around the periphery of that platter; titanium for its delicate, multi-counterweighted pickup arm; and threadlike drive belts and electrical filaments, culminated in a coruscating, predatory structure that seemed best fitted for frenetic submarine life. Once Elke switched on the controller resting on my sternum, I was apparently linked wirelessly to this thing, and both of us to Elke's desktop computer and the Siemens Connexx Trainable-Hearing-Instrument Fitting Programming Interface. She now washed the vinyl disc in a Spin-Clean Record Washer—a yellow plastic trough with rollers and brushes filled with distilled water and one capful of vinyl-washing fluid—lovingly turning the disc on the rollers with gloved fingers, three times clockwise, three times counterclockwise, then removing and drying it with delicate pats of a pristine white, lint-free cotton cloth drawn from a drawer with rubber seals meant to keep dust out. Clamp the disc to the platter with the acrylic puck, flick up the retro toggle power-switch in its steel housing, gently lower the tiny coffin-like myrtlewood cartridge into the vinyl groove, and ... nothing. I heard nothing.

"I hear nothing," I said, but to no one, because Elke had left the booth, closing the double doors with a whoosh of expelled atmosphere and leaving me in a vacuum. I could just see her through one of the two triple-glazed portholes in the wall, starting to work the Connexx program almost before she had fully settled into the Aeron. I had come to the Jungebluth (there were partner audiologists I never got to meet) to derail my complicity in Célestine's delusions about Romme, about the insects in her breast, about Pyongyang, assuming that my inquiries there would deliver some proof that Romme was living in Paris or Rome and that he had not been kidnapped by any of the Kims, and that he was not the director of *Judicious*. This would naturally have encouraged a gentle easing of Célestine out of her compelling body narrative, perhaps with the shock treatment of a meeting with Romme in our apartment once I had contacted him. Would there arise some sort of Capgras syndrome response from her, a denial that the Romme I presented her with was the real Romme? Would she claim that he was an imposter surgically created by the Kims in order to delude the world and, specifically, delude Célestine? These, then, were my own fantasies, which were summarily crushed by Elke's evidence that Romme had spent time in Pyongyang functioning as a technical consultant, that "some kind of filmmaking" was involved, and that he had been "kidnapped"—Elke used the word innocently, unbidden by me—"by the depth and passion of the culture there, mesmerized and delighted to the extent that he wished to live there for an indeterminate length of time."

I was the one who was delusional, not Célestine; or at least I was haughtily and unjustifiably dismissive of her instincts and her sensitivity to some aberrant realities that neither of us had been capable of conjuring up before. Had her left breast become a bagful of dangerous insects? Was that any less conceivable than the invasion of breast tissue by rampaging rogue milk-duct epithelial cells? Well, yes, of course it was, but what if the "insects" were Célestine's metaphor for something more medically plausible? What if that was the only way she could express her very real awareness of a unique pathology?

The acrylic platter of the Spotheim-Koreneef device was spinning hypnotically, its corona of glittering weights, like stacks of coins, shimmering with nano-crustacean avidity. And now, through my portholes, I could see the Connexx program reduced to a window on Elke's monitor, streamers indicating that it was feeding its settings and parameters—everything controlling my Siemens Pure micon receiver-in-the-canal instruments—to another, larger window, which displayed a mixture of Korean syllabic blocks and English words. This was the fitting program devised by Romme and his nameless North Korean Juche comrades which was designed to be used in conjunction with the *Crickets* album and the neo record player, and to which I had agreed to submit my entire auditory existence for realignment. According to the booth's Swiss Federal Railways station–style clock, the process took one hour and seventeen minutes, during which time I was projected into a mildly sinister audio landscape of threatening hums, chirps, and stuttering clicks, as well as raspy, non-human breathing (through valved insect spiracles?) and a variety of pulsing, fluid ripplings which suggested the movement of non-human blood through minute, multi-chambered tubular hearts. My interpretation of this auditory world was obviously much shaped by my experience of the *Judicious* film, Célestine's inventive pathology, and the album cover, and this interpretation could well have been recorded and analyzed somewhere in the internet ether, because apparently the response of my eardrums and the associated organic machinery inside my head to this soundscape being fed back to the North Korean program (it was called, innocuously, "In Tune with Nature," I later learned) was tantamount to a reading of my brain's electrical activity that was much deeper and more meaningful than a normal EEG. I idly wondered if the increasing stress on my shrunken bladder could affect the results and derange my programming; I really had to pee. We had agreed that most of the changes would be funneled to Program 5, my former Music program (which attempted to balance the sounds of all musical instruments and voices as per normal hearing), and that Program 1, Universal, would be left completely untouched for reference. A rocker switch on my left instrument allowed me to cycle through the six programs, which included TV (Program 2), Noisy Environment (Program 3), Outdoor/Sports (Program 4), and Telecoil (Program 6, for special telephone use). I asked Elke to name Program 5 Vertegaal, and that's how it showed up on the LCD display of my Tek wireless controller.

I walked out of the Jungebluth Clinic with my ears tuned to my safe, unaltered Program 1, unaccountably fearful of walking on the streets of Vanves while on Program 5—what could happen?—and having forgotten where the Smart Fortwo was parked, as was increasingly usual for me. Fortunately, my iPhone, which was now propping up my failing brain, had the GPS coordinates ready at hand, and its Maps turn-by-turn guidance system got me around the three corners to the little vehicle, which looked so dapper in its Matte Anthracite replaceable body panels. I was aware that I was taking inordinate pleasure in small, technological events and objects, and that this was probably a semiconscious tactic meant to evade confronting certain agonizing life events which were probably not resolvable and were destined to cause unrelenting pain and distress; yet the pleasure was real, and I took it greedily. Once I was in the car, I thought, I would switch to Program 5, the Vertegaal, and allow the new settings to flow sounds never before perceived through my brain; but then I didn't. My rationale was that the electric car was too quiet, too well insulated—against temperature changes, in order to save the battery, but effectively damping sounds as well—to really deliver anything spectacular, and then I would be disappointed, and then I would get depressed. That was the rationale. But was the whole exercise not really about one thing: the left breast of Célestine? Why play with toys?

I arrived back at our apartment with my head buzzing as though *it* were the vessel full of truculent insects; perhaps it was my head that needed to be removed. Célestine was not there. I could not possibly read. I switched on the TV and began to watch the MotoGP world championship motorcycle race from Aragón, broadcast on delay. I knew nothing about MotoGP, but was immediately entranced by the machinery, the strange, padded, hunchbacked leather riding suits bearing ceramic sliding pucks Velcroed to their knees, the futuristic helmets, and the ferocity of the racing. The commentators discussed the increasing sophistication of the electronic controls on even these elemental machines, a worrisome thing, they said, because it took so much control of throttle, traction, braking, pitch control and even lean angle away from the riders that one wondered whether riders would soon be rendered obsolete. Needless to say, the questions of technology raised by the racing stimulated me and happily distracted me, especially since the technologies of MotoGP and Siemens hearing instruments were seeping into each other so that I was soon feeling traction control, anti-lock braking, g-force sensor, and electronic-control-unit elements beginning to operate in my ears. It occurred to me that the speakers of our poor old Loewe, only banal stereo, not 5.1 or 6.1 or beyond, were still quite good, and I was tempted to switch to Program 5 just to see what it would do to the unearthly sound of those multi-cylindered motorcycles. Would it create a brilliant form of Grand Prix motorcycle-empowered hearing? My index finger was actually hovering over the rocker of the left behind-the-ear module when I heard Célestine's keys jingling as she approached the narrow landing outside our door. Mild claustrophobia normally kept her from using the compact elevator, so she could be heard from quite some distance down the spiraling stairs. I switched off the TV as two Spanish riders started their final lap in the lead, to the wild delight of the Aragón crowd, but the half-life decay, the aftertaste of blended MotoGP/hearing-instrument engineering, remained for quite some time.

WE WERE IN THE HABIT of having our most intense, most abstract and intellectual conversations in bed, usually fully clothed but not always. Even if it began as something mundane, something merely functional, in the kitchen or in front of the Loewe, once it drifted into that territory that we subliminally recognized, we ourselves drifted, as if randomly, into our small bedroom and would lie down together without having missed a beat in the rhythm of our talking (the pillows occasionally making my Pures squeal petulantly with feedback), and with the conversation sometimes ending with a profound nap, or profound sex, both the nap and the sex infused with the thematics of our talk. There were pens and stubs of pencils strewn everywhere in the bedroom, evidence of our habit of scribbling notes for future papers, articles, letters to editors, at any moment of the day or night, during or following our bed sessions. We made sporadic forays into the world of voice-recognition spoken-note-taking using iPad or iPhone, but inevitably reverted to the handwritten word. We both had appalling handwriting that required considerable decipherment even by the writer, but the very act of decipherment was comforting, the contortions of the scrawls conveying emotion and nuance that no perfect pixels could embody. Speaking the words seemed to release them into a void in which they could evaporate unexpectedly; writing them seemed to encase them safely within our skulls, where they could leisurely ripen.

Célestine headed for the bedroom first, tossing her keys into the wooden Chinese bowl we left on the glass half-moon table by the door, kicking off her shoes and flopping down on the bed with a long, slow sigh. As usual, I followed her, half-sitting rather than stretching full out, my shoes already off.

It was apparent to both of us that we were going to talk about Romme Vertegaal, with no preliminaries, no banter about parking difficulties or what was missing in the refrigerator. Earlier in the day, she had been to the Entomological Society's office again, hoping that her contacts there had some news of Romme's whereabouts or latest projects. She had turned to them in desperation after our colleagues at the Cannes Film Festival were unable to provide any enlightenment. *Judicious* had been handled entirely by a North Korean government film and media agency, and they never had any interaction with the director of the movie himself. It had been hinted that he had somehow disgraced himself in Pyongyang and was lucky not to find himself in prison. There had never been any chance that he could accompany his movie to Cannes as most directors do; the festival had decided to accept this onerous condition in the hope that it would at least open the door to more interchange with North Korean artists. The executives of the festival would not accept Célestine's contention that Jo Woon Gyu was not Korean, not Asian at all, but was a French national born in Holland. Disbelief and dismissal soon turned to irritation, and Célestine's entreaties—phone calls, emails, street interventions outside the Paris offices of the festival—quickly became moments of embarrassment for everyone that were best forgotten. The pair of us were used to becoming embarrassments in political and social causes of all stripes—it was a badge of honor; you could not worry about dignity or reputation when it came to hot-button issues—so this in itself was not hard to take, but the emotional stakes in this instance were very high, and Célestine in bed next to me was enervated, dispirited.

"Look at this," I said, handing her my iPhone.

She covered her eyes with her arm, flexing her fingers so that her forearm muscles bunched rhythmically, exuding anguish and aggravation. "I can't look at your ironic little pictures right now. Please." I was in the habit of bringing back cell-phone photos of things I encountered during the day, just like a dog with an amusing stick in its mouth. I believed I took these photos in innocent amazement at the richness of mundane reality, but Célestine, on the contrary, detected revulsion and existential dismay skulking under every shot. I no longer contradicted her on this point.

I slid down on the bed until we were side by side. "This picture has a very special irony that you'll want to experience. I promise." She rolled over abruptly and grabbed me by the hair with both hands, inducing my Pures to complain bitterly. I used to pull them out of my ears and toss them onto the night table at such moments, fearing an interruption of intimacy, but we had gotten so used to their companionship that it never occurred to me to do that now. "A promise like that is a dangerous thing," she said. "I'm in a perilous, slippery state of mind. One of your shots of inane parking signs could push me right over the edge. And I'd never come back." She kissed me a full, openmouthed kiss, then pulled away as though shocked by what she had done, her own little act of irony. "Well, let's see it. I'm not going to be easy to impress."

I recovered my iPhone from where it had hidden itself in the folds of the duvet and again conjured up the photo I had taken of the *Listen to the Crickets* album. With a flourish, I gave the iPhone to Célestine.

IT IS DIFFICULT TO FIND Crisco in Paris, but not impossible. As well, friends visiting from America got in the habit of bringing us Crisco—not in the spray cans, but the preferred cardboard box containing the four-hundred-and-fifty-four-gram wax-paper-wrapped white block of vegetable shortening. Once we discovered the use of Crisco as a sexual lubricant and an antidote to vaginal atrophy, I could never again see the Crisco logo (the red letters over a white ellipse with a golden drop of oil serving as the dot over the letter *i*) without getting a melancholy erection. At the age of sixty-two, Célestine was still voluptuous and sensual, but of course well advanced in her postmenopausal life. It was typical of her to search for a metaphor, or perhaps an analogy, to help her absorb a change as fundamental as the transformation brought about by her menopause, particularly where sex was concerned. She found it when we participated in a panel, part of the Festival Lumière at the Grand Lyon Film Festival, whose subject was "Sex and the Disabled in the Cinema." Our postmenopausal sex was immediately illuminated by the testimony of our fellow panelists, who were not specialists, but merely six aficionados of cinema who incarnated a spectrum of human disability from relatively minor (a non-functioning right arm owing to a childhood stroke) to major (motor neuron disease at the advanced Stephen Hawking level). A strong sense of invention, leavened by an even stronger sense of humor, and the suppression of embarrassment at the sometimes grotesque acrobatics required, seemed to be the key, spiced by the exhilaration of being forced to understand and, more, to graphically discuss, precisely what the purpose of the sex really was—a woefully ignored aspect of sex for most of the enabled.

Secretly, I lusted after Célestine as I always had—secretly, because it was not allowed that I could somehow evade our synchronized aging by lusting now as I had always lusted. I was allowed to express my desire to her, but it was necessary for her to laugh it off in disbelief, the delusions of an old man, possibly the first signs of senility, if not dementia, in her own private senex. It was as though my unabated, youthful lust was by its very existence a reproach to her for her own brutally truncated lust, now feebly supported by the stratagems I've just described. I could not tell her how our past sex blended smoothly into our present sex for me, how her past body modified the reality of her present body. Even as anal sex was not possible for her now, still the old, vividly recalled anal sex was vitally alive and present for me, happening somehow concurrently with vaginal sex. And of course, my body was changing too, as I'm sure you've guessed even without reference to internet photos and videos, and I felt that her menopause was also mine. The transformation of our bodies was locked in a rigorous synchrony, and perhaps beyond synchrony: we were too close in all ways not to have affected each other causally. As her body changed (and that change, of course, is invisibly gradual until one of those startling moments of revelation, when the light slanting in from an oddly placed skylight rakes cruelly across the skin, the veins, the toenails, and changes forever your perception of what your lover is) I at first willed my esthetic for womanly beauty to change in order to accommodate her transformation, so that she remained as beautiful and as desirable as ever before, though she was different. And the difference itself became provocative and exciting, as though sex with her was also sex with a new, exotic person who demanded new sexual protocols and new perversities, until I didn't have to will that change anymore because that esthetic had permanently changed; I was no longer attracted to the same women, and it was a blessing and a relief, and a curious thing. An unexpected corollary was the realignment of the esthetic concerning my own body, which could now absorb the stringy musculature, the mottled skin, the haggard cheekbones, the reptilian wrinkles, into its category of acceptable male beauty. Yes, we were both still wonderful.

After I described my adventure in Vanves to Célestine in obsessive detail, all in explanation of the album cover photo, we made desperate, triumphant, celebratory love, inevitably embracing the theme of Romme Vertegaal and his odyssey as we imagined it. While we were on a trip to Mexico, whose purpose was an exploration of leftist politics and philosophy *à la mexicaine*, we discovered that our sex had independently segued into a meditation on Frida and Diego, with a flavoring of Trotsky (Célestine was always Frida, but I occasionally was Trotsky in that delirious country of sexual self-annihilation; later on, when we revisited the theme, I was sometimes Frida, Célestine sometimes Diego), and had distinctly Mexican surrealist folk-art overtones. From that point on, we would often consciously choose the themes of our sexual sessions as though collaborating on a collage or sculpture project, and would afterwards discuss their textures and sensory effects. We wrote a joint piece about it for the "Annals of Sexuality" section of *The New Yorker*, which caused some small controversy. Now, just post-Vanves, there emerged a new layer in our constantly evolving, composited sexual structure (which always reminded me of the use of layers in Photoshop): Célestine's uncharacteristically desperate longing for Romme. I could be Romme in our fantasy—I certainly knew him better than I knew Diego Rivera—but the jealousy was there even though we allowed each other lacunate lovers, and the jealousy was dissolving the layers and producing a disharmonious mess. Is there anyone who has not felt jealousy over a lover's past lovers, a jealousy made all the more ferocious the more it is unjustified, the more it is secured in the past, mockingly protected by the vault of memory? So yes, triumphant, celebratory, but anguished in its emotional complexity, at least for me, and made more agonizingly poignant by Célestine's apparent serenity, her ease even with the by-now-inevitable pain that came with penetration. I hated allowing Célestine to fuck Romme using me as a Romme surrogate.

We were both subdued by the end of it, Célestine holding my hand over her left breast and squeezing it with distracted cruelty. But then she startled me with a sudden, whimpered exhalation, followed by a terrified gasp. A shot of adrenaline projected brainward and flushed me with a familiar, unmoored anger. When I first got my hearing aids, which were primarily tuned to augment those higher frequencies which are usually the first to disappear with age, it is true that the world instantly became louder and more harsh; it was difficult for someone whose aural landscape had so gradually become more and more muted and dulled to believe that this was hearing as experienced by most people, that this harshness was just the restoration of higher sound frequencies that had been lost. But the most disorienting aspect of this new soundscape was that sounds now carried too much emotion, too much meaning, so that a single sneeze was an expression of rage, the closing of a bedroom door was a pointed separation that would need healing, the smacking of a pillow to reshape it in the middle of the night was an explosive assault that caused my heart to pound with reflexive anger. A recalibration of my reaction to the intensity of sounds was urgently demanded, and though I was constantly recalibrating, those unexpected shots of adrenaline still persisted and confused me. I wanted to jerk out of bed and slam the bedroom door and go for a petulant walk in the wet, dark streets, muttering to myself about spousal insult and betrayal. But I recalibrated.

"Tina."

"You feel them, don't you?" she said. "They're going crazy in there. It's not possible you can't feel them."

"The insects."

An exhaled "yes!" like the report of a high-powered rifle. "Do you think it's the Romme Vertegaal gestalt that's animating them? The entomology, the North Korean connection ...?"

She twisted around to face me. On her face was a terrible, frantic joy. "Program 5," she said. "Switch to that and you can hear them. That's what it's for, isn't it? It's obvious! Romme knew this moment would come!"

"I don't know what Program 5 is for. Even Elke couldn't tell me precisely what it was for. I let her create it because of you, because of your

North Korean obsession, and of course because I was curious, even about my hearing, what its potential might really be. We know that Romme was brilliant, so let his brilliance open up my head if it can. That's what I was thinking. But honestly, I've been afraid to switch to it, partly because I think it'll be disappointing, be just a bland expression of harmonic filtering, who knows what. Elke was very proud of her work with that difficult analogue-vinyl-to-digital routine, and I hated to frustrate her by being so timid, but she let me go when I promised her that I would report back in detail after I'd had the courage to experiment with Program Vertegaal."

I could not tell Célestine that I had another motivation in letting Elke Jungebluth manipulate me: I had become terrified that Célestine would make good on her promise to travel to North Korea in order to seek out Romme, to reconnect with him and to give her insect problem to him, all within the context of a farcical political rapprochement with the North Korean dictatorship. On one level her stratagem was complete madness, a fantasy, and on another it confirmed—I felt this with crushing pain—that she still loved him, loved him in a way that she did not love me, and that I was trapped in a wretched telenovela I would never escape.

Célestine cupped her left breast in both hands and offered it to me. "Switch it on and listen," she said, with a breathless intensity whose hopefulness utterly deranged me. What husband has not avidly played the role of voyeur in his own house, watching the reflection of his wife in a window as she examines her vagina or anus with his chromed shaving mirror, one leg propped up on the white metal bathroom chair, searching for some real or feared lesion, polyp, secretion, or telltale discoloration? I would often catch Célestine examining her left breast in the most unconventional way: for sound, rather than sight. She would pull it up towards her left ear, her head cocked, manipulating it ruthlessly, as though it truly did not belong to her but was a ludicrously wrongheaded transplant or recent pathological growth, prodding it in order to provoke the insects into an aural frenzy loud enough to be recordable by the iPhone that sat propped up against a Kleenex box, the VU-meter of its Voice Memos app twitching with every rustle. Now it was my turn.

I hesitated, paralyzed. Her hair was wet from our exertions, glistening black and gray strands striping her cheeks. One strand was caught in the corner of her mouth, and I hallucinated that it was the leg of an enormous black-and-gray spider inadvertently exposed, patiently waiting inside her mouth for the insects to emerge. I forced myself to gently pull the leg from between her lips, which parted slightly to aid me, and swept it back over her ear. "You know, you've always been able to hear things that I've never heard, even with my very sophisticated bionics," I said. "And you've never been able to successfully record the sounds of your insects. You've admitted that."

"But this is Romme. This is Romme's gift to both of us. It's been created by his brilliance and by his understanding. This is a new thing." She glowed as she said this, and the glow tormented me. She reached up with one hand, the other now palpating her breast, and touched the Pure module behind my ear. (I had chosen dark silver for its color, vain enough still to want it to disappear in my unruly nest of silver hair, which one of my students described as "confrontational philosophy hair, though not as intimidating as Schopenhauer's hair.") I took Célestine's hand away from my ear, leaving it to hover uncertainly, and I reached up for the program switch behind my left ear and pressed it, methodically cycling through the programs from 1 to 5. Each cycle was accompanied by a unique sequence of musical tones cleverly designed to indicate which program one was entering, and because Célestine could hear those tones, when I arrived at Vertegaal her eyebrows immediately rose in bright, girlish expectation.

"The oven fan has been left on. I can hear it now," I said.

Célestine laughed and pulled my head towards her breast with exaggerated nonchalance.

And then I heard them. The insects. They were there inside her breast, and I could hear them.

THERE ARE APPARENTLY BIOMARKERS present in exhaled breath which can be analyzed by a mass spectrometer for indications of many kinds of cancers and other diseases. Could there be an equivalent in exhaled or otherwise emitted sounds? Could Romme Vertegaal and his North Korean colleagues be in the vanguard defining a revolutionary new medical diagnostic system? Could my innocent, pragmatic Pure hearing aids have been transformed into an audio analogue of the mass spectrometer by the *Listen to the Crickets* program? In the light of day, none of this would stand up to scrutiny. But there, in the bed with Célestine, it was darkest night, and I could hear the insects in her left breast, and they sounded alive and present and real. I had always suspected that insects have what I think of as "species personalities"; that is to say, not personalities as individuals, but as individual species, so that certain of the nymphaline butterflies—the admirals, commas, anglewings, tortoiseshells—all have a habit of landing on your head when you are trying to catch them, and when you move abruptly, they fly off, only to circle and return to the top of your head—behavior you would never see in a monarch or a tiger swallowtail. In Célestine's bunched breast, now covered with the liquid sheen of excitement, there were eight species of insects I could discern, all by the sounds they made, sounds which generated an image in my mind of the organs—legs or wings stridulating, tymbals vibrating—which produced those sounds. As part of my life's philosophical enterprise I had—naturally, it seemed to me—been drawn to entomological studies, because I could not see how a philosopher could avoid engagement with the existence and meaning of such forceful yet utterly non-human life-forms. It always amused me to observe the pathetically desperate hunger expressed in popular culture for life-forms on other planets, when underneath the very feet of these seekers of aliens, and roundly ignored by them, were the most exotic, grotesque, and fabulous life-forms imaginable. But as a student of insect life I could not become more than a dabbler, so immeasurably deep is the subject. The lecture I delivered at the Club Immédiat, which I titled "Entomology Is a Humanism"—a playful, though pointed, reference to Sartre's famous lecture "Existentialism Is a Humanism"—incorporated most of the substance of my entomological learning, and is there for all to see in all its shallowness. I could not, in other words, accurately name the species of every insect represented in Célestine's breast. And how many of them could there be? Was there only one specimen of each species, so that the answer would be eight? Or, following the paradigm of Noah's ark, was there a male and female of each animal? A cicada, certainly. A mud-daubing wasp. A robber fly. An assassin bug. Several species of ant. My mind swelled with odd, comically disorienting images that seemed to bring along their own sound tracks: the savage swarming of the *marabunta,* the billion-strong soldier-ant army in the 1954 Charlton Heston movie *The Naked Jungle*; a show on the Discovery Channel examining insect parasites that turned their hosts into zombies serving the needs of the parasites; a YouTube parody of *The Green Hornet* in which the masked hero is actually a hornet that is fatally swatted by his Japanese sidekick, Kato, whose sound track was "Flight of the Bumblebee," complete with theremin hornet-buzz effect as per the old radio show. (I wasn't sure whether I had actually seen this *Hornet* video or hallucinated it.)

I pulled away from Célestine in horror and confusion, and she laughed a small, sympathetic laugh and released her breast, which seemed for one hallucinatory moment to ripple with inner turmoil before finding its innocuously normal position of gravitational repose. It was, as I've said, my favorite breast, the larger and more accommodating one (the left one is usually larger, apparently because of the way the heart pumps blood), but now this breast was overwhelmed by waves of meaning and symbolism even beyond the metaphorical freight which those long-suffering organs are accustomed to bear. It dissolved almost cinematically before my eyes into a rapidly cycling series of objects—a bag, a nest, an egg, a yurt, a hive—each one of which provoked an excruciating emotional response which left me trembling and drained.

"You know now, don't you? You know now," she said, studying my every tremor with involved curiosity.

But I didn't know. For obvious reasons, I could not believe my ears—in the most literal sense. It occurred to me that the insect sounds I thought I heard were actually being generated by my hearing instruments themselves, and not being passively received by them. Could they not have been programmed to fabricate those sounds, their creative computing power barely stressed by what they were ordinarily required to do? Could Romme, in concert with Elke, have constructed this unlikely elaborate scheme in order to drive me insane or, even more perversely, to seduce me into collaborating with Célestine in the deepening of her own insanity?

The look on Célestine's face was so benign—no, more, benevolent, even saintly—effortlessly overflowing with compassion and understanding and kindness, that I could not bring myself to voice these cavils at what was obviously a near-religious cathexis for her. And then again, I could still hear them, and I had the sense they were speaking to me, though I could not understand what they were saying.

I could understand what Célestine was saying. "Now you see why we have to cut this off. We have to do it before they spread everywhere. We don't have much time." She said this sweetly, gently, without apprehension. It disturbed me that she said "we," though her desire to have my approbation and support was normal for us; but in this context, it discharged a sinister undertaste which must have altered my expression. "I want *you* to do it," she said. "Why would you leave it to anyone else? It's something we've talked about, and now it's here."

I imagine it's incomprehensible to a young couple that they might one day be talking in many modalities—sometimes joking, sometimes despairing, sometimes brutalizing—about killing each other or mutilating each other. It's common enough to find articles about the ethics of euthanasia and pulling the plug on your spouse under dire medical circumstances, or the logistics of accompanying your wife to the Dignitas clinic in Zürich to end her life, but Célestine and I often found ourselves proposing hypothetical acts of violence which only peripherally had to do with aging, senility, and easeful death. She would castrate me; I would cut off her breasts—both surgeries committed with kitchen utensils ready at hand. She would strangle me with an old bathrobe belt; I would stab her with the twin-horned, sharp-pointed titanium sculpture I was awarded for my pamphlet "Consumerist Cinema"; we would take an overdose of barbiturates and lie down in our bed together, holding hands, in the manner of *The World of Yesterday*'s author, Stefan Zweig, and his young wife, in the Brazilian city of Petrópolis. We offhandedly devised many imaginary scenarios during the course of any given day, a habit that began as acerbic banter between two hypersharp intelligences, whose function seemed to be to absorb the venom of normal mundane tensions, anxieties, jealousies, resentments, and nano-betrayals, but gradually transformed into a daily hedge against death, an acknowledgment of our painful ephemerality, and a bid to take the kitchen utensils of mortality out of the hands of happenstance and put them back into our own drawer.

You can begin to understand, then, the accumulation of circumstances that created our gestalt. I went from humoring Célestine, not certain whether she was beginning to suffer from dementia or was, rather, deliberately developing a fantasy, a willed hallucination involving a unique form of apotemnophilia, to inhabiting this complex psychosis completely. It's too bad you never got to sit in a room with Célestine. You would have felt her power to seduce and hypnotize.

THE NIGHT TRAIN TO MUNICH left Paris Est at 20:05 and was the first leg of our journey to Budapest. We had chosen the City Night Line *Schlafwagen* Cassiopeia, operated by Deutsche Bahn, to be followed by Austrian Railways' Railjet high-speed train into Budapest's Keleti station, in order to accommodate Célestine's newly emerged fear of flying, or rather her fear of cabin pressure change, which might aggravate her own small passengers. It can't be denied that the sense of occasion promoted by many hours of rail travel was also part of the transit stratagem, meant to validate the purpose of our trip and to lend the whole enterprise some of the credibility which it was lacking. For one must ask, as I'm sure you are, just how insane was Célestine, and how irresponsible was I to be complicit in that insanity. She was so convincing in the invention of the details of her malady and the conspiracy surrounding it that it took on a compelling substantiality, like being swept into the reality of a brilliantly written novel or charismatic movie: it's not that you believe in its literalness, but that there is a compelling truth in its organic life that envelops you and is absorbed by you almost on a physiological level. I remember experiencing a small earthquake in Los Angeles—only a four-point-six, I think—when I was there as a guest of the Academy the year they decided to develop a special Oscar for Philosophy in Cinema. A small earthquake, and yet the forced awareness that the earth beneath your feet was volatile, not stable, was terrifying, and for days afterwards I was sure I could feel the earth trembling and threatening. I live with it still; it is ready to strike me at any moment, a special vertigo which is now part of my very physiology.

Célestine was like that earthquake. Célestine was also like that first LSD trip, the one you perhaps took in a deli in Brooklyn, where suddenly the colors all shifted towards the green end of the spectrum and your eyes became fish-eye lenses, distorting your total visual field, and the sounds became plastic, and time became infinitely variable, and you realized that reality is neurology, and is not absolute. Célestine was a personal hotspot, emitting her own special Wi-Fi signal which connected you to the Célestine web, and only the Célestine web. There was of course an element of unconditional support, a solidarity with one's primary partner in the world adventure no matter where it took you both. I was now shoulder to shoulder with Célestine at the barricades, just as she had been with me during my short-lived lunatic political career (which almost landed us both in prison and taught us the old lesson about philosopher-princes).

We took a deluxe two-berth Comfortline compartment with an en suite toilet and even a shower, complete with toiletries, which we never used. Unusually, Célestine wanted the upper berth, which she normally said made her feel like a piece of carry-on luggage stowed in the overhead bin, but now made her feel as though she were flying over the green canopy of a Caribbean island rain forest. She clambered up the white metal ladder, hooked to the upper berth by our resolutely cheerful sleeping-car attendant, like an eight-year-old girl on her first trip away from home. I must confess that the perforated plastic card-key lock system and security dead bolt inside the compartment completely killed that old Orient Express sense of exotic bonhomie, and replaced it with the feeling that one had been admitted to a rolling minimum-security prison for white-collar criminals heading, possibly, to the grotesquely ornate St. Gilles lock-up in Brussels. (For some reason, I flashed that the criminal/philosopher/artist Jean Genet was also riding on this prison train and was feeling quite at home.)

Before she ascended, Célestine sat on my bed and kissed me with as much passion and sensuality as she could while keeping her mouth shut tight, as was her new habit, the unspoken fear being the migration of insects from one body to another. I missed the mouth that fell wide open at the first touch of my lips, fell open with the evaporation of social will and any hint of reservation or resistance, the mouth that mindlessly invited—no, begged for—complete invasion and possession. I wondered if that mouth would ever return, perhaps immediately on our return trip from Budapest. And after the kiss, the by-now-ritual hearing-aid stethoscopic examination of the breasts and abdominal cavity, Célestine pulling open the top of her pinstriped cotton pajamas (they looked like the New York Yankees' home uniform, though she never wore them at home) and giving her breasts to me, now not her lover but her diagnosing physician. I could hear the vibrations of the rails in her flesh, and I could hear the insects too, clamoring for my attention and creating little capsules of sound that, in the overheated compartment, began to say rhythmical, nonsensical things to me, the way you might hear voices in the motor of a treadmill you were jogging on, or in the gnawing of an electric pencil sharpener. But so strong is our desire for meaning, an innate desire, it seems, that we construct meanings where there are none.

So too, the insect voices speaking to me from deep within Célestine, for by the time she left my bed for her own flight deck, the nonsensical, rhythmical things had become sensical, sequential, gnomic things that were full of meaning. I could still hear them through the upper bunk, shifting in tone and clarity as Célestine shifted from back to side. The insects knew why we were going to Budapest, and they were feeling persecuted. I turned off my Pures and put them into their puck-like container, which sported separate niches for each instrument, both receivers, and extra batteries, but as I placed the container on the fold-out table crammed tight to my berth and turned out the light, the insect-voice residue was still strong in my ears, like a bubbling, chittering excrescence of wax.

And so we rocked and rolled our way through a dreamy nighttime landscape towards Munich, and then wrapped ourselves in the modernist, leather-clad luxury of the Railjet, which left Munich at 09:27 and arrived in Budapest at 16:49, after pauses in Salzburg and Vienna.

YOU KNOW HERVÉ BLOMQVIST, of course. He sent you to me, and that was very much in accordance with his assumed role of social enabler and political provocateur, with a special emphasis on combining the two. He met Zoltán Molnár when Molnár, a notorious Hungarian surgeon who at times had been sought by Interpol for his involvement in the illegal international trading of human organs for transplants, and who was in the habit of materializing as if by magic as the proprietor of pop-up transplant clinics in places like Kosovo and Moldova, slipped surreptitiously into Paris to conduct clandestine seminars on the politicization of the human body and the response of the international medical establishment to that politicization. According to Hervé, who was, as you know, an intimate member of our intellectual family even as a student, Dr. Molnár flaunted his vested interest in subverting the establishment of government regulation of the organ trade, while at the same time making an inflammatory case for the humanistic benefit of that regulation. Let poor people in impoverished countries sell their kidneys to the rich, he said. It's organic capitalism of the best kind, and is good for everybody, and should be monetized and industrialized to the maximum degree.

Naturally we googled the good doctor to the maximum degree before we made an appointment for Célestine's mastectomy at the Molnár Clinic on Rákóczi út in Budapest. We eschewed the offer relayed by his office of a package deal which included a Malév flight and a room at the Gellért; we wanted some distance between ourselves and the very enthusiastic doctor, and the all-inclusive deal, which involved meals at a restaurant called La Bretonne, felt like an entrapment, an intimacy urged with such intensity that it bordered on the salacious. And yet, what we were seeking *was* intimate, *was* perversely salacious, and we were aware that our diffidence was an emotional paradox which would not stand up to rational scrutiny. Only Dr. Molnár, Hervé assured us, of all his many subterranean contacts in the medical world garnered during his sub-rosa gamboling, would agree to allow me to perform Célestine's mastectomy under his supervision. Only Dr. Molnár, said Hervé, with that disarming boyish sweetness that lightly masked a rather ruthless intelligence, only the good doctor would see that the removal of Célestine's insect-infested breast was a neurological imperative and not a psychiatric one. Molnár was of the school that believed apotemnophilia arose from a congenital cerebral dysfunction and that its symptoms could be relieved only by complying with the patient's wish for amputation. Needless to say, it pleased both Molnár's and Hervé's sense of anarchy and social subversion to support this view, and it didn't take much for Molnár to absorb Célestine's case into his already edgy caseload. He had presided over only one other apo event: a male twenty-eight-year-old sex worker in Cologne who wanted to remove his left leg below the knee and who, frustrated by the reluctance of any doctor to amputate when there was no apparent physical reason to do so, tried on several occasions to jam his leg under a moving tram, causing great consternation in the city's Stadtbahn offices, not to mention the streets themselves. After the man visited the Molnár Clinic (according to the colorful emailed brochure originating in Romania), the patient's life improved on every level, including the professional, for he found a thriving specialized clientele in his new incarnation which he had never known existed.

And so we encountered the flamboyant doctor in his lair in a dense industrial suburb of Budapest which housed, among countless other international corporations, the Israeli Teva Pharmaceuticals Industries Ltd.

This proximity to legitimate medical businesses gave some comfort to me and Célestine, although the clinic itself was undeniably shady, located, as it was, totally underground in the poured-concrete entrails of an enormous, deteriorating complex. We found ourselves in the windowless Executive Director's Consulting Room, slumped in red-and-yellow butterfly chairs that had somehow survived the sixties, waiting for our preliminary tranche of instruction from the *chef* himself. On the walls were posters in several languages, which seemed to be extolling the virtues of medical tourism in several countries—Jordan, South Korea, Mexico, India—none of which was Hungary.

"My luminaries!" he sang out. "I am thrilled to have you here. I have been rereading both your works in preparation for our glorious collaboration."

"Collaboration?"

"You will forgive my enthusiasm and my presumption. But you must accept that what we are here today to do with each other cannot be subsumed under the mantle of medical procedure alone. For me to put the scalpel into your hand, my dearest Monsieur Arosteguy, is basically a crime, you understand. Though I fully comprehend the emotional ownership of the breast involved with the husband and the wife. In the light of that ownership, the alien surgeon is an intruder, a rapist, a violator. Why should he be allowed to sever that most beautiful organ from that beloved body? Who the fuck is he anyway? No, only the husband should have the right to do that intimate severing with all its resonances of personal history. And so on. But legally it's a crime. So what's the solution in our heads? In my head, the solution is that we are not committing surgery, but are creating an art/philosophy/crime/surgery project. The three of us. A collective. The Arosteguy Collective Project. Do you agree?"

Célestine and I glanced at each other and could see that we were immediately in sync. We were overwhelmed, horrified, and also delighted. After all, the normal terror in the face of life-altering surgery did not exist for

Célestine. Like that poor boy in Cologne, she was ready to throw her breast under the steel wheels of the tram if there was to be no surgery. So focused was she on the removal of the insect-sac, as she had taken to calling it (myself, I found this repugnant, but I could say nothing), that she had lost all fear of clinical misadventure, of death on the operating table. In this context, the pretentious rhapsodies of our good doctor leavened a potentially somber occasion with a dose of playful metaphysics, however suspect, that we found surprising and welcome.

Even more surprising, perhaps, was the seriousness with which he conducted his tutelage over the next few days. He had arranged our "gathering" to overlap a colleague's procedure—only a lumpectomy, unfortunately, but still it was the breast, and of course still illuminating for one who had never been in an operating room—and insisted that we both "audit the performance." I will spare you the details, but not my reactions: it was sensational and exhilarating to the point that I began to question my sanity, or more accurately my mental health. After that audition I could not wait to take up the scalpel, which Molnár first had me do in a bizarre fashion: he had commissioned a Molnár Clinic app for the iPad and designed an electronic scalpel which allowed one to perform several kinds of virtual breast surgery on the iPad itself. It reminded me of the early days of frog dissection over the internet, but of course was immeasurably more sophisticated—freakishly so, even incorporating (the perfect word) breasts of different sizes, races, and nipple/areola configurations.

Célestine was eager to try out the app, and she became particularly adept at the radical mastectomy, in which not only the breast tissue is taken but also the axillary lymph nodes and even the chest muscles. She seemed drawn to the Asian breast model, and I attributed this to her complex relationship with her Vietnamese general practitioner, Dr. Trinh. Célestine was amused by this idea but didn't accept it as valid. In any case, she and Molnár had many intense discussions about the need, or lack of need, for a radical mastectomy in her case. Ultimately, she felt that it was not indicated, given that her insects were not analogous to a metastasizing cancer which might invade her lymph nodes; a simple mastectomy would suffice. We agreed that the three of us would write a paper on the collaboration of the patient with the disease, and then, as a consequence, the patient's collaboration with the physician on the nature of the treatment of the disease.

Molnár tried his best to maintain professional decorum throughout our clinical education, but he got quite drunk at what seemed to be his own restaurant, La Bretonne, and we actually had to endure his sobbing and wailing in happiness as we toasted each other with a particularly medicinal apricot *pálinka*. "I have so much respect and love for you. I have resisted documenting everything, so much respect is invoked. But I am proud to be interpeded within your long-standing love affair. I feel that I am a lover to you both, in the way that I have read that you have taken on some students as lovers in the past. And yet, and yet I am also your teacher in this enterprise, and you are *my* students. This is something so delicious and tart, it forces tears to spring from my eyes." This is not something you want to see in your surgeon, and it did rattle us. It caused us an anxious night in our suite—they had upgraded us spontaneously—at the Corinthia Hotel. But the next morning our doctor presided over our iPad surgery session with full, dispassionate propriety, responding perhaps to the distancing effect that working on an anonymous African breast, delivered by the iPad's HD Retina display, had for all of us. Molnár assured me that when I began to cut into Célestine's flesh, the effect of the cool light of the surgical lamps and the masking-off of my wife's face would have the same effect, and I would have the detachment to be an excellent surgeon. "See how steady your hands are? Beautiful. Philosophy is surgery; surgery is philosophy. You are a natural. You have been rehearsing this your entire life."

It would not be until after the surgery, later in the hotel, when I could, all by myself, remove the surprisingly large and clumsy surgical staples with the disposable white-plastic-handled staple remover, no more sophisticated than something you'd buy at an office-supply store, that the emotion would kick in, that the vast and deep reservoirs of our personal history together would overflow, and we would be overwhelmed by what we had done.

But here, at the turning point of both our lives, mine and Célestine's, and in a sense yours as well, dear Naomi, is where I have to end the narrative which has submerged me, and to surface again, and come back to you.

11

"IT WAS NASTY OF YOU to speak French to me. Cruel. Are you always so cruel? You're a cruel person?"

"You told me you just forgot all your French. You never said the language traumatized you."

"I thought you understood."

"I thought I did too."

Chase was wearing jeans, black stockings, loafers, and a formfitting stretchy black T-shirt with long sleeves sporting thumb holes. Her thumbs were in those holes, and her hands were half covered as a result. Nathan thought he recognized the style from something Naomi had bought at a store called COS in Charles de Gaulle Airport. He was normally oblivious of the details of clothing. It was like being tone deaf, he thought, a genetic thing, nothing you could do about it; only the general impression ever remained, never the details. When Naomi said, "What was she wearing?" he would fumble for an intelligible answer, and it became a major item in their large storehouse of self-directed jokes. But where Chase was concerned, fashion was evasion, literally a cover-up, and so he forced himself to mentally download the details and store them; and in some cases, like now, as they made their way up the carpeted stairway to the third floor of Roiphe's house, he resorted to surreptitious technology in the form of his muted iPhone, recording her from behind when she wasn't looking.

Chase had acknowledged the banning of the doctor from her domain upstairs—"father issues," she said flatly—and had outlined the rules of engagement for Nathan: no photos up there, no note-taking or voice recording, no reports to Daddy. All those things might come later if she was comfortable with his presence after the first go-round. At the top of the stairway was a small landing overlooking the atrium formed by the spiraling staircase. It was gauzily lit by diffused daylight from the fussy art nouveau skylight above, and connected four doors, all of them closed and, he assumed, locked.

"Which door would you like me to open, Nathan?"

He had seen what was behind one of the doors—her bedroom—when Roiphe had taken him on his late-night excursion to Chase's tea party, but of course he was not going to mention it; in any case, he was not sure which door it was, so disorienting had that night been. "Maybe you should decide that," he said. "I'd just be guessing."

"Yes, I suppose I should shape the narrative for you." She turned to the door farthest left, pulled out a set of keys on a braided ring, and opened it. "I have a secret color code for these keys so I don't get confused. See these little stickers? Okay. Come on in."

Nathan followed her into a short room featuring a steeply sloped ceiling with a gabled dormer whose window looked out into the bristling, serrate leaves of a large chestnut tree that were showing the brown blotches of fungal blight, with crisping edges curled like the vegetable equivalent of Dupuytren's contracture. Chase flicked on the overhead gimbaled halogen lights and gestured towards the device sitting on the floor at the far end of the room. It looked something like a European clothes dryer, but one with a very high-tech powder-coated steel chassis bathed in violet LED mood light.

"Well, what do you think?"

"Your 3D printer?"

"The FabrikantBot 2. This is the very rare floor model. It's got a huge build volume. Most of them are desktop."

"Looks good. What do you fabricate with it?"

On a night table next to the FabrikantBot was a twenty-seven-inch iMac which Chase now woke from its cozy electronic slumber. Once she had typed in her password, a window snapped up which depicted a congenial green landscape with shadowed mountains, clouds, and blue sky in the distant background; various chunky control icons dotted the landscape's periphery. On the lawn-like foreground sat a mesh graphic of a cubic volume within which perched a stylized pink great horned owl. Chase kneeled before the computer and began to massage the wireless Magic Trackpad beside the keyboard. The owl responded by rotating in all directions with flawless three-dimensionality. "This is a file I downloaded from thingiverse.com. That's a communal website where you can find thousands of 3D modeling designs uploaded by the community, all for free—bicycles, engine models, anything. It's all STL files—I think that means stereo lithography, or something like that—and all the digital modeling programs understand those files. If I were to hit the Fabrik button here on the screen, the printer would start to make me this little owl."

"That would be great," said Nathan. "I'd love to see it in action."

Chase nudged her cursor up to the cardboard-carton Dropbox icon in her menu bar and opened the Dropbox folder. "Well, okay. I've got a new design waiting right here for me. It's something my friend in Paris has sent me. I don't know what it is. Let's see. It's an STL file, so I drag it into the virtual build space of the FabrikWare program so that

I can scale it up or down and play a bit with his design. Oh, gosh. I'm embarrassed!"

Gosh. The owl had disappeared, and there on the screen was an eccentric, unapologetically erect penis, presented in the same bland and cheery pink as the owl. Chase turned to Nathan, gray-green eyes vibrant, shining. "Are you okay with this, Nathan? Another man's sexual organ?"

He had somehow missed the radiant power of her eyes until just now; probably, he mused, a function of too much looking through a lens. "Pretty much okay, as long as I don't have to play with it." She laughed a conspiratorial laugh. "And who is this other man? I mean, is it just a CAD/CAM design fantasy or what? I mean, what I'm seeing is not normal."

"Oh, no. Hervé would never do that. He subscribes to the philosophy of the *cinema verité* filmmakers of the sixties." Nathan noted that she pronounced the French words in a risibly Anglicized way.

"They wanted to document reality in an authentic way, right? Even when they were making fiction films. But how does that equate here?"

"Hervé uses a handheld laser scanner on real objects in the real world—his version of the shoulder-mounted Eclair NPR camera all those *verité* guys used. Incredibly expensive, but he got an arts grant from the Ministry of Culture and he has some sketchy patrons. He doesn't design. He might combine, and so on, but the basis is always real-world scanning."

"So he scanned someone's penis with a laser scanner?"

"It's not dangerous if you know what you're doing. It's done for movies all the time—actors' faces get mapped onto the faces of stuntmen so that it looks like they're doing really dangerous stuff."

"Not sure someone would want that penis mapped onto their own."

Chase blushed. "It's Hervé's penis, of course. He's not shy about his condition, believe me. He's managed to turn it into quite a popular tourist attraction. It wouldn't curve that much if it weren't erect. I'm sure he had a friend help him with that part of it. Maybe one of his patrons."

"So now that it's on your computer, what are you going to do with it?"

Chase went back to the trackpad. "So you've dropped your file into this virtual build space, and then the interface gives you the tools to rotate it, like this, turn it around, scale it up or down. I think I'll make it bigger than it really is, just for fun. The software lets you know when you've exceeded the physical build volume in the machine, so you can't make that mistake. Then you get the software's slicing engine to julienne your virtual object before the machine creates the physical object, layer by layer. They used to call it 'rapid prototyping'—a very nice term."

"You know how big it really is? Your friend's penis?"

"Oh, I've seen it many times. Now watch." She hit the Fabrik button and the printer came to life, the print head beginning to surge back and forth with relentless energy on its steel rails. "You see this roll of pink filament back here, on this spool attached to the chassis, looks a bit like a big fishing reel? It could be any color, but I happen to have this intense pink. It's made of PLA, polylactic acid, it's a renewable bioplastic. So the print head pulls this filament spooled in the back up through this clear tube here, see? It's pulled up into the extruder, which heats it up and squirts it out through a macro hole onto the build platform, which, as you can barely see, is slowly descending as the model is printed out layer by layer. You can find tons of videos on YouTube of stuff being printed with speeded-up motion. It's mesmerizing. Really a lot of fun. The platform sinks down like an elevator and the object kind of mushrooms up on top of it. This thing is probably going to take two hours to build, it's got so much detail."

The print head had already laid down a pink disc—rather small and plaintive on the substantial translucent build platform—which represented a slice through the root of Hervé Blomqvist's penis. Mesmerizing enough, but Nathan was primarily mesmerized by Chase, who had snapped compellingly into focus the moment she engaged him through the lens of the FabrikantBot 2. She was displaying an unexpected geeky passion that was even deeper than Naomi's, and for Nathan that was pure, dangerous sex.

"And what exactly is the condition that your friend … Hervé …?"

"Yes, Hervé Blomqvist. We were students in Paris together."

"Does he expect you to actually do something with that? The thing he sent?"

"Oh, he knows that I will, and he probably has a good idea what that'll be."

Nathan could only imagine her using the emerging device as an oversized dildo, and immediately got an erection that fused unpleasantly with the image on the computer. "What's the condition that makes his penis take that extreme bend halfway down its shaft?"

"Three French doctors," she said.

"What?"

"Hervé said he was plagued by three French doctors: Dr. Peyronie—that's what the penis has; Dr. Dupuytren—contracture of the tendons and then the fingers so your hand goes like this"—Chase made a claw with her left hand—"and that often goes along with Peyronie's; and Dr. Raynaud—his feet sometimes go purple from lack of blood circulation whenever it gets even just a tiny bit cold. Three French doctors. Sounds like a nursery rhyme, doesn't it?"

"You seem to know this guy fairly intimately."

"We were a very tight group there, at the Sorbonne. It was exciting." *Sorbonne* pronounced the way a Midwesterner who had never heard of French might have pronounced it, with the accent on the first syllable: *sorbn.* Nathan wondered if she would gradually evolve an elaborate meta-language which would annihilate any trace of French in her speech and thinking, the way *le schizo* Wolfson had done in transforming English into a compound of Hebrew, French, German, and Russian. It was, in a way, the inverse of

Samuel Beckett writing some of his works in French in order to get away from his mother tongue and thus force himself to write, he said, with greater clarity and economy.

The printer was shuttling back and forth, laying down its strata of PLA on the build platform, which ratcheted lower and lower as the object, the renewable bioplastic penis, grew up like a stalagmite in a cave. It worked with measured enthusiasm, without irony, happy to be creating an extruded twisted erect penis, happy to be creating anything at all. Nathan felt weird to be identifying with the FabrikantBot, but he was. He could understand that feeling of being happy to create anything at all, to just be creative, and it suffused his trepidation about his Roiphe project, the phantom book called *Consumed*, which he thought maybe the FabrikantBot could print out for him. Why not? Renewable organic plastic books by the thousands.

"I would love to do the veins in blue or purple, and just the head in pink or red, but this version of FabrikantBot only does one color at a time, and you can't combine them in one object. I've been doing a lot of painting, but it would be great to not have to. I'm trying to get my father to spring for the next iteration, but he's resisting. The RepliKator 3 has dual heads and uses a hot build platform and I think you have the option of using ABS plastic and it's more expensive. But it's not just the money. He wants me to show him what I've been doing, and I don't want to."

"Well, he probably wouldn't want to see Hervé's penis, although we know he's seen plenty of them before. Maybe just not in this context."

"Oh, but Hervé doesn't just send me penises."

They left the FabrikantBot contentedly chugging away and stepped out onto the landing. Chase locked the door, then turned to the adjacent door. "That one's my bedroom, and the next one is my bathroom, and that one"—she turned to the facing door—"the one we're going to look at, is my art room."

Chase flicked on the lights in a room that was a mirror image of the printing room, although this one's dormer window was shuttered. There were two rough wooden trestle tables: a very long one the size of a picnic table, and a shorter, square table crowded with cans and tubes of paint, brushes, strips of cloth, rectangular plastic palettes with lids, painting knives, jars of water.

"See, there, I told you about the painting. You can paint directly on PLA with acrylic paint. You can sand it first too, if you want to create different textures. It would be perfect if I had a sink in here, you sometimes need water, but the bathroom's right next door. It's kinda messy right now."

Chase turned away from the paints and stepped over to the big table, on which rested many large, lumpy objects covered by a bed-sized canvas sheet. Standing before it, she paused and took a deep breath—with odd reverence, thought Nathan—then leaned over and began to carefully fold back the sheet. Now gradually exposed were the thermoplastically replicated body parts of a mutilated and dismembered female human, distributed in no discernible order. They were painted crudely, but convincingly enough to induce revulsion in Nathan, reminding him of a horrifying butcher shop he had once come across in a small town in Spain. A single hacked-off breast, chunks of thigh and calf, fingers separated from one hand, a torso split into quarters, a startled head cut open and splayed with swollen tongue protruding. Almost every square inch of observable skin surface had been gouged, as though savaged by the mouths of a large school of piranhas, and each gouge had been lovingly detailed with necrotically dark-red acrylic paint.

"Hervé sent me these, piece by piece," she said, tossing the neat bundle of the sheet under the table. "I've arranged them and finessed them with paint." She turned to Nathan and leaned back against the edge of the table, hands behind her. "You know, I wanted to call this work *Consumed*, but my father beat me to it. Unless you can convince him to give your book another title."

Nathan recognized the tortured body parts from the photos that Naomi had directed him to. In the aggregate, they were Célestine Arosteguy.

"YOU ACTUALLY DID IT, THEN. You cut off your wife's breast with her consent." Naomi was thinking journalistically and legalistically; it was an astringent approach she had to take in order to keep her balance in the thick liquid night of the late Tokyo summer. They were outside in the drab, desperate garden because the house had become too hot, too sultry, too intimate and airless. She was sitting on a lichen-stained concrete replica of a hand-cut stone bench pushed back against the far wall. The heavy-lidded orange lights built into that wall splashed her face with a medicinal glow like a disinfectant, sculpting her with deep, flushed shadows. Arosteguy paced around the garden in front of her, occasionally kicking at some piece of household garbage obscured by the darkness that rippled in cross-currents before him.

"You know, a colleague of mine—I won't tell you who it was because you would look him up—we were at a strange karaoke event, in Paris, not here, and I was forced by circumstance to sing the song "Je t'aime … moi non plus" like Serge Gainsbourg, with the colleague singing the Jane Birkin part in falsetto. I only did it as an homage to Salvador Dalí, who is quoted in the song's title referring to Picasso's communism. Gainsbourg had asked Birkin to sing it so that she sounded like a little boy, and my colleague did that too, with no apparent effort. It was a moment of revelation about him that I could have lived without. And after that kitsch moment of bonding he told me that he had a savage dream, and the dream was that in a moment of passion he would cut a woman's breast off. He was actively looking for a woman who would agree to let him do it for money, and also a doctor to guide him. He was a very fastidious and scrupulous man. I don't know if he ever realized his desire."

"Is that how it felt to you? Was it sexy? Was it passionate?"

"I enacted surgery. I committed surgery. And Célestine was right, as always. I wanted to keep the breast, preserve it somehow, take it to the taxidermy shop on Rue du Bac, something, even if grotesque. I couldn't let it go. I really did feel that she was diminished by its loss, but even more selfishly, that *we* were diminished, our life together, our sexuality. I can't imagine the complexity if we had had children that she had breastfed. And I said these things to her, but she wouldn't let me keep it, and Molnár was on her side—for psychological reasons, he said, as well as health, as well as legal. Imagine being stopped on the train back to Paris ... But for her it was simple: destroy it and everything inside it, like a wasp nest you've pulled down from the eaves with a fishing net and stuffed into a garbage bag. Burn it and the winged adults and the white grub larvae and the eggs. Burn it."

Naomi had no doubt that Arosteguy was lying about everything (well, perhaps not some of the details of their personal life and habits), that his confession was a novel, an art project, and that he was making her his collaborator in its shaping and its dissemination. But this did not dishearten her or even challenge her sense of journalistic integrity, which, to be truthful, was always only a theoretical thing, a professional playing card, secondary to entertainment and the continuance of work, or even tertiary, with her own creative fulfillment, never spoken of, a surprising first place. If the lie was complex and enthralling—and it was, it was—then there might be a book in it, with the ever-present desire to dig for the chimeric truth driving it on, providing the suspense, and no need ever to certify that truth. She could lead her readers to wonder if the photos of Célestine's body parts would reveal the presence of *two* severed breasts, thus refuting the mastectomy tale she was being told. She could press the prefect of police, M. Vernier, for this information without explaining its importance to him. She could try to examine the torso herself, the actual torso—this was an exciting thought; but had it been preserved as evidence or had it already been buried or cremated?—to see if the left breast had been surgically removed, stitched and healed, rather than brutally hacked off. The photos she had seen only revealed the torso's left side, and a shadow obscured the wound. Was this deliberate on the part of the police? Were they even police photos? Had Arosteguy posted them himself?

"But didn't you enjoy it, the cutting?" she said. "On some level? Now that I know you . . ."

"You would like to inhabit my body as I approach Célestine lying on the table, inhabit me as in those sci-fi movies where a warrior climbs into a giant robot nine stories high and operates its immense arms and legs from inside the robot's glass head."

"Yes. Exactly like that." Of course she was recording, and of course he knew it. The Nagra sat on the faux-stone beside her, blinking happily. He wouldn't perform without a recording now, she was certain, like a poet working in the oral tradition who had been contaminated by the advent of the recording device and so insisted that all improvisations be saved for posterity.

"All right, then. I approach her body, and it is her *body,* because her face is hidden in a sterile cloth tent erected around her head. And it is not exactly Célestine, because her color is wrong, she's blue and green, and so in a sense is not alive, not sensible." The French often got that last word wrong in English, Naomi observed; in French it meant sensitive, responsive, sentient. "And her smell is wrong, a harsh disinfectant smell. And I swear to you, her breast is outlined and bisected with dotted purple Magic Marker dashes—cut here!—like some terrible nightmarish cartoon, a large teardrop shape with the nipple in its center.

"Molnár is hovering over my right shoulder, my scalpel side, whispering to me, his prize pupil, urging me on, sensing my reluctance and fear, but also sensing—you will not be surprised to hear—that I have an erection, and I am suddenly flooded by the emotions of my karaoke colleague, as though his words of that night have swarmed my brain and have become my words, my thoughts, and now I am about to fulfill both our dreams by cutting off the breast of my wife.

"I am about to make the first cut. Molnár has cautioned me not to think in terms of perfection, of making the perfect cut, because that leads to paralysis; it's impossible with flesh in any case. 'Look at that footage of Picasso making his drawings: no hesitation,' he says. In a sense, no thought at all, just pure instinct and a desire for the reality of the drawn line, whatever it happened to end up being, a certainty that it would be right. But still I tremble when I first sink into her breast the hot needle of that terrible electronic scalpel, with its disposable blade for disposable flesh."

Arosteguy had been pacing constantly as he spoke, and so now, when he suddenly stopped, it had the impact of a gunshot. "It's too banal," he said.

"What is?"

"This voice-over description. This talking-head interview."

"Oh, no! What do we do?"

"I need you to bare your breast and then I reenact it. We collaborate. How great for your article or even a book. How dangerous I am. How brave you are. How perverse and yet somehow sweet."

"But can't people see us here?"

"We're *gaijin*. They don't care what we do to each other, or even what Japanese citizens do to us. Remember Sagawa? And many other crimes against *gaijin*? Not worth worrying about. And sex surgery? This is Japan, my darling." Arosteguy had been fumbling around in the pockets of his corduroys and now produced a short, thick, Japanese Magic Marker with a very thin tip, which he brandished like a cigar. "We will play doctor. You will be Célestine, the willing, excited patient. I will direct your performance. I will play two roles: the somewhat reprehensible but roguishly charming surgeon, Dr. Zoltán Molnár; and then the entirely reprehensible and ponderously unappealing French *philosophe*, Aristide Arosteguy. I will direct my own performance but will entertain any suggestions offered by my co-star regarding stagecraft. And we will cover the entire process of breast removal as far as I remember it." The effect of their communal drinking was beginning to manifest itself in his slurred pronunciation and the general mistiming of his mouth and his body. Naomi had been matching him drink for drink—sake and then beer—primarily to keep his narrative rhythm from faltering, but she now regretted it, certain that her own timing must be deranged even though she couldn't gauge it—a bad sign for her.

As she began to unzip her fleece hoodie, Naomi felt doubly whorish: she was going to expose her breasts in a Tokyo backyard; and she was doing it knowing that it was only for the article, for the book, for the perversity of the narrative and the commercial value of her Arosteguy project, taking it so far off the rails that it was probably irresistible to any publisher, paper or electronic. The feeling did not daunt her; she was enjoying the transgressive whorishness of it in the most childish way. A huge advertising blimp floated into view overhead, its flanks lit up by an animated slideshow featuring a line of Finnish fitness equipment. Naomi watched dreamily as a miniature collapsible treadmill, suitable for modest apartments, was demonstrated, and imagined Célestine and Ari treading side by side in Paris. As though induced by her fantasy, Arosteguy took two resolute steps towards Naomi, fell to his knees at her feet (groaning slightly as the bursitis swelling the tip of his right knee expressed itself), laid the Magic Marker on the bench, and took her hands in his before she had managed to completely unzip. "Let me unbox you," he said.

"Do what?"

"You know, those unboxing videos you see everywhere on YouTube. They are the epitome of consumerist fetishism. I love them. You watch as an anonymous Vietnamese teenager lovingly opens the box he has just received which contains ... One of those, possibly." Arosteguy flicked his fingers towards the Nagra. "He is in ecstasy—we can ascertain this only from his voice and his boyish hands with the edgily bitten fingernails, the camera never wandering from the box and its contents—but he is a master of delayed gratification, as are his thousands of viewers. He will slit the tape holding the box shut with a special box-cutting knife. He will first take out the smallest inner box containing the charger and charging cords and the instruction manuals in several languages. He will fastidiously cut open the tiny heat-sealed plastic baggies holding the battery and the earphones and the adapters. And then finally, with a tremulous flourish, he will lift out the bubble-wrapped object of desire itself, the electronic device, saying, with feigned nonchalance, in lightly accented English, which is the language of consumerism, 'And, well, okay, so here it is ...'"

So here it was: Naomi's left breast, unwrapped with a tremulous flourish by Arosteguy, though not without some difficulty, because she was by happenstance wearing her white compression sports bra—she had thought she might find time to go jogging around the neighborhood—and the sports bra's slender metal front clasp had, with the familiar innate maliciousness of small mechanical things, seized, forcing Naomi to twist it open for him before allowing him to complete her unboxing. She was traveling with only two bras this time around, and she would have preferred to be wearing the lacy black Victoria's Secret underwire with removable straps, but the whole procedure seemed to be occurring on an intellectual level, and he didn't seem put off by the white bra's unsexiness.

She sat braless, hoodieless, and mysteriously comfortable, her hands spread and resting palms up on the bench as Arosteguy dangled the bra from a finger, letting it rotate gently in the provocative light of the garden like an unexpected flounder. "Afterwards, we fitted Célestine with a special mastectomy bra. It had a pocket on the left side for a prosthetic breast. It was called Amoena, I think, a very beautiful, classical name. Actually two pockets, as though it were waiting for her to lose the other breast. The breast form called Energy Light, Size 4, seemed to match her remaining breast perfectly, though the missing one had been larger. All a question of balance and symmetry and weight and social acceptance. The inside of the prosthetic had a transparent bubbly surface, like bubble wrap, to allow breathing, but it still got hot and sweaty, though there was the promise of a NASA-developed material which could maintain normal breast temperature. The outside was flesh-colored and had a not very enthusiastic nipple at the tip, and its consistency was remarkably malleable and lifelike, though too homogeneous in feel to be a real breast. She wore it twice, I think, and then abandoned it. I used to find it perched on a bottle of liquid paracetamol in our laundry closet next to the washing machine, like a conical Chinese hat. In fact she stopped wearing bras altogether, and made a fetish of wearing tight sweaters and T-shirts that emphasized her amputation, saying that as a child she had a cat with one ear, and now she was one herself."

"I don't think I could be so brave."

"You can't know how you would react, which is why we must reenact. We shall become reenactors, like those guys who refight the Battle of Waterloo with those old muskets, with their anachronistic little blue earplugs securely in place." Arosteguy began to manipulate her left breast in a dispassionate, utilitarian manner, lifting it with three fingers like a baker appraising a nascent pastry, pinching it gently above and below the nipple, then folding it to demonstrate where the scar would end up being. His face was very close to her, and she could feel his breath on her skin, hot from his mouth, slightly cooler from his nose. She gave herself over to the sense that she was channeling Célestine, that part of her body was not her and could easily be parted with; she found that thrilling. "Tina was completely awake and alert, and sitting, as you are now, when Molnár marked up her breast. I would be speaking Hungarian to you now if I could, as Molnár spoke to his staff members over his shoulder, in order to produce the authenticity and strange clinical magic of that moment. He told them to give me an Ativan, because I started to wilt, to faint like a small girl; I could not allay the anxiety that washed over me. The Ativan was very subtle and effective; I could feel everything except the anxiety. Célestine, on the other hand, was calm and solicitous; she smiled and petted me and pitied me as the great doctor began to draw a child's treasure map on her breast. Like this." The tip of the pen felt hot—Naomi was sure that it was the thought of the electrocautery needle that made it feel that way—as Arosteguy tracked out with confident dashes a large teardrop shape with its point near her armpit and its body angled towards her sternum, encircling her nipple. He then marked a line from end to end through the nipple. "This is the line of the scar."

"The nipple would be gone?"

"There was discussion about sparing the nipple and also a possible reconstruction of the breast. Molnár launched into a very pompous meditation on the social significance of the breast and lactation, and on the evolutionary innovation that the mammal represented. Tina just laughed and said that she was intrigued by becoming half a boy, and that she would only be interested in a boy's nipple for that side, not a woman's. The doctor talked to her about the difficulty of imbalance. She said that it would be a duality, not an imbalance, and that she looked forward to it."

Arosteguy drew back, marker in hand, to study his work. Naomi looked down and lifted her breast with her left hand to share the study. "It makes me think of those teardrop tattoos that prisoners have on their cheeks," she said.

"I had a student with one of those. It was disturbing to look at. He often covered it with makeup."

"It usually means that they've killed someone." Arosteguy pondered this in silence; she had the impression that he hadn't understood the import of the tattoos, and so some meanings and understandings were consequently shifting in his head; she could almost feel the blocks rearranging themselves, and thought of Tetris, her favorite childhood computer game. "I'm sure you could get someone here in Tokyo to give you one," she added thoughtfully. "I would go with you and document it."

He tilted his head up to face her again and laughed an openmouthed laugh. "Perhaps I'll need two of them. Are you ready for me to cut you?"

IF ONLY SHE HAD BEEN able to trust Yukie. Naomi scrolled through the photos that Arosteguy had taken of her lying on the concrete bench in the garden, her eyes closed and mouth open in mock anesthesia, her marked-up breast looking pleasingly full, its nipple erect (would Célestine's have been erect at the moment of cutting, pleading in its own way to be spared, or would it have retracted in fear, her bravado caving at the last moment?), her arms pressed against her sides so that they would not flop down from the narrow bench, her right breast demurely covered by her hoodie. But the badly focused, awkwardly framed images reminded her that handling a camera was not an innate human capability, and that even under the duress of alcohol and sexual weirdness, the media-savvy Yukie would have produced sharp, well-composed photos that she could use to accompany her long piece or book. They would have said so much about Naomi's approach to the latest flavor of parajournalism, which involved an artistic collaboration between subject and journalist and by its own definition was self-limiting to very rare pairings of the same. It had occurred to her that the ultimate expression of Tom Wolfe's "saturation reporting" was possibly at hand: the copycat murder of the journalist, with the murderer finishing the piece and filing it, complete with photographs and videos. She remembered studying the concept of parajournalism at Ryerson University in Toronto, journalism that mixed the factual with the invented without attribution; but in her work with Ari, as she was beginning to think of it, the fiction, the creative invention, was all his, and since he was her subject, his fiction was admissible.

Yukie's photos would have been better technically, there was no doubt, but her presence would have completely altered the biochemistry of the project. And on closer scrutiny, she saw that Ari's photos were expressive of something thrilling and terrifying: Naomi's merging, in Ari's mind, with Célestine. Of course, she looked nothing like his Tina, but in the intensity and macrophagic voyeurism that was evident in his shooting of her, Naomi felt a desperate attempt to re-create his lost wife. He had begged her for the macro lens so that he could get close, the lens she had borrowed from Nathan and still kept—undoubtedly for this moment—and he consumed her body with that lens (the awkwardly named Micro-Nikkor 105mm f/2.8G IF-ED), and it was that lens that became his electrocautery needle. While shooting her, he had told Naomi that he had been able to smell Tina's flesh burning as he cut her, that Molnár—spreading her breast open with a pair of stainless-steel rake retractors to provide a clear target—had told him to avoid breathing in what he called surgical smoke, because it was toxic. He had not recorded his surgical escapade in any way other than mentally but remembered acutely the Bovie knife, named after its inventor William Bovie, and he kept thinking of the Bowie knife, the huge, cleaver-like fighting knife named after Jim Bowie of Alamo fame. The trim cautery itself seemed innocuous, the flat-bladed metal tip, like a small screwdriver, fitted into its yellow housing, the playful blue plastic handle, yellow power button, blue power cord. It had emitted surprising little lightning flashes as it cut, like a miniature welding torch flickering inside the translucent tent of skin created by the rakes, the layers of breast tissue vaporizing into white smoke with no more than a whisper. "Her breast tissue looked like yellow custard. I felt like Sagawa even thinking such a thing."

"And when you opened it up, did you find a bagful of insects?"

"Of course not," Arosteguy had said. "Of course not. But afterwards, in recovery, Célestine was so happy, so satisfied, that the question was never asked, and the answer was never offered."

After he cut her up with the camera, Arosteguy seemed to fall into a reverie, or perhaps a near stupor—he certainly outstripped her in drinking—and Naomi tried to bring him out of his elusive state by offering to draw one or two teardrops on his cheek, engaging him in a discussion about whether the teardrops should be filled in—indicating murder—or just outlined and empty—indicating attempted murder. It was an oblique lead-in to what she wanted to be a straightforward discussion of how Célestine went from being a euphorically happy mono-breasted apotemno-philiac to a mutilated corpse, but after accepting two solid teardrops—no explanation for the two murders they agreed they represented—which she drew on his damp right cheek in purple marker, he slumped and swooned, and she put him to bed like a child (he insisted it be her bed), after helping him stagger and lurch up the narrow staircase, feeling the full weight and heat and sweat of him.

In the morning, she realized that she must have fallen asleep beside him on the bed. Her laptop was still open and on the floor where she had been sitting last night, back against the bed, feet jammed against the wall, scrolling through his photos of Naomi performing Célestine on the operating table. Lying in bed, she had dreamed that she was Célestine, Tina being cut up, but not on the operating table. She was in the famous Paris apartment of the Arosteguys, and she was on an uncomfortably small marble slab being carved and eaten by a photorealistic Ari, a solicitous and appreciative one, who commented on and savored every morsel of her while she herself encouraged him in his efforts to disjoint her and, of course, to sever her breasts, and then finally her head, which never stopped being aware and never stopped smiling fondly, even when he began to eat her lips. When she rolled over towards the sleeping Arosteguy, so strong was the half-life of the dream that she worried that her head would fall off and bump off his shoulder and onto the floor like a soccer ball. But he was no longer in the bed. As she walked the few steps towards the bathroom, she felt as though she were floating on the forceful tide of oblivion which her dream had generated deep in the waters of unconsciousness, and in this floating, which was a cathartic and liberating sensation, she felt closer to Arosteguy, from whom it must have emanated, so strongly did his desire for obliteration radiate even in the most mundane moments. Jammed behind the sink's Hot faucet she found a crumpled piece of Cute-brand facial tissue streaked with watery purple, and she assumed that he had wiped away his two tears. Had the tears represented Célestine and, figuratively, Naomi, and had he now absolved himself of those two murders?

He was not downstairs. The house was empty except for her. Three days later, it still was.

THE FRANTIC BANGING at the front doors terrified Naomi, who cowered for some minutes in Arosteguy's bedroom before daring to creep down the stairs, flinching at every repetition of what she felt was a focused assault on her solitude. She was experiencing the odd doubling in memory of her own arrival at those doors, only now she was playing the role of the reclusive, neurotic *philosophe*—she felt haggard and unshaven, and her unwashed hair felt Arosteguy gray to her—and the unknown at the door was playing, unwittingly, the newly arrived Naomi. Her three days of burrowing into the life of Ari as incarnated by his house and everything in it was no doubt partially responsible for this shift in identities, but there was a willfulness about it on her part as well. She had not yet washed off the surgical guidelines on her breast the way Ari had washed off the murderer's tattoos she had so lovingly applied to his cheek. (That had seemed callous to her, and even a rejection.) She had not changed her clothes from her garden surgery outfit; she had not left the house to forage for food; and, pathologically, she had not browsed the net, or even opened her laptop or turned on her tablet. She had not felt any sense of violation of Ari's privacy when she went through every drawer and shelf and cupboard and cabinet in the house precisely because he had abandoned himself by leaving without a word and not returning, abandoned Arosteguy-in-his-Tokyo-house the way a hermit crab casts off its borrowed shell when it has outgrown it. Naomi gratefully crawled inside that shell and became its new tenant, a female Arosteguy, who was close to Célestine, but was not Célestine.

She had not been downstairs since it had gotten dark. When she switched on the same pallid, watery lights that had greeted her on her first arrival at the house, that sense of Naomi-at-the-door was heightened to the point that, on sliding the doors open, she expected to see herself. To her confusion, she did recognize the woman at the door, a woman in a crisp open-collared navy business suit who was teary-eyed and obviously emotionally stricken, and Naomi could not understand how that could be. The woman stared at Naomi, her fist frozen in mid-knock, her mouth slack with disappointment and shock at what she was seeing—namely, Naomi. *"Qui êtes-vous?"* she said, with an absurd, barely contained outrage.

"I'm Naomi. Who are you?"

The woman lowered her threatening fist in slow motion, seemingly unaware of its independent life. "Where is Ari? Does Ari live here? Does he live here with you?" The English into which she slipped in response to Naomi was confident, overly forceful, and shaped by a hybrid French-German accent.

"This is the house of Aristide Arosteguy. He is not here now. What is your name, please?"

"I'm a friend. I was waiting for him and he did not come to me ..." Unexpectedly, she began to sob, and as her thin face crumpled and she turned away from Naomi in shame, thus exposing a comically protruding ear, Naomi realized that she was Arosteguy's—and Romme Vertegaal's—audiologist, Elke Jungebluth.

Once inside, sitting in the larval beanbag chair with a hot tea in her hand, Elke dealt crisply with her various errant fluids—the tears, the snot—using the Cute tissues Naomi had brought her from the bathroom. "It took me some time to connect with Professor Matsuda at Todai. This was the contact that Ari had given me. He did not want me to know his address directly. To protect me, he said. I am a French citizen, and his is a scandalous criminal case. And so on. But it was understood that I would come to Tokyo to meet with certain technicians of the Democratic People's Republic of Korea. I am an audiologist. Some of our hearing instruments are of North Korean origin. Perhaps Ari mentioned to you that he wears them?"

"He told me that they were German. Siemens, I think."

A rueful smile from Elke. "They were what you would normally call Chinese knockoffs, except they weren't Chinese. They were North Korean, and not just imitations, but of special North Korean design. It is true that they were stamped with Siemens markings, but it was in the nature of camouflage rather than commercial deception. We have a French electronics manufacturer standing by, very eager to get into the audiology market. The brand name will probably be Eternal President's Voice." A secret inner smile. "I have ambitions beyond my immediate métier, as you might have guessed. And so Ari had agreed to test them for us before we dared to expose them to the Western markets, and we arranged for him to report to me at my hotel here." A catch in her voice. "But he never came. We texted, he was on his way, and he never reached me. I brought my mobile audiology station with me. We were going to finesse the software before my engineering contacts returned to Pyongyang. It's a big problem for me now. I'm not really prepared to deal with the North Koreans without Ari's feedback. They can be very harsh in the face of disappointment. Are you Ari's new girlfriend? You seem to be an American."

"I was born in Canada. I have dual citizenship." Naomi was not sure why she thought this was an appropriate response, but there was something in the references to France, Germany, and North Korea that tasted of passports. She peripherally wondered if Canada had any sort of diplomatic relations with North Korea that France or the US did not. She might have to open up her Air and hit the net again, though it had been liberating to pretend the net didn't exist for the last three days. "I'm a journalist. I'm covering the Arosteguys' story for some magazines. I was surprised too when he didn't show up." This last deliberately ambiguous. She knew that her own bedraggled appearance belied her objectivity re Ari; she and Elke were quite a pair.

"Elke, did your North Korean colleagues know about Ari? That he was acting as a test subject for you?"

"Of course. It was his standing in the international community that made it interesting for them. That he would turn to North Korea for technology of such a personal nature. The emotion of hearing, of communication, of speech and language. Perhaps you've come across some of Ari's children's philosophy books? They're all wonderfully illustrated by Célestine. So charming and wistful. They say that Kim Jong Un was given some of them to read as a child of ten years and absorbed them immediately, and that's why the Arosteguys have such status in the DPRK. They are seen as being fervently anticapitalist and anti-consumerism. It's possible, of course, that they have been somewhat misunderstood." A wry pause followed, during which Naomi was able to flagellate herself for having read only the three Arosteguy airport primers, which probably left her as advanced in

Arosteguyan political philosophy as the then ten-year-old inheritor of the Kim dynasty. "And there was a personal element involved as well."

"Romme Vertegaal," suggested Naomi.

It was not that her eyes were of different sizes, as Ari had described them, but that they were not aligned properly in her face, the left being substantially higher up than the right, giving her a permanently quizzical look, as though skeptically raising an eyebrow; and now that she *was* raising an eyebrow, the net effect was indeed comical, but also somewhat disturbing, smacking as it did of insanity and deformity. "I see that Ari has taken you deeply into his confidence," said Elke, sweeping her hair back with both hands and plumping it up a bit at the back.

"He was anxious that I should have enough information to write ... intelligently."

"Well, some of that information is not for public consumption."

"Like Program Vertegaal?"

"Yes, like that. It has some dangerous edges to it—commercially, politically, neurologically, and, as Ari pointed out repeatedly, philosophically."

"Elke, did your North Koreans, did Romme himself, know that you were to meet Ari at your hotel? Did they know when?"

"What are you suggesting?"

"Was Ari planning to go to Pyongyang himself? Perhaps with you?"

Elke dropped her gaze and blushed. At that moment, it was obvious that at some point Elke and Ari had been lovers, his humorous description of her homeliness notwithstanding. "Not originally, no. But I did hear from Professor Matsuda that the Japanese government was thinking of deporting him, returning him to France—there is apparently a gray area or two in the treaties between France and Japan. And of course Ari is not a Japanese national. I imagine he might have been forced to consider going beyond Japan to North Korea."

"He would have told you, wouldn't he? He would have taken you with him."

"I would have loved that, of course. But somebody had to stay in Paris to coordinate. And truly, there are enough of us in North Korea."

"Enough? Who is there?"

"Romme, of course. And then there is Célestine Arosteguy."

"In Pyongyang? Right now?"

"Yes."

"How can that be? Célestine is dead."

"No, she's not. She is with Romme in Pyongyang. I Skyped with her this morning—she has a special internet connection that is only allowed for certain foreign celebrities. Closely monitored, of course. Her hair was cut in Approved Hairstyle Number 3, very short and tight." Elke made emphatic chopping hand motions along her jaw to illustrate the cut, one of eighteen government-approved for women in the DPRK. "She looked very different, but adorable. Just adorable." A pause with a faraway smile while she visualized Célestine's new North Korean look, and a small shake of the head in wonderment over the infinite adaptability of this superb woman. Elke returned her gaze to Naomi, smile fading rapidly. "She didn't mention to me that she expected Ari to join her."

"But there is a criminal homicide investigation going on in Paris regarding her murder, her dismemberment. There are photos."

"This is something orchestrated by Romme for Kim Jong Un. It is a virtual murder. Don't ask me how it was done, but it's a Vertegaal specialty. He would have had particular, shall we say technical, help from Paris."

"What kind of help?"

"There was a brilliant student of the Arosteguys who became very enamored of Romme. And he is a wizard."

"Hervé Blomqvist."

Elke laughed a resigned laugh.

"Hervé, yes. So the French would rather have Célestine be dead than to think that she has, in a cultural, non-technical sense, defected to North Korea. It's entirely possible that they know the truth and have decided to accept the cover-up presented to them: she is just dead, murdered by her husband, who has also proven to be a traitor to France—again, in a cultural sense, which is to the French a betrayal worse than political betrayal. I would not be surprised to read that Ari was kidnapped by North Korean agents and bundled off to Pyongyang to help the new young dictator polish his special North Korean philosophical social policy. It would be the kind of subversive fiction generated by the French to offset Ari's genuine desire to cast off his old, deeply French life for a new, vibrant Asian one. But what a ménage they will be up there, if that's in fact where he's gone. The three of them." Elke would obviously have loved to make it four of them.

"Could that have been what happened? The kidnapping of Ari? On his way to meet you. And they were waiting for him?"

"They probably could have just talked him into it. If Matsuda knew about the possible deportation, they did too. Maybe that was enough."

"But if Célestine is alive as you say, then Ari has committed no crime. He could go back to France an innocent man."

"There was more involved in that investigation than just the supposed murder of Madame Arosteguy. Many crypts were broken open. He did not want to go back."

"Sex with students? Is that what you mean?"

"An approved learning tool for three thousand years, now considered an atrocity."

Naomi had found all of Arosteguy's electronic paraphernalia strewn around the house, including some thumb drives and SD cards that she had not had the heart to explore, and this suggested that he had expected to return to the house. He had left three European phones as well, including an ancient Nokia and a prehistoric two-toned Sagem, all of them chipped, dented, scraped, scratched, and generally disheveled, in keeping with the personal esthetic of their owner; you could feel them falling out of various pockets onto various hard and wet surfaces just looking at them, and she felt a pang of separation at the thought. He must, she concluded, have taken his pink Japanese LG DoCoMo flip phone with him. She decided that she could not trust Elke with the possibility of accessing Ari's electronics.

"Elke, did you happen to record that Skyped conversation with Célestine? I'm surprised she left herself that vulnerable. And did she not care that people thought she was dead? Or was she even aware of that? If it were ever posted on YouTube ..."

Elke stood up. "You have been very kind to me. I shall try to connect again with my DPRK technical affiliates, who seem to have disappeared along with Monsieur Arosteguy. If this continues, I shall return to Paris to lick my various wounds. I'm sure you understand." And she stepped around the low table, bent down, and kissed Naomi on both cheeks. She smelled of sour caked makeup and anisette.

Once Elke had left, Naomi rumbled the house again from top to bottom, only this time it was not an expression of longing and abandonment, but a focused hunt for hard and possibly hidden information. She assembled all devices that could be considered information-bearing entities on the living room table, and she included her own arsenal of electronics just in case she needed to remind herself of critical words that Arosteguy had spoken which only now would reveal their true import. The appearance of the real Elke, who was absolutely as described by Ari during his long "confession," which Naomi had comfortably, even happily, taken for lies, or at the very least, artful delusion, had snapped things into focus like a phase-detect DSLR camera.

The programming of the hearing aids, the connections with North Korea, all the most hallucinatory, paranoid imaginings, were real, and the consequences for her proposed article, now obviously needing to be a book, were that she was miles further from the totality of the story than she had ever thought. Could she go to Pyongyang herself as more than just a tourist under the strictly controlled jurisdiction of the state-owned Korea International Travel Company? She understood that journalists, particularly of the North American variety, were rarely granted visas. Would Romme Vertegaal give her an interview by Skype or, much preferably, travel to meet her somewhere? Would this put her in danger? And was Célestine really alive and in the capital of the Hermit Kingdom? Could Elke's Skype event with Célestine have been faked? It would be easy to create a monologue for a virtual Célestine, animating the many images and voice recordings that she had trailed behind her over the years; or, given the stutterings and audio glitches expected when Skyping at such distances, adroit operators could create the semblance of a conversation, of specific responses to comments or questions. It would be a nuclear event if Naomi could track and confirm Célestine's fate. Or was Elke just lying? Perhaps Naomi would pick up the thread of her nascent Elke relationship once she was back in Paris.

And then finally she found the coffin-shaped red plastic 64 GB Verbatim thumb drive wrapped in plastic film and sunken clumsily into the greasy cream contents of a white jar marked, in English, "Kanebo Moistage W-Cold"—it seemed to be an olive-oil-based cold cream, though Ari's blotched and pebbly facial skin belied any use of such a balm—and the growing heap of electronica became irrelevant except for the MacBook Air, which she would use to scour the drive's contents. She thumbed the slider to extend the USB connector and slipped it into the Air's left-side USB port. It would be two more days before she found herself scrolling through images depicting the dismemberment and cannibalization of Célestine Arosteguy.

12

THE FEAR MADE NAOMI feel closer to Ari, almost to the point of a destabilizing fusion. As her own fear of kidnapping by DPRK agents amplified (they would probably pose as entomologists or audiologists), she was certain that she was picking up that vibe from Arosteguy himself, and that he in turn picked up hers. This fusion, however, proved to have its own usefulness. Once she had found the Verbatim drive and discovered that it was encrypted, she felt she had to *become* Arosteguy to stumble upon the drive's password. She spent the two days after Elke left crawling nanoscopically through Arosteguy's electronics, none of which had even the simplest password to protect it. She combed through his Contacts app, his email, his desktop littered with disparate thumbnails of photos (some in 3D, though she never found the necessary 3D glasses), folders, magazines, technical PDFs, user manuals. She trolled the websites revealed in the History menu of his Safari browser, desperate for any clue that would unlock the thumb drive. She delved into arcana in his old MacBook Pro that she had never paid attention to before: Disk Utility encryption; FileVault; recovery keys;

the Keychain Access app in Mac Utilities. She plunged deeply into security forums on the net and came up with a few passwords that Arosteguy had used for some political and philosophy websites that demanded them; but he had obviously been careless about, or more probably disdainful of, securing anything at all, apocalyptically inviting, she felt, the world's swarms of viruses and scams to come and overwhelm him, to take his machines and his past life away, to leave him stripped and dripping, as she had herself seen him more than once.

She could not leave the house, of course. She could not risk being rendered to the Democratic People's Republic of Korea, to one of the undocumented gulags, concentration camps, apartment prisons, there to rot while the boy deity Kim Jong Un matured and hardened into a ripe old age, attended to by his court *philosophes* Aristide and Célestine Arosteguy, who would be unaware that she was so near. She knew that this scenario was ridiculous, and yet it stirred painfully in her viscera as a living and undeniable creature, and when she accidentally tripped onto the official, rather sumptuous English-language webpage of the DPR of K, as they called it (it was in Ari's browser history, and finding that he had visited it many times chilled her to the bone), she jumped back from the screen of his laptop and immediately slammed it shut, terrified that the webpage could track her, could send her Tokyo coordinates directly to the deadly entomologists, who would kick down her door, muscle her into a waiting Audi, blindfold her, drug her, expunge her. She blamed her creative paranoia on a lack of protein; she had been reduced to eating nothing but plain instant ramen noodles for three of the four days since Ari's disappearance, nothing else edible having been left except for a small bottle of soy sauce, which lasted just over one day.

She was in the bathroom when it occurred to her that the Verbatim stick might have been encrypted by someone other than Ari, and this thought depressed her and led her to consider flying to Paris to seek the help of Hervé Blomqvist, whom Elke had labelled an IT genius and who would have reasons to help her unravel the mystery of Célestine's fate. Or would he? Tina might in fact be dead, and Hervé might be implicated in some way, either in the murder itself or in some aspect of covering up details. A perilous course to take, then. More depression. Naomi opened the jar of cold cream in which the thumb drive had been hastily (it seemed to her) concealed and began to smear some over her cheeks, which, like most of her skin, had become hot, dry, and stinging. When she used "kanebomoistagewcold" as a password, the Verbatim unceremoniously unlocked with that delicious metallic Mac padlock sound effect; when the drive appeared on her desktop, it called itself "La mort de Célestine."

THE NAME WAS PROVOCATIVE ENOUGH. Was Ari being direct and Célestine was dead, or was Ari being ironic, given that Célestine was not dead, and her death had been faked? And was it Ari himself who had named the drive, or had it been someone else? Opening the drive, Naomi found two folders, "Vidéo" and "Photos." She opened the video folder and there found one long QuickTime file called "PRIVATE." It was not password protected, and so when she double-tapped her trackpad, the QuickTime Player opened on a mysterious frame, which, when she tapped the play triangle, revealed itself to be an extreme close-up of Célestine's mastectomy scar, just a Rothko-like abstraction until the camera pulled away to expose a calm and thoughtful Célestine submitting herself to the camera clinically, without carnality, as though for a mammogram. The revelation of the scar triggered a shot of adrenaline in Naomi: first, because the mutilation of Célestine was shocking; second, because it meant that at least part of Ari's confession was true, though the cause could still have been cancer rather than an apotemnophile's hallucination about a buzzing horde of insects nesting in her breast. The camera moved over to Tina's right side, prompting her to take her remaining breast in both hands and offer it to the lens, compressing it analytically and accentuating its engorged nipple. The camera was still very close to her, making it difficult to determine where she was lying, or even if she was lying; the force of gravity on her breast, which would have at least hinted at whether she was upright or flat on her back, was negated by Tina's breast-holding, and the camera spent some time in extreme close-up mode, surveying Tina's face and then body, tracking down her only slightly protruding belly until it arrived at her thinning bush of graying pubic hair, where it lingered as Tina rotated her hips gently towards the lens. Naomi estimated from the detail of the pubic hairs, especially as the camera moved, that the video bit rate was reasonable, probably the AVCHD high standard of twenty-four megabits per second. The color was very good; the room was apparently lit by muted daylight coming through a window somewhere to the right, the skin tone cool and accurate with no yellow contamination by incandescent lights.

Eventually the camera backed away, floating languorously, so Naomi could see that Célestine was lying, not on a bed, but on a worktable set up on a mezzanine overlooked by massive wooden ceiling beams. The beams—pockmarked oak smeared with a white glaze—were of a now-extinct size and configuration that suggested they were medieval, and thus that the apartment was likely in the Jewish Marais section of Paris. It was not, then, the apartment of the Arosteguys. Célestine, somehow comfortable lying exposed on the rough butcher-block surface of the table, continued to intimidate Naomi, who was certain that if she had a mastectomy she would never allow herself to be photographed naked, much less reveal her wound publicly.

When a slim-hipped naked young man entered the frame, Naomi immediately knew it was Hervé, even before he walked around the side of the table to place his hooked penis in Célestine's coolly accommodating mouth. He brought with him something metallic that looked like a ray gun from a 1950s sci-fi movie, pale blue and silver and trailing a black cable. The muscles of his forearm were taut from supporting the substantial weight of the mysterious device. The naked young woman who entered from frame right, however, she did not immediately recognize, even after the woman had knelt at the head of the table in order to kiss and lick Célestine's mastectomy scar, her sinewy left arm stretching out so that her fingers could burrow into Tina's pubic bush. It was not until the camera drifted into a low-angle close-up that Naomi could identify Chase Roiphe, the star of Nathan's Toronto portfolio, and some of the pieces began to click into place.

But not all. After less than a minute of casual sex play among the three of them that seemed more like a social ritual than a hot orgy, Hervé stepped back from Célestine and became absorbed in the manipulation of a complex array of buttons on the body of the ray gun. Chase also detached from Célestine, who seemed to understand this as a signal to pose for what Naomi assumed was some kind of 3D capture. Tina swept back her long gray hair and draped it behind her so that it hung over the end of the table like a curtain. With a laugh, she then arranged herself into a grotesque, contorted pose, which Chase helped her to achieve by minutely adjusting the angles of her asymmetrically bent legs, splayed fingers, twisted arms, arched neck. It struck Naomi that she was playing the role of a tormented corpse in a 1960s Hammer horror film.

Chase stepped back to watch as Hervé squeezed the trigger on the pistol grip of his ray gun and began to sweep laser light over Célestine's body; a grid of red crosshairs, emanating from the device's twin space-pod-like nozzles, undulated like a ghostly manta ray over the contours of her flesh. Hervé brushed Célestine delicately, meticulously spray-painting every inch of her body with the light as she fought to hold the arranged position, her belly contracting with laughter as some unheard words were spoken and jokes were cracked. The camera floated gracefully around the trio, at times moving in to follow the sweep of the lasers and then tilting up to catch the expression on Chase's face, so full of love, excitement, amusement, sensuality. The camera also took a moment or two to linger on Chase's athletic breasts, her erect nipples, and her pubic hair, which was dirty blond and luxuriant and not at all in the modern prepubescent-shaven-porn idiom which Naomi loathed; if you looked only at their bodies, the two youngsters could have been siblings, Chase's a female version of the bicycle-hardened physique of Hervé. Now Chase closed the eyes of Célestine, as one might close the eyes of a cadaver, in preparation for Hervé to work the scanner over her face, but abruptly, the video ended. Naomi could not be sure that the camera operator was Arosteguy (the framing and movement were so assured!), but she knew he was there somewhere, watching and guiding.

Ultimately, she was disappointed by the video, wondering if after the scanning, whatever it was intended to do, there was sex among the four of them, and wishing that somehow she could have seen that instead. The confirmation that Chase Roiphe was sexually intimate with Hervé and the Arosteguys was of course valuable, and established the luscious necessity of a focused visit to Toronto, to Nathan, and to the Roiphes. Naomi was now convinced that Chase's bizarre trauma was connected with the death of Célestine Arosteguy; the mouth aspect, the French-language revulsion, the self-mutilation, the eating of her own flesh, were too perfect. She quit QuickTime Player and double-tapped the "Photos" folder, which popped open to reveal two sub-folders: "Célestine est morte" and "Des photos pour M. Vernier."

THERE WERE 147 JPEGS in the "Célestine est morte" file, which Naomi immediately decided to import into Lightroom so that she could catalogue and organize them with all her other research photos. As the thumbnails of the images loaded into the Import screen, she saw that they were all black and white and had been deliberately degraded in quality to give them a vintage feel in the Hipstamatic style—very contrasty, heavy vignetting, digital grain added to mimic Kodak Professional Tri-X panchromatic 35mm film, the old high-speed standard for newspaper and documentary journalism. All were starkly lit by a harsh on-camera flash in the tradition of the 1940s Speed Graphic flashbulb crime-scene photos of Weegee, and it occurred to her that the subtle linking of these images to socially historical crime photos was an attempt to authenticate them, because now that the importing was concluded and Naomi could examine them full screen in Lightroom's Library module, they struck her as quite obviously posed and theatrical and manipulative, qualities that disturbed her even more than the content of the images itself.

The setting was not the attic workroom of the video, but the now-familiar space of the Arosteguys', not much changed from its configuration in the various interviews that Naomi had seen. The sequence of the photos told a little story. Célestine is dead and has been dismembered, as per the police photos, with her body parts strewn randomly around the apartment and her torso on the couch. Hervé, Chase, and Arosteguy himself, gradually revealed to be completely naked as the shots' perspective widens and they emerge from behind various elements of furniture, take their turns biting small pieces from her thighs, her hips, her shoulders, her belly—but never all three in one frame, which suggests that one of them is always assigned camera duty. Blood is dripping from their mouths and from the bite-sized wounds they are creating, and there is a glazed, zombie-like affect to all their faces which somehow embraces primordial pleasure as well as toothy efficiency. Célestine's severed head, hair swept back as in the video but now parted to display a crudely cracked-open and hollowed-out skull, sits on the small table next to the old Loewe TV, watching the ghoulish trio with half-closed eyes (her brain is eventually to be found on the kitchen drainboard). And most shockingly—in a way that Naomi felt only she could appreciate—Célestine's torso begins the session with two full breasts, and when all the mouths have had their way with her left breast, violently ripping and tearing and seeming to eat it on camera, what is left is a raggedly circular bloody wound, not a clever mastectomy scar. Her right breast, though also savaged, remains attached to the torso.

The missing breast. Naomi obsessively scanned the face and body of Arosteguy in every photo in which he appeared, searching for a hint of mischief, of irony, of theater and performance. She wanted him to be sending her a message that said, "I was fantasizing for you about the mastectomy, the Hungarian surgery. It never happened. What you are seeing now is the reality. We three are cannibals and we ate that breast." But she found nothing but ritualistic solemnity on the faces of all three. And it was bracing, in a distancing, Brechtian V-effekt fashion, for her to see Ari's naked body in this context, from this perspective, so familiar in its powerful fullness, its slope-shouldered monumentality, that she could feel the weight of him on her, could feel his teeth in the meat of her shoulder, and yet also feel how separate she was from him, how alien he truly was. In the video, Célestine's body had reminded Naomi of the famous sequence of photos of the nude Simone de Beauvoir taken by the American photographer Art Shay in a Chicago apartment's bathroom. They both had the same good muscular rump, slightly heavy legs showing age-puckering behind the knees, and slim waist, though Célestine had fuller breasts, and Naomi had never seen a photo of Beauvoir with her long hair down (even primping in the Chicago bathroom after her shower, she wore high heels and her hair up in a tight chignon). Or perhaps Naomi was forcing a physical connection when it was really the seduction of students that linked them, a scandal even in those days before political correctness, and for which Beauvoir and her eternal president Jean-Paul Sartre were infamous. She had never discovered a nude photo of the tiny, toad-like Sartre.

The title of the third folder, "Des photos pour M. Vernier," was ominous in its implications even without being opened: it suggested that Arosteguy at least, and possibly Hervé and Chase as well, had collaborated with the prefect of police, Auguste Vernier, by sending him photos of their crime, and this proved to be the case. In the nine JPEGs in the folder (these were in color and not archly Hipstamaticked), the apartment has been abandoned by the trio and left to Célestine's poor segmented corpse. When Naomi double-checked her video and photo crime files, she saw that these exact photos were all that had been presented by the police and by the press as evidence of the murder of Célestine Arosteguy; there were no photos generated by the police themselves, and this of course led Naomi to wonder if the police in fact had possession of the body parts, or only photos of them provided by the unknown criminal or criminals. Was it only the photos and Célestine's disappearance that launched the Préfecture's investigation, or did they also have some physical evidence of her murder? Did they have any of the "Célestine est morte" series of photos as well? The titling of the Vernier folder suggested that they did not. If they had, they would undoubtedly have picked up Hervé for interrogation and possibly tried to extradite Chase Roiphe as well. What, then, was the purpose of that series? Was it being held back for the purpose of blackmail? Who would be the blackmailer?

It was as she was considering how best to approach a face-to-face interview with M. Vernier, and how that might tie in with a trip to Toronto to conduct her own sly interrogation of Chase Roiphe, that her laptop pulsed with that spooky Skype outer-space-fish ringtone. She jerked mindlessly in surprised sync with that pulse, so disembodied had she become. Skype had been kept running just in case Ari tried to get in touch, but this call was from Nathan. She slid the cursor over the green Answer button, tapped the Air's trackpad, and immediately was looking at the very worried face of Nathan in his basement bedroom in Toronto.

"I can't see you," he said.

Skype's default was no video. Naomi slid the cursor over the video-camera icon with the red line running through it, but she couldn't pull the trigger. "I don't want you to see me right now," she said, the words ragged, as if shredding on her teeth. She hadn't spoken for days. Nathan looked stressed and gaunt, although it could have been the connection, which was not good, and his voice being out of sync exacerbated the pangs of separation and loneliness that she immediately felt on seeing him. She was terrified to activate that little frame in the bottom right corner of the Skype window, which would show her not only to Nathan but to herself. She was sure she would see a female clone of Arosteguy at his most disheveled and confused, so mingled had they become in her head. Though she felt no guilt over her affair with Ari, given Nathan's Hungarian adventure, she could still smell the sex of her last few days—it had comforted her, trailing around like a cloud of perfume—and felt that Nathan would smell it too if he could see her. She did not want to inflict that on him, at least not now.

"Why not? Omi? Why not see you?"

Though his image was wrinkling and slip-sliding, she could read his tightly controlled concern and it pained her. "Will you allow me to come to Toronto? Cross-fertilization?"

Her voice was little and childlike, and her unheard-of submissiveness disturbed Nathan greatly. "What do you mean by 'allow'? That doesn't sound like you at all. What's going on? Are you in trouble? Do you want me to come there? I will, you know. Just say it and I will."

"I wouldn't want to step on your toes or anything. You've got your thing going with the Roiphes. You don't need me messing it up."

"I'd love to see you here. It wouldn't be a problem. But 'cross-fertilization'?

You mean Chase Roiphe's connection to your French philosophers?"

"Yeah. That's what I mean. She might know some stuff. I'm kinda at a dead end. I dunno. Maybe."

"You sound really down. Is there something wrong with you? Physically? Let me see you." Nathan was thinking that Arosteguy had beaten Naomi up, or that she had even gotten into a sick kind of dominant/submissive sex with him that had spilled over into her working life, and her little-girl voice was the expression of that. He closed his eyes for a few seconds, imagining that when he opened them he would see Naomi's face floating in his Skype window, battered and bruised and broken like one of those TMZ photos featuring celebrity abuse. The window remained dark.

"I'm just tired and dragged out. You don't need to see me like that. It's not a big deal."

"Yeah. Okay." Nathan knew not to push it. "So? You coming to Toronto? I'm sure I can set something up with the Roiphes. If it's interesting, maybe we collaborate on one big book. Who knows?" Nathan knew he was taking a chance suggesting such a thing; maintaining the separation of church and state was a big deal with Naomi; combining forces with anyone was always a stern test of her basic insecurity, her fear of fusion that would inexorably lead to annihilation, and she rarely allowed it to happen. But he was desperate to enfold her somehow, to draw them back together, and he couldn't think of any other way to do it, despite the risk of a major backfire. When she didn't flinch, however, Nathan realized he could not take it as a good sign.

"I might have to stop off in Paris first, but, yeah. I'm coming to Toronto." She managed to hit Mute a beat before she burst into heavy tears which jetted out of her eyes and onto her keyboard and trackpad. When she swiped at the wetness with the sleeve of her hoodie, she disconnected Nathan.

PROFESSOR MATSUDA had manifested fear, and that had made Yukie Oshima fearful herself. He would not meet her in a noodle shop or a restaurant or anything associated with eating, though that was not quite how he framed it. Yukie got the message anyway, so they agreed to meet as if by accident in a sleek, modern store in Shibuya which declared itself, in English, in white Comic Sans font on a red banner background, a "Comic Speciality Store and Cafe." It was not a venue he would ever willingly enter on his own—Shibuya was listed on travel websites as "the fountain of teen trendiness"—but then neither would any of his colleagues. This was not a rendezvous to be noted.

He was as natty and proper and controlled as she had remembered him, and she, she was certain, was as loopy and dangerous as he had remembered her. During the student uprisings at Todai, the university had clandestinely sought Yukie's advice on how to present its conservative case to the youth of Japan—it would not have been seemly for an academic institution to have engaged spin doctors and PR hacks on its behalf, though that's what it was doing—and Matsuda had accepted the role of point man for Todai in that endeavor, though reluctantly; the shyness, propriety, humbleness, and obscurity of the man, all attributes which made him perfect for the job, also made it excruciating for him. Now he was shoulder to shoulder with his unlikely collaborator (he had earnestly wished never to see Yukie again, though of course would never express this) at a bookshelf fronted by trays teeming with graphic novels and the Japanese version of comic books, which were more like paperbacks than the classic comics of vintage America. He could not bring himself to flip through any of the colorful offerings, as Yukie was doing when he arrived, particularly because she had stationed herself in front of a collection of BBC books—the initials stood for Be-Boys Comics, which flaunted the Mars male symbol in black on a yellow square as its logo—and was leafing through an edition that featured on its cover two long-haired, windswept men with very feminine occidental features who managed to embrace face to face while riding on a motorcycle. Typical of the woman, thought Matsuda. She would know he found this offensive.

On his approach, Yukie had turned to face him and bowed, eyes down, hands clasped before her, manga book still in hand but now firmly closed. "Professor Matsuda-san. I thank you for the meeting."

Matsuda had nodded in return. "You have asked me for the French professor's address. I have tried to contact him to gain his permission, but he has not responded. He has also missed several classes and appointments, and that has caused some worry. I agreed to meet you because I fear that something tragic has happened to him and thought that you might perhaps have some information that could ease my worry."

"My Canadian friend was staying at his house. She emailed me that the professor had left the house and not returned for days, but now she no longer answers my emails, my texts, my phone calls, and so I am worried about her as well. I try not to imagine all the things that I can imagine. I must go to that house and see what the reality there is."

Matsuda picked up a book and nervously hefted it in his hand without looking at it. "You will not see any reality in that house," he said. He turned to Yukie with a disturbed, clenched smile. "Strangely, the house is owned by the Japanese Collective of Medical Entomology. Why they would need such a house I have no idea, but it was provided to the philosopher as a courtesy, I understand, by the collective itself, as arranged by the Department of Philosophy at Todai." He turned to go, momentarily forgetting that he had a book in his hand, then turned back. As he replaced the book, he muttered, "Of course, the philosopher was for some reason interested in the use of entomological warfare in China during World War Two." He shook his head in dismay. "Airplanes spraying plague-infected fleas and flies onto an unsuspecting populace. He mentioned to me that the North Koreans still allege that during their war with the South, the

Americans and their new allies the Japanese conspired to bring Japanese entomological warfare to the Korean peninsula. A strange coincidence."

Yukie was dazzled by the twists and turns, sensing a wonderful story with international weight but not at all certain she could connect the dots. "Professor-san, are you suggesting that there is a link between the renting of the house from the collective and the sudden absence of our colleagues? What could that possibly be?"

Matsuda did not smile. "And will you also be turning this affair into a publicity circus?"

It was uncharacteristic of Matsuda to be so blunt, not to mention vengeful, and Yukie took it as an indication that there was something complex and worrisome about Arosteguy's disappearance that went deeper even than the French domestic murder scandal. She immediately thought that Naomi was dead and that Arosteguy had killed her, but for reasons that had nothing to do with sexual passion or deviancy. She could not fathom what those reasons could be.

"I would just like to have my friend Naomi back," she said.

AND SO YUKIE FOUND HERSELF standing in front of the open gate of the Arosteguy house taking photos, like a tourist, she thought, at the Bates *Psycho* house on the Universal Studios back lot in Hollywood (as she had actually been at the time of Naomi's Santa Monica escapade)—a very unwelcome association. Though her new Sony RX1 camera was renowned for its low-light capability and she was eager to exploit this, she had waited until the morning after her "accidental" meeting with Matsuda to go to the Arosteguy house, wanting the fullest of full daylight surrounding her. Still, once she had documented the garbage-strewn front garden and slid open the unlocked front door, she found darkness waiting for her in the house, and soon she was shooting at the widest aperture, f/2.0, with Auto ISO all the way up at times to 6400 at the camera's preferred shutter speed of 1/80 of a second. The widest, most open, most accepting aperture, the one providing the narrowest, most demanding depth of field. She and Naomi had joked about the sexuality of camera apertures, that they needed to write a woman's monograph on the symbolism and cultural relevance of the mechanics of image-making as it related to sex, so that, for example, stopping down the fixed 35mm lens's diaphragm—elegantly composed of nine leaf-shutter blades—to a tight f/16 would be the equivalent of executing a Kegel pelvic floor exercise. But beyond that, she had learned so much about photography from her friend, and here she was, using that knowledge to document this house, which was filling her camera with its devastating atmosphere of Japanese urban despair reflecting her own; the camera was inhaling it through that lens aperture, and would exhale it into Yukie's flat from the screen of her computer when she got home again.

A 35mm lens did not give you a very wide perspective—it was certainly not a lens for architecture—and so Yukie, wanting to document every cubic meter and to disturb nothing, began to combine shots in Panorama mode in order to deliver something of the cramped, stingy scale of the place, and alternated this with rotating the middle ring on the beautiful Carl Zeiss lens into its macro focusing position so that she could get very close to the details, which, she hoped, on study back home, would divulge some clues as to what had emptied the house of its two mysterious *gaijin*. There was no immediate evidence of the house having been professionally tossed or rumbled, though certainly it was a mess; random drawers had been left hanging open, tubes and jars left unsealed, books and papers strewn everywhere among empty bags of ramen noodles and chips. On the other hand, there were no electronic devices to be found anywhere, other than the modest TV set and its controller and set-top box. No computers, iPads, cell phones, hard drives, laptops, or chargers, cables, or peripherals for any of the same, and this was beyond what could be construed as normal; you might take a couple of devices with you on leaving your house, but not your desktop, not your fax machine (still a force in Japan, unlike the West), not your printer.

As she made her way up the cabinet-like stairway, she could not keep her paranoia completely in check. Would it be Naomi who came streaming out of a second-floor doorway and down the stairs towards her, carving knife raised high, violins stabbing away with predatory beaks, or would it be Arosteguy himself, squeezed into one of Naomi's dresses, an old-lady wig insanely askew on his head? That was almost preferable to what there actually was: nothing and nobody. Once safely upstairs, Yukie could smell Naomi everywhere, and there were traces of her—underwear, makeup—in every corner, like the kind she had left in Yukie's apartment, sheddings of her skin that could not have been accidental, that were assertions of Naomi's existence, claims of territorial possession. She would come back someday, they said. Don't forget me.

Yukie was not familiar with the neighborhood surrounding Arosteguy's house, but the unlocked door might not indicate anything unusual; on the other hand, given Naomi's growing paranoia as expressed in her emails, it did seem strange that the door wasn't locked.

As Yukie walked away from the house, she turned one last time to photograph it from some distance down the street, which, like the house itself, displayed only provocative traces of people—bicycles with front-mounted wire-mesh baskets tilted on their kickstands, odd-sized wooden planks lashed together and leaning against a doorway, potted plants randomly placed on the roadway's narrow curb—but no people themselves.

Maybe the story was the story of the house, a house owned by Japanese insect scientists and rented to a fugitive French philosopher. Maybe that was the story.

"MEANT TO ASK YOU: Where is Célestine's left breast? Omi."

The text floated in a pale-green dialogue bubble amid a bead-chain of increasingly frantic gray-bubble texts from Nathan, wondering where exactly she was, and who belonged to the strange Japanese phone number being used. It was a cell number, something he recognized from earlier calls from Naomi, who had borrowed Arosteguy's phone (81 for Japan, 090 for a cell), and he suspected that this too was an Arosteguy phone, or possibly one belonging to Naomi's friend Yukie, but until he heard something specific from his texter, he could not be sure that the SMS was authentic. What did it mean? He had studied the crime-scene photos available on the net, and it was true that Célestine's left breast had been somehow amputated and was not seen in any of them, but given the grotesque cannibalistic elements of *l'affaire Arosteguy* and the paucity of photos, this was not an obvious question for anyone to ask. Particularly Naomi.

Nathan's iPhone lay unforthcoming on the plastic wood-grain surface of the table, right next to the simple white plate bearing two overcooked pork chops, a mound of corn, three tomato slices, and a pleated paper cup of apple sauce. The small steak knife had a gnawed handle worn streaky gray from a thousand machine washings. A glass bowl held his plain green salad. He had come back to the Coach with some unspoken symbolic intent, though he was not sitting as deeply into the room as he had first sat with Dr. Roiphe. He preferred to sit closer to the multiple windows at the front of the restaurant, where he could watch the low-key action on the street called Spadina Road. From this vantage point, the Village really felt like a village, like the two-story main street in some small town in Indiana. Across the street: an Edo-ko (a chain Japanese restaurant); a What A Bagel!; a midscale Italian restaurant called Primi; a One Hour MotoPhoto struggling to come to terms with the total annihilation of film technology. It was clear to Nathan that he was not really there, despite the clarity of the details of the restaurant, the food, and the street. His reality had been displaced by Naomi's—no surprise, really, and not for the first time. Or perhaps it was just that her narrative was more compelling than his, and so Chase was now part of Naomi's adventure, not Nathan's. He knew that he had precipitated this by letting Naomi in on Chase's past history in Paris. But how could he not? She would have done the same for him. He didn't understand the significance of Célestine Arosteguy's missing left breast, but if the text proved to be authentic, he was sure he would soon be gently interrogating Chase on Naomi's behalf. Gloom settled in as he attacked the chops. What was he doing there, really?

The first forkful was barely in his mouth, the touch of it generating more thoughts of his first meeting with Roiphe, when the doctor himself materialized as if summoned by the mere mental imaging. He walked with a hunched urgency, adjusting his strange straw hat—not the Tilley this time—which seemed to need a bit of rotating to feel just right, gaze locked onto the pavement until he was at the restaurant's door, at which point he straightened up with a start, pivoted theatrically, and entered. Nathan kept eating, following Roiphe's progress with dreamlike interest, and it soon became evident that the doctor was looking for him. He veered right once inside, taking a few steps towards his own favorite booth at the back of the restaurant, squinting in the sallow light of the hokey glass carriage lamps on the wall, then turning back and methodically scanning the room through his big distorting glasses until he spotted his target. Nathan's single window seat—flaunting, like all the seats, a big floral pattern in pink, green, and black—forced Roiphe to sit sideways on the bench seat under the window and then to twist from the waist in order to face Nathan. Certain that Roiphe would think of their first meeting, Nathan expected an amused, caustic comment on what he was eating, and perhaps a meditation on Jews eating pork, but the doctor was all business, all worry.

"Chase is very, very upset," he said. "I suppose you've heard about it."

Nathan had to finish chewing before he could respond. He remembered observing Roiphe chewing his own pork chops, and how he seemed to be having trouble that was possibly caused by slipping dentures. Absorbing Roiphe on top of Naomi, Nathan felt as though he himself had dentures that were slipping. He found it difficult to speak. "Chase? Heard? No. Heard what?"

Roiphe took his hat off and started to play with the brim. He was backlit against the window, and his thinning hair looked particularly vulnerable and wispy. "That French professor of hers. Arosteguy. You haven't heard? It's all over the internet. Too soon to hit the papers."

"What … what about him?" Nathan immediately felt sick. He didn't want to hear it, certain that whatever it was meant bad news regarding the mysteriously unresponsive Naomi, even though Roiphe would be oblivious of the Naomi aspect. Nathan had been careful not to let the doctor know about what was going on in Tokyo; he would be too interested in Naomi's Arosteguy project for comfort.

Roiphe shook his head at the incomprehensible weirdness of it all. "They finally found him. Found his body."

Nathan put down his knife and fork. "His body? What does that mean?"

The air-conditioning wasn't working in the restaurant, and Roiphe began to fan his face with his hat, the backlight from the windows strobing through the straw and bringing Nathan to the point of migraine. "Well, he's dead. That's what that means. His body. Apparently he collapsed in the middle of some huge intersection in Tokyo. Some witnesses said blood came dribbling out of both of his ears. Sounds like a cerebral hemorrhage to me, although, well, you never know."

"But you said something. They *found* his body? They had to find it?"

"Apparently, once some ambulance picked him up, they misplaced his body. Or the police took it to do an autopsy and didn't let the media know about it for three or four days. Something. Some mystery about it. The witness stuff was suppressed until later. He was a fugitive. The French cops wanted him back in Paris. Maybe that was it. Delicate situation."

"Jesus. Fuck."

"What. You knew him."

"No. *You* knew him."

"Well, I met him once or twice. He had weight. He had substance. I didn't trust him with Chase, but there's a paranoid old father for you. And speaking of which, Chase wants to see you. Said she needs you for some solace, whatever that means. Obviously it has something to do with her professor. I dasn't think of it. I dasn't. Never seen her so depressed. Disturbing for a parent." Roiphe used his hat to gesture towards Nathan's pork chops. "But you should just sit here and finish those first. I'm sure she'll be able to hang on."

Nathan pushed his plate across the table. "I think I'll go now. Where is she?"

"Up in the workroom. Hey, if you're serious about not finishing those. I'm prohibited, I'm persona non grata up there, so I might as well stay here."

Nathan slid out of his seat and stood up. "You go right ahead."

Roiphe lifted the plate and floated it, wobbling, over to the table in front of him, which stretched the length of the windows. "I'll expect a full report, natch. For the book. Eventually. And could you tell them to bring me a fresh knife and fork on your way out?"

By the time Nathan hit the sidewalk, Roiphe was happily trimming off the edges of the pork chops where Nathan had made cuts, evidently contaminating them, and fastidiously lifting the trimmings with his new knife and fork onto the butter dish, where they were safely isolated. Nathan waited until he had walked half a block, well out of the doctor's view, before he stopped in front of the grandiosely named Village Market—

"Variety/Greeting Cards"—intending to open his phone's Safari web browser. He needed to know just what he was walking into. As giggling schoolgirls tumbled out of the Village Market's ancient green door and pushed by him clutching *Archie* comics and Kit Kat Minis, he found himself looking at blurry, tweeted photos of Arosteguy lying facedown on the square paving stones of a narrow, crowded pedestrian street in Akihabara, the games and electronics mecca near Tokyo Station. The handsome square head, the large staring eyes, the long, unruly gray hair matted with the blood which flowed from his ears and curled into the granite interstices. Taken at night under the many varieties of artificial light illuminating the street, the photos displayed surreal colors and vague focus, but Nathan thought he saw bits of organic material—brain? inner ear?—spattering the shoulder of Arosteguy's jacket and soaking in the pooling blood. The lack of good light and the jostling of the crowd made the one relevant video he could find on YouTube even more of a surrealist smear. It was shot handheld and walking from behind Arosteguy, with two or three shoppers between Arosteguy and the camera, which was framed to highlight the whirlpool of neon above the crowd. At the bottom of the frame, out of focus, you could see something that looked like smoke or a liquid spray, like a messy backlit sneeze, spurting from Arosteguy's ears, at which point his head jerked back and dropped out of frame, and the holder of the camera seemed to stumble before the image looped skyward and then cut out. It would have struck Nathan as farcical if he hadn't seen the Twitter photos first, the ones in which Arosteguy looked quite horridly dead.

The inevitable mutating variations were all over the net, but basically: fugitive cannibal French philosopher found dead in Tokyo street. There had been, as Roiphe had suggested, some mystery surrounding the interval between the loading of the body into a special small ambulance that was capable of threading its way through the backstreets, and the release by the Tokyo Metropolitan Police Department of the report concerning the noted *gaijin*'s collapse, which seemed to involve a catastrophic cerebral event. The president of France commented only that the death of M. Arosteguy was a mercilessly compounded national tragedy and that his body must of course be returned to France for burial in the Cimetière du Montparnasse where it belonged, in the company of Sartre and Baudrillard. The desire by Tokyo police to conduct an autopsy under their own control was deemed inappropriate by French authorities.

CHASE HELD HERVÉ'S L-shaped penis in her hand and dipped its root into a glass pot of white glue. It had been painted to resemble a wormlike larva—a meaty translucent yellow with tobacco striations delineating its body segments, and two black-stippled ovals on the upper shield of the glans representing the chemo-sensory organs found on the larval head.

"I invented my own parasitoid infestation for her, for Célestine. I felt she deserved her own species, something that lovingly lays its eggs in her—we never see what the adult form looks like—and then the maggots hatch and start eating her from the inside out. They spend most of their lives burrowed into the bodies of their hosts, gently nibbling, so they don't really need eyes. And it's really magical and spooky when they finally emerge, poking through, waving around all together, synchronized like those weird women's Olympic swim teams."

She turned away from the paint table and took a half step to the body-parts table, where about two dozen of Hervé's penile fellows protruded from Célestine's 3D-printed body parts like immense parasitic fly larvae. After a moment of deliberation, with one hand held under the current penis/larva to catch any glue drippings, Chase delicately planted the creature into a bloody, ragged hole just above the knee of the left leg, giving it a twist to settle it in like a lightbulb in a socket. Some of the penis/larva units had been cut down to different lengths so that they presented a more varied diorama of parasitic emergence, although Nathan thought that their uniform ninety-degree signature Hervé bend worked against the illusion of randomly squirming maggots seeking the light. He thought as well that the entire effect of the piece would be enhanced if the body parts were arranged as a complete body instead of like prime cuts in a butcher's display fridge—the symbolism of the head between the legs, for example, striking him as too obvious, too desperately provocative—but he was reluctant to criticize her work for any number of reasons, not the least of which was the fear that she would ask him to donate an erect penis scan of his own in order to provide larval variety to the work. Collaboration with Nathan was in the air in the Roiphe household, but Nathan himself remained wary.

Light poured down over Chase like a shower of clarity from the angled skylights. She was wearing a schoolgirl uniform—short-sleeved white sailor blouse complete with stripe-edged antimacassar, unbuttoned at the throat; loosely knotted gray-and-burgundy-striped tie; and short box-pleated gray skirt—which he recognized as belonging to Bishop Cornwall School just down the street. But she was not wearing the requisite burgundy jacket, gray knee socks, or black oxford shoes; her feet were bare, as were her legs and her arms, and, raked by the light from above, the hundreds of tea-party scars stood out in relief so that she seemed to be swarming with ants the color of dried blood. It created a strange alliance between her and the worm-eaten Célestine, which, it was clear, was the desired effect. She knew he was studying her.

"I'm too shy to do this live onstage, putting my Célestine together, but maybe you could video me and we could project it. I could take her apart and put her back together again. I think your super camera does video too, doesn't it?"

"It does, sure," Nathan lied. "They all do now." Nathan could just see a video with his name attached being presented to a French court; he could barely imagine the confusion it would cause. Well, it would be a unique vantage point for the writer of the definitive article on what was spiraling awkwardly into the Arosteguy/Roiphe/Blomqvist case. "The uniform is a nice touch. Were you a Bishop Cornwall girl?"

"I was, briefly. My mother kept the uniform. I was shocked that I could still fit into it. I found it in the basement by accident—only, I guess, not by accident. It was in a moldy cardboard box with the school logo on it. That kind of racy bishop's miter. You can still smell it, the mold." Pause. "I had a wonderful art teacher there."

Chase's luscious enunciation of the word *wonderful*, preceded by a telltale flick of the tongue over the lower lip, strongly suggested delicious, forbidden, teacher-student sex, probably involving that very uniform. "To be explored" was the mental note. "So the uniform is part of the performance?"

"Asians love schoolgirls in uniform. They say the Japanese can buy used schoolgirl panties from vending machines. And from shops hidden away in apartment buildings. *Burusera* shops, they call them. The smell is very important; it adds value to the commodity. I wonder how Marx would have dealt with that? I'm not talking about the moldy smell. *Sailor Moon.* Did you ever watch that? It was a manga series that became an anime." She sang the first few bars of the *Sailor Moon* theme song in a husky, sweet voice, only slightly off-key:

Fighting evil by moonlight
Winning love by daylight
Never running from a real fight
She is the one named Sailor Moon!

NATHAN HAD HEARD IT BEFORE. A young cousin from Newark named Leslie had been obsessed with the schoolgirl destined to become a magical warrior who fought to save the galaxy, all while wearing her—admittedly stylized—schoolgirl's sailor suit. "The Asian element surprises me. For the performance piece, I mean. Does that come from Tokyo?"

"There are many reasons Professor Arosteguy went to Tokyo. It had nothing to do with extradition treaties. He was always fascinated by the Asian version of consumerism, particularly Japanese, so complex. We keep texting. Kind of compulsive."

Texting? Now? From the Tokyo morgue? Nathan tacked. "Maybe you need to dress Célestine Arosteguy's corpse like Sailor Moon. Just to tie things together."

Chase allowed him a quick glance over her shoulder, then turned back to her paint table, where there were only two more larvae, pre-painted and waiting for installation. "You know, that's a really good idea, the Sailor Moon thing. She is a magical warrior, Tina is."

"And your many insect bites? Also good for the performance?" Now that her mini-mutilations had been unceremoniously unveiled, he felt he had been invited to notice them, also without ceremony. He could easily see her onstage, clipping off bits of her flesh and eating them while the wide-eyed Célestine corpse looked on with affectionate approval.

"Wow. I hadn't thought of them that way. You probably don't realize how perfect that concept is."

"I'd like to realize."

"I'd have to totally poach you from my father for my own project. Are you still positive for Roiphe's?" So casual a throwaway line was this last that, for a beat, Nathan thought he must have mentioned his affliction to Chase, but then understood it could only have come from her father. Was that a betrayal? Did it indicate a more open relationship between father and daughter than the doctor had suggested? What context could there have been for that discussion? It occurred to Nathan that he did not remotely have a handle on the Roiphes.

"Not sure. The symptoms have subsided. I have three weeks' worth of pills to go. Why?"

Mischievous smile. "I remember reading about Calvin Klein's daughter. Every time she pulled down a lover's pants, she was confronted by her father's name on the band of his underwear. A total sex killer. I have to wonder what it would be like to be infected by my father's namesake disease."

"Acquiring it is more pleasant than living with it. But … could be part of the performance."

"Could be."

"And could we say, then, what the meaning of the performance actually is?"

"We can't worry about meaning. Ari proposed to us that meaning is a consumer item. Some people manufacture it through religion, philosophy, nationhood, politics, and some people buy it. But an artist is not a manufacturer."

"And will you ever get the rest of your French friend Hervé to perform with you?"

Chase laughed a surprisingly hearty laugh. She held the second-last of Hervé's replica penises up in the air and whirled it around a few times like a football pennant, then turned back to the Tina-thing, looking for the right socket to plug it into.

"Maybe not. This is the best part of him."

"And speaking of parts."

"Yes. You asked me a strange question when we were coming up the stairs: Where is Célestine's left breast?" Chase decided on a wound in the Célestine-head's cheek, but after holding the penis/larva in place, she seemed to feel that it was too long, overpowering. At the paint table, she began to trim it back from the root end with an X-Acto craft knife.

"That was the question." From Roiphe's testimony, Nathan had expected to find a weepy, devastated Chase waiting for him in a darkened workroom. Instead, she was as luminous as the room itself, and patently playful. "Do you have the answer?"

Chase put down the knife, turned around, and crossed her arms, tapping the glans of the bioplastic penis against her lips. The maggot paint, long dried, left no marks. "It's not really *your* question, is it?"

"It's a question asked by a journalist in Tokyo who was working on a story about the Arosteguys. About Célestine's murder." A journalist. Nathan had distanced himself from Naomi without thinking about it, but immediately felt guilty for never having outlined his relationship with her to Chase. Then again, that was not a short outline. He let that dog lie.

"A journalist you're in constant touch with? Trading stories?"

"Journalists are too paranoid to trade stories. Sometimes they help each other with details."

With a spasm that seemed almost painful, Chase detached herself from the table and ambled towards Nathan, arms still folded, the abridged penis now lowered and hooked over her left biceps; its oval sensors seemed to be looking up at Nathan. "And so if you get an answer to the question, if you come up with the answer, you'll just email it to your journalist friend? You'll quote me? And then what I say will become evidence in a murder case? Something like that?"

"I would protect you. You'd be an unnamed source."

Chase now stood in front of Nathan, combatively close. He was not at all sure that he could protect her. Would that be under French law? International law? Canadian law? He had no idea. But he wanted the answer to the question even more, now that he saw what was swimming around in her eyes.

"That would be so nice of you. To do that. Protect me," she said. "What would you think if I told you there really wasn't a murder case?"

"You mean the French police don't have a case to make against your old professor?"

"No, I mean what if there was no murder to be a case?"

"Madame Arosteguy . . . Mrs. Arosteguy died accidentally?"

Chase had actually flinched at the word *madame*! This was exactly like the reaction *le schizo*, Louis Wolfson, would have had to hearing even one word spoken to him in English by his one-eyed mother or his stepfather, and it left Nathan unaccountably thrilled and distracted. It just emphasized how much the Chase story was interwoven with Paris, the Sorbonne, with language, the Arosteguys—in other words, the French story. Perhaps there was no other way to do the piece justice than to collaborate with Naomi just as she had proposed. But where was Naomi? The worry sank into his gut like that X-Acto knife. Maybe he needed to meet her in Paris and not wait for her to come to Toronto.

"Mrs. Arosteguy didn't die at all. Mrs. Arosteguy is still alive. That's what I'm suggesting."

"Then what happened to Célestine's left breast?"

"You're closer to it than you could ever imagine."

Nathan slid out from under Chase's gaze and walked over to the body-parts table. From close up it looked like a makeshift autopsy table strewn with the rotting detritus of a particularly confusing homicide. He turned back to Chase.

"Am I getting warmer?"

"No. You're cold. Very cold. You were warmer standing in front of me." Nathan returned to her.

"Okay. I don't get it."

Chase took his hand and placed it over her own left breast. She was not wearing a bra; the cotton of the sailor shirt was unexpectedly rough. "Do you feel it?" Nathan could only shrug. He was out of the game, not comprehending. "I ate it, Nathan. I ate her breast, at least most of it. What

I could stand to eat. It's not something I think any other animal would eat, not the milk glands anyway. They were horrible. We left the rest of it in the apartment so that the cops would have some flesh to do their DNA thing on. That's why they think there was a murder." He let his hand slip off her breast and onto her arm. The little scars felt like a bad heat rash. She twisted away from him, strolled over to the table, and leaned over the body parts. Using the penis as a comical viewfinder, she began making camera shutter noises by sucking air in past her teeth. Click, a leg, click, a hand, click, a foot. She swiveled back to Nathan. "That and the clever special effects photos."

"It was actually hers? The breast? She was ... alive when you ate it?"

"She had always wanted to amputate it. She was very passionate about that. She had some intense body dysmorphic disorder thing. I think Ari took her someplace where they helped him do it to her himself. A collaboration. They froze it and brought it back to the apartment. Left it in the fridge for the cops to find. There was still part of a nipple, a lot of skin, fatty tissue, not much gland."

"If she's still alive, where is she?"

"We don't know. She's an enigma."

Nathan nervously wiped the back of his hand across his lips. He knew it was a revealing gesture but was compelled to prepare his mouth for his next words. "You do know that Aristide Arosteguy is not alive."

Chase's face lit up with the most radiant smile. "I looked at everything I could find on the net. Well, not the French reports, of course. And at first I was incredibly hurt and shocked and saddened. I wanted to vomit my heart out. Because he means so much to me. The professor. My philosopher. But then I realized." Nathan thought her face would lift off her skull and float around the room with joy.

"And then you realized."

"He's not-alive the way Célestine is not-alive. They are together somewhere, and I will see them again. I don't mean in some lame afterlife. They'll call for me when they're ready, when their new lives are ready to be lived. And I'll go to them, wherever they are." As if to begin that journey, Chase turned back once again to the paint table, where she dipped the larval root into the glue pot, then conveyed the thing to the wound in Célestine's cheek just below the cheekbone. After a moment's reflection, she gently eased it into the waiting socket, gave it its ceremonial twist, and took a step back to get a proper perspective. The new, shorter larva now competed directly for attention with the head's swollen and bruised protruding tongue. Chase gave a little "ha" of satisfaction.

SAMUEL BECKETT, apparently, had Dupuytren's contracture in his right hand, which caused his outer fingers to curl inward and made shaking hands difficult and embarrassing. This pleased Hervé Blomqvist, who, while researching famous people who had Peyronie's, looking particularly for those who rode bicycles, had discovered that many Peyronie's victims also suffered from Baron Dupuytren's, which suggested an immune system pathogenesis rather than a bicycle-riding problem. Hervé could now count himself one of that exclusive club, noticing a new ugly chevron-shaped swelling of tendon sheath in his left palm (he thought of shark gills) which would undoubtedly lead to an eventual contracting of his little and middle finger—a condition called "trigger finger"—to the point where he would no longer be able to straighten those fingers. He was willing to bet that Beckett had Peyronie's too—he seemed to have had an appropriately contracted sex life—but doubted that there would ever be confirmation of that fact. He hefted the Creaform portable 3D scanner, which he had just used to scan his penis, still partially erect, and fantasized scanning Samuel Beckett's penis as well as those of any number of other famous Peyronie's sufferers. His current scan was more detailed than the one he had sent Chase Roiphe earlier in the day, but she probably didn't need it. No, this one he was sending to Romme Vertegaal, somewhere in North Korea that was not Pyongyang.

The FabrikantBot 2 was chugging away downstairs, printing out the latest parts for the Juche Idea People's Universal Folding Bicycle, meant to replace the flawed components of the bottom bracket internals which had caused Hervé so much grief as he rode the assembled prototype around the confines of his Rue Beaubourg flat in the 3rd arrondissement. The tight, acrobatic turns that were required had managed to lock up the pedals, and the pedals would not let go until they and their cranks had been completely disassembled and reassembled. A detailed Skyping of the photos and videos documenting the problem drew a quick response from Romme, who had somehow become the Universal Bicycle's project manager. So positive and helpful, really, and definitely meriting the gift of a return printable scan.

Romme was intimately familiar with Hervé's sex organ, of course, having helped guide it into various orifices during the wild days of the Arosteguys' *séminaires,* which inevitably drew the obvious puns involving the words *séminal* and *semence,* and anything else related to sperm and semen. Hervé imagined that they must be very prudish in North Korea, as such repressive regimes always seem to be, and hoped that Romme would be alone in whatever ramshackle studio had been provided for him when Hervé's gift penis began to print out, though there was a perverse tickle of pleasure at the thought that Romme might be caught holding an ABS replica of his Peyronie's-twisted member by a strict cadre supervisor, and as a result be cast into the darkness of a reeducation camp like Jongori, Camp No. 12, about as far away from the capital and humanity as you could get.

But perhaps Romme would apply to the Peyronie's scan the special effects makeup required to turn an ABS or possibly bioplastic penile replicant—muted and bland in uniform gray or powder blue—into a vibrant, living thing full of color and pores and texture. He doubted that Romme himself had such artistic skills, the kind that Chase had shown under the tutelage of the SFX team they had been assigned: Arthropoda Souterrain Effets Spéciaux, a French-Korean firm specializing in gargantuan arthropods for schools and scientific displays. It was a strange choice to say the least, given that arthropods did not bleed red blood, nor did they have skin, but Romme had been steadfast in using them because they could be counted on to be reasonably discreet; and, to be fair, they brought great gusto to creating fleshly things that no lobster or cricket ever incarnated—torn tendons, ruptured blood vessels, exposed hormone glands, splayed muscles—bringing to life Célestine's tortured body parts, photos of which had convinced the *préfet* that a murder had in fact been committed.

It had ultimately been Chase who did the dog's work, the Souterrain boys needing to be kept at arm's length so that they would not be tempted to blow the whistle on Hervé when the crime-scene photos hit the net. Only Chase could have been entrusted with building the edible prosthetic left breast and the wound-FX application worn by Célestine that had covered the mastectomy scar in the cannibal series of photos. And it had been the original of that breast that was the clincher, the only body part actually found in the Arosteguys' apartment: a pathetic, mutilated bowl of flesh bearing tooth marks and half a nipple found in the fridge, which was easily DNA certified as belonging to Célestine Arosteguy (her distraught sister Sophie, manager of a group of chalets in Chamonix, had been desperate to provide samples). He wondered if the *préfet* had had the presence of mind to have the breast teched out for cancer, but public momentum seemed to be demanding a cannibalistic murder. More thrilling that the breast had been ripped off and eaten than surgically removed. Complications were not yet welcome; they would be, eventually.

The breast-in-a-soup-bowl evidence had not been formally released to the press (the delicate, handmade Astier de Villatte earthenware bowl had been chosen specifically by Célestine for the purpose, and was not a customary luxury), but when Hervé had been interrogated by a quite cool young guy wearing an extremely narrow, double-breasted, six-button Costume National suit, striped in black and gray, with a zippered black sweater and no tie (Hervé couldn't help but wonder if the suit was a rental calculated to make him feel at ease with this cop), and then later by the *préfet* himself, who wore something navy, subdued and conservative, which Hervé suspected was Gucci, it became obvious that what Aristide had called the cheese in the mousetrap had been taken, and the police were quite confident that they had a major homicide on their hands, despite the lack of an entire body.

The cannibal photos would be released around the world at what Romme called "the politically effective moment." (Romme had promised to digitally alter the faces of Hervé and Chase, but Hervé was now thinking he would like to be at the center of the ensuing firestorm, whatever the consequences.) What this meant, Hervé could only guess. He could see that the coronation of Aristide as a refugee in Pyongyang would be a slap in the face of the French government, which was currently harassing the DPRK over their nuclear testing; that would be even better than the actor Gérard Depardieu's giving up his French passport in disgust over his tax rate and receiving a hastily mocked-up Russian passport from President Putin himself. But the cannibal photos? The very staging of Célestine's death itself? Were they comic-book illustrations of the horrors of capitalism, of the insatiable, all-devouring Western consumerist ethos? The expected pronouncement by Aristide on his safe arrival in the capital would undoubtedly clarify everything.

Hervé tapped the trackpad of his MacBook Pro and dragged the STL file encoding his penis into a special Korean version of Dropbox. The sending of such a file, no matter what its actual content, was the signal developed by him and Romme indicating that a Skype session was wanted.

Despite the regime's apparent affection for M. Vertegaal, he was constantly monitored by a pleasant team of five or six young cadres of both sexes, and was officially restricted to a living range of thirty-five kilometers from the center of Pyongyang, though Romme said that he had been able to bicycle alone beyond the first military perimeter, where the adolescent soldiers seemed shocked and flustered at the sight of a Westerner but were nevertheless very polite. Lately, however, Romme had been escorted in an elite "2.16" car (Kim Jong Il had been born on February 16, and the luxury cars whose special white license plates began with those numbers did not have to stop at roadblocks and checkpoints) to a research facility of some kind far from the capital, so secret that he would not talk about it even to Hervé, who was used to functioning as Romme's safety valve; in this case, the valve had been firmly shut off. Hervé could sometimes feel the presence of the cute monitoring team, and could even see them hovering anxiously in the background of Romme's Skype window, at which times Hervé and Romme would speak elliptically, often in English, knowing that the team was more adept at French. Their excuse, only grudgingly accepted, was that for technology, English was the appropriate language. At times, Hervé feared that Romme had in fact been exiled from the capital, a form of punishment that fell short of doing time in a reeducation camp but was scary enough.

Hervé had expected a coded email message appointing a time for a Skype session in return for his STL file, but almost immediately he heard the fishy Skype tone bubble up, and in no time was looking at the face of Romme Vertegaal in all its moody glory, Romme seeming fit and splendid in his many badges depicting members of the Kim dynasty. Hervé clicked the video-camera icon and a small window showing his own face popped up at the bottom right of the lower toolbar. He liked the way he looked, and thought that the two of them were very hot in an internationally subversive and dangerous way, definitely material for a big movie someday.

"*Salut*, Romme. Are you in Pyongyang?"

"Hervé. Thank you for your funny file. Amusing memories. I need eventually to talk to you about the FabrikantBot deal. My colleagues are worried about US sanctions against the DPRK, as usual, and are concerned to hide the North Korean origin of the FabrikantBot machines. Would it make sense to set up a French plant somewhere rather than a German one? It would be similar to the pending Eternal President's Voice hearing instruments gambit we have with the FrancoPhonics corporation. This and other considerations.

"But now, we need to discuss the geo-coordinates of Aristide Arosteguy. We have lost him. We don't know where he is. You've read the reports about his death; you've seen the tweeted photos. We're not convinced. The detail of the exploding hearing instruments has made us cautious. We feel that this is meant to be a message to us. Madame A. is extremely upset and has been disturbing the peace of the Korean Friendship Association. She was working on my next film script with the Juche Idea Study Group Film Unit, and they were eagerly awaiting the input of Monsieur Arosteguy. As you know, they are both still much revered for their support of *The Judicious Use of Insects* at the Cannes Film Festival."

"I'm shocked to hear this," said Hervé. "I had some nice desperate emails from the Canadian girl saying that the *philosophe* had disappeared after leaving the Tokyo house for unknown reasons. We know that he was on his way to meet our DPRK agents under the guise of a hearing-aid appointment brokered by Elke Jungebluth. Of course, it would have been appropriate for him to disappear *after* that meeting. I thought that he would be with you, that I might even see him in this window with you and have some words with him."

"We have lost him. He never arrived at the woman audiologist's hotel in Tokyo. Our agents were with her, as arranged with Arosteguy himself."

"Could there have actually been an electronic intervention? Could the hearing instruments have been tampered with, or perhaps substituted at some point with lethal intent? We know that Seoul did not want Arosteguy to end up in Pyongyang."

"We cannot rule it out. It is known that the Soviets used exploding headphones in the 1960s in Bulgaria to kill the defecting orchestra conductor Solovyov."

"And the Canadian girl? Naomi Seberg?"

"We do have her, thanks to you. She is in transit. An inconvenience meant a slight change of plans involving a long journey by train. We expect her within a week. Madame A. is curious to meet her."

"Her mental state? The girl?" Hervé needed concrete details; he deserved them. He did feel a giddy twinge of guilt for having put Naomi in play with Romme and the North Koreans, but he was sure she would be excited by the drama, would thank him later, as they say. And perversely, he himself was excited by the drama, by the fact that he had actually influenced international events in a quasi-criminal way. It was he who had pointed out to Romme the danger to their exploit represented by Naomi, even though he had been instrumental in connecting her with Arosteguy. His motives were, as usual, mostly opaque, even to himself, but definitely involved the deliciousness of mixing volatile and explosive elements and then standing back to watch the cataclysm.

"Subdued. Our team has been gentle with her, but of course the events have been stressful. They told her that she would be with the Arosteguys, and that seemed to mollify her, but of course now that's not entirely true. It will be interesting to see how she reacts. I'll have her Skype with you when I can."

Hervé observed Romme with some sadness, feeling that he had not seen the real Romme, the wickedly funny, engaging, and intellectually seductive one, in any of the Skype sessions from the DPRK. He missed that Romme, and wondered if there was really any of that Romme left; he had spent so long there under surveillance, shaping himself to fit the requirements and the fantasies of the regime, that perhaps the new shape was irreversible. At some point, Hervé thought, he must surely travel to Pyongyang himself, even as a humble tourist, to see if his prince's kiss could revive Princess Romme.

"But where did they pick her up? At the airport?"

"Strangely enough, they found her at the house rented by our operatives for Arosteguy in Tokyo. She had been living with him. She was sitting by the door with her suitcases all packed, ready to go somewhere but not sure where that should be. I'm reading the report right now." Indeed, Romme's eyes were not quite where one's eyes normally were when Skyping. Few people actually looked into the camera, or even knew where it was on a Mac, so tiny and occult was it, sunken within the screen's top bezel. Romme was looking far left of the Skype window, squinting with the effort of reading and translating the North's very particular dialect. "Our people felt it was important that she had packed not only her own personal belongings but also all of Arosteguy's, including electronics. There was barely any need for the team to strip the premises."

"Another victory for Kimunism," said Hervé, knowing he was treading on dangerous ground; irony and satire were not correct modes of discourse in the DPRK, though that made them very useful for monitored conversations, because, through lack of exercise, they were also not at all comprehended. It had been Ari who proposed the term *Kimunism* for the strange form of xenophobic nationalism practiced under the Kim family dynasty; it was not really socialism, nor was it communism in even the Maoist form, despite the heaviness of its cult of personality. Ari had felt that it was the severity and chimeric plasticity of the system, so provocative, that made it appealing to French intellectuals, and he did not exclude himself.

"There is another thread left hanging," said Romme. "I hope you've been keeping up correspondence with your little friend Chase Roiphe."

"Oh, yes. I sent her the same STL file that I sent you. It was just a few hours ago."

There was a sudden, dangerous change in Romme's features, a subtle deadening of expression, accompanied by an intensity around the eyes, that subverted Romme's normal Skype look, which was a cheerful, enthusiastic, unquestioning perkiness, the kind demonstrated by North Korean news readers. Hervé hoped Romme's handlers could not decrypt it; it was a warning to Hervé. "I appreciate the playfulness, but perhaps that was not the most sage thing you could have done."

Hervé was not used to reprimands from Romme; the game was that they were equals, young French technocrats with a future on the international techno-political stage, where cyberkampf was the name of the drama being played. But when it came to their strange liaison with North Korea and the young president, Kim Jong Un, they were not equal. It was Romme who had first traveled to the Hermit Kingdom on a technology visa, and Romme who had become involved in the burgeoning subterranean, quasi-legal tech markets, almost as a foreign subversive at first, and then as the acknowledged leader of the revolutionary, hands-on, Juche technology sector. Romme had been an older student of the Arosteguys, and easily enlisted Hervé in his scheme to build a small empire within an empire in North Korea. With Hervé's collusion, the philosophy couple too were recruited, so beautifully did their musings on consumerism and politics mesh with the retro-radicalism of the Hermit Kingdom.

And now Hervé realized that he had indeed made a mistake, in fact more than one mistake. It caused him anguish to know that he was afraid to tell Romme about his art project with Chase, that he had sent her the STL files that had allowed the 3D printing of the alleged mutilated body parts of Célestine. Chase had, in her attic workroom in Toronto, evidence that could prove that Célestine Arosteguy was not dead, that the incriminating photos of those body parts were only photos of bioplastic replicas, doctored by the SFX team to suggest the results of a hideous murder and subsequent butchering.

"I wanted to keep her close and to remind her of the lightness of our sexual play with the Arosteguys," he said. "I thought she needed something radical to snap her out of the depressive state of mind she had fallen into. She told me that I should not have forced her to take bites out of Madame A.'s amputated breast, and that she was sure that some of her own DNA would be discovered eventually because of that. She has a point, unfortunately. When we discussed placing the remains of that breast in such a way that it would convince the Préfecture that a cannibalistic murder had been committed, we omitted to think about saliva as a source of DNA."

"How unstable do you think she is?"

"It's a very volatile situation there in the Roiphe house in Toronto. The Canadian girl's journalist boyfriend is there, living in the house, looking for a story. I think he will soon find a story he didn't know existed. For instance, in her fugue state, as she calls it, she mutilates herself and eats tiny bits of her own flesh. She says she's aware of deliberately creating a kitschy drama but at the same time feels compelled to act it out. Her father has allowed this boyfriend, an American, to witness her behavior. His name is Nathan Math. He writes usually on medical subjects."

A pause. "I believe you need to go to Toronto to visit Chase Roiphe. You need to assess the situation there. And then, if you need assistance, we do have assets there to do whatever is required."

"Ah," said Hervé. "That would be suitably cathartic. So, financing for the voyage at the usual source?" The disbursement of the Vertegaal development funds involved a complex set of interactions beginning with the issuing of money drafts in tugrik, the Mongolian currency, by the Golomt Bank in Ulan Bator, which then underwent a series of conversions and transfers resulting in the deposit of euros or dollars, as circumstances demanded, in a commercial account in the name of Hervé's corporation,

Trois Médecins Français, at the Quai du Président Paul Doumer branch of the Crédit Agricole bank (former sponsors of a Tour de France–winning cycling team), all this to disguise their origins as North Korean won.

The image of Romme in the Skype window opened its mouth to speak but then unaccountably froze, then stuttered in a disturbing computer-graphics-creation kind of way, then disintegrated in a shower of sparkling pixel flakes. After a pregnant pause the Skype window itself crashed, leaving a momentary square black hole in the middle of the desktop's swirly cosmic image of the Andromeda Galaxy, the default Mac OS X (Lion iteration) wallpaper. (Lately, he avoided using personalized desktop wallpaper for security reasons; in the past, he would have featured Colnago beauty shots.) Staring blankly at that sinister new hole in the universe, his umbilical brutally cut, Hervé for one moment imagined that he might not have been communicating with the real Romme Vertegaal.